GONE IN THE NIGHT

Mary-Jane Riley is a former BBC talk show presenter and journalist. She has covered many life-affirming stories, but also some of the darkest events of the last two decades. Mary-Jane is married with three children and two dogs and lives in rural Suffolk. *Gone in the Night* is her fourth novel set in East Anglia and featuring journalist Alex Devlin.

 /maryjanerileyauthor
@mrsmjriley

Also by Mary-Jane Riley

The Bad Things
After She Fell
Dark Waters

GONE
IN THE
NIGHT

MARY-JANE RILEY

KILLER READS

A division of HarperCollins*Publishers*
www.harpercollins.co.uk

KillerReads
an imprint of HarperCollins*Publishers* Ltd
1 London Bridge Street
London SE1 9GF

www.harpercollins.co.uk

This paperback edition 2019

First published in Great Britain in ebook
format by HarperCollins*Publishers* 2019

A catalogue record for this book
is available from the British Library

ISBN: 978-0-00-834026-1

Set in Minion by
Palimpsest Book Production Limited, Falkirk, Stirlingshire

Printed and bound in the UK by CPI Group (UK) Ltd, Croydon CR0 4YY

MIX
Paper from
responsible sources
FSC
www.fsc.org FSC® C013604

*For my parents, who did so much to
encourage my love of books*

PROLOGUE

He watched them kill her. Not a needle in her arm, not a quick bullet in the brain, but blows to the head with a large, heavy rock – one blow to each temple. Then they rolled her over on the plastic sheeting they had laid on the floor and stove in the back of her head. The iron, meaty smell of her blood mingled with the sweat of her killers.

He tried to remember her name.

They would throw her into the sea and let the water and the rocks cover up their dirty work. She might never be found – after all, the sea doesn't always deliver the dead back to the living.

Or maybe they would take her to one of the many out of the way foot crossings on the Norwich to London railway line. He didn't have the strength or the will to intervene. Not yet. All he could do was watch and commit it to his memory. Commit that last look she gave him, that last sad, defeated look, to his memory.

By the time her body was found, there would be no evidence that she had been murdered.

CHAPTER ONE

DAY ONE: MORNING

Cora Winterton dabbed concealer under her eyes and applied shocking pink lipstick to her lips. She peered at herself in the mirror, then grimaced. She looked terrible. Nothing a few good nights' sleep and some decent meals wouldn't cure, but she wasn't going to get those any time soon. Working nights was a bitch. Especially when she didn't get much sleep during the day. Couldn't do it. Even after all these years her body clock wouldn't adjust to hospital shifts. But she wasn't going to put it off any longer. She couldn't pretend any more that Rick had moved sites or was staying in a hostel. Besides, she had been around all the obvious places, and plenty of the not so obvious ones and there was still no sign of him. But she had to check once more, there were still some people she hadn't talked to.

Where was he?

Her head began to swim. She leaned forward and grabbed the sides of the washbasin, trying to breathe deeply and evenly. Lack of food, lack of sleep, worry about her landlord putting up her rent – all of that. More deep breaths and her head felt better.

Two cups of coffee, one cigarette and another application of lipstick later and Cora emerged into the misty gloom of the early morning. It was a good time to see the people she wanted to talk to – before they moved on to start their begging in shop door-ways, or to find breakfast at one of the hostels in the city. She hurried down the steps and out onto the pavement, striding along to the underpass, glad she'd brought her umbrella.

With its walls of graffiti and stench of urine, the underpass linking her end of town with the shopping area was a favourite spot for the dispossessed and the vulnerable. Often it was littered with cardboard, empty drinks cans and bottles, old bits of clothing used as bedding, sometimes used needles. Although there had been an attempt to make the bare concrete walls more cheerful by covering them with paintings of Picasso-like figures in lurid colours, Cora often thought someone could die down here and never be noticed. Today it was the rowdy crowd, drinking cheap cider and knock-off spirits, leaning, or in some cases sagging, against the wall.

'Corrrrrra.'

'Hey, Tiger, how are you?' She smiled at the man who had pushed himself away from the wall and staggered towards her, ignoring the catcalls from the other men and women. 'You're up early.'

'Keepin' warm,' he said, holding a can aloft. 'Pissin' freezin'. Coppers moved us on this mornin'. Honestly, no bleedin' hearts in them.'

'Can I get you a coffee?' she said. 'A bit of breakfast?'

'Nah you're all right. Bit of cash'd be nice.'

'Tiger—' She shook her head.

'I know, I know, I'd piss it up against the wall.' He cocked his head to one side. 'Are you still lookin' for Ricky-boy?'

'Yes. Why, have you see him?' Her heart leapt.

He shook his head. 'Nah. We miss him though, don't we?' he shouted out to the others.

A general rumble of noise floated around the underpass. Tiger shrugged. 'Sorry. Can't help you. He's a good mate, though. Find him soon, yeah?'

4

'It's okay,' said Cora, 'there are plenty of other places I can look.' The familiar darkness settled around her head. She was never going to find him, but she had to keep looking.

And that was the depressing thing, she thought, as she tramped around the city in the drizzle that was getting harder and colder by the minute, there were plenty of other places to look, even in a city like Norwich which never used to have a homelessness problem. Now it seemed to be everywhere. People sleeping in shop doorways, in car parks, alleyways, even by the traffic lights outside the station.

And it was Martin, outside the railway station, bundled up in his sleeping bag, covered with old tinfoil, and lying on a bed of newspaper and used pizza boxes with his beloved dog, Ethel, who gave her the first bit of hope since Rick went missing.

'Yeah,' said Martin, sitting up and accepting a cigarette and a takeaway coffee from her with trembling fingers. 'I saw Rick 'bout two weeks ago. Before I went to Yarmouth. Piss poor place that. Two weeks was enough.' He hunched his shoulders against the wet.

Cora nodded. That was the last time she'd seen her brother, when she had tried to persuade him to spend at least one of the freezing nights in a homelessness shelter.

'He had a smoke with me. Told me 'bout some men who'd come calling.'

'What sort of men?'

Martin tugged the sleeping bag around his neck trying to stop the rain trickling down. He shivered. 'You know, well-dressed, well-fed types. One of them wearing a suit, for fuck's sake. Looked like Mormons. Wanted to know about him.'

Cora frowned. God-botherers? Do-gooders? Or the men they were expecting to see? 'And what did he tell them?'

An early morning commuter tossed a few coins in the bowl that was always by Martin's side. Ethel sniffed the bowl, but turned away when she saw there were no tasty biscuits in it for her.

Martin looked down, focused on the ground. 'He said he told them he had nobody and he didn't want no help from no one, unless they had a job to offer him.'

There it was. The guilt that squeezed her, that had made her search frantically for her brother whenever she could these past few days, that had interrupted what little sleep she had managed to grab for herself. The argument she'd had with Rick the day before he disappeared. When she'd told him she was done with helping him. It was time to call it off. She was frightened about what might happen.

It had started out as nothing really, as many arguments do. She had sought him out at his usual spot behind the solicitors off Unthank Road. Two of the lawyers looked after him occasionally, giving him food and coffee. Cora was forever grateful to them. That day she had gone to find him, determined to persuade him to have his hair cut – had offered to pay. There was a new Turkish barbers that had opened, she told him. They would do the lot. A wash, a cut, even a beard trim. Why would he want that, he'd said, he was perfectly happy with how he looked. It was necessary *now*, she knew that, he told her, shaking his head.

Cora had wanted to cry. Rick's hair and beard were long and matted. Grimy. She hated that ratty beard. It symbolized how far they had fallen. He looked uncared for, unkempt. And she told him so.

'I live on the streets, Cora. That's what happens,' he told her. 'This is what I wanted. And now it's perfect.'

She wanted to stamp her foot. 'But you don't have to. We can stop this. You can come home with me.' She'd had enough.

'No.' He had that steely look in his eyes.

She knew she ought to stop, but she couldn't. 'Rick, I don't want to do this anymore.'

'Well, tough. Because I do.'

'I can't bear it. I can't bear to see you on the streets with no

one to care for you and no one to love you. I want you with me.'
She dashed away the tears that were trickling down her cheeks.

'I thought you understood, Cora.' His voice was hard. 'This
has to be done. This is my life now.'

'I don't know why you're punishing yourself,' she whispered.

'Yes, you do.'

'Please, Rick. Come home with me. Or at least let me find you
a place in a shelter for a few nights.'

'Stop it.' He sighed. 'Cora, this is exactly what you do. You
come here offering to pay for me to have my hair cut, trim my
beard, probably put pomade or whatever that stuff is on it, but
it would make a nonsense of everything. It would make a nonsense
of my life. Of our lives. Of what I need to do. I have a purpose.
Leave it, Cora, leave me alone, let me get on with it, like we
agreed.'

'I want us to be together. I'm not strong enough without you,'
she whispered.

'You are. You're stronger than anyone. Now, leave it, Cora,
for fuck's sake.'

And she had seen that anger in his face, the anger that could
spill over into something altogether more frightening, and she
had turned and left. Almost running in her haste.

'That's right, Cora,' he shouted after her. 'Run away. Just like
you always do.'

She stopped and turned. 'You know what, Rick? You're a loser.
You think you're making life easier for me? Well you're not.
You're bloody not.'

And since then she hadn't been able to find him. And how
she bitterly regretted the words she had flung at him so carelessly,
so thoughtlessly.

'Rick didn't tell you about a job, then?' she asked Martin now.

'Nah.' He smiled at her. 'He didn't say anything.' He stroked
Ethel, who snuggled up even closer to him.

'But it was after he spoke to them that he disappeared?'

'Well, couldn't rightly say the two things were, like, connected, but—' Another shrug of his shoulders.

Cora wanted to know. She wanted to know right now whether the two things were connected, who the men were, what they had wanted with Rick. Whether he had done something really stupid.

'They haven't spoken to you then, Martin? These men?'

'No, I ain't seen them. Rick told me to be careful of 'em though. Come to think of it—'

'What?'

'Nobby said he'd been spoke to by some blokes.' He sniffed, hard. Ethel moved away for a moment, then came back to his side.

'Nobby?'

'Yeah. He used to hang out in the doorway of the old bank. Said it was the nearest he'd ever get to any moolah.'

'Okay.' Cora tried not to show her impatience.

'I haven't seen him for a while. Or Lindy.'

'Lindy?'

'Lives in the grounds of St Peter Mancroft. By the hedge.'

'Thanks, I'll go and check it out.'

Cora could see Martin's eyes beginning to close. 'Martin, how about a night in the shelter?' she said softly, reaching into her pocket for a biscuit for Ethel, who took it from her with careful teeth and a fair amount of slobber.

'Nah. Thanks, Cora.'

She put her umbrella down by his side.

8

CHAPTER TWO

DAY ONE: EVENING

He was shivering, his teeth chattering, water dripping off his hair as he crawled out of the river and onto the shingle. The tee-shirt and boxer shorts he was wearing were sodden, clinging to his skin. He paused on his hands and knees, panting, exhausted, and looked around. There were lights in the distance, but not at this point of the harbour. Not here. Surely no one would have seen him?

The night was dark, there was neither moon nor stars, for which he was grateful. Less chance of being spotted.

Had he been missed yet?

He couldn't stay here. He had to get moving. Get up. *Get up.*

His body was too heavy. He tried to unfurl, to stand.

So much effort.

He could do this. He'd been fit once. Muscle memory, that's what he needed.

He gritted his teeth.

His head was pounding, there was a sickness in his stomach. He mustn't think of what he'd had to leave behind. All that work, all those chances he'd taken and he'd had to get rid of it when he realized they were on to him. When he knew he had to escape.

Right away. And he'd left her behind too. He'd wanted her to go with him, but she wouldn't. Said she would slow him down. She would have done, and they could have made it together. Until it was too late for her.

Come on, *come on*.

Almost up. He stayed for a minute, back hunched, hands on the top of his knees, still shivering, always shivering. He couldn't remember when he'd last felt warm, when his head was clear, when he felt well. He couldn't remember.

A car. He needed a car.

Shapes grew out of the shadows. A shed, boathouses made of timber, two fishing boats resting on the concrete. The smell of fish and diesel in the swirling air.

He listened.

All he heard was the wind whistling around the edges of the buildings, then he became aware of the wind drying his body, his clothes, making him shiver more deeply, right down to his bones, to the damaged organs in his body.

Cold.

Cold was a killer.

He took a deep breath and staggered towards an old shed. Hugging its perimeter, he peered around the corner.

Nothing. Nobody.

Lights, though. On the car park. Not many, but enough. Had to keep away from those.

He set off in a crab-like run, fear giving an edge to his strides. He was better now, had to be better, had to get to freedom, had to leave this place behind.

He risked a glance over his shoulder, back at the island. Lights twinkled in the distance, making the buildings look benign. There were no signs that someone – him – had escaped. No floodlights, no shouting. But then there wouldn't have been, would there? Too risky, even for them. He tried to listen, to see if he could hear the sound of a boat, a speedboat perhaps, coming to find him.

10

Nothing, even the wind had stopped its moaning.

Either he hadn't been missed or—

The alternative was too awful to contemplate. He couldn't have come this far for them to be waiting for him, just around some corner.

He ran. Past houses towards the road. Down the road. And there. An explosion of relief. Lights. A pub. Perhaps he could get a car. Out here, in the country, they could be careless with their security. He began to pray he was right as his breaths became ever more shallow, the kicking he'd received in his ribs making itself known.

There were cars in the car park. Swish cars, nothing old, nothing he could hot-wire. Frantic, breath coming too hard now, he looked around. A BMW. A Mazda. A Land Rover. A couple of Fords. Which one? Which one?

He limped over to the Land Rover, his muscles seizing up more with every step.

It was dirty, mud-splattered. The windows were open halfway. He peered inside. The floor was littered with empty sandwich packets, beer cans, tissues. There was an old, hairy blanket on the passenger seat. It smelled of damp and dog.

He pulled on the driver's door. His hand bloody hurt. It opened. He leaned across and pulled down the sun visor. A bunch of keys fell onto the floor. He thanked fuck country people were so trusting.

As he jammed the key into the ignition, something made him stop. Listen. He clamped his lips together so he wasn't hearing the chattering of his teeth. He slowed his breathing, told himself to be calm. There it was. A faint sound. Was it a motorboat? Coming from the island perhaps? His heart began to jump in his chest, and he turned the key in the ignition.

A noise like a giant clearing his throat came from the engine.

He turned the key again – so hard it could have broken off.

The engine turned over once, twice.

11

Cold sweat was dripping into his eyes.

It fired. He said a thank you to a god he hadn't believed in for a very long time.

Without waiting to listen, or even to look to see if anyone was coming for him, he released the handbrake and pushed his foot hard on the accelerator.

He hadn't turned the lights on, and the corner came up too quickly. He turned, hard. Made it round on two wheels, tyres screeching. The Land Rover bounced back onto four, he was thrown out of his seat, then back down. He breathed again.

Where were the lights? Where were the fucking lights? It was so dark. No moon. No stars. No street lights. No more comforting lights from the pub.

He looked down for a likely looking switch.

Where the fuck was it? Where the—

There. Light.

He looked up to see a pair of eyes in front of the windscreen reflected in the headlights.

He screamed and slammed on the brake, wrenched the steering wheel first one way, then the other.

The Land Rover lurched across the road, hitting the hedge on one side. Somewhere in his subconscious he heard the side of the vehicle being scratched by thorns, twigs, branches. Then, before he could think any more, the Land Rover was thrust, skidding, to the other side of the road.

A tree loomed in front of him. Once more he hit the brake.

He felt himself being propelled forward. Tried to throw himself across the seats. Slammed into the dashboard. His head thrown backwards then forwards. He was weightless. Felt a shower of glass. Time stretched, contracted, stretched again. Something trickled down the side of his face and into the corner of his mouth.

Rick's last thought was of his sister.

The deer, unharmed, trotted off into the forest.

CHAPTER THREE

DAY ONE: EVENING

The sky was alive with a shower of red and green and yellow sparks as one rocket after another exploded in the night air. Beyond the lake, Catherine wheels crackled and whistled and Roman candles fizzed and hummed. Watching from behind the French windows, men and women in party clothes holding champagne glasses oo-ed and ah-ed their appreciation, grateful the wind had died down so they could enjoy the display. Alex Devlin sipped her warm tap water and wished she was at home, tucked up in bed with her hot water bottle.

'Enjoying the fireworks?'

Alex turned to see a man looking down at her, a smile on his face. Mid-forties, she reckoned, swept-back black hair with wings of grey. Soft crow's feet at the corners of his eyes. Laughter lines by his mouth. Could be anger lines, of course. All this she registered in a couple of seconds.

'They're very impressive,' she said, carefully.

He raised an eyebrow. 'Hmm. Does that mean "impressive but a waste of money"?'

A smile tugged at the corners of Alex's mouth. 'You may say that, I couldn't possibly comment.' She turned back to watch more of the display. More rockets exploding in the air. She could feel the man's eyes on her.

'I saw you earlier. With someone. It looked as though you were having an argument.'

'Really?' She wasn't sure how to react. She wanted to ask why he was watching her and what business it was of his, but she didn't.

'I know it's none of my business …'

Ah.

'But I was watching you …'

Right.

'Only because I was worried …'

Of course you were.

'Worried?'

He shrugged. 'I don't like to see couples arguing. It can lead to all sorts of things.'

'"All sorts of things"?'

'I'm sorry. I'm digging myself into a hole, aren't I?' He smiled wryly.

Alex laughed, the tension slipping from her shoulders. 'Just a bit.'

'Tell me.'

'What?'

'About the man you were arguing with.'

'Why?'

'So I know who I'm competing with.'

'"Competing with"?' Alex still tried not to smile. The arrogance of the man. She turned to look at him properly. Beautifully cut suit, blue tie, blue handkerchief poking out from the breast pocket, but yes, grey eyes. Wolfish.

'Drink?'

'Drink?' She was confused at the sudden change of subject.

He nodded to her empty glass. 'More champagne?'

'I'm drinking water.'

'Are you sure I can't tempt you? You look as though you might need a glass.'

'Really?' She didn't look that shaken, surely. Still, she did feel as though she could do with some alcohol at this particular moment. Sod it. 'Okay. Why not?' Now she did allow herself to smile fully at him.

He clicked his fingers and a woman, impeccably dressed in a white shirt and tight black skirt, glided towards them, bearing a tray at shoulder height. Alex wasn't sure whether she was supposed to be impressed or not. She wasn't. In fact, after the evening she'd had, it would take more than an imperious clicking of fingers and a solemn waitress bearing booze to impress.

The woman handed her a glass; Alex drank deeply, hardly appreciating its coldness and the pop of bubbles on her tongue.

'Looks like you needed that,' he said.

'I did. Thank you.' She took a more delicate sip, wanting to savour it this time.

'Who was he?' The man leaned against the window. The fireworks had ended.

Alex sighed. 'He was a friend who wanted to be more than a friend.'

He was David Gordon, the head of a charity for the homeless in East Anglia, who had invited her along to the event at Riders' Farm – an event not in aid of his charity, but for one concerned with refugees. He liked to pick up ideas, he told her. Also, he said, the Riders were big donors to Fight for the Homeless and it behoved him to be there. Alex thought at the time his use of the word 'behoved' was rather sweet and old-fashioned.

She had found David an interesting person to interview for *The Post*. He had come into money and had decided to put it to good use. He wanted to make the lives of homeless people more normal, he had told her earnestly. To fight the root causes of homelessness. It was no good merely giving money to beggars on the street, you had to put that money to good use. To fight drugs, robber landlords, the benefits system. And to that end he had set up a hostel in Norwich and another in Ipswich where people could go and not have to account for themselves in any way, but would be helped with whatever problem they had. No one would ask them questions.

Finding out about David's hopes and ambitions had been the sort of freelance job she liked best. A good subject, an interesting cause. She'd enjoyed herself, so when he'd asked her to join him at the function at the Riders' farm, she'd agreed. She'd heard that the event at the rather splendid farm was the place to be seen. Not that she was interested in being seen as such, but there could be some people here who would make good subjects for future features she enjoyed writing. And she might even get a news story of some sort out of it. She badly wanted to up her news credibility with Heath Maitland, the news editor at *The Post*.

The evening had started off so well, with David taking her to a delicious early supper at the nearby Dog and Partridge.

The party was well underway by the time they arrived at Riders' Farm. Alex could hear the strains of a jazz band as they walked towards the large oak front door up the path lit by dozens of bamboo garden torches and strings of fairy lights hanging from the bare branches of trees.

At first David had been the very model of attentiveness, making his way through the packed rooms, introducing her to all sorts of people from the chief executive of a local hospice to the raddled drummer of a famous band of old rockers. The great and the good were in evidence everywhere. Suffolk's Assistant Chief Constable was chatting to a prominent surgeon from Ipswich Hospital. The Chief Fire Officer was listening to the Lord-Lieutenant of Suffolk – a post currently held by a countess. And the canapés were delicious and the champagne cold.

'When do I get to meet the Riders?' Alex asked, after spending several minutes in the company of the pompous High Sheriff of Suffolk, complete with the gold medallions of office, who was telling her how the city council was about to adopt a zero-tolerance policy towards beggars on the streets.

She couldn't wait to get away.

'There's Marianne, the matriarch, I guess you'd call her.' David nodded across the room.

Marianne Rider was tall and elegant, wearing a crimson dress that was nipped in at the waist and fell to the floor. Her silver hair was carefully twisted in a chignon and diamonds glinted in her ears. As if she knew she was being looked at, Marianne Rider turned and stared at Alex. The woman's face was tastefully wrinkled, though the number of lines around her mouth denoted a heavy smoker. Her lipstick matched her dress. A silver necklace glinted across her collarbone. She didn't smile. She turned back to continue talking to the man next to her.

Alex almost shivered. She felt snubbed. Marianne Rider did not look a cosy sort of person.

'And that's her husband next to her, Joe Rider,' said David.

Joe Rider was as tall as his wife and stood dutifully nodding at whatever she was saying while sipping from a glass. His dark navy suit was stretched across his paunch. He was sweating slightly, and he ran his fingers around the inside of his collar as if it was restricting his breathing.

'I can't see the three sons, but they must be around somewhere,' said David. 'Apparently Marianne likes the family to present a united front, so they always have to come to these events with their wives.'

'Wives? You make it sound as though they've got several each.'

David laughed. 'One of the sons is on his third wife, but I don't think all three have to attend. Still, I'll introduce you when I see them.' He tried to sound casual, but Alex could hear the excitement in his voice. She didn't like to tell him that she had done a bit of research before the evening and knew a little about the Riders. They were an old farming family who owned a lot of land in Suffolk, an awful lot of land, including an island off the coast. An island about which there were all sorts of stories, stories of strange lights and noises at night. Screams carrying over cold air. Bodies washed up on beaches. Local people said the island was haunted.

'… diversification. Are you listening to me, Alex?' David stared at her with irritation.

'Sorry.' She tried to look contrite.

'What I was saying was that they have diversified and done very well out of it. They have "forest lodges for the back-woodsman" on some of their land.'

'For townies to "experience" the countryside, I suppose,' said Alex, grinning. 'Yes, I read about that.'

'There's also a centre for holistic therapy, complete with yurts, and a couple of barns that can be used for corporate events or as wedding venues. Of the three sons, Simon, the youngest, is married, and has a degree in chemistry or something. The eldest, Lewis, is on his third wife as I said, and the middle son, Jamie, has just got divorced. There we are. A potted history.'

Alex wondered if she was meant to give him a round of applause.

The evening continued. Alex was now drinking water, much to David's annoyance.

'I need to keep a clear head, David,' she told him more than once. 'I've got to do an interview in the morning.'

'But you shouldn't waste all this,' he said, sweeping his arm around the room.

'I'm not, I'm enjoying talking to people.' Some, anyway.

'But—'

It was almost as if David wanted to get her drunk.

And just before the fireworks started he had manoeuvred her into the cold air of the garden for 'a walk to clear their heads'.

'My head is perfectly clear, thanks, David.'

'Come on, don't be a spoilsport.'

He was beginning to get a little bit annoying. She took a deep

18

breath, she really didn't want to ruin the evening. 'What do you mean? I'm not a spoilsport, and anyway, it's bloody cold out here.' She rubbed her arms, trying to get rid of goosebumps. She tried to smile at him. 'Come on, let's go back into the warm.' There was something about the way David was looking at her that was making her nervous.

He lunged towards her.

Startled, Alex jerked her head back. David stumbled, and she tried – and failed – to suppress a giggle. Then she saw his face: puce and furious.

'David, I—' she said, searching frantically for words to let him down gently, knowing her laugh had been cruel.

He grabbed her shoulders, pulling her towards him and managing to plant a wet kiss on her mouth.

'No, David.' She wriggled out of his grip, resisting the desire to wipe the back of her hand across her lips.

'Why not? Aren't I good enough for you?' He flushed, his lips wet and flabby.

'Don't be silly. I see you as a friend, that's all.' She tried a smile. 'I'm not looking for a relationship right now.'

'With me?'

'With anyone. I am sorry, David.'

'You led me on.' His face was suffused with anger, the veins in his neck like cords of rope.

Alex was taken aback. 'I don't think so.'

'You did.' He thrust his chin forward, hands in fists.

Had she? Not to her knowledge. 'David—'

'Oh, forget it, you're just like all the others.' He marched off, leaving Alex even more confused. That had come out of absolutely bloody nowhere and there was no way she had 'led him on', as he put it. She really didn't have any desire for a relationship at the moment. She'd been there, tried that.

'It was David Gordon, wasn't it?'

The man's voice brought her back to the present.

'I'm sorry?'

'Fight for the Homeless charity?'

'You *were* spying on me,' she said mildly. 'David and I were outside when we argued.'

The man threw back his head and laughed. 'Caught. I promise I wasn't being pervy, I was merely looking out of the window when I saw the pair of you.' He shook his head. 'Arguing. Is that what you call it nowadays. Poor David. Never has much luck.'

'I don't think luck comes into it. I hadn't encouraged him at all when he—' She stopped. What was she doing explaining herself to a stranger? He had no right to know anything about her. She was irritated with herself. She put her glass down on a tray being carried by a passing waiter. 'If you'll excuse me, I must leave.'

He put a restraining hand on her arm. 'Wait. Do you have to?'

'Yes. I have to be up in the morning for a radio interview.' She looked at his hand. He let it drop.

'How intriguing.'

'Not really.' She gave him a brief smile as she turned to go.

'Stay.'

She looked at him. 'I really do have to get home.'

'I'm Jamie Rider,' he said as if she hadn't spoken. He put out his hand.

Alex took it. She had known it was Jamie Rider, although he was far more impressive in real life than the photos she had found of him had led her to believe.

'Alex Devlin,' she said, shaking his hand.

His grip was warm and firm. 'The journalist.'

'Oh dear. You said it like it was a cross I had to bear.' She laughed, lightly.

He laughed. 'Not at all. Your book is like a bible for my mother.'

She gave a wry smile. The book. All the profiles she had put together about interesting people, the stories she had written about the danger of suicide forums on the Internet, the investigations she had done into dodgy business practices, all this counted for nothing against a book she had been commissioned to write after an article of hers had appeared in the paper about extreme couponing. The art of collecting coupons and vouchers and spending them well was a very popular subject. Popular enough to write a book about and for the book to get onto the bestseller lists. Popular enough to give her the cash to put a deposit down on a waterfront apartment in Woodbridge.

'That's good to hear,' she said, thinking he was either having her on or was trying to ingratiate himself with her. After all, what possible pleasure would the imposing and somewhat terrifying Marianne Rider take in cutting out coupons from newspapers? It didn't go with the red dress and frosty look.

'Perhaps you could sign it for her some time?'

'Of course.' Really? she thought. 'And you. What's your niche on the farm? The backwoodsman lodges, the yurts or the haunted island?'

Jamie Rider threw back his head and laughed. 'You make us sound like a family of weirdos.'

Alex raised an eyebrow.

'Ah. You think we *are* a family of weirdos.' He nodded. 'Fair enough. But I don't have anything to do with any of those projects. Never have. I'm far too boring. I work in the city.'

'Banking,' said Alex.

'You've been doing your research. I'm impressed.' He didn't look impressed. 'Yes, banking. Very dull.'

'Not at all,' she replied, trying to sound politely convincing. 'I'm sure it has its own delights.'

Again he laughed, and Alex found she enjoyed hearing it. It made her smile. 'But now,' she looked at her watch, 'I really must be going.'

'No. The night is still young.' He frowned. 'You can't disappear like some sort of Cinderella, not when I've just found you.'

'I have been here all the time, and I'm afraid I must disappear. So, please excuse me.'

'Can I give you a lift? I mean, since you and David ...'

She shook her head. 'I'll be fine, thank you.'

'But the roads.'

'I know the roads. And maybe I brought my car.'

'Maybe you did, but you have been downing the champagne. And, if – as I imagine you did – you came as David Gordon's guest, then you will have lost that lift home.'

'Not necessarily. I'm sure he would take me home if I asked.' Actually, she was bloody sure he wouldn't. 'In any case, the fresh air will do me good.' She was enjoying the banter but she really did want to get home to her bed so she was fresh for the radio interview in the morning. Besides, she didn't want or need any complications in her life, and Jamie Rider looked as though he could be a very big complication, if she let him in. No, she would go outside and order a taxi.

'Fair enough,' he said. 'Maybe I could see you another time? Show you around the farm? Book you in to realign your chakra?'

'Maybe.' She smiled, graciously, she hoped.

Chakra indeed. It really was time to leave.

22

CHAPTER FOUR

DAY ONE: LATE EVENING

Cora didn't see the two men until it was too late.

Normally, she would catch the last bus home after an evening shift at the hospital, but tonight she had worked late thanks to an emergency admission and so she'd missed it, but a colleague gave her a lift part of the way, dropping her on Unthank Road – not too far for her to walk. However, this was Norwich, and there weren't many people out late at night in that part of the city, which was well away from the nightclubs and the pubs the students frequented, so she hurried along, trying to make herself as inconspicuous as possible. Once or twice the hairs stood up on the back of her neck and she looked over her shoulder, convinced she was being followed, but she saw nobody.

She decided to take a shortcut through Chapelfield Gardens that was lit in part by sickly yellow sodium lights. A couple meandered along in front of her, hand-in-hand. She passed a group of four men, swaying with booze. They called out to her; she ignored them.

Two men stepped out of the dark in front of her. She stopped, smiled.

'Excuse me,' she said, pleasantly, hoping they would stand aside.

They didn't.

'Excuse me,' she said, more loudly now, her heart fluttering in her chest. This was not a good situation. Still they didn't move. She glanced around, wondering if she could shout for help, but the gardens were now empty. The two men moved smoothly to flank her either side, pressing her between their bodies. Both were much taller than she was.

'Cora,' one of them said without looking at her, 'you shouldn't be walking around on your own.'

'Especially not here,' said the other. 'In a deserted park an' all.'

'Have you been following me?' Her mouth was dry. Fuck it, she'd been right.

Man Number One, who was thickset with rubbery lips, smiled at her. 'Since you left the hospital,' he said, cheerfully. 'We'd been waiting for you to leave. Though you didn't make it easy, missing your bus and everything. Good job we had our car parked nearby. Especially as parking can be hell at NHS places, don't you find?'

'I don't know who you are,' Cora said, keeping her voice low and even as if she were talking to a frightened child, 'but I would advise you to get out of my way.'

'Or what, Cora?'

His lips were wet with saliva; it was all Cora could do not to shiver.

Then the two men began to hustle her along the path so fast that her feet were barely touching the ground. Her heart began to beat even faster.

'What are you doing?' She tried to wriggle free, but the two men merely gripped one of her arms each and carried on walking. All she could hope for was that they would pass someone and she could shout for help.

The group of drunks. There they were, ahead of her.

'Help,' she shouted, though it came out more like a whisper.

She gathered her breath, opened her mouth. One of the men punched her in the stomach. She bent over, winded.

'All right, mate?' she heard one of the drunks say as they hurried by.

'All right,' said Man Number One. 'A few too many. Y'know.' He laughed.

'Fuckin' do,' said the drunk. They all laughed. Cora was still trying to catch her breath.

'Look, Cora love,' said the skinny man on her left, as they turned out of the gardens and began to walk down the road. 'We don't mean you no harm. Not intentionally, anyway. This is just a little warning.'

'A warning, that's right,' said Man Number One, squeezing her shoulder hard. 'Stop poking around, asking questions.'

'Yeah, poking your nose in where it's not wanted.'

'Looking for Rick, you mean?' she said through gritted teeth. Her stomach hurt. 'Is that what it's about?' It was all she could think of.

'Yeah.'

'Why?'

'Why what?'

'Why shouldn't I look for Rick?'

'It's not just that. Boss reckons you interfere too much and people'll start talking.'

'Listening, you mean.' Anger made her bold. 'They might just start listening.' She tried to shake them off, but they held on even tighter. Rain had begun to fall.

'Whatever.'

'Who's your boss? One of the Riders? Which one?'

Her question was met with laughter. She knew she was right.

They were now in an alleyway at the back of a row of shops – Topshop, she thought. MacDonald's. No one to hear her.

25

'Boss knows you like chatting to the homeless,' said Skinny Man, dragging her towards one of the large grey industrial wheelie bins, 'so we thought you could spend a bit of time being in their gaff.'

Okay, she thought, so they were going to dump her in a bin to make a point. To frighten her. And they'd done that all right. She was frightened. And getting cold from the rain. But at least she could climb out of the bin when the men had gone.

All at once Man Number One grabbed her arms and jerked them behind her back, wrapping gaffer tape around her wrists. Before she could scream, Skinny Man had slapped tape over her mouth, wrapping more tape around her head. Fear coiled in her stomach. Man Number One pushed her and she fell heavily on to the ground, banging her head on the hard concrete. Her vision went black for a moment and she felt sick. Then more tape was wrapped around her legs from her knees to her ankles, before she heard one of them push open the lid of the wheelie bin, and then she was tossed inside like a piece of rubbish.

'Take this as a warning,' Skinny Man said, smiling down at her.

The lid slammed shut.

The smell hit her first. The sweet tang of rotting food. Fried onions. Mouldy old rags. Body odour – from old clothes? Chips. The sourness of beer. There would be maggots, she knew there would be maggots. Fat. Crawling. Wriggling. She was lying on cans. Bottles. Cardboard containers. Lying on all sorts of rubbish. Slime. In the dark. Terror rose in her throat. Bile too. No, she must not be sick. Not be sick.

Another thought: would the bin be emptied tonight? Her terror grew so it was almost uncontainable. She could scarcely breathe. She had heard about this. Knew it had happened to homeless people, or drunks who thought they'd found somewhere safe for the night. And then the bin lorry came along, scooped up the bin and emptied it into the lorry where the contents were crushed before being taken to the landfill site. Her body would never be found. She would never be able to help Rick. To bring those who deserved it to justice.

Oh, Rick, where are you?

She tried to throw herself against the side of the bin – for what? To topple it? To make a noise? No matter, however many times she tried, nothing happened. It didn't move. No one heard her. She tried to stand up, but kept sinking down into the rubbish. She screamed, but the tape muffled her cries. It was dark. It stank. She was wet. Cold. Her throat hurt. There was no air. No air. She closed her eyes.

She had no idea how long she had been lying in the bin, but now she heard it, the noise of a lorry on the street nearby. Could it be the bin lorry coming to collect the rubbish? To collect *her*?

Fear made her freeze.

Light. Not light, but not dark either. Fresh air. Rain on her face.

'Here let me help you.'

Someone – a man – leaning right over the edge of the bin, holding out his hands. She tried to shuffle towards him, carefully, so she wouldn't sink any further into the filth. He grabbed her under her arms and hauled her up and over the lip of the bin. Her shoulders burned. For the second time that night, she landed on the hard concrete.

The man jumped down off the pile of crates he'd been balancing on, and bent to tear the tape off her head and mouth.

It hurt like hell.

He produced a knife and cut her wrists and calves free.

'Come on. Leg it.'

A bin lorry came around the corner.

Cora held on to the man's hand and legged it.

Chapelfield Gardens again. Cora sat down on a bench.

Her rescuer wrinkled his noise. 'You stink.'

Cora looked at him, at his trousers held up by a tie, his stained knitted jumper underneath a buttonless coat out of which protruded much stuffing. 'You can talk.'

Her rescuer grinned. 'Maybe. Glad I got you before the crusher did.'

Cora nodded, then began to shiver. 'How did you know I was there?'

Her rescuer shrugged. 'A man gave me some dosh, told me where you were and told me to get you out. Preferably before the lorry.'

Now Cora laughed. 'Thank you. Do you know who the man was?'

He shook his head, putting his finger to his lips. 'Hush money, that's what he said.' And he ran off down the path.

Cora couldn't stop shivering.

CHAPTER FIVE

DAY ONE: LATE EVENING

Alex hunched into her coat and pushed one hand as far down into a pocket as she could. The other held her phone with the torch light on so she could see her way. The weather had turned from clearsky cold to stormy in the time she had been at the charity event. If she looked at the ground, the wind wouldn't whip across her skin. The stars were hiding behind furiously dark clouds.

It hadn't been her greatest idea. To attempt to order a taxi to come to the middle of nowhere on a weekday night. Or any night, thinking about it. It wasn't as if she could call an Uber, or that there was a plethora of taxi firms in the area. The two firms that did answer her call said they were too busy. Alex imagined them shaking their heads ruefully as they put the phone down.

Why hadn't she ordered one earlier?

Because she hadn't realized she would need one.

So she began to walk, reasoning that it wasn't too far to Woodbridge. And when she got a decent signal again, she would give one of the taxi firms who hadn't picked up another try. Or, when she reached the Dog and Partridge, where she'd had supper with David, she might be able to persuade the owner's student son to take her home for a bit of cash.

On reflection, perhaps she should have let Jamie Rider drive her home. Still, she'd had a lucky escape from David. Where had that mauling come from? She hadn't encouraged him; there was no way she was even interested in him. Or anyone, for that matter, especially now her life was coming together at last. She didn't feel as though she was being buffeted by the winds of chance any more and was finally feeling at peace with herself. The guilt that had weighed so heavily on her for years had lifted. She had a new start. Finally, she knew she deserved it.

All she needed now was a juicy story to get her teeth into. It was all very well having a bestselling book – and she wasn't complaining, it had bought her independence as well as the new flat – but she did want to be taken seriously. She'd been writing features for *The Post* for a long time now. She wanted something else, something worth doing. She'd had a taste of it eighteen months ago when she was delving into the proliferation of suicide forums on the Internet and the financial shenanigans of the previous editor and owner of the newspaper. She'd enjoyed writing that copy.

The rain began to fall, gently at first, then it came on harder, running icily down the back of her neck. Damn. She was going to get properly wet now. And cold. She tried to protect her phone. It would be the last straw if that was ruined. And her feet were hurting. Those damn heels. Why hadn't she brought flat pumps to change into? Because she hadn't thought she was going to have to walk home, had she?

She had talked to Heath about more work, about her desire to be taken more seriously. Heath, whose looks, charm and inherited wealth belied a sharp operator, was the owner of *The Post* as well as its news editor. He wanted to be hands-on, he'd told Alex during one of her rare visits to London. She had told him she wanted more excitement in her working life. He'd stretched out his long legs, pushed his floppy fringe out of his eyes and said, 'Well, you don't want a staff job on *The Post*, I know that. Don't sit around moaning, Alex. You're a freelance, a self-starter, even if you do have enough money at the moment. It might not always be like that. You call yourself an investigative journalist, so get out there and find something to investigate.'

Tough love.

For a few days she'd been hurt, resentful, but she knew he was right – damn him. It was up to her to find stories, to get stuck into something.

Her phone buzzed. She peered at the screen. Her sister. Her heart used to sink when she got a call from her, but now it was like being phoned by someone – ordinary, was that the word? Probably not. Normal? What was normal these days? What she meant was that she didn't go into worry mode as soon as her sister's name cropped up on her phone. Or in conversation.

'Hey, how're you doing, Sasha? It's a bit late.'

Though she knew her sister didn't sleep much, not these days. She might be stable, her mental health issues on an even keel, but sleep was the one thing that eluded her. Too many thoughts in her head, she'd told Alex. Too many regrets.

'Alex, guess what?' Her sister was bubbling with excitement. No preamble. 'There are critics coming up from London for my exhibition. Real-life critics want to view my paintings. Mine! What if they don't like them? They might hate them. You will be at the preview, won't you? You will be there?' Her words came rushing out, tumbling over each other.

'Whoa, slow down, Sasha,' said Alex, smiling at the sheer joy in her sister's voice. 'Of course I'll be there. It's at that swish gallery in Gisford, isn't it? I'm not far from it now, actually.'

'Really? Is that where the charity do was then?'

'Nearby. A big farm. Big landowners. Pots of money.'

'I know the ones. Pierre told me about them.'

'Pierre?' Alex grinned even though Sasha couldn't see her.

'The gallery owner. And not my type. So, you know where it is, there is no excuse for you to miss it.'

'I wouldn't miss it for the world. The date's in my diary.'

'I'm so glad you'll be there. It wouldn't be the same without you. Can you believe it? Extremely famous people have exhibited there and now me. Me. I hope Mum'll come too.'

'You deserve it, Sasha. You've worked hard.'

'So how was the charity gig? You were going with that bland bloke, weren't you?'

'David. And he's not bland. His work is very interesting,' she replied, tartly.

'So how was David?' Her sister was teasing her.

'The do was a bit dull, in all honesty. And David was, well, not for me, shall we say.'

'Do I detect something not right, my darling sister?' There was amusement in Sasha's voice, and it gave Alex such pleasure to hear it. For years her sister had been so very fragile, doubled under the weight of guilt from which Alex thought she would never recover. But she had, as journalists such as herself were fond of saying, 'turned her life around', and was making a pretty good success of her art – something she had started as a hobby only relatively recently, but a hobby that had turned into a passion, and a passion that was quickly becoming a career.

'Put it this way—' Alex began, but then her words were interrupted by a beeping sound. Damn. The phone battery must be low. 'He was persistent.'

'And?'

Beep. She knew she should have charged her phone before she left home.

'And, nothing.' Alex suppressed a shudder as she saw in her mind's eye those wobbly lips coming towards hers. 'He's not my type,' she said, briskly. 'Worthy and all that, but not my cup of tea.'

Beep.

'So you won't be bringing him to my preview?'

'No.'

'That was pretty definite. Anyway, I must go. Art to create and all that. See you.'

'Sash, hold on—'

But her sister had gone. Damn. She'd been about to ask her to phone a mate to come and fetch her.

Beep.

And that was it. The battery was dead.

'Bloody hell,' she muttered, shaking it as if that would bring it back to life. 'Stupid, stupid woman.'

Definitely dead. No chance to ring Sasha or anybody else now.

She looked up. The light was fading fast. The wind was even sharper now, and the rain like needles on her face. There was a slight ache behind her temples. She didn't think champagne was meant to give you a hangover. And she had drunk plenty of water. She bent her head lower and trudged on, regretting once more declining that offer of a lift. Her hands were numb, even inside her gloves.

All at once she became aware of a flickering orange light in her peripheral vision. Was she imagining it? Was her brain more alcohol-fuddled than she realized? On. Off. On. Off. She began to walk more quickly.

There. She peered down and could just about make out marks on the road. Skid marks?

She stumbled on.

Then, around a corner and out of the dark loomed a vehicle on its side in the ditch with an indicator light flashing lazily. She hurried towards it.

Judging by the tyre marks and the torn vegetation the Land Rover – for she could see it was that – had lurched from one side over to the other, then hit a tree before coming to rest in the ditch.

The front of the vehicle had caved in and the windscreen had been smashed to smithereens. Glass littered the road and the verge. A strong smell of petrol made her head hurt even more. Christ. Gingerly, she made her way over to the open driver's door. No one inside. She looked in the back. Nothing. Then she heard a groan coming from a few feet away.

A man was lying on the ground like a ragdoll, his clothes half-flayed off him, his face a bloody mess. He groaned again. Rain diluted the blood that ran off him in rivulets. She hoped he looked worse than he was.

She knelt beside him and took his hand, swallowing hard. 'It's going to be okay. I'm here. You're going to be all right.' Her tears welled up at the lie.

'Cold.'

Alex shrugged off her coat and laid it on top of him. 'There. Now look, I've got to leave you.' She peered into the unyielding darkness, wondering where the nearest house was. She thought she wasn't too far from the pub, but how far? What did she reckon? The darkness was oppressive, and she had lost her bearings. The pub could be around the corner or a mile away.

'No.' A hand gripped her wrist strongly. 'Don't leave.'

She put her hand over his. 'I've got to. I've got no battery on my phone, I can't even make an emergency call. I need to fetch help. Do you understand?'

'Yes. Don't go. They'll come. Here,' she felt him press something in her hand, 'take this. My sister—'

'Please. Don't talk.' Her voice sounded desperate and she knew it. She was desperate. She had to get help – he was in a bad way.

She crumpled the piece of paper in her hand while trying to tuck her coat around him, oblivious to the fact that she was becoming soaked through. His skin was clammy. His breathing was becoming laboured. She could hardly bear to look at his poor, bloody face, but she made herself, and there was a flicker of recognition in her brain. He was wearing a gold chain. That, like his face, was familiar. She'd seen this man somewhere before, she was sure of it.

Before she could process the thought, she heard the sound of a car coming fast along the road. Thank God, thank God. 'Help is coming,' she whispered to the man.

His eyes opened. They were dark pools among the blood and torn skin.

'It's going to be okay, I promise.'

'No,' he said. His eyes closed. 'It's not.'

Alex leapt up as she saw headlights careering towards her and waved frantically. 'Stop. Please stop.'

Two men jumped out of the car and hurried over to her.

'You have to call the police. And an ambulance. There's a man who's been seriously hurt—' Alex could hardly get the words out in her haste.

'It's all right,' one of them said, turning the collar of the red Puffa jacket that strained against his body up against the rain and walking over to the injured man. 'We've got this. We'll take him to hospital.'

'We shouldn't move him.' Alex was agitated. She wanted proper help. People in green with stethoscopes. The reassuring lights and sound of an ambulance. Her head throbbed.

The man shook his head. 'Can't call an ambulance. No signal.'

'But—' She was going to say she had been on the phone to her sister not long before, though she did know there could be a decent signal one moment and none the next in this part of the world.

'If we don't take him to hospital he might die anyway.' The man in the too-tight jacket whipped her coat off the injured man. 'This yours?'

Alex took it back and put it on over her wet clothes, then realized she was still clutching the bit of paper the injured man had given her. She shoved it into her pocket.

The two men heaved the injured man into the car, almost stuffing him onto the back seat. He groaned in pain.

No, this wasn't right.

Alex had a half-memory from a First Aid course she had done years before that told her a casualty shouldn't be moved if at all possible. But then, even if there was a phone signal, how long would it be before an ambulance came to this rural road? Perhaps the only answer was to let these two men take him to hospital.

'Be careful, you'll hurt him even more.'

'Don't worry.' The second man turned to her. His dark wool coat was glistening with raindrops and he had an unmistakable air of authority. 'We'll get him to hospital.'

'Which one?'

'Which what?' He shut the car door on the injured man as the man in the red Puffa went to the driver's door.

'Hospital. Oh never mind, just get him there, will you. And hurry, please.'

'Don't worry, we will.'

'Hang on,' she said. 'Here.' She delved into her bag and pulled out a business card. 'Take this. Give the police my number. They'll probably want to talk to me. And could you let me know—'

'Police? Yes, of course. I'll call them.' He snatched the card from her hand. 'We'd better get going.' He jumped into the car and it drove off, wheels spinning on the tarmac.

Alex watched it go. Something didn't feel right. But her head was fuzzy and she couldn't grasp what was wrong.

The orange indicators of the crashed Land Rover continued to flash, and in the strobing light Alex saw a solitary trainer, soaking in a bloody puddle.

CHAPTER SIX

DAY ONE: LATE EVENING

He was in a car, he could hear an engine, feel his body jar as it went over bumps.

What had happened to him?

A crash, that was it. Driving too fast. Something on the road. A deer? A deer on the road. Hit his head. Hard. Men came. How many? Two? Was there someone else there as well? Think, for fuck's sake, think. It was all just out of reach. The men picked him up and tossed him in a car. He was hurting and he wanted to cry out, but he didn't. Again, instinct kicked in. He played dead. Almost dead. He was in a bad place.

The car stopped. The two men in the front seemed to be arguing. Something about 'cover it up' and 'as if it hadn't happened'. What was that all about? One of them banged the steering wheel.

He tried to open one eye. Couldn't. Stuck. Rubbed his hand over his eyes, Christ his hand was sore, then managed to open them, a little bit.

The men were getting out of the car. He strained to listen to their argument. He couldn't make out any words, but he could smell salt, diesel. A port?

37

Wait a minute. The estuary again. They were going to take him back. Where to? He didn't know, couldn't remember, but he knew suddenly and with absolute certainty that if he went back he would never leave.

He emptied his mind of all extraneous thought and concentrated on moving his limbs. He ignored the pain that shot through his shoulder as he tried to open the car door as quietly as he could, praying they hadn't put any internal locks on. The two men were still arguing.

He held his breath as the door opened. He rolled off the seat and onto hard concrete, jarring all the bones in his body that were already screaming with pain. He could hear the men's argument more clearly now.

'We keep quiet about this, right?' The first man's voice was gruff, slightly accented. Local? He wasn't well enough versed in the Norfolk and Suffolk accents to be sure.

'They'll find out, you know that.' Definitely Essex.

'Look, we get him back, patch him up and he'll be back at work in no time.'

Back at work. Flashes of memory. Taken underground. Kept underground. Packing boxes. Trying to talk to others who were doing the same thing. Learning they'd been taken. *Taken?* What did that mean?

Rick heard one of the men inhale deeply, then he saw a cigarette butt thrown onto the tarmac and ground underfoot.

Hurry, his brain screamed. *Hurry.*

Through sheer force of will, he made himself get onto his hands and knees – *Christ, that hurt* – and he started to crawl away. He glanced around, trying to take in his surroundings. There was no light from the moon or stars. As his eyes grew accustomed to the dark, he made out a few cars parked here and there, an unlit streetlamp. He had painfully made his way to one of the other cars. Now what?

He heard footsteps, running. Expletives, not shouted but

38

spoken quietly, angrily. They were looking for him. He saw their shoes coming nearer to the car. They were going to find him. Then:

Laughter. Chatter. A group of people? The laughter died away. 'Can we help you?' a voice called. Friendly.

'No.' Rude. aggressive.

'From round here, are you?' The voice was less friendly.

Rick chanced a look around the back of the car. He saw the two men who had picked him up with their backs to him. They were facing a crowd of, what? Six, seven men? Maybe out of the pub, walking off the booze. The right side of aggression. For now.

'Look,' said the first man, the one in the smart coat, 'we don't want trouble.'

'Nor do we,' said the group's spokesman. 'Gisford is a quiet little village where nothing happens because we don't want anything to happen and we always remember strangers.'

'Okay, okay. We're going.'

The men who were trying to take him somewhere he didn't want to go – wherever that was –got into their car and drove off, fast. Where were they going? And how long before they came back looking for him? He didn't have much time.

The laughing group wandered away, and Rick slowly came out from behind the car.

He was on some kind of harbour front. Concrete. The sea lapping at the edges. Across the water – the estuary he had swum across? – there were lights. Is that where he had come from? He had a bad feeling in his gut about the island across the water.

Keeping to the shadows, he limped away from the sea as fast as he could and towards a small road. It was dark, apart from the odd twinkle of light here and there from behind an upstairs window of a house. It was late then.

Better keep away from people. Vehicles. They might come back for him.

He set off down the narrow lane, looking for a gate or somewhere he could get off the road and hide. But there was nothing.

Then he heard an engine. A car. Had to be them.

He crouched down, then rolled under – thank fuck – a hedge, hardly daring to breathe.

The car went past him. Slowly.

He was comfortable here. Wanted to sleep. Only for a minute. He closed his eyes.

Rick thought he remembered French doors opening out onto a stone-flagged patio. A small retaining brick wall. A table and chairs and parasol. Green parasol. Maybe grey. Did it matter?

It did.

His whole body ached.

He kept his eyes tightly closed, shutting out the cold and the dark, the sound of a tap dripping and the dank smell of rotting vegetation, and tried to feel the warmth of the sun on his head and the scent of newly mown grass in his nose.

He thought hard.

There was laughter, he was sure of that. A child's voice, pure and high. His child? Sister? Brother? His head was so muddled. Had been for years. He shivered but felt the sweat roll down his back.

Wait.

Back to the sunshine.

A woman. Small. Blonde. Smiling at him. His wife. Her name? What was her goddam name? He wanted to cry out in frustration, but something told him to keep silent. Helen, that was it. But as soon as he thought of her name the dark began to roll in again. Why? What had he done?

Water. He'd swum across the estuary. Dark. Cold. He'd climbed into a car – hadn't he? Yes, yes. He'd been on his own, though he'd wanted to take Lindy. But she didn't make it. Why not? What happened? Was she here?

And who was Lindy?

The blonde woman? No. She was definitely Helen. Don't think about Helen.

And he'd left something behind, something important.

He shivered. And realized his body was a mass of aches and pains. He ran his tongue around his mouth and felt a couple of loose teeth. Tried to lift his head.

Fuck that hurt.

He gritted his teeth. Lifted his head again. Let it fall back. Too much pain.

Where was he? It wasn't hot enough to be the desert, not cold enough to be Norway or Russia, so where the hell was he?

He could do this, he'd been trained to withstand all sorts. He'd been trained by the—

What was he thinking? That he'd been trained by the army. Fuck, yes. Heat. Desert. The girl with the almond eyes. Push them away.

Army. That's who he was.

He opened his eyes. Saw brown spikes and brambles. His face throbbed. The dripping tap was rain falling off tree branches onto the ground beside him. Cold seeped through him from the earth. He was under a hedge? What?

He flexed his fingers, tried to move his legs, his arms. Instinct told him to keep his movements small and quiet. There had to be a reason he was under a hedge.

Hiding?

That had been such a bad idea. Could have been fatal.

He had no idea how long he'd been under the fucking hedge, but he had to gather himself and move. Even more, he needed to feel his body – at the moment he was numb and that was not a good thing.

Trying not to cry aloud with the pain of it, he rolled out from under the hedge and onto the road.

The full force of the rain hit him hard, opening the cuts on

41

his face, and within moments he was soaked through. At least, he thought grimly, it would wash away some of the blood and the dirt and the grime.

He lay still for a moment, then gritted his teeth and tried to stand.

His blood roared around his body and the mild pounding in his head became ever more fierce. His head swam and he thought he might black out or throw up or both. More deep breathing. Tried to throw his mind elsewhere. Back to sunshine, to laughter, to the hazy feeling of happiness he couldn't quite grasp.

Then, at least, he was standing straight. Only had one trainer on. Not good.

He shook his head, felt the loose teeth rattle. Spat out blood, but no teeth.

His body was stiff and weak. And it was fucking painful, especially his shoulder. He couldn't move his arm properly. Had he broken it? Dislocated it? He tried to waggle his fingers and winced. Yep, that worked. Not broken then. Blood was running down his arm onto his fingers. He craned his neck to look. A nasty gash running from shoulder to elbow. Not only dislocated but sliced open. And it didn't look great. Pieces of grit and mud and grass in the wound. He'd have to find somewhere to wash it.

Christ he felt sick. He started shaking again. Hot. Feverish. The shaking filled his body, stretched from the top of his head to his toes. Falling to his knees, he let the vomit spew out of him, retching until his ribs hurt and there was nothing more to come.

He closed his eyes.

He wanted, no needed – what? He had a memory of being given something, something that made him feel good. It made him feel good but also like a – zombie, that was it. Someone useless, without sense or a mind of their own. He'd been given it quite recently. Who by? Those men? He didn't want to feel like that again, like his body and mind were jelly and nothing could make an impression on them. No, he wanted to feel like himself again, but somewhere in the deep recesses of his mind he knew he didn't like that self. That self hurt people.

He stood up again. Slowly. Looked around. It was still dark, though the rain had abated. Right. He needed to get dry, to try and clean his wounds and to get some rest. Then maybe he could think about what he would do.

And at all costs he must avoid those men.

CHAPTER SEVEN

DAY TWO: MORNING

Alex stepped out of the Forum – a modern building constructed of glass that housed the city's library, a café, a shop and television and radio studios – and into the grey and drizzly daylight. Norwich was getting ready for work, and people splashed to and fro huddled under umbrellas. The market stallholders were busy pulling back the awnings over their stalls and putting goods out on display – all manner of things from spare vacuum cleaner parts to high-end leather goods. The smells of bacon and coffee from the fast-food outlets wafted over to Alex, making her stomach rumble.

The interview down the line to BBC Scotland had gone well, even though she'd been stuck in a small cubbyhole behind the Norfolk radio station's reception and had to imagine the jolly-voiced person at the other end of the microphone. Still, at least the presenter had read her book and had formed some interesting questions about it. He had even gone on to ask her about her other work, though obviously didn't want it to get too serious, as he cut her off when she began to go down the mental health route. It seemed she was destined for evermore to be known for her love of coupons.

It made her back itchy. Ever since she had begun her career – one that was blown off course almost straightaway when she became pregnant after an unfortunate one-night stand in Ibiza – she had lurched from one freelance job to another. Heath was right, she had to get off her backside and find herself a project, a decent story. If she wanted to be taken seriously, she had to do something serious. Sure, she had won a lot of professional acclaim for that series on Internet suicide forums, but she knew she was only as good as her last article. Or book. And if she didn't want to be remembered for all eternity for a book about finding and using money-off vouchers, then she had to get on with it and stop feeling sorry for herself. Give herself a new sense of purpose.

Alex yawned. Sleep had been elusive overnight, images of the crashed car and the broken man flashing through her mind. The blood. The look on his face. Frightened, not relieved when those people turned up to take him to the hospital. She had a nagging feeling that the whole set-up was wrong. Why hadn't she been more insistent that they told her exactly where they were taking him? Too much drink. Befuddled brain, maybe.

And there had been no call from the police. There had been a crash, a man had been injured, she was a witness. The man in the coat said he would call the police. They would want to talk to her.

Then she remembered she had given one of the men her card. There was no excuse for them not to call. Right. She wasn't going to wait, she was going to call round the hospitals – there weren't that many in the area – and find out the state of the injured man. It had been, what? About eleven o'clock when she left Riders' Farm. Allow about fifteen minutes for the walk down the road and then another three quarters of an hour for them to get to a hospital, so, it would be somewhere around midnight when he arrived, a bit longer if they went to the Norfolk and Norwich Hospital. She turned and went back into the Forum.

45

Five minutes later and she was in the radio cubbyhole again. The man on reception had assured her that it wasn't going to be used until lunchtime and said she was welcome to make her calls from there and could he have her autograph. For his mother. Of course.

She took her damp coat off again and settled down and spent fifteen frustrating minutes on the phone. No injured person had been brought in by one or two men at midnight to any of the hospitals she called – Norwich, Ipswich, Great Yarmouth and Bury St Edmunds. She even tried Colchester just in case. The only road traffic accident victims had been taken to hospital by ambulance.

'Sorry, love,' said a kind nurse at Colchester. 'Are you sure you weren't mistaken? Maybe the man wasn't that badly hurt after all and they took him home.'

Had she been mistaken? Could the blood and bruising have been superficial? You did hear about people walking away from horrific crashes without a scratch on them – perhaps that was it?

No, he had definitely been in pain, definitely needed hospital treatment.

'Maybe. Thank you for your help.'

'I hope you find him, love.'

Her journalistic instincts were beginning to kick in. It didn't smell right. How could someone seemingly so gravely injured disappear off the radar? The only explanation was if the men in the car hadn't taken him to hospital at all. But why wouldn't they? Perhaps the more pertinent question was: who were the men in the car? And how was she going to find that out?

Coffee, she thought, to help the brain function. She picked up her coat from the chair and looked at it. The same one she'd been wearing last night. And the injured man had pushed something into her hand that she'd stuffed into the pocket. Reaching inside, she took out a damp, crumpled piece of paper and carefully

46

smoothed it out on the desk. The ink had run, blurring the letters and numbers, but she could just about make them out. A name and a phone number. She stared at it. No time like the present.

The phone was answered after the third ring. 'Hello?'

'Is that Cora?' asked Alex.

'Who is this, please?' The voice on the other end was wary.

'Cora, my name is Alex Devlin. A man gave me your name and number last night.'

'What do you mean, a man gave you my name and number? What man?' Wariness had given way to suspicion.

Alex hesitated. Something told her not to go into the events of last night on the phone. 'Look. It's a bit of a story. Can I come and see you?'

'But I don't know you. You could be anybody.' Her tone was hostile. 'And I'm busy. This is a scam.'

'Wait.' Alex didn't want her to put the phone down. 'I'm a journalist, Cora. I freelance mainly, you can google me. I'm quite harmless. Honestly.' She injected a smile into her voice.

There was a silence at the other end of the phone. For a minute Alex thought Cora had hung up.

'I see you,' said Cora. 'Articles for a London paper and a book on—'

'Yes,' Alex said hastily. 'I know it doesn't sound too serious, but I do know what I'm doing.'

'Do you?' Another silence. 'Okay.'

'Where are you? Only I'm in Norwich at the moment and I'd like to come as soon as possible.' All at once she realized Cora could have been anywhere in the country.

'I live in the city, on the Ipswich Road.'

Alex looked at her watch. 'I can be with you in about ten minutes?'

In fact, it took less than that for Alex to find Cora's flat, which was up two flights of stairs in a sixties block with tidy grounds.

It was the second one along the walkway, with a honey-coloured wooden bench beneath the kitchen window and pots of straggly, struggling herbs by the door. She rang the bell.

A petite and too-thin woman with dark rings under her eyes and a blooming bruise on her cheekbone answered the door. She was wearing jeans tucked into Doc Martens and a sloppy black jumper. Her vibrant red hair was coiled messily on top of her head. She made Alex feel like an elephant.

'Alex?' Cora dragged deeply on the cigarette she held between two fingers.

Alex smiled. 'Yes. Thanks for seeing me.'

'You'd better come in out of the rain.'

The flat was clean and tidy with an overlying smell of smoke, but there were touches of colour and flamboyance in the shape of velvet cushions and rainbow throws. Dramatic photographs of landscapes were on the magnolia walls. Alex stared at them. They made her feel as though she was there, standing in that landscape.

'Good, aren't they?' said Cora, nodding at the photos and handing Alex a mug of coffee. As her sleeve slipped back, Alex saw three swallows inked on the inside of her wrist.

'Fabulous. Where are they from?'

'They're my brother's work,' she said, and Alex saw a darkness creep into her eyes. 'Please, sit down and tell me why you're here.' She held herself slightly aloof.

Alex curled her hands around the mug, warming up. A washing machine whirred in the background. Cora obviously wasn't one for small talk. 'Last night I came across a car accident,' she began, searching for the right words. 'A man had been thrown out of a Land Rover. He was badly hurt.'

Cora was still. 'I don't see what that has got to do with me.'

'He gave me a piece of paper. It had your name and telephone number on it. Could he be a relative? A friend?'

Cora didn't move. 'What did he look like?'

Alex knew that question would be coming, but it didn't make it any easier. 'Cora, it was difficult to see. It was dark, he was covered in blood. There was one thing though—'

'Yes?'

Alex had thought about this. She had remembered feeling something strange as the man had thrust the piece of paper into her hand. 'I think he only had three fingers and a thumb, or at least, there was something strange about his hand.'

Cora gave an intake of breath and stood up abruptly. She went over to the bookshelf. 'Is this the man you saw?'

Alex took the photo frame from her. It was a picture of a young man in battle fatigues, smiling, looking fit and happy. From the looks of it, the photo had been taken in a desert army camp of some sort. Afghanistan, perhaps? She looked more closely. The thick black hair, the shape of the face. As she'd had when she'd seen him on the road, she felt a flicker of recognition. 'I think it could be,' she said. 'He didn't have any hair as such though – it was only stubble.' Then she nodded. 'I'm almost sure.'

Cora exhaled. 'That's my brother, Rick. He's missing most of the little finger on his left hand. I've been looking for him. I haven't seen him for two weeks. He had long hair and a beard last time I saw him.'

Alex shook her head. 'No beard. No hair. Stubble on top. But I think it could have been him.'

Cora stood, stubbing out her cigarette. 'Where is he? Which hospital did you take him to?' Her eyes were feverish, she looked as though she was ready to break out into a sprint. 'I'll get my coat.'

Alex put out her hand to stay her. 'That's the thing, I didn't take him to hospital.'

'What do you mean?'

Alex tried to avoid Cora's glare. 'My phone had run out of battery, so I couldn't call anyone. I was about to go for help when

49

two men turned up. They said they would take him, make sure he was seen—'

'So, which hospital?' Cora rubbed her face, as if trying to keep herself alert.

'I'm so sorry.' Alex's heart twisted, she could understand Cora's desperation. And she felt so stupid – how could she have let it happen? 'I don't know. They didn't say where they were taking him. I've rung hospitals all around the area, but without any luck. Could he have gone home?'

'Home?' The laugh Cora gave was harsh. 'That's just it, He doesn't have a home.'

Alex was puzzled. Then, with a sudden insight, she got it. And she remembered where she had seen the man before. 'He's homeless, isn't he? I've seen him around Norwich.'

'Yes.' That single word held years of pain. 'But all this talking isn't getting us anywhere near finding him. I'll try the hospitals again. I'm a nurse, I know the way it works. Sometimes you might get hold of the wrong people or something. Did you try the James Paget at Gorleston? You probably forgot that one.' Alex saw her hands shaking as she began to punch in numbers on her phone.

'Cora—'

She looked at Alex, eyes blazing. 'Let me do this. I need to know.'

Alex looked on helplessly. She knew she had done her best to find the man – Rick. She had spoken to every hospital press officer, even the chief exec of Ipswich who she was on friendly terms with. But Cora had to see for herself.

CHAPTER EIGHT

DAY TWO: MORNING

Detective Inspector Sam Slater jogged and splashed down the muddy path through the trees to the pedestrian crossing over the railway line. It was a miserable day, with lowering clouds and gusts of rain. A miserable day to kill yourself.

He reached the track, and, as he opened the gate festooned with warning notices and one giving out the number for the Samaritans, he saw that the train had come to a standstill about a hundred metres down the track. It was travelling towards Ipswich, probably carrying people to work in the town, or further afield to London. The air ambulance was preparing to land and Sam knew forensics would be along soon to gather up what was left of the body. He could imagine the scene on the train: commuters on their mobile phones cancelling meetings, phoning bosses to explain why they would be late. Because they would be late. Some would be complaining, demanding their Delay Repay forms and muttering about compensation. Few would spare much of a thought for the driver who had probably heard the dull *thwack* against the bottom of the train, a hollow crunch as metal hit flesh. He would probably hear that sound for the rest of his life and know that he had been the unwilling instrument in someone's death.

Engineers in hi-vis tabards and safety helmets had turned up to check the train for damage before it would be allowed to move on.

Slater walked down the track and past the train.

She had been lying on the rails before she was hit, thought Slater. She had been decapitated, he could see that, and various limbs were strewn along the track, along with shreds of material. There were long streaks of blood along the line and on the clinker under the track. If he looked carefully near his feet, and he tried not to, he could see white bits of bone and grey brain matter. He wondered how much forensics would actually retrieve before the rain washed it all away. Not that it mattered. Railway suicides were cut and dried.

Police Constable Edwards was taping off the access onto the track, and Slater thought of the angry people waiting on platforms for trains that were either delayed or cancelled. That was the trouble. A delay for one person was another's final journey.

Slater took one more look at the scene – at the engineers, the paramedics from the air ambulance and the train driver who was sitting by the side of the track oblivious to the rain. Soon there would be posies of flowers, ribbons and teddy bears – there were always teddy bears – by the crossing gates that would wither and turn brown and rot with time.

Nodding to Edwards and the extra officers who had turned up, Slater turned and jogged back down the muddy path which was now more churned up than ever.

CHAPTER NINE

DAY TWO: MORNING

Cora couldn't stop her fingers from trembling as she began to dial the numbers of the hospitals in the area. She knew many of the nurses on shift well. Working on the bank – essentially free-lancing – meant she had worked at hospitals all over East Anglia at one time or another. But ten frustrating minutes later, after some helpful calls and other downright hostile ones, Cora had drawn a blank. It was as Alex Devlin had said, no one of her brother's age or description had been taken to A&E the previous night.

So where was he? What had happened to him? Why couldn't he get in touch with her? And what was he doing on a lonely road in a Land Rover? She thought back to last night and the 'warning' she'd been given. She gingerly rubbed her cheekbone. There had been a reason for that. Whatever he was doing, he was getting close, whether she liked it or not.

She threw her phone onto the kitchen table. 'Take me through it again,' she demanded, tapping out another cigarette and lighting it. One day she would stop, just not now. She was so tired and her head was swimming. 'If you don't mind?' she said suddenly, remembering her manners.

Alex took a deep breath.

Cora concentrated hard, occasionally blowing out smoke through the corner of her mouth as Alex told her what had happened once more, only interrupting for clarification.

'And you've no idea who the men who took Rick away were?' They didn't sound like the same ones that had picked her up, and anyway, the timing was wrong.

'None. I'm sorry I didn't ask more questions. It had been a long day and I had been at this charity event at Riders' Farm and—'

'Riders' Farm?'

'Do you know it?'

Cora laughed harshly. 'Oh yes. The brothers Grimm and the witch and the wizard.'

Alex raised her eyebrows. 'Wow. Those are certainly some monikers.'

'As rich as Croesus but with the morals of alley cats.' She stopped. What was she saying? For all she knew this Alex Devlin might be best buddies with the Riders. 'Sorry, that was a bit harsh. But they are big donors to one of the hospitals where I work. Everybody has to bend the knee when they walk past. And they love it. Smug bastards.' She ground out her cigarette in a saucer. 'They like women too. Correction. They like to control women. So I've heard.' She added quickly.

'I take it they're not the most popular family around here?'

'You could say that. Others might say they've brought employment to the area, tourists.'

'But you say?'

The look on Alex's face was open and friendly. But she was a journalist. And Cora didn't want to be part of her story.

'So this event,' she said finally, ignoring Alex's question, 'who did you meet?'

'Jamie Rider, among others.'

'And what did you think of him?' She lit another cigarette

from the one she'd been smoking, trying to push away the memories of her mother sewing curtains for the Riders, babysitting those damn boys while leaving her and Rick to fend for themselves. Her mother baking scones for Marianne Rider's coffee mornings. Her father tugging his forelock and calling Marianne Rider 'Ma'am' and Joe Rider 'Sir', as if they were the bloody queen and bloody Prince Phillip.

Alex narrowed her eyes. She looked as though she was about to say something, but then thought the better of it. 'He was charming.'

'Charming. Right.' She nodded.

Alex leaned forward. 'Why do I think you know the Riders better than you're admitting to?'

'King's Lynn,' Cora said, banging her forehead. 'Why didn't I think of them? It could be possible he was taken there. And I know several of the nurses in A&E.'

She picked up the phone and stabbed out a number.

'Margot is phoning me back,' she said after a minute's chatting. 'She thinks that they may have had someone brought in, so she's going to check.' Her leg was jiggling up and down. She slapped her hand on her thigh to stop it. 'Tell me more about you, Alex. You're from this part of the world, aren't you?'

Alex nodded. 'Yes I am. Sole Bay up the coast is where my heart is, but I needed a change, and thanks to people's love of saving cash I was able to buy a flat in Woodbridge. So here I am.'

Cora nodded. 'I did see it, when I looked you up. Your book, I mean. Sounds like a great idea. A bit like that woman who cooks on a shoestring or bootstrap. Jack somebody. It's all about saving money.' She looked away. 'I also read about your sister and all that happened.' She pulled on her cigarette wishing that damn phone would ring.

Alex didn't flinch. 'She's had a tough time, but she's doing well now. I'm proud of her.'

'I'm proud of Rick,' said Cora. 'He's had one or two problems, but we were dealing with them together, and—' she chewed her lip. She had to be careful, Alex was too easy to speak to.

'It must be difficult, with him being homeless.'

Alex's voice was so gentle it almost made Cora cry, so she busied herself with the kettle and cups and a box of teabags. She wished that phone would bloody ring.

'It's not great, I have to say, but we manage.'

'You manage?'

Careful. 'We used to live around here, near the coast anyway, but had to leave when I was eighteen.'

'Had to leave?'

Sharp.

Alex was too on the ball. 'Sort of. Anyway, we were living near Bury St Edmunds and Rick was working on a farm. When I qualified as a nurse, Rick decided to sign up for the army.'

'So, how did you get here?'

The kettle boiled. Steam curled under the kitchen cupboards. Cora poured water onto teabags in mugs. 'Rick was here. I wanted to be near him, so I followed him to the city and managed to get on the bank. Plenty of work at the hospitals around here.' She smiled sadly. 'Everyone going off with stress, you see. They need agency nurses.' She squished the teabags against the side of the mug, poured some milk in and handed one to Alex. 'Sorry. More caffeine. Rick saw action in Afghanistan. Watched his friends get blown up, maimed. But it was on his second tour that the worst happened.'

'Go on,' said Alex.

She sighed. 'There was a young girl – look, you've got to know that part of the reason they were out there, in Afghanistan, was to "capture hearts and minds".'

Alex nodded. 'I know. I read about that.'

'They would give out sweets to the kids, help the women, helped the men if they could. And they were winning. They were.'

'A young girl?' prompted Alex.

Cora gripped her mug even tighter. 'Rick was at some sort of checkpoint. The girl came towards him. She was fifteen at the most, he reckoned. But she was already beautiful. Lovely eyes. As she came closer, Rick said he saw tears in those eyes. She spread out her hands. And then—'

Cora stopped, took a deep breath, gathered her thoughts. Every time she told this story – and she tried not to tell it often – she had to damp down the tears, talk about it as though it had happened to someone else and not her brother.

'She blew herself up.'

Alex drew a sharp breath.

Cora knew the stark brutality of her words was shocking, but there was no other way to say it.

'I'm so sorry,' Alex said.

Cora gave a brief smile. 'It doesn't end there. One of his friends was killed and Rick received shrapnel wounds. He came home but he was a different man. Helen – Rick's wife – got her husband back in one piece, but he wasn't the man who'd left for Afghanistan, and no one seemed to care. He tried so hard for so long. He even held down a job in security for a year or two. The photography helped for a while – it had been a hobby of his for years – but it didn't keep the demons away in the end. He would lose his temper at the slightest thing, just fly off the handle.'

'Did he hurt his wife?'

'Once. And that was it for Helen. She worried he would hurt the girls.' Cora saw Alex's questioning look. 'His daughters.' She gripped the sides of her mug to stop her hands trembling. 'They were only four and five and they didn't understand why Daddy had changed towards them. I think he was pushing them away deliberately.'

'So Helen threw him out?'

'Not exactly,' said Cora, sadly. 'He left before, as he put it, he did any more damage. He also said that every time he looked at

57

his girls he thought of the girl in the village and how she'd been young and carefree not so many years before. But when he left he had nowhere to go. Or nowhere he wanted to go. So he got on a bus and ended up in Norwich.'

'On the streets.'

Cora sighed. 'Not straightaway. He had some money and he stayed in a hotel, then a hostel. But then the money ran out.' She shrugged. 'He went on the streets. Said he'd met someone who could help him get a good pitch, that sort of thing. I tried to get him help, but Rick didn't want the bit that was offered. Said he didn't deserve it. Said no one could understand what he was going through. And I suppose they couldn't. I came this way because I wanted, no, needed, to keep an eye on him. I couldn't bear the thought of him being all on his own. But he didn't seem to care whether I was around or not.' The best lies contained a grain of truth.

'And Helen?'

'Moving on. She took the girls to her parents in York. My nieces. I won't see them grow up now.' She sniffed, rubbed away some tears from the corner of her eyes. 'We – Helen and I – know now that he was suffering from a head injury and post-traumatic stress disorder. Still is. He didn't tell us it was so bad. We didn't understand.'

Alex took hold of one of her hands. 'I've been there, Cora. Regret, lost opportunities. I know how guilt can eat away at you until it takes over your whole life. You have to let it go or it will destroy you.'

How Cora wished that bloody phone would ring.

'And what about you?' asked Alex.

'Me?' Cora sniffed. She lit another cigarette.

'Yes, you. You're entitled to a life too, you know. Rick made his choice. It doesn't mean you have to give up your life.'

'I'm not.'

'Okay.'

'Really, I'm not, so can you leave it, please.' She made her voice deliberately sharp. There was no way she wanted this woman, this journalist she hardly knew, to start poking her nose into that business. Finding Rick, well, that was another matter. She would just have to make sure she kept Alex Devlin pointed in the right direction, didn't allow her to veer off course. She jumped up and wrapped her arms around herself. 'This isn't getting us any nearer to finding Rick.'

'No. But I wanted to get a sense of who he is.'

'Perhaps if you hadn't left him to be taken in a strange car to God knows where you might have done just that.' Cora knew she sounded mean and unforgiving but she couldn't help it. Alex had got under her skin.

Alex picked up her bag. 'That's unfair, Cora. He was probably taken to a hospital and left before they could treat him. I'm sure he's fine. That could be the answer. I'm really sorry I didn't do better. I hope you find him soon.'

'Please don't go.' Cora grabbed Alex's arm. 'Look. He would have been in touch with me by now.'

'Really? How?'

Cora could see the doubt written on Alex's face. 'He always finds a way to get a message to me.' She sat down again, her shoulders slumped. Up and down. Mercurial, Rick had told her that once. 'Sit down. Please.'

Alex sat, though Cora could see it was with reluctance.

Cora's phone rang. She snatched it up. 'Hello?'

It took Margot on the other end only a few seconds to tell her that she'd been wrong. Someone had been brought in to A&E, but he was an elderly man of seventy-five.

She threw the phone down. 'No luck there.'

'We will find him, Cora.'

'When I went looking for him, one of his mates, Martin, said that a couple of blokes had spoken to him, to Rick I mean, a few days before he disappeared. And that he wasn't the only one.'

'The only one what?'

'Who these men spoke to.'

Alex frowned.

'Martin said they'd been talking to Nobby and Lindy, two more of the homeless, and he hasn't seen them since either.' Cora leaned forward. 'Don't you see? These men could be the ones who picked Rick up. Maybe he didn't want to go with them. I don't know, maybe—' she waved her hands around, 'maybe they forced him in some way. Maybe,' she said, warming to her theme, 'maybe they were the ones who picked him up off the road? Come on, you're a journalist, you must know how to find missing people. You can get into all sorts of databases and stuff.' And the more she thought about it, the more she thought it would be a good idea to have Alex on board. She really was worried about Rick, what he was trying to do was dangerous. Then there were those goons last night. She rolled her shoulders. Bloody hell, she ached. And her head ached.

'Cora, have you told the police that Rick is missing?'

Cora began to laugh, but knew she had to control herself before the laughter became hysterical. 'Do you think they care if someone who lives on the street is missing? Of course not. They'll only say he's moved on or fallen in with some criminal gang or gone somewhere else to score.' Her finger made patterns in crystals of sugar left on the table. Besides, she did have an idea where he might have gone. Before. But now, after this supposed accident?

'Maybe. But he would probably be classed as a vulnerable person and more would be done to—'

'Really?' Cora was all sharp sarcasm.

'Look,' said Alex, 'I'll have a word with a friendly copper to make sure he hasn't been picked up by them for some reason or other. I'll phone him on our way to see this Martin who you know. We can try the hospitals again later. But let's not sit here doing nothing. And maybe we should report him missing. Cover all bases, yes?'

60

Cora drummed her fingers on the table. Last night had been a warning. Don't poke your nose in, don't stir things up. Well, fuck that. She was bloody well going to poke her nose in where they didn't want it and Alex Devlin could help her do just that. Reporting Rick's disappearance to the cops wouldn't help find Rick – the dozy buggers wouldn't lift a finger – but it would piss the Riders off.

She stood. 'I'll get my coat.'

CHAPTER TEN

DAY TWO: MORNING

Alex had walked through the underpass many times before, lowering her gaze so as not to attract the attention of the winos and the druggies, always feeling slightly apprehensive. But with Cora they became individuals. The woman knew them by name, laughed with them, told them off for their filthy language. And Alex thought she was doing something for society by buying the *Big Issue* and occasionally giving to Crisis at Christmas. But it was Cora who was doing the right thing, seeing the homeless as people, with names and personalities and lives.

'Still not found 'im then, Cora?' A man with badly discoloured teeth and wearing a tatty flat cap waved a bottle of cheap cider at her.

Cora shook her head. ''Fraid not Tiger.'

'Perhaps he's got himself a girlfriend. A bed for the week, you know?' He leered at her.

She took no notice of the leer. 'Maybe. But I'm worried about him. When was the last time you saw him?'

Tiger shrugged. Pursed his lips. 'Well, it ain't changed since the other day. Coulda been last month. Or three weeks ago.' He tapped the side of his head. 'My memory's not so good these days.'

'Has anybody spoken to you recently?' asked Alex.

'Besides the cops?' There was general laughter. He stared at her. 'And who are you anyways? Are you a copper? Or a do-gooder?'

Alex tried to smile as easily as Cora, though her heart was thudding in her chest. 'Neither. I'm a journalist.'

'You can write about me then,' said another man, swaggering up to her. 'Tell my life story. How I got here. You'd never believe I was an accountant in a past life, would you?' His sour alcoholic breath wreathed around her.

He was right, she wouldn't have believed it, but she knew perfectly well that anyone could become homeless – most people were only a couple of missed rent or mortgage payments away from it.

'Gambling,' he said, before hawking and spitting to the left of her. She didn't move a muscle. 'Lost everything. Had a good life once, everything going for me. Now look at me. No house. No wife. No kids. No life.'

Alex looked him straight in his rheumy eyes. 'I would like to write your life story,' she said firmly. She lifted her voice. 'All of your stories.' Her words echoed around the underpass. 'I mean it. If you want me to. But first we want to find Rick.'

'What about the coppers? Maybe they've picked him up.' A challenge.

Alex shook her head. 'Not as far as we know.' Alex had rung Detective Inspector Sam Slater on the way to the underpass and he'd checked for her. No one had been taken off the streets early that morning or late last night, with or without any injuries.

A girl – who could have been aged anywhere between twenty and fifty – peeled herself off the wall. 'Have you talked to Boney?'

'We were going to go and see Martin. He was the last person to see Rick.'

Alex couldn't help but notice the glances that went around the group. 'What?' she said.

'Haven't seen Martin since yesterday,' said the girl. 'Din't turn up for the soup round last night. He allus turns up for the Sally Army soup round. Greedy bugger. Wasn't there today neither. Ethel was tied up to the lamppost. Guess she's gone to the dog pound. He could've moved on, I suppose. Back to Yarmouth.'

Cora shook her head. 'No, he didn't like the place.'

The girl shrugged. 'Boney'd know. He knows everything.'

'Where do we find Boney?'

Cora tugged at her sleeve. 'I know where he is. Come on.'

Half an hour later and Alex found herself in the corner of a car park on the outskirts of central Norwich helping Cora pull at a sheet of corrugated iron.

'If we just push this along like so—' panted Cora. 'We can shimmy—' She squeezed her small frame through a narrow gap in the fence she had made. 'Voila! Easy-peasy.'

Taking a deep breath, Alex followed.

'Is this what I think it is?' said Alex, looking around at the lichen-covered gravestones that sat, higgledy-piggledy in a small area of waterlogged grass. Some were leaning so precariously it would give a health and safety inspector nightmares. In between the overgrown graves and forgotten chipped weeping angels was long grass dotted with molehills.

'It's an old Jewish cemetery,' said Cora as they made their way through the wet grass. 'Years old I'm told. It's forgotten by almost everyone except Boney and his crew. I think some historians want to make it some sort of protected area, restore it and all that. Put in a visitor's centre I shouldn't wonder. But there's no money, apparently. So for now, it's home to Boney. And his, er, mates.' Her mouth was set in a line.

'So who exactly is Boney?' Alex was curious.

Cora sighed. 'He helps the homeless people in the city. Finds places in hostels for them, gets the soup run out to them. Takes a small cut, but, hey, he's got to earn a living, I guess. Gets them

64

good pitches, makes sure they're not turfed off them by someone new to the area – he even has a couple of coppers in his pocket who turn a blind eye to some of the people on the streets. Some might say they're not doing their job; I think they're showing a bit of humanity.' Her expression grew dark. 'But Boney's also responsible for the never-ending supply of drugs – heroin, crystal meth, Spice, you name it, he can get it. Says it helps.' She shrugged. 'Maybe it does. Oh, he can also supply a dog.'

'Ethel?' Alex asked, thinking of Martin.

'Yes.'

'Where are they then? Boney and his friends?'

Cora nodded to an even more overgrown area of the cemetery, in which stood a shed. 'That's where the caretaker used to store his tools,' she said.

The door opened and a cadaverously thin man dressed in skintight jeans and a very grubby Parka stood in the doorway. His head was shaved, showing the outline of his knobbly skull, and his whole face was covered in what Alex thought were Maori-type tattoos. His bottom lip, eyebrow and cheek were pierced, and one of his earlobes had been stretched so it hung fleshily down.

'Cora.' Boney had a high-pitched voice but with a cultured accent. Alex wondered what his story was and whether he might tell her sometime. Could make a good article. He smiled and held out his arms. His incisors had been filed to sharp points. 'Long time no see.'

Behind Boney Alex saw a disparate group of men and women, girls and boys, all thin and grubby and all dressed in what looked like cast-offs. Many of them didn't look more than teenagers. She was reminded of the Lost Boys from *Peter Pan* and her heart bled for them. She thought of her own son, Gus, and how easily he could have ended up as a lost boy, but thankfully he had weathered the crises that had beset him as a teenager and as a young man trying to find his way in the world.

Now he was safely at university with his girlfriend. He'd be back soon for a weekend of rest and relaxation and she couldn't wait to see him.

Cora ignored the open arms and folded her own. 'Boney.'

'Still looking for that wastrel brother of yours?'

'Yes. Please, Boney, have you any idea where he might be?'

Alex stepped forward, she needed to be at the front of this. 'And Martin. Apparently he's gone missing too, together with Nobby and a woman called Lindy. That's four people.' She lifted her chin.

'Who might you be?' Boney's tongue flicked out of his mouth and played with his lip ring. His eyes gleamed.

'I'm Alex.' She wished he wouldn't do that with his tongue and the ring, it was really disconcerting.

'And what have you got to do with our delicious Cora?'

'I'm a friend. I'm helping her look for Rick.'

'First I've heard about Cora having a little friend. Usually too busy with work and looking after Rick, isn't that right, Cora? Always helping the fucking cripples.'

'Shut up, Boney.' Cora brushed his words aside. 'And Rick isn't a cripple. I've helped you and now it's payback time. That was the deal if you remember. One good turn and all that. You know everything that happens on the streets. You must have heard something about Rick. About Martin.'

'And Lindy. And Nobby,' said Alex, wondering how exactly Cora had helped Boney in the past.

Boney's eyes narrowed. Now his smile was dangerous, his teeth vicious. His followers shuffled impatiently behind him. As yet, none of them had said a word. 'If you take my advice,' he said, enunciating every word and sounding like a school teacher, 'you will forget about Lindy and Martin and Nobby and, yes, even Ricky-boy, and get on with your lives. Nice shiner you've got there, Cora. I'd've thought you got that message last night.' He turned his head sharply and his eyes bored into Alex. 'You too,

Alex Devlin. Don't think I don't know who you are. Journalist.' He spat out the word.

Alex was shaken but was determined not to show it. 'If you know who I am then you know I like to write about social issues.' She was pleased to hear her voice came out evenly.

He pulled at his earlobe. 'Really? Social issues.' He laughed. 'What bollocks. Social fucking issues. Want to write my life story?'

'I might,' said Alex, determined to stand her ground and not be intimidated. 'Can't promise anything though.'

Boney did nothing for a moment, then a smile curled his lips. 'Fuck me. Ballsy. I like that. As for you, Cora, no can do, I'm afraid. I guess your old bro has just buggered off. Like the rest.' He shrugged. 'It happens.'

'I don't believe you, Boney,' said Cora, hotly. 'You know everything that goes on. And you owe me.'

'I owe you nothing. Now, get out of here. Before I make you go.'

'What'll you do?' said Alex, emboldened. 'Call the police?'

'Come on, Alex.' Cora tugged at her sleeve. 'He's not going to help us. I should have known his word's not to be trusted.'

Boney's mocking laughter followed them out of the cemetery.

'So, what was the favour you did for the charming Boney?'

They were sitting in a coffee shop back in the city trying to get warm and dry, two sausage rolls and two cups of coffee in front of them. Alex couldn't feel her toes.

'I stitched up one of his gang members after a knife fight,' said Cora, her hands shredding a paper serviette. She looked down at what she was doing and gave a hollow laugh. 'See, I don't know what to do with my hands when I can't smoke.' She shaped the pieces of serviette into a pile.

'Drink some coffee.' Alex pushed the cup towards her. Cora curled her hands around the china mug. 'Had Rick been involved? Is that why you did it?'

67

'Got it in one,' said Cora. 'A fight between the homeless guys and some youths from the city. Boney and his boys waded in. I didn't want the coppers coming along, shutting Rick away. He wouldn't be able to stand that, you see. But Boney. I thought he'd be as good as his word. That'll teach me. I won't make that mistake again,' said Cora. 'At the time he said he owed me one. Would repay me. Shows there's no honour among thieves.' She shook her head. 'But you know, I can't believe he doesn't know *something*.'

'You're right.' Alex took a sip of her coffee. 'I've been doing this job for so long now that you develop a sixth sense for when people are lying. And he was lying.' Alex put her cup down carefully. 'What happened last night, Cora?'

Cora's head snapped up. 'What do you mean?'

'Boney said that you had a message last night. What did he mean? It's something to do with that nasty bruise on your cheek, isn't it? And you've been moving as if you hurt in other places too.'

'Oh, that.'

'Yes, that, Cora.'

Cora drank some coffee. 'Couple of thugs tied me up and threw me into a wheelie bin.' Alex gasped. 'Told me to stop poking my nose in where it wasn't wanted.'

'Cora – anything could have happened. The bin lorry could have come and—'

'It very nearly did. But whoever was behind it didn't want me to die. Not yet anyway. They paid someone to let me out just in time.'

Alex looked at her steadily. 'Who do you think's involved?'

'Dunno.' Cora avoided her eyes.

Alex didn't believe her.

'You asked me about the Riders.'

'So?' Still Cora didn't – or wouldn't – look at her.

'You don't like them.'

'No shit, Sherlock. Look, leave it, Alex.'

Alex put down her coffee cup. 'You think it's one of them.'

'I said, leave it.'

But Alex didn't want to 'leave it'. She decided to try another avenue. 'So Boney knew about it. The wheelie bin thing, I mean.'

'It would seem so.'

'Do you know his real name?'

Cora smiled, a real smile that lit up her face and chased away the pasty edges. 'Someone on the street told me once. Nigel.'

Alex raised an eyebrow. 'Nigel?'

'Nigel Bennet.'

Alex grinned. 'He doesn't look much like any Nigels I know.' She fished her phone out of her bag. 'Let's see if Google knows who he is.' Her fingers stabbed at the phone. 'There are five Nigel Bennets on LinkedIn, but I can't imagine his business would have a profile on there.' She scrolled some more. 'A few on Facebook. Unlikely too.'

'He's not really going to be on social media, is he?' Cora sounded impatient.

'No, not now maybe, though it's always worth checking. He could be like one of those stupid people who post pictures of money and goods they've stolen. Now let's see …' She turned the phone round to Cora. 'Look, there are a couple of Nigel Bennets in images. But I can't tell if any of them are him. Especially without the—' she gestured at her face.

Cora smiled. 'You mean the piercings, the long lobes and the sharp teeth?' She squinted at the screen. 'Nor me. Too fuzzy. You're not going to find him there. I wouldn't bother, if I were you.'

Alex put her phone away. 'You're probably right.'

'What do we do now?'

'Now,' said Alex, smearing some Colman's mustard over her sausage roll before popping a piece into her mouth and deciding not to pursue the Nigel angle for the moment, 'we report Rick missing – yes we will,' she emphasized as she saw Cora about to interrupt. 'He's a vulnerable person and if he's on the police radar then they'll look out for him.'

Cora frowned. 'If you really think—'

'I do,' Alex said firmly.

'Okay. Then what?'

'I'm not sure,' Alex said, thinking it through. 'But Rick is missing. So are Martin and Lindy. And Nobby. Do you suppose there are others? After all, as you rightly said, no one really cares if someone who is homeless isn't seen for a while. People just think they've moved on, or have been banged up for one reason or another.'

'Are you seeing a pattern in this?'

'Maybe.' She knew who she should be speaking to, though she really, really didn't want to. She sighed. 'I am friends – sort of – with the guy from Fight for the Homeless.'

'David Gordon.' Cora flicked a piece of the serviette on the floor.

'You know him?' She was surprised.

'Bit self-serving. Doesn't really care about the homeless, only about his reputation.'

'I'm not sure—'

'Take it from me.' She moistened her fingertip and dabbed flakes of puff pastry from her plate. 'I like this sausage roll. Is there any more?'

'Here,' Alex pushed the plate across to Cora, 'help yourself. Anyway. I think I'll go and see him, find out if he knows anything.'

'And in the meantime, Rick is still missing.' Cora looked at Alex, her eyes suddenly sharp.

Alex nodded. 'Yes, he is. But we will find him. I promise.'

'Really?' Her voice was part hopeful, part scathing.

'Yes.'

Oh, Alex, she said to herself. There you go again, making promises you may not be able to keep.

CHAPTER ELEVEN

DAY TWO: MORNING

A weak grey light filtered through the gaps between the trees. Rick groaned and opened his eyes. The taste in his mouth was worse than the bottom of a parrot's cage and the pounding in his head threatened to split his skull in two. The smell around him was awful, too. Vomit, sweat, unwashed bodies, well, one unwashed body – his.

The smell evoked a memory: a concrete room underground. He was lying on a thin mattress, covered by a couple of blankets. There were two or three electric heaters dotted around, so there had to be electricity. Not that those heaters did anything except maybe take the edge off the freezing cold.

He thought hard. He hadn't been the only one there. How many? Two? Ten? More.

The memory faded as another bout of sickness overcame him.

He had to fight this.

The night had been full of dreams of white space, white noise, swaying snakes, insects crawling over his skin. When he woke up from the nightmares – which was often – he would be sweating, his heart pounding. He vomited more than once. Was he ill? No, it was that stuff they'd put into his veins, or rather, the lack of it.

Withdrawal symptoms. That's what this was.

More disjointed memories. Being tied down, straps across his chest. A tourniquet around his arm. A stab. Darkness and vivid dreams full of colour and sound.

And was that responsible for his loss of memory or did that come from the car accident?

Car accident. Yes, he remembered that. Swimming in icy water, finding a car, crashing it, being picked up and put in another car, escaping. Walking, keeping to the shadows, away from the road, until he found this barn. He'd managed to take off the wettest of his clothes and crawl underneath some old sacking.

Wait.

Rewind.

There was a woman somewhere in that mix. Softly spoken, kind eyes. He'd given her a piece of paper. What was on that paper?

Nothing. Couldn't remember. It would come back to him, wouldn't it?

What was he doing here?

He became aware of another pain. His arm. He twisted to look at it. A long gash. Throbbing. Needed stitches, maybe.

Priorities: clean water; food; dry clothes; dental floss to stitch the wound; a needle. Or better still, a decent bandage. And he needed shoes.

He reached for his clothes. They were damp and they stank. Nevertheless he pulled them on – didn't want to frighten the horses. Or the cows. Or the pigs. He guessed he was on a farm from the other smells that surrounded him – good, clean farm smells compared to his body odour.

But it was getting light, so had to be after seven. Damn, he needed to get moving.

He looked around. In one of the corners he saw round bales wrapped in plastic. With a combination of his hands and teeth and shutting his mind to the pain in his head and his arm, he managed to tear a hole in the plastic and grab a couple of handfuls of the straw inside. The straw hurt his hands. So sore. He wanted to cry out. He rubbed himself down, feeling as though he was doing something to get himself clean. Though not enough.

He threw the straw to one side and peered at the palms of his hands. They were a mess. Looked as though he'd suffered burns on his right hand. Left was not so bad. He'd need to find something to put on them so they didn't become infected.

He limped to the barn door, pushed it open slowly and peered out.

The day was grey and misty. Cold too. He shivered, but his forehead was hot.

He could see more plastic-covered bales of straw stacked up across the concrete yard. He heard the sound of cows and pigs on the still air. There were some fairly ramshackle sheds about fifty metres away, and that's where he reckoned the sound was coming from. Looking to his left – fields. Some ploughed, some showing a scant green carpet. To his right, a farmhouse. Square, solid. Smoke coming from the chimney.

The front door opened. A woman came out. Rick didn't move, didn't want to catch her eye. He saw her whistle, and two dogs came bounding out of the door towards her.

Fuck. They might catch his scent.

But the woman clipped the leads onto the dogs before they had a chance to sniff him out – at least, that's what he hoped.

The dogs – Labradors, he thought – suddenly pricked up their ears and looked towards the barn. He would bet their noses were quivering.

'Come on,' he heard the woman say. 'If you want a proper run we've got to go now.'

She turned and locked the door, before pushing the key under a large flowerpot.

A flowerpot? Laughter bubbled up inside him. Surely not?

'Right. Let's go.' The woman turned and set off in the opposite direction, the dogs now more interested in walking her than in him.

Rick listened carefully. He heard a dog barking in the distance. Different dog? The drone of a tractor somewhere. There had to be a farmer and maybe someone – what – milking cows? Or whatever they did on farms these days. But there wouldn't be too many people around.

A loud bang made him drop to the ground and cover his head with his hands. Blood was roaring around his body and he was shaking with fear. Pictures flickered into his mind: sun reflecting off sand, a soldier laughing, sweat beading his forehead where it met his helmet. A group of children walking. A girl, peeling off from the group. The girl looking at him. Her head becoming a mass of blood and brains and bone.

Another loud bang.

Rick had to bite his tongue to stop himself whimpering. It's all right, he told himself. It's all right. You're in England. England. It was a bird scarer, that's all.

Funny how he knew that.

His heart rate gradually slowed. The shaking subsided. The blood began to flow normally around his body.

His mouth was dry.

He got up off the ground. Looked around again. Still nobody. Ignored his aches and pains and did a crouching, crab-like run to the front of the farmhouse, scrabbled under the flowerpot for the key, and let himself into the house.

In the dim gloom of the hallway his mind was clear, focused. He could do this. After all, he'd been in the … the …

In the army.

Why did he keep forgetting?

Don't dwell on it. Priorities.

He crept down the hall and found the kitchen. It smelled vaguely of wet dog, but was fuggy and warm, thanks to the Aga

74

in the corner. He could smell fried bacon and toast on the air and his mouth watered. Priority: food.

There were crumbs on the work surface next to the Aga. A knife, greasy with butter lay next to a plate that had the remnants of bacon and egg on it. His mouth watered, and it was all he could do not to pick the plate up and lick at it.

He opened a cupboard door. Biscuits. An unopened loaf of bread. A jar with no label. It was honey. Chocolate bars. Muesli bars. He didn't like those at the best of times, but beggars couldn't be choosers. He stopped for a minute. Somehow he'd known he didn't like muesli bars. That was progress. Of a sort.

He took the items out of the cupboard and put them on the work surface.

There was an old biscuit tin at the back of the cupboard. He opened it and found several £5 notes and plenty of coins. Somewhere, in the past, he had known someone who had kept money 'for a rainy day' in a biscuit tin. His mum. He had a sudden clear memory of her reaching up to the top cupboard and pulling the tin out and putting money in it. He could almost hear the clattering of the coins as she dropped them in.

He pocketed some of the money. Didn't take it all.

He looked around.

The fridge in the corner made him stop. It was covered in magnets that pinned messages, takeaway menus, colourful drawings and photographs to its door. There, in the middle of it all, a photograph of two girls, smiling for the camera. They could only have been about four or five, the same age as his girls.

His girls. Briony and Bethany. His heart twisted. Helen – his wife, Helen – had taken them away from him. For a moment he felt an almost uncontrollable anger, then he remembered it was his temper that had been the problem. He had hurt Helen. She didn't trust him not to hurt the children.

He closed his eyes briefly, willing the tears not to come. His girls. He had lost his girls.

75

No time to mourn now.

He shook himself, and spied several large bottles of water on the floor next to the fridge. He took four, put them next to the food.

But his movements were slow and clumsy and he had to hurry.

Hanging from a hook on the kitchen door was a canvas bag. *I heart Labradors* was the logo. Oh well. Maybe he did. And his luck held – there was a thin waterproof jacket hanging behind a couple of heavier coats. He took that too, promising he would bring it all back. One day.

After putting everything in the bag, plus some clingfilm and kitchen roll, he made his way stealthily upstairs, carrying the bag.

He found the bathroom. In the cupboard there were plasters, antiseptic wipes, bandages, painkillers. No dental floss, but there was a roll of gaffer tape. Probably had a few accidents down on the farm, he thought. Or maybe someone had leg ulcers. He'd heard gaffer tape was good for those. He tried not to take it all – he didn't want the family, the woman, to know immediately that stuff was missing.

He threw three paracetamols into his mouth. They almost stuck in his throat, but he managed to swallow them dry.

He looked at the shower. Went out onto the landing. Then went back and looked carefully out of the bathroom window. Could see nothing, hear nothing. He would chance it.

It was quick and cool so as to create as little condensation as possible but so damn good to wash the dirt and general shit off himself. His whole body was a mass of cuts and congealing blood that stung as the water cascaded over him. How he wished he could have shaved the stubble off his face. Step too far.

He dried himself off and saw new bruises blooming on his skin, together with old ones that were fading. How had he got those? No time to worry now. He looked at his arm. Needed fixing.

He wiped around the shower with the towel before carefully

hiding it among the washing in the laundry basket in the corner. Then he reached inside the canvas bag for the gaffer tape and antiseptic cream.

With the edges of his wound pulled together and arm neatly bandaged with the tape and the burns on his hand treated with the cream, he padded along the landing and into a bedroom. He found a drawer with several pairs of jeans in it. Tee-shirts too. And a couple of jumpers. He pulled on jeans, a tee-shirt and a jumper, ignoring the shafts of pain that raced around his body and wondered how long it would be before they were missed. Hopefully a long time.

Trainers. Three pairs under the chest of drawers, all of them men's. He pulled a pair out. A size too small, but they would have to do. He pulled them on.

He started as he heard a whistle. Then a woman's voice. 'Vera? Ollie? Come. Bloody hell, come. *Come.*' The woman's voice was at once frustrated and furious. 'Damn you dogs.'

Christ.

The sound of a door opening downstairs.

'You two can stay outside. You're filthy.' A cacophony of barking ensued.

Thank God for that.

Think. Come on, you've done this sort of thing before. Think.

He went over to the bedroom window. He was in luck. There was a flat roof below.

He eased the window open, then climbed out and dropped onto the roof, trying not to cry out from the pain. He hoped the wound on his arm hadn't opened up.

As quickly as he could he went to the edge of the roof and jumped into a flower bed. At least it was a soft landing, but he still had to grit his teeth as his whole body was jarred and he felt every bruise, every sore bone.

There was a soft pounding, then panting and the two Labradors came racing around the corner towards him.

Oh fuck.

He prepared himself to kick out at them and then run like hell, but the dogs merely trotted up to him and started licking his face and neck until he was covered in slobber. He chuckled and scratched them under the chin. 'Well hello you two.' It seemed a long time since anyone or anything had given him such an enthusiastic welcome, or had pressed their warm body against his.

Reluctantly, he pushed them away. 'Gotta go now,' he said.

He couldn't see anyone around, so he walked purposefully and painfully towards one of the sheds on the outskirts of the farmyard, reckoning if he looked as though he was supposed to be there, anyone who saw him wouldn't question him. Unless someone recognized the clothes he was wearing.

There was hot breath on his legs. The dogs had followed him. 'Go away,' he hissed. 'Home. Now.'

'Vera! Ollie!' The woman was calling their names. The two dogs turned and ran off towards the sound of her voice.

Rick quickly got out of sight behind the shed.

He waited ten, fifteen minutes. Then set off limping at as brisk a pace as his battered body would allow. Though where he was going or what he was going to do, he had no idea.

There must be somewhere he could go – there had to be.

The rain began to fall steadily.

CHAPTER TWELVE

DAY TWO: MORNING

'I'm not sure about this,' said Cora, lighting up one of her never-ending cigarettes and puffing furiously on it as they walked to Bethel Street Police Station to report Rick missing. The rain had stopped for the moment, but the sky was still the colour of pewter.

Alex stopped. 'Why not? It can't do any harm, and there's no time like the present.'

Cora sighed. ''Spose not. But what if he turns up tomorrow and he's just been somewhere else?'

They were standing on the pavement, and people tutted as they were forced to step off the pavement to avoid them.

Alex took hold of her shoulders. 'Then there's no harm done. Come on.'

'Christ, who put you in charge? Bossy cow.'

'I'm not—' Oh, what was the point of arguing? None at all, that's what. She took a deep breath. 'I was just trying to help, that's all.'

'I bet Boney would've opened up to me if you hadn't been there.'

Oh for goodness' sake. 'Okay, Cora, I get it.' Alex was fed up, defeated. 'I'll leave you to it. Do me a favour, though, will you?

If Rick turns up, let me know. You've got my number.' She turned to go. She really didn't need the hassle of someone like Cora. She would have to hope and pray the woman's brother did turn up and she would have the grace to tell her. But it seemed obvious she and Cora were not going to get on.

Cora grabbed her arm. 'Hang on.' She gave a crooked little smile. 'I'm sorry. I've never been good at accepting help. It's always been me and Rick against the world. Mum and Dad were, well, let's just say they weren't really there for us.'

'Oh?'

'Yeah.' She ground out the cigarette under her boot. 'Come on. We're like those old dears in the supermarket who stand chatting with their trolleys blocking the way. Irritating.'

Alex pushed open the door of the police station and the odour of fresh paint mingled with sweat and despair hit her. The pale green walls were bare, waiting for their covering of wanted posters and signs that would make anyone feel like a criminal.

'Can I help you?' The officer on the front desk sported a shiny forehead but a pleasant smile.

'Cora?'

But Cora had the look of someone who was trying to distance herself from events. Alex sighed. It was up to her, then. She began to tell the officer what had happened. He took notes, his face impassive.

'Has he gone missing before?'

Alex turned to Cora. 'Has he?'

'Has he what?'

'Gone missing before.'

A look of panic washed over Cora's face and Alex's heart sank. She knew what was coming.

Cora cleared her throat, her face was pale. 'Yes, he has. More than once. The first time he took himself off to Brighton for a few days. It was when he was still with his wife. Nobody knew where he was. But he came back. The second time was just after he'd arrived in Norwich. He was sleeping in a tent and some bastard slashed it during the night. So he scarpered. Never said where he'd been.'

The officer writing down all the details stopped. 'It's not unusual for him to go missing then?'

'I suppose not,' said Cora, folding her arms and looking fierce.

'But officer,' interrupted Alex, 'I told you about finding him on the road and two men saying they would take him to hospital but now we can't find him?'

'You did.'

The officer's eyes were kind, thought Alex.

'Though, if I may say, by your own admission you'd had a fair bit to drink.'

'But—'

'And maybe he did get picked up and maybe he asked them to stop so he could get out. And he's gone to find a bit of peace somewhere. War veteran, didn't you say?'

Both women nodded.

'Look love. I'll put in a report. We'll have a chat with some of the others on the streets and go from there.'

'The Land Rover,' said Alex, suddenly.

The officer stood patiently, pen poised, eyebrow raised in a question.

'I found him by a Land Rover. He'd been in a crash, I told you. Perhaps you could send someone to look.' Alex tried not to sound as though she was telling him what to do. And why hadn't she thought about that before?

'Look?'

'For clues,' said Cora, nodding.

'Clues?' The eyebrow was raised again.

'Yes,' said Alex. 'You might find something there that'll at least tell you we're not making it up.'

'Right.' The officer didn't look convinced by their story. 'Tell me again where the Land Rover crashed.' His pen was poised.

Alex told him about the road from the Riders' Farm towards Woodbridge.

'The Riders?' He raised his eyebrow. 'Don't want to tangle with them.' He wrote down what Alex told him.

'Why do you say that?' Alex was intrigued. The Riders' influence stretched far and wide, it seemed.

The officer didn't answer.

'Why shouldn't we tangle with the Riders?' Alex persisted.

'Influential, aren't they.' He shut his lips tight and Alex sensed they weren't going to get any more from him.

'Okay,' she said. 'What about CCTV?'

The officer sighed. 'Clues, CCTV. Let's start with his mates, shall we, before we spend money on wild goose chases?'

'I'm sorry,' Cora said to Alex as they walked out of the police station into the cold air. 'I hadn't thought about him having gone missing before.'

Alex squeezed her arm. 'Don't worry, you did really well in there.'

'I'm not good at police. Or police stations.'

'Not many of us are.' But when she looked at Cora she realized her dislike for the police went deeper than a normal person's. 'You've had a bad experience.' It was a statement.

'What did you mean about CCTV?' Cora said, ignoring what Alex had said.

'I wondered if there was any near where he slept. In case it showed him speaking to those men the other day. I thought if I could identify them as the ones who picked him up then it might add more to our story. I might go and have a look myself later. Where was he again?'

'His usual place was at the back of an alleyway behind Able and Paul Solicitors on Unthank Road. Do you know it?'

Alex nodded. 'And any idea when they spoke to him?'

Cora thought. 'I'm not sure, but it might have been mid-morning.'

'Right. I'll give them a ring.'

'Good.' Cora yawned. 'Do you think the cops'll go and look for the Land Rover?'

'I don't know, Cora, but you look whacked.' She thought she had never seen anyone look so tired.

'I am. I'm exhausted. Do you mind—'

'No, you go and have a sleep. Have you got to work later?'

Cora nodded. 'I'm on a late shift at the N and N, so I'd better get some rest and get ready to go out. Um – thanks, Alex, for believing in Rick.'

Alex stared at her. 'Don't be silly. I should have done something more when those men took him away.'

'Do you think something has happened to him?'

Alex sighed. 'Oh Cora, I don't know. I just think it's odd that not only does Rick seem to have disappeared, but Martin, Nobby and Lindy. Surely it can't be a coincidence?'

'Perhaps someone did offer them all a job or something?'

Alex made up her mind. 'I'm going to drop in on David. If anyone would know whether someone is offering homeless people somewhere to work, then he will. I'll call you later.'

Cora nodded, then walked off quickly, her hand in her pockets, shoulders hunched, as if she had all the cares of the world on her shoulders.

Alex watched her go. Then a thought struck her and she went back into the police station.

'Hello again,' said the officer, looking as though he was trying to look interested in what she had to say.

'I'm sorry to bother you again,' said Alex, sweetly. 'But if a dog was left tied up to a lamppost, what would happen to it? Would it go to the dog pound?'

The officer gave a small smile. 'No. No dog pound.'

'So?'

'So it would be taken to the local animal sanctuary. Here.' He pushed a leaflet across the desk.

Alex put the leaflet in her pocket.

She checked her watch. Probably a good time to ring Heath, fill him in, see if he was interested in a series of articles for *The Post*.

'Alex, good to hear from you,' he said when her call finally connected. 'What have you got for me? I could do with some good news – this management lark isn't always fun, you know.'

'You're news editor, not management.' Alex was amused.

'Both, my dear, both. And I had to bollock a poor lowly intern who could have landed us with a hefty libel suit.'

'Then you shouldn't have asked them to do something they weren't qualified to do,' she replied, tartly.

She could almost feel him puffing his chest up. 'I'll have you know—'

'Heath, cut the crap. This is me, you know.'

'I know.' His voice was soft. 'We are linked for life as the gods would say.'

Alex did not want to think of the time when Heath had been so grievously injured helping her chase a story she thought she had lost him. 'Heath. Please.'

'We are. Isn't that what Shamans abide by? Or white witches? Or wizards? Someone anyway.'

'Enough of that. Next you'll be spouting about the wisdom of Odin or Athena and telling me you've turned mystical.'

'Trying to lighten the atmosphere. I have a hard job here, I'll have you know. What do you want to talk about? Don't tell me. You want to write a book about winning competitions on the back of cereal packets.'

'Heath, will you please listen?'

'Sorry. Go on.'

'I want to talk to you about rough sleepers who are disappearing off the streets. And before you say anything, I think they really are disappearing, not merely moving on.'

'Go on.'

84

Alex filled him in on what had been happening, knowing she would have his full attention. He groaned when she told him about Boney.

'You will be careful, Alex. He sounds vile.'

'He is. But imagine what his story might be. And imagine the scoop we would have if there really is something sinister going on with these people disappearing.'

'I can almost hear you rubbing your hands with glee. And the plods aren't interested?'

'Not at the moment. I'll see if I can make them interested,' she said, thinking about her friendly copper, Sam Slater. 'It would be good to have one on our side.'

'What else?'

'My next move is to go and have a chat with David Gordon, the head of one of the main homeless charities around here. If anyone knows what's happening, he should.'

'Good plan. Is he easy to get to? Do you know him well?'

She decided not to tell Heath about David hitting on her, he would only tease her for evermore. 'Well enough. So, you'd be interested in the story?'

'You know I am. Go for it.'

David Gordon's offices were in an old Georgian house just away from the city centre. Alex had always thought they were a bit grand for a small, local charity. But then perhaps they got the building for a peppercorn rent from a benefactor. Probably the Riders as part of their charitable work. They were an interesting family, to say the least and she wanted to find out more about them, but first she had to get this out of the way.

As a journalist, Alex was used to awkward situations, but seeing David again after his clumsy pass made her feel strangely nervous. She had to put her job hat on and feel confident, that was all. Shoulders back. Metaphorically speaking.

She went up the steps and was about to push open the grand

glass door, when someone pushed it hard from the other side, almost knocking her off her feet. A tall man in a sharply cut pinstripe suit came rushing out.

He stopped.

'I do apologize,' he said. 'I hope I didn't hurt you?'

She shook her head. 'Not at all.'

He flashed her a smile, showing a set of too-white teeth in a tanned face. He had sharp cheekbones, a very smooth forehead and full, almost girlish lips. He seemed familiar, but in that instant she couldn't quite grasp his name or where she had seen his face.

'Good. Must look where I'm going next time.'

Alex watched him hurry down the street, then pushed the door gingerly in case someone else was to come racing out.

'Hello,' she said to the young girl on the desk who looked up when she spoke. Earrings went all the way down the outside of one of her ears. 'Is David about, please?' She looked around, taking in the framed photographs of Norwich buildings along one wall, the beautiful chandelier hanging over the desk, and the sweeping staircase with its polished bannister. David obviously liked to give a good impression.

'Do you have an appointment?'

He was that busy? 'No, but I'm a personal friend.'

'I'll have to—'

Alex leaned on the desk and gave what she hoped was a friendly smile. 'Tell him it's Alex. I'm sure he'll see me.' She pushed one of her business cards across the desk. 'It's important that I talk to him.'

The girl picked up the phone and spoke into it, then looked up at her. 'He says he's very busy but can spare you a couple of minutes in a little while if you're able to wait?' Her voice went up at the end, making the statement sound like a question.

Alex didn't let her smile drop. She seemed to be doing a lot of that lately. 'I can wait.'

It must have been half an hour before David appeared, walking down the staircase like a celebrity from *Strictly Come Dancing*.

'Alex,' he said, his voice verging on curt.

Alex brought back the smile. 'I wonder if I might have a word?'

'It'll have to be quick.' He stood expectantly.

'Er – here?'

'No reason why not, is there?' The hostility came off his body in waves. Alex felt sorry for him, she must have really hurt his ego.

She shrugged. 'Okay. I wanted to ask you about some of the people on the streets. I believe they use your hostels too, on occasion.'

'Most likely. But then we hardly take a register. That's the whole point of our places. People who haven't got anywhere else to go can come and have a good meal and a safe night's sleep without feeling like they're being monitored.' He looked around, as though he was hoping for someone more interesting to come along.

'I know that.' Alex damped down her impatience. 'I wanted to know if you'd heard any talk, any rumours, about people going missing?'

'People going missing?' He enunciated each word as if she were saying something extraordinary.

Alex tried again. 'Homeless people, disappearing off the streets?'

He gave an exaggerated sigh. 'Alex, my dear. By their very nature homeless people move from one place to another. They get moved on, they decide to move on, they—'

She waved her hand. He was a pompous prick. 'I know all that, David. But this is more than that. Apparently a couple of men – usually well-dressed – speak to them and then a day or so later they're not around.'

'Like who? Who have these men spoken to?'

'Lindy. Nobby. Martin. Rick.'

He frowned. 'Lindy. I know Lindy. Yes. She is pretty unstable. There's every chance she could have hooked up with someone, she never did like to be on her own. So maybe she went off with a couple of men. Who knows? Rick? Post-traumatic stress I believe. His sister is a nagging bitch – so he told me. Nobby often takes himself off to Lowestoft for a few weeks and then comes back again. And Martin? I can't believe he would "disappear".'

'Well he has. And left Ethel.'

'His dog?' He frowned, stroking his chin. 'That does surprise me. Though maybe he couldn't afford to feed her.'

'You told me, David, that when you're on the streets having someone, something, to love and look after can keep you sane. That you feed your dog before yourself.'

'True.'

'So why would he leave Ethel?'

David took her by the elbow and steered her towards the door. 'Look, Alex. I have enough on my plate without you bothering me about two or three people who have decided to go walkabout. It happens. They don't stay in one place all the time. You know that. I try my best but I can't help everyone. Sometimes I'm – we're, the charity I mean – able to help someone live a better life, but more often than not they slip through the cracks. Sometimes they go elsewhere. Like Nobby to the seaside, that's a popular one—'

'I know.'

'And sometimes they think that life just isn't worth living. Have you thought of that?' He stuck his chin out.

They were standing on the step outside the building now. Alex looked at David. He was pale and he had lost weight from when she had first met him to do the original interviews.

'Are you all right?' she asked.

'Of course I'm all right, why shouldn't I be?'

'Because,' she began slowly, 'the David I interviewed for the paper was passionate about changing lives, and was passionate about his people. You seem … different. Worried.'

'I'm fine, Alex, thank you.' He sighed and his shoulders slumped. 'We're having a bit of trouble with funding at the moment, but it'll all work out in the end.' He rubbed his eyes. 'I don't mean to come over as unfeeling, but there are more than ninety people in Norwich alone without a home, and hundreds in Norfolk and Suffolk, so the whereabouts of a couple of them who will have gone off to pastures new can't concern me at the moment. Alex …' He hesitated. 'I remember you telling me you wanted to do more in your life, more worthwhile journalism, find a big story. You don't think you're trying to make this something that it's not?'

Alex stared at him. Why had she said anything about that to him? 'No, David, I'm not,' she said finally. 'I'm trying to help a friend, that's all. Thank you for your time.'

She walked away before she either hit him or burst into tears.

The encounter with David had made Alex feel unsettled. Was he right? Was she helping Cora because she wanted it to be something more? Was she manufacturing a story? Maybe Nobby, Lindy, Rick and Martin had simply found somewhere else to go. But all of her instincts pointed to there being more to it. It didn't smell right. It was no good having a hunch, though, if you couldn't back it up with evidence.

Why had David been so jumpy, so worried, so tired? What was it he'd said? They'd been having some trouble with funding? Then it clicked into place. She knew where she had seen the man who had almost knocked her over as she was entering the building. He was Lewis Rider, the eldest of the Rider brothers. She had caught a glimpse of him at the charity function and had seen his picture online. David had said the Rider family were great supporters of his charity, so it would seem logical that Lewis Rider was seeing David. Perhaps, though, the money troubles couldn't be so easily solved.

If David wasn't going to be any help, then she'd have to find someone else who might be ...

'Why do I think this is only going to be trouble?'

DI Sam Slater answered his mobile with his customary laconic tone. He made Alex smile. And had done ever since she met him at a 'press meet the police' PR kind of day – excruciating for all sides, though it did at least mean that officers and journalists were more than voices at the other end of the phone to one another.

'Have you got a minute?' She didn't wait for Slater to answer, but launched straight into her story, telling Slater all that had happened, right from the very beginning. 'So can you send someone out to look at the Land Rover site? I think it would be worth it.'

He sighed. 'Look, I'll see what I can do. But—'

'Thanks, Sam, I owe you.' And she cut the call.

Good. She had someone on their side. But she wanted to see the crashed Land Rover for herself, see if she could find anything that might help pinpoint Rick Winterton's whereabouts.

This was turning out to be a long day.

CHAPTER THIRTEEN

DAY TWO: LATE AFTERNOON

The home was an almost elegant building, with three sides set around a lawn and well-kept flower beds – there was always colour in them, whatever the time of year – the pink and purple of cyclamen, the yellow of winter aconites, the red of Japanese quince. He knew these flowers and shrubs because he had made it his business to know, so he could talk to Rosie about them. She had always loved her flowers and her garden, and Sam Slater fancied he saw animation in her face when he took her outside to see them here.

He put his phone back in his pocket, knowing he would have to cut this visit short. Luckily, he wasn't too far away.

As he walked into the front reception he was struck again by how unlike any of the depressing care homes he had trudged around when trying to find help for Rosie this was. So many were institutions, with harried staff, good care but the bare minimum. No time to spend with the people living there. Institutional food, institutional entertainment. And he had wanted her to be somewhere special, where she was cared for and cherished because she was Rosie, not because she was another 'client'. He wanted paintings on the wall, thoughtfully chosen, a restaurant, Farrow & Ball paint. The smell of fresh air. And he had found it here at Lime House. There was even a hair salon and Jo Malone toiletries, for Christ's sake.

'Hello, Sam. Rosie's looking forward to seeing you,' said Marcia on the front desk, all cheerful smiles and cheerful demeanour.

He signed himself in and went along the corridor to Rosie's room. He stood at the doorway, looking at the cheerful space that, when the sun shone, was full of light.

Yes, he had chosen well. It was all worth it. It had to be.

She was sitting, well wrapped up, in her specially adapted wheelchair, waiting for him. At least that's what he liked to think, that she knew he was coming and was looking forward to it.

He fixed a smile on his face and went in. He kissed her cheek.

There was no reaction, and hadn't been for some time. Rosie was in the last stages of Huntington's. How he hated that single word and the way it had taken his beloved wife away from him in a few short years. Would he have married her if he had known this was coming down the tracks?

Hell, yes.

He loved her fiercely, and although in the last couple of years he knew he had to start living again, his love for her had not diminished.

His phone vibrated in his pocket. He took it out, looked at the screen, his expression darkening. He pressed 'decline', turned it off and jammed it back in his pocket. That particular devil would have to wait. He didn't want this visit spoiled.

He sat down, took his wife's hand, and began chatting to her about the flowers and the rain, which had begun to softly fall.

CHAPTER FOURTEEN

DAY TWO: LATE AFTERNOON

The road from Riders' Farm towards Woodbridge was slick with water, and big puddles had formed at intervals along the side. Alex had to drive carefully. The afternoon light was already threatening to fade.

She tried to remember how far along the accident had been. What landmark did she remember seeing?

None, was the honest answer. She hadn't been taking a lot of notice, more intent on listening to Sasha's happiness than anything else. Was that oak tree familiar? What about the hole in the hedge? That gate? Hang on. She thought hard. There had been a T-junction with a signpost to Gisford. And only a few metres past that one of those road signs warning drivers to beware of deer. She knew only too well they could leap out of the hedgerow right in front of the car.

It was around here somewhere.

There. The sign to Gisford and then the one depicting a deer. It had a hole through its centre where someone had been practising with their air rifle.

Alex pulled onto a convenient farm track.

She was glad she'd had the foresight to bring her wellie boots with her, as the side of the road was wet and muddy. She wrapped her scarf tightly around her neck and jammed her bobble hat on her head. The wind was getting up and the sky was threatening to unleash a deluge.

She walked on, brushing up against the thorny hedge, sometimes catching her coat on a bramble. She stepped into the road, hoping to see police tape fluttering like a banner in the wind somewhere up ahead. Not for the first time she asked herself why she hadn't had her wits about her when she came across the crash originally. Why hadn't she picked up the trainer in the puddle? Maybe it would still be there.

She stopped. Surely she should have come across the wreck by now?

She crossed over. There was a ditch and a line of trees along this side. She thought hard. The Land Rover had turned over by the last tree in the row, the driver – Cora's brother – having swerved to avoid a head-on collision with its trunk. Or that was how it looked.

But there was nothing. Nothing at all. No sign of a Land Rover. No sign of a crash. No skid marks – though with the amount of wet mud on the road from farm vehicles, they would have been covered up or washed away within hours of the crash.

She looked carefully at the tree where she thought the vehicle had overturned – she was certain now this was the place. She began to feel excited. Was that a scrape in the bark? Or just nibbles from deer? She traced the mark with her hand.

It told her nothing.

The trainer. That had been in a puddle nearby.

Too many puddles. Of course the rain would have washed so much away.

There was the sound of another vehicle coming fast down the lane. A door slammed. DI Sam Slater sauntered into sight, hands in his pockets, dressed casually in jeans and a leather bomber jacket.

'Sam,' she said. 'I didn't expect to see you.' She stood up.

He shrugged. 'I had a bit of spare time, so I thought I would come and see what you were on about.'

'I'm honoured.'

'Don't be. I didn't want to take an officer off a really important job, that's all.'

'I don't think—' she was about to say she didn't think his comment was fair, but from his point of view, it probably was. She smiled. 'Thank you. The trouble is, I can't find it.'

'You're at the right place?'

Alex nodded. 'Look.' She pointed to the tree. 'There's a scrape on the bark, where it has come away.'

Sam went up to it, felt the mark as she had done. 'Could be a deer. They like bark, particularly from young trees.'

'But it could also be from a vehicle.'

He looked more closely. 'No sign of paint.'

'There's no sign of anything. And I'm sure this is the place.'

'Shall we walk up a bit further, just in case?' He strode on ahead. Alex had to run to catch up with him.

'You think this is a waste of time, don't you?'

Sam stopped and looked at her. 'Alex. You're a good journalist, one of the best. If you believe something's happened, then I'm almost inclined to believe you. That's why I came out here today. I can't afford to waste time, not with budgets as they are. Christ, we're not even investigating some crimes like shoplifting and criminal damage these days. But—'

'But what?

'Alex, people like him disappear all the time. I know you reported him missing, and that was the right thing to do and wheels can be put in motion, but a lot of the time they don't want to be found. And you've given me absolutely no reason to think he's a bona fide missing person. He moves around and he's disappeared before, always turning up.'

'"Wheels put in motion". I see. Because he's homeless you don't bother.'

'That's not fair, Alex,' he said quietly. 'Look.' He waved his arm around. 'We've walked a long way and there's nothing. All I can say is if there ever was anything here, someone has done a bloody good job of tidying it up.'

'Exactly, Sam. That's what's happened.' Surely Sam could see what she was getting at? 'Somebody has cleared it all away.'

'And why would they do that?'

'Come on, Sam. You're the copper.' Why couldn't he see? 'To cover something up of course.'

'Alex, we're not on a TV show, you know.' There was impatience in his voice.

'I know that, DI Slater.' Alex tried to damp down her irritation. She sighed. He was right, though. There was nothing here.

When they got back to the tree, Alex hunkered down to examine the ground around it. There had to be something.

'I must to go now, Alex.'

'Fine.'

'Alex—' he hesitated. 'I know you believe there was a crash, but—'

'But what?'

'You had been at a party. Perhaps your thoughts are a bit muddled.'

She bristled. 'My thoughts were not and are not muddled, party or no party.' She paused. 'Could you at least find out if anyone reported a Land Rover being stolen?'

He sighed. Heavily. 'I'll have a look, Alex. I can't promise anything.'

She nodded. 'Thank you for coming anyway.'

'See you around, Alex.'

She heard him walk away.

Well, sod him.

Alex started scrabbling about in the undergrowth, but there was nothing there – not even a sweet wrapper. Then the heavens opened and rain came gushing out of the sky. It soaked her hat, her scarf and her coat in minutes. She could even feel water trickling down the inside of her wellies. Rivulets of water were running down the road and the light was well and truly fading now.

Bloody hell.

She didn't want to give up.

One last look.

She switched on her phone torch and shone it around and about the tree. She was about to give up when she saw something reflected in the light. Crouching down, she put her hand on the wet grass at the side of the road. Two small pieces of glass. She thought back to the crash. The windscreen had been smashed, so had the indicator lights. Glass had been everywhere. This could be from that. Something the clear-up boys, for she had no doubt there had been clear-up boys, had missed. She scooped up the glass with a hanky she found in her pocket, and wrapped it up carefully before making her way back to the car. The afternoon hadn't been entirely wasted, after all. She would see what Detective Inspector Sam Slater said now she had some actual evidence.

She started the engine, put the car into reverse and let off the handbrake. The wheels spun, the engine roared, and her little Peugeot didn't move. She gritted her teeth and tried again. Useless. The pouring rain had made the farm track a mud pit and the car was well and truly stuck.

Now what?

She got out and squidged her way to the boot, taking out a red and blue striped picnic blanket. She'd never used it on a picnic, but it could help here. Kneeling in the mud, she laid it as close to the back wheels as possible, went back into the car and tried again.

Nothing. Apart from spinning tyres and a ruined blanket. She banged the steering wheel in frustration. Well, that was great. Just what she could do without. She lowered her head on to the steering wheel.

A knock on the window made her jump.

A man in fisherman's oilskins and a wide-brimmed hat dripping water was smiling at her. He motioned for her to put the window down.

'Alex Devlin, isn't it? What are you doing in this neck of the woods?'

All at once she recognized the charming smile. 'Mr Rider—'

'Jamie, please.'

'Jamie, I—' What was she doing? She thought frantically. 'When I was walking home the other night I dropped my scarf. I was hoping to find it. It's got sentimental value, you see. I got it when I went to Venice. Have you been to Venice?' For God's sake stop babbling.

'I have as a matter of fact. Beautiful. One of my favourite places. Can I help at all?'

'Help?'

'I've got the four-by-four here, I could pull you out.'

She felt a twinge of annoyance. What was it to be? Stay here in the car along with her pride, or accept the humiliation of being pulled out of the mud?

'It could happen to anyone. Being stuck in the mud, I mean. And it is a particularly nasty day.'

Suddenly her irritation drained away. There was no point in looking a gift horse in the mouth. Or the offer of help from a man with a four-wheel drive.

Five minutes later and Alex was back on the road, Jamie Rider's face at her window once more. 'Okay?'

'Thank you,' she said. 'You must let me buy you a drink sometime.'

He cocked his head to one side. 'How about you come up to the farm for one? Let me show you around?'

'Well—'

'Please?'

She could have sworn his eyes twinkled. Or maybe it was just the rain.

What was the harm? It could be an interesting way to find out more about the Rider family.

She smiled. 'I'd like that. Thank you.'

'See you tomorrow for a quiet family supper,' he said. 'I'll send a car.'

'That won't be—'

'Until tomorrow.'

A car? What was the reason behind that? To show off or to show who was in control? Or perhaps he was planning to get her as pissed as a rat and have his wicked way with her? On the other hand, maybe he was simply being nice. Time would tell.

As she drove away, she glanced in her rear-view mirror to see him standing in the middle of the lane watching her as she went.

She also noticed two thick streaks of mud on either side of her face.

CHAPTER FIFTEEN

DAY TWO: LATE AFTERNOON

Left or straight on? Did it matter? Where was he trying to go? And why hadn't he found a bloody map in that farmhouse place, then he might have some idea of where he was.

Rick had pushed his way through hedges and across ditches to find the road again in an attempt to give himself some sense of direction. Where was his physical strength? His mental strength? Had that place (whatever that place was) sapped it all from him? He was better than this, he knew he was.

He sheltered behind a tree and pressed another three paracetamol out of the blister pack. His headache was still raging. He wasn't sure if it was the rain making the air around him misty or whether his eyes and brain were playing tricks on him.

He was trying to keep off the roads, but the mud from the fields had made each footstep heavier than the one before. He had slipped into deep puddles, and the jeans he was wearing were sodden and heavy. The waterproof jacket was soaked through, no protection from the rain that fell and fell and fell some more. He had eaten most of the chocolate bars, had torn off hunks of bread and dipped them in the honey, savouring the sweetness, and he had drunk two bottles of water. His body had been craving nourishment. He must have been deprived of it for some time. Weeks? Days?

Left or straight on?

He heard the sound of an engine. Not a tractor, more like a car. Or a van. Most likely just a car. Someone out for a drive, going to work, visiting a friend. Anything. Nothing to be worried about. Too much of a coincidence if it was them. Nevertheless, he flattened himself against the tree, hoping now the mist was real and wasn't just in his imagination.

Lights came into view. A white van, travelling pretty slowly. He pressed himself even more against the tree, wishing he could disappear inside it. He'd seen that white van before, he was sure of it.

He risked a glance.

Two men in the front. Faces turned. Looking. Dog in the back, head through the gap in the seats, panting, drooling. Could he really see that or was it his fevered imagination? Dear God.

It was them, he was sure. He recognized the bull neck and bright red jacket of one. He always wore that too-tight bright red jacket. Rain or shine. Every time he took Rick to work in the lab.

The lab. Where had that thought come from?

On the island.

What was it for? Suddenly his hands began to sting. The burns on his hands. Something in the lab. What, though?

And not just a lab, but there were also booths with beds and comfy seats in one of the sheds. That shed had been warm. He had seen them. He had talked to—

There had been women there. Women wearing perfume. How had he got there? He remembered being in the car park behind the solicitor's and two men coming to talk to him, offering him a job. Next he knew, he was in the back of a van that smelled of fish. Fish and the sea. And something else. Misery.

Then there was that niggle of memory, a niggle that said his arrival on the island was something planned. But he'd had to leave before he wanted to. He shook his head. It would come back. It had to.

The van slowed down. The men inside were probably debating whether to go left or straight on.

They stopped the vehicle and got out. He wondered whether to stay behind the tree or make a run for it. But he was not at his best, he knew that. He was weak from wounds and lack of decent food. Those bloody muesli bars gave him no sustenance at all. But the two goons were fat and overfed. Pumped themselves full of steroids and thought they were fit. He balanced on the balls of his feet and took a deep breath.

Then he heard the sound of a zip being pulled down, and the splash of urine as it hit the ground near his tree. Once more he kept still. Told himself not to move a muscle, not to breathe. To wait.

The sound of the zip being done up.

'Come on, mate,' shouted the other one from the side of the van. 'We've gotta keep looking.'

'All right, all right. I needed that piss. Stuck in that van all day with you.'

'Fuck off, Gary and come back here.'

'What about food? We've eaten all those doughnuts.' Gary began walking back to the van, his tread heavy. 'I'm bloody starving.'

'Perhaps we'll find a KFC somewhere.' Laughter.

'Yeah, right. More like some poncey vegan place with people in flat sandals.'

'Who stink.'

'Worse than our lot.'

'Anyway, we've got to find Rick before anyone else does. You know the harm he could do, and we'll be toast if that happens.'

'Yeah, I know.'

The door slammed, the engine revved, the vehicle moved away down the road.

Rick let out his breath in one long sigh and sank down on his haunches. He held his throbbing head in his hands. That had been a lucky escape. He'd almost given himself away.

But what harm could he do?

It was what he had seen on the island. To do with the women – and more. He pounded his forehead with his fist. he needed to remember more.

Until he did, he had to keep walking.

The road down which the white van had gone was wider, better kept, more used. The one to the left narrowed, tufts of grass grew down the middle at intervals. Less traffic. Straight on probably led to a town, to safety, to people. Left went nowhere. Maybe to the sea. To the wild. To where he couldn't hide. There was a sign, covered in dirt. By-way to Gisford, it said. He knew that place.

The white van went straight on.

He turned left. Towards Gisford.

CHAPTER SIXTEEN

DAY THREE: EARLY MORNING

The early morning wind blew off the North Sea and knifed straight through Sam Slater's overcoat. The sea spray combined with the driving rain to lash his face and the faces of police officers and specialist crime scene investigators. He knew his skin would be sore by the time he reached the inside warmth of a police station. Sand stuck to his shoes and the waves crashed like angry fists onto the shore as he made his way across the beach to talk to the investigating officer.

'What have you got?' he asked, rubbing his hands together to try and coax some feeling back into them.

'Sam. Turning up like a bad penny. Unidentified male. About all we know for certain at the moment.' He wrinkled his nose. 'Face has been picked clean by gulls and fish. Been in the water some time, the pathologist reckons. And the smell from the corpse suggests a few weeks of decomposition. The sea has done a lot of damage, as have rocks. Might not even have come from around here. I mean, we have had bodies washed up on the beaches here that have started in the Netherlands. Not natural for a body to float, of course. We're made up of sixty per cent water, did you know that?'

Slater shook his head.

'He'll only have floated for as long as there was air in those lungs, then he would've dropped like a stone. Or a dead body.'

There had been too many of these, Slater knew that. It was the third body that had been washed up on a Suffolk beach in the last three months. One had been minus its limbs and head, never to be identified. He knew his colleagues in Norfolk and Essex had been puzzled by the sudden increase in bodies landing on their beaches. Could any of them see a pattern? Surely not. It was all coincidence. Most of them were seen as people who wanted to kill themselves. A couple were so badly decomposed the Home Office pathologist couldn't say whether it was suicide, accident or murder. Given the state of the country and politics and all that, Slater thought there were plenty of reasons for topping yourself. People thought wading into the sea to die was an easy option. But it took an iron will and a real desire for death to keep wading.

For how much longer would they put these down to suicides?

'So,' said the officer, 'we'll be doing the usual round of appeals for information, maybe even a facial reconstruction. There'll be a post-mortem, of course, but unless that throws up anything suspicious, we won't have much to go on. Sometimes we never identify them.'

Slater almost felt sorry for him.

'Any missing person investigation that he could be linked to?'

The officer looked out over the grey sea. 'Not that I know of.' Then he turned to Slater, as if something had just occurred to him. 'What brought you down here anyway, Sam?'

Slater shrugged. 'I heard it on the radio. There've been too many suicides recently. I'm leading a task force about it all. Anyway, I'll leave you to it.'

The officer nodded. 'Of course. I'd heard about that nugget

of bureaucracy. They must have thought you didn't have enough to do, you know. Too much free time.' He laughed.

Slater laughed. 'As if,' he said, and walked back up the beach, carefully placing one foot in front of the other.

CHAPTER SEVENTEEN

DAY THREE: MORNING

The wind had howled around the apartment block all night. Alex had woken up several times to hear the *thump thump* of boats' fenders against the harbour wall. She'd also heard the waves crash onto the walkway between the apartments and the harbour and guessed the nearby railway line would be flooded.

She squinted at her clock. Time for another five minutes of shut-eye.

Her phone played David Bowie's 'Starman'.

Gus.

She sat up, stifling a yawn. 'Hi darling, how are you. I'm looking forward to seeing you next week.'

'That's just it, Mum.' Her son sounded awkward. 'I'm afraid I can't make it.'

Disappointment filled her. She had been so looking forward to seeing him and catching up with whatever was going on in his life. It felt a very long time since she had been able to talk to him without Martha there. Much as she liked his girlfriend, Alex wanted time with Gus, the two of them. Though perhaps it was unfair of her to expect this. He and Martha had been together for some time now. Her mother's job was done and she didn't half feel useless sometimes. Perhaps another reason why she wanted to get her teeth into something substantial and make a difference to someone, somewhere.

'That's a shame, Gus.' She tried to smile, thankful it wasn't FaceTime.

'Martha wants me to go to this gig with her.'

Alex wanted to ask if there wasn't someone else she could go with, but bit her tongue.

'I can't say no, Mum. Even though I don't like the band.'

Yes, you can, she said to him, silently. You can say you haven't seen your mum in ages and you promised her a visit and— She took a deep breath, pushing the thought that maybe Martha was a selfish cow right away from her head.

'No, that's fine, Gus. You can come another time soon, perhaps?'

'Of course I will. Really soon. I'll ring you and arrange a date.' He sounded relieved. 'And thanks, Mum?'

'What for?' She kept her voice light and bright.

'Understanding.'

'That's what mums are for.'

After saying their goodbyes, Alex was in no mood to sleep, besides, she had a phone call of her own to make.

Pulling an old jumper over her PJs, Alex went to her desk. There, nestling in a piece of kitchen towel, were the pieces of broken glass she had picked up on the road where the accident with the Land Rover had happened. She had no idea whether they were from the indicator or headlight, or even the windscreen, but she wanted to show them to Sam so he could check it out, though when she'd tried to call him last night she had frustratingly only got his answerphone.

This time he answered.

'Sam, it's Alex. I've got something that might be interesting.'

'Right.' His voice was careful.

'Yesterday, when you came with me to find the Land Rover—'

'And we didn't find anything.'

'I think I have.'

'What do you mean?'

'After you left, I dug around some more—'

An impatient sigh. 'Alex. You should let it go.'

'Maybe I will, but first listen, please. I found some pieces of glass that I think could have come from the Land Rover.'

'And?' Now there was only weariness in his voice.

Alex ploughed on. 'And if I give it to you, could you have it tested or something?'

There was another sigh, then silence for a moment. 'Forensics would have to look at it.'

'That would be great.'

'But you know very well what budgets are like. As I said to you before, we are being squeezed until more than our pips squeak—'

'I know all that, Sam. But this could be important.'

'Even if we find that it is glass from the Land Rover, how does that help you?'

'It means I'm not going mad. It means you might actually take me seriously, believe that I saw Rick Winterton at the accident.'

'I do believe you saw him.'

'No you don't. If you did you'd be wondering why the Land Rover had disappeared. And you'd be helping me look for him.'

'Look. Next time you're in Norwich drop it in at Bethel Street. I'll pick it up from there. Okay?'

'Couldn't I bring it to you today—'

'No. I'm busy,' he cut in. 'I won't be around until tomorrow at the earliest.'

'Okay.'

'Sorry, Alex. I don't mean to be abrupt, but I've got a lot on at the moment.'

'Right.' Though yesterday, thought Alex, he had time to come and see what she was doing.

'It could be glass from anything, you do know that?' Sam went on. 'A Coke bottle, a different car accident, anything.'

'I know. Which is why I'm asking you if you'll get it tested. Please. But I do have a feeling about this, I really do.'

'Alex?'

'Yes?'

There was a pause. 'If something had happened to me, I'd want you on my case.' He cut the call.

After a shower and a hasty breakfast of yoghurt and honey, Alex locked the door of her apartment and ran down the stairs to the main door. The rain was coming down in buckets again. Damn, she was going to get really wet if she had to leave her car too far away from Able and Paul. After she had told Kate Able the whole story about Rick's disappearance the solicitor had been very accommodating on the phone, agreeing to let her take a look at the CCTV.

'Miserable, isn't it, dear?'

She turned to find a man in a wheelchair sorting through the free sheets that were left strewn on the ledge by the post boxes.

'I'm looking for something to read.' He sighed. 'I get so bored with re-runs of *Star Trek* and *Friends*.'

'Mr Watson, isn't it?'

'John, yes.' He gave a laugh. 'And this is Stumpy.' He pointed to his stump. 'Not very original, but, hey-ho. We cripples have got to get our amusement from somewhere.'

Alex bit her lip, trying not to laugh at John's political incorrectness. She knew from one of her other neighbours that his leg had been amputated a couple of months before. It couldn't be much fun having to cope on your own with one leg and sitting in a wheelchair. 'Look, if I can help at all—'

'Thank you, my dear. Be careful what you say because I am well known for taking advantage of anyone who wants to come to my aid in any way. And do forgive my sartorial mistake of sandal and sock but it's the only thing that keeps me steady at the moment.'

Alex looked down at his feet and rather liked the bright pink sock with large blue hearts on his single leg. 'I wouldn't dream of saying anything about your attire.'

John laughed. 'Must go now. I've got to go and fit Leggy on and have a bit of a walkabout.'

'Leggy?'

'Leggy goes onto Stumpy.'

'I see,' laughed Alex.

'Have a good day,' he said cheerfully.

And with that he deftly turned his wheelchair and went into his apartment, newspaper free sheets under his arm. Alex made a mental note to call in on him and see if she could do anything for him – despite what he'd said.

After a long journey from Woodbridge to Norwich spent peering at the rain through a windscreen being cleared by inadequate wipers, Alex was able to park near the solicitor's office. It was a stroke of luck, and she made it to the reception desk without getting absolutely soaked.

'Grim out there, isn't it? I don't think it's ever going to stop. Like some sort of Biblical flood,' said Kate Able as she collected her and swept her along a bright corridor and into a small room in which every available space was taken up by books or papers or both. It smelled of coffee and a flowery perfume with a very faint undertone of cigarette smoke. 'You're a journalist, yes? And you're investigating Rick's disappearance? And the police don't think he has disappeared?' Kate Able glared at Alex, her painted eyebrows raised inquisitively. She had sharp eyes and sharp features and Alex thought she would be sharp in court.

'No. I mean, yes. I mean, I'm not sure what's happened to him.'

'And how will looking at our CCTV help?'

Alex didn't want to say she had a hunch that the two men

who had spoken to Rick were the same two men she'd met at the scene of the accident because it seemed such a remote possibility and she felt silly even thinking about it.

'I don't know,' she said. 'Just a feeling I suppose.'

'Journalistic hunch, eh?' Kate Able smiled. Then she said, 'I don't want you to think we let anyone look at our CCTV, but Rick is a good guy, and having him there kept the real dirtbags away from the alley. We did try to help him, you know,' she said, frowning. 'But he said he was happy where he was. We used to give him coffee and meals, and our junior knitted him a hat and gloves for Christmas. I wish we could have done more, though. Ex-army, wasn't he, yes?'

Alex nodded.

'Now let me see.' Kate Able put on a pair of glasses that added to her intelligent look and started pecking at the keys on her computer. 'Take a seat next to me, yes?'

Alex looked around, eventually taking a pile of papers off a stool and sitting on that.

'I can get it all up on here. If I just …' Kate Able frowned as she concentrated. 'That's it.' She sat back in the chair. 'Yes. If you see.' She pointed at the screen; Alex craned her neck to take a look. 'I've pulled up camera two, which is the one at the back. I mean, we only have two and camera one is at the front, so it makes sense to have camera two at the back, yes?'

'Yes,' said Alex, faintly.

'And I guess we want to look at a date a few days before he went missing, yes?'

'Sounds good.'

'Okay. Let's start on the Tuesday at, what? About ten o'clock?'

'Earlier than that. Maybe eight thirty, to be on the safe side?'

'And end at one p.m., I think. Here we go.' She pressed 'play'.

Alex peered over her shoulder. The pictures were surprisingly clear. And it wasn't chucking it down with rain. The unlovely yard was like any other back yard behind a business: two or three wheelie bins, a pile of old planks of wood, a fat pigeon scratching the ground more in hope than expectation, and a couple of parking spots, one occupied. 'Presumably for staff?'

Kate nodded.

The downside was that the camera only covered part of the yard.

'Where did Rick sleep?'

Kate pointed to a doorway right in the corner of the shot. 'There. If you look carefully, you can see the edge of his sleeping bag. He's normally up and about by this time. Has a smoke. Reads a book. See? There he is.'

Alex looked. She watched as a man came into view holding a cup of coffee, steam curling off it. His hair was dark, long and matted. His beard was full and straggly and threaded with grey. He was wearing a thick, long overcoat. Khaki? Alex couldn't be sure. But the man in the accident had stubble on his head and was clean-shaven. Could she be mistaken? Maybe it wasn't Rick in the accident.

Then he held up his coffee to the camera and waved.

'Can you pause it there,' she asked Kate. Yes, there it was. The little finger – half of it was missing. It was definitely the same man.

Rick looked up to the camera, grinned, and blew it a kiss.

Kate went through the rest of the morning on fast forward. Nothing changed.

On Wednesday morning, a car drove slowly into the yard. Alex's heart beat faster.

'That's Damien Pemberton,' said Kate. 'He often gets Rick a coffee when he makes his own first thing. See, he's getting out of his car and chatting to Rick now.'

Damien Pemberton. She should check him out. 'What does Rick do with himself during the day?'

'He goes into the city to find himself a meal, see friends, that sort of thing. I know he often goes to the library and reads the newspaper or a book.' She smiled. 'He says it's a bit noisy some-times, but he enjoys the warmth.' She turned her attention back to the screen. 'Let's see what else happened.' She pressed the button.

The CCTV fast forwarded through the rest of the morning. Alex saw Rick march out of the yard, probably on his way into the city. A cat slunk in, pissed against the wood and slunk off again. A white delivery van drove in and drove out again. The next two days looked much the same – Rick drinking coffee, talking to one of the partners, going off into the city mid-morning. The cat. The delivery van.

'You have a lot of deliveries,' Alex said.

'What? Hmm. Not really. Could be for the accountant next door. The back entrance to his office is in our yard. No right of way, though.'

On Friday things changed. Rick was sauntering, coffee in hand, out of the yard when Alex noticed two men going up to him, just within sight of the camera.

'Stop,' said Alex, 'Can you go slowly?'

'Sure.'

The film moved along jerkily. Alex leaned forward. Frustratingly, the two men kept their heads turned away from the camera as if they knew it was there. Well, they probably did; it didn't disguise itself. But there was something about the set of their shoulders, their walks. Or was she imagining it?

One of them glanced up.

Alex stifled a gasp, and Kate Able paused the film. The man was one of those who had taken Rick away the other night. Thick neck, meaty features, jutting forehead. And the red Puffa jacket.

'You recognize him.' It was a statement, not a question.

Alex nodded slowly. 'Yes. I think he was one of the men who took Rick away after the accident.'

'Are you sure?'

Was she? Yes, pretty sure, but she felt she had to be careful what she said to this sharp lawyer. 'Not entirely,' she said, eventually.

Kate shifted in her chair. 'I'm sure there's a simple explanation for all this, you know. Perhaps these men are friends of Rick's. And he was happy to let them take him after the accident you told me about. Perhaps he really doesn't want to be found.' She frowned. 'Strange though, he always said he wanted to look after Cora. I said to him if that's what he wanted to do then he ought to get himself some sort of job.'

'What did he say to that?'

'I think he snorted.'

Alex smiled. 'Probably not too easy in his situation. Getting a job, I mean.'

'Hmm. He also said he had unfinished business. Whatever that meant. So, now you think you have recognized one of the men, what are you going to do?'

'Are you able to print that picture?' Alex asked. Maybe someone would know who the man in the red jacket was.

'Sure.' Kate Able pressed a button and a printer perched on top of a filing cabinet rattled into action. 'I'll do you a few copies, just in case, yes?'

'Can you move the video on in slow-motion?' said Alex. 'I'd like to see how long they stayed talking to Rick.'

The two men walked up to Rick, who seemed to square up to them – certainly the body language didn't look friendly. The man in the red jacket pointed at Rick, maybe even jabbed his shoulder.

The second man, who was wearing a dark overcoat and a tartan scarf, grabbed his arm.

Rick shook it off and turned away.

Alex almost felt the anger radiating out from the film. She couldn't quite see the face of the man with the scarf – could he be the second man who had picked up Rick the other night? She squinted, but he was adept at keeping his face away from the camera. It was so frustrating.

All at once things moved fast.

The two men and Rick were talking. Were they arguing? She couldn't tell. Then Rick's shoulders sagged and he nodded.

A white van – could it be the same van she had seen going in and out of the yard over the week? – drove fast into the yard, then out of the camera's vision.

A few seconds later the van sped out of the yard. Kate kept the film running. For the rest of the day there was no sign of Rick.

'Can you try the weekend, please? And Monday?'

'Sure. Yes.' Kate pressed the button.

No sign of Rick. Over the weekend, a party of youths went into the yard and urinated against the wall. Kate tutted. They left their fast-food wrappers soaking in a puddle. Kate tutted some more. The cat wandered in and out. The fat pigeon and some of his mates puttered about, pecking at the remnants of the fast food. It rained a lot. On Sunday, Damien Pemberton drove in, parked his car and hurried into the office.

'Oh,' said Kate. 'I wonder what he was doing at work on a Sunday?'

Monday morning and there was still no sign of Rick.

Tuesday morning and still no sign.

Kate paused the film. She sighed. 'It looks as though he went in the van with those men, though we can't prove it.'

'You don't think he just walked out of the yard?' Alex had to ask the question even though she was convinced he had gone in the van. She felt it in her bones.

'No, not that we can see. Though sometimes he did avoid the camera altogether. He said he didn't want all his movements known. When he said that he laughed, but he meant it.'

Right. Another idea struck her. 'What about the van? Can you zoom in and see the number plate?'

'I can try.' Kate clicked some more and focused on the plate. She shook her head. 'It's too dirty. I'd say deliberately. There's no way we can see the number. Sorry.'

116

Alex sat back, deflated. She sighed. 'Thanks though, Kate. You've been a great help.' She gathered up the printouts of the picture of the man in the red jacket.

'Hang on, let me put the sequence on a memory stick, then you've got it if you need it. You never know when some clown might wipe the file clean thinking we don't need it anymore.' Kate busied herself clicking buttons. 'There,' she said, handing the memory stick to Alex. 'You know, I'm a lawyer, and I should be encouraging you to go to the police if you think something's happened to Rick. I should be going to the police. But—'

'There's no evidence,' Alex finished for her. 'And he could have got into the van of his own accord. But why was he driving around Suffolk in a Land Rover two weeks later?'

'What are you going to do now?'

'Do what most journalists do: go and talk to people. Trudge around a bit, see what happens. Try and rattle a few cages. The trouble is, I don't know whose cages to rattle. Not at the moment.'

Alex cast her eyes around the underpass. She felt vulnerable without Cora's protection, but as far as she could see there was only one person wrapped up in old clothes and newspapers. Perhaps everyone else had found somewhere more comfortable to sleep. She took a deep breath and said, 'Tiger.'

He opened one eye. 'What the fuck do you want.' Recognition crept slowly across his face. 'Cora's friend.' His voice was slurred, and several empty white cider bottles rolled on the ground beside him.

Alex's heart sank. How likely was she to get anything out of him? She tried a smile on for size. 'That's right. Look, I've brought a McDonald's. I thought you might like it.' She put the paper bag containing the burger and chips, together with a cup of coffee, down beside him.

'Ta.' He struggled to sit up, stale alcohol fumes wafting towards her. He began to stuff the burger into his mouth. Alex waited until he had finished.

It was now or never.

'I want to know whether you've seen this guy down here.' She held the picture of the man in the red jacket in front of his face.

He squinted at the paper. 'Bleeding 'ell, what's that?'

'It's a photo. Of a man.'

'What you showing it me for?'

'Have you seen him anywhere around here? Talking to people?'

'People? What – you mean people down here?' He yawned widely.

'When I was here with Cora—' Alex settled herself down on an old magazine on the concrete floor, 'she told me that Martin had said two men had been seen talking to Rick, Nobby and Lindy before they disappeared. Now Martin's gone too. This is one of the men seen talking to Rick. He was caught on camera.'

'Bleddy nineteen eighty-four. Big Brother always bleddy watching us.' He rolled his eyes.

Alex grinned, relaxing a little. 'I know what you mean, but sometimes it has its uses. Take a look, Tiger, have you seen him before?'

He took the picture out of Alex's hand with nicotine-stained fingers.

'Two of them you say?' He frowned. 'Gotta ciggie?'

Alex reached into her bag for the emergency packet of cigarettes she always carried with her. They often proved useful.

'Ta,' he said, after he had lit the cigarette. 'You know, I have seen him.' He jabbed at the paper. 'With another fella.'

'Down here?'

'Mebee. No. It was at the hostel. The Fight for the Homeless one down Magdalene Street. Stupid name for a charity if you ask me. They were talking to some of the guys there.'

'At the hostel?'

'Yeah. Maybe they had some jobs on offer or summat. It

happens occasionally. People come round. Sometimes its dodgy like selling dishcloths door-to-door. Other times it could be labouring work.'

'But surely they would have had to have gone through management to be allowed in?'

Tiger snorted. 'Management. Puffed up little pricks. Anyway, I wouldn't know about that. I go for the grub, that's all.'

She smiled at him. 'Okay, thanks, Tiger. You've been a great help.'

'Anytime, lassie.'

'You're from Scotland, aren't you?'

'Aye, originally. Came down to the bright lights. Marriage broke up. Had nowhere to go and no job and nothing to keep me in Glasgow. So I came here. Streets paved with gold. My arse. Anyway.'

'Why do you sleep here and not get a place in a hostel? Like the one on Magdalene Street?'

'Ah, those places are not for me. Too much sharing, you know, bathrooms and toilets. And the meetings they wanted you to go to. And the curfews. They do a good meal there, though.'

'I thought the Fight for the Homeless hostel was different, more like a home from home? No checks and stuff?'

Tiger looked at her through narrowed eyes. 'Aye. That's what it says. But you still have to be in the place at a certain time or you don't get no bed. That's what Lindy told me anyway. She went there for a while when the weather was bad, but some of us want to be on our own, however dangerous it might be. One day I might join the Poles who've set up camp in the middle of a ruddy great roundabout. Sounds almost like a camping holiday.' He grinned. 'Anyhow, ta for the food and the coffee. Come anytime. But not when the teenagers are around, okay?'

'Teenagers?

He sniffed and took a large hanky out of his pocket and wiped his nose elaborately. 'They like to have a bit of fun on a Saturday night by kicking our arses.'

'Can't anyone do anything about it?'

'The polis you mean? Nah.' He tapped the side of his head with a nicotine-stained forefinger. 'Yer mental if you think that. An' we can't do nothing in case we get banged up for it. Lose me pitch then, wouldn't I?' He laughed.

Alex didn't know what to say.

'Ah, look at the face on you. Don't you worry now. Do you want to leave that bit o' paper wi' me and I can show some of the others?'

'Thanks, Tiger.' She passed it over to him.

'It's a good job nobody else is around at the moment or they'd all be wanting a MaccyD.' He winked at her.

Alex grinned. 'I lucked out then. Bye, Tiger. See you soon.'

CHAPTER EIGHTEEN

DAY THREE: MORNING

The heavily tattooed young man behind the hostel reception desk gave a cursory glance at the picture Alex showed him.

'Nope,' he said. 'Never seen him.'

'Take a closer look,' pleaded Alex.

The man barely acknowledged it or her. 'Nope,' he said. 'Definitely not.'

'Can I go and ask inside, in case someone else has seen him, it's very important?'

'Who are you?'

'Alex Devlin. I'm a journalist.'

'Journalist?'

She ignored the sneer in his voice and tried to curb her impatience.

'Haven't got you down.' The young man didn't look at anything.

'Got me down where?'

'In the book.'

Alex couldn't see any book.

She leaned on the high counter. 'If I was homeless, would you let me in?'

'But you're not, are you? And for all I know you could be wanting to give us bad publicity.' He stared at her.

Bloody hell, it was so frustrating. Perhaps she should sit down on one of the primary-coloured seating blocks in the window and wait it out.

'Alex. What are you doing here?'

Alex wheeled round to see David Gordon behind her, no welcoming smile on his face. She was still in his bad books, then.

'You can't get away from me, can you.' She gave a little laugh but the joke fell flat. Very definitely still in his bad books. She waved the picture of the man in the red jacket at him. 'I have a photograph of one of the men seen talking to Rick Winterton before he disappeared. I want to see if he and his friend spoke to any of the others we can't find at the moment.'

David's mouth made a moue of disapproval. 'You're not still chasing this, are you, Alex?'

'Yes I am, David. I need to get to the bottom of it.'

'It's that sister of his, isn't it? Goading you on? She's a troublemaker, you know. How much do you know about her? Very little, I would say at a guess.'

'I don't need to know much about her. She's hurting, I'm trying to help and I might get a damned good story out of it. In fact, I will get a damned good story out of it, one way or another.'

David regarded her steadily. 'Ask Cora about the Riders.'

'She knows about the Riders. Why wouldn't she? She was brought up here.' Alex was determined not to let David get to her.

He laughed. It sounded hollow. 'She knows them better than you think. Ask her.'

'What do you know, then, David? What do you know about the Riders and Cora?'

'The Rider family are great supporters of Fight for the Homeless,' he said, stiffly. 'I count Marianne and Joe Rider as my friends. If they have reason to not want to engage with Cora Winterton then that's good enough for me.'

'Engage with – what the fuck are you talking about, David?'

'Ask Cora Winterton.'

'I will,' she replied, frustrated.

'And as for these two men you're so keen to find, what do you think? That they kidnapped Rick? And Lindy? And Martin? And who else? Nobby? What, in broad daylight? Because they haven't been seen for a while?' His pompous tone grated on Alex.

'No,' she said, annoyed at his sneering. 'Not necessarily kidnapped. I don't know – maybe they offered them a job and—'

'Well that's just it, isn't it? They were offered jobs, maybe picking lettuces—'

'In January?'

'All right, parsnips then.' He spread his hands. 'Anything. A lucky break.'

Alex nodded. 'Okay. Don't you think it's odd that they're going around asking people? Why not put an advert out?'

'An advert?' scoffed David. 'Come on, Alex. These people don't read adverts.'

'All right. But they came here and spoke to your clients.'

'Here?'

'Yes.'

David turned to the tattooed young man. 'Did you know about this, Tyson?'

Tyson sniffed and pulled at his ear. 'Er. Don't think so.'

'You don't have any sort of register, do you?' asked Alex.

'You know we don't. We do record people's names though. Health and safety and all that. But we delete them the next day. We want this to be a safe space where our clients don't feel hounded.'

She steadied herself, she wanted to sound pleasant. 'Can I go in and show the picture around? I mean, it is lunchtime and someone might have seen them.'

David huffed and puffed. 'Very well. But don't pressurize anyone, do you understand?'

'I won't. Thanks David. And, as for the other night—'

'That's all in the past. I don't want to dwell on it,' he said stiffly. 'As far as I'm concerned it's all over and done with.' He straightened his tie. 'I'll see you around.'

Alex nodded. 'By the way, David. Cora—'

'Yes?'

'She only wants to find her brother, that's all. You can't blame her for that. He's her only family.'

'Are you sure about that?'

'What do you mean?'

David shrugged. 'I'd be careful about her agenda if I were you, that's all.'

The dining room was alive with chatter and the smell of school dinners and sweaty feet. The chatter was coming mainly from the volunteers, dishing out the steaming mince and potato from large stainless steel dishes. Men and women, in various states of cleanliness, lined up to be served, taking their lunches over to communal tables where they ate with determination. Alex guessed it was probably the only hot meal they would get that day.

As she went around the various tables she was greeted mostly with indifference – too busy eating to want to look at a grainy photograph.

Until she reached the far corner of the room.

A woman with hair that had once had highlights but was now peppered with grey took the paper from Alex. She squinted at it, then brought it closer to her face and tapped it with her finger.

'I saw him,' she said. 'With another fella. They were talking to some of us—'

'Did they talk to you?'

She shook her head, and Alex's mood plummeted. For a moment there she thought she was onto something.

'Do you know what they were saying? To the others, I mean?'

The woman shook her head. 'Not really. Thought they were

religious types. You know, trying to save our souls and that caper. Mine went black ages ago.' She grinned, and Alex could see the mischievous light in her eyes that must have made her an interesting woman until misfortune took her life away.

'I speak to them.'

Alex turned to see a young woman of about twenty-five with long black hair and large, soulful eyes. Although she had the defeated air of someone for whom life had been too hard, she was clean and her threadbare clothes well cared for.

'Really? This man?' Alex showed her the picture.

'Yes. It is they. I speak to him and another man.'

'The other man, was he wearing a red quilted jacket?'

She frowned, thinking. Her face cleared. 'Yes, he was. And I speak to them because I am interested in their job. I hear them talk to another girl. I want a job. I did not come all the way from Lithuania to end up here.' She looked at her surroundings with disgust. 'But my boyfriend who brought me here, he ran away with someone else. I could not pay the rent on my flat. So.' She shrugged. 'I am here. For now.'

'And what was the job?' Alex was beginning to feel excited.

She shrugged. 'Cleaning. They said it would be good for me. And if I was interested they would be back.'

Alex tried to sound nonchalant. 'And did they say when they would be back?'

'They say soon. Maybe in two days' time.'

Alex nodded. 'Thank you—?'

'Karolina.' She drew herself up tall. 'My name is Karolina.'

'And are you interested in what they said Karolina?'

Karolina bit her lip. 'They promise me the work. They say it is good money and somewhere to live. They do not say where. I have heard stories about these things, where they take your passport away and don't give you money. Where they say you have to pay your way out. Where you end up selling yourself. I don't want that to happen. But I do need somewhere to live.'

Alex saw the indecision in her eyes. 'Karolina. Please don't go anywhere with these men. Not until you've spoken to me. Please.'

'Who are you?'

Alex gave her a card. 'My name is Alex Devlin and I'm a journalist. I'm trying to find out more about these two men. I'm not sure how genuine they are.'

'I see. Thank you, Alex Devlin. I will try to speak to you. I will ring you. I still have my mobile phone. It is precious to me. It has pictures of my family on it.'

Alex smiled. 'I'm glad you've got reminders of home. Phone me, yes?'

Karolina nodded.

CHAPTER NINETEEN

DAY THREE: LATE MORNING

Alex drew up in her parking space and wondered what the hell she had done. Even though the window had been wide open all the way back, the smell in the car was indescribable – somewhere between rotten eggs and rotting meat with a sweet top note. She looked across at her front seat passenger.

'So, Ethel. Is your stomach this bad all the time, or is it merely nerves?'

Ethel looked mournfully straight back at her, all grey hair and brown eyes, a rope of drool hanging from either side of her jowls. She was shivering.

Alex smiled and stroked the dog's head. 'Come on, let's get you inside.'

The people at the dog's home had been only too glad for her to take Ethel away. They knew Alex from articles she had done about the shelter, and it was so full of abandoned dogs that they couldn't wait to see Ethel go to a good home – at least temporarily. 'Until we know where his owner has gone,' Alex said to them.

Now, armed with a large bed, a lead, a dog bowl and some dog food and biscuits, Alex led Ethel up the stairs to her apartment.

Ethel stood trembling in the doorway.

'Come on, sweetie,' said Alex, proffering a biscuit in the shape of a duck, 'let's get you inside.'

Ethel sniffed at the biscuit suspiciously, then opened her mouth to take it. Alex slowly pulled her hand away, willing Ethel to follow the biscuit into the apartment. Ethel took a step. Then another. And another. Until Alex gave her the biscuit and shut the front door quietly behind her.

Ethel lay down by the door, putting her head on her paws, her ears cocked.

'Okay old girl, you stay there for now, I'll take the bed through and make it cosy for you.'

She walked into the main room and put the bed down on the wooden floor in the corner of the sitting area, near the balcony. It was light and airy there, the room always flooded with the early evening light that was reflected off the River Deben, and she thought Ethel would be happy. She wondered how well house-trained she was, and thought probably not very, considering she had been living on the streets with Martin. She would have to remember to put some newspaper down when she went out and hope for the best.

She sighed, wondering at the wisdom of her actions.

Going over to the balcony doors, she opened them and went outside, hugging herself against the biting wind. The boats were bobbing up and down, and the sky was salmon pink. She breathed in the air, the smell of the river, a mix of vegetation and mud – a great improvement on Ethel's smell – thinking how much she loved the wide East Anglian skies, the sense of space and freedom. The day was fading fast, the clouds in the distance looking like a dark mountain range.

A sharp bark brought her back inside. Ethel was standing, watching her, her long ragged tail swishing back and forth. She trotted up to Alex, nails clicking on the floor, and nuzzled her, the smell of old dog wafting around her. Then she went into her new bed, turned around several times before flopping down and closing her eyes. She didn't exactly fit in the bed, her legs, head and tail all hung outside of it, but she looked contented enough. A few seconds later she was snoring. Loudly. Alex looked at her expensive scented reed diffuser and wondered if it would cope with the dog's odour.

Glancing at the old railway clock on the wall, Alex realized she hadn't got long before she had to get ready to go to Riders' Farm. Jamie's driver was picking her up in – what – an hour, an hour and a half? She wanted to make some notes about what she had found out since she had let Rick Winterton disappear with the two men at the accident.

She opened the door of her study and stopped. There was something … something not quite right. A sense of the air having been disturbed. Something she couldn't quite put her finger on.

Stepping into the room she did a quick check. There was her computer, in front of the window with a view past the Tide Mill and across the river. By the side of it her notebook. Pens, one with the lid on, two with lids off. A dirty coffee cup. Two stacks of books precariously balanced. Sheets of A4 paper on her desk by the keyboard with recipes downloaded from the Internet. Nigel Slater's three onion soup and an Australian blogger's chicken shawarma. Had she taken those papers off the printer, or left them on there because she couldn't be bothered to bend down and get them? Think. She shook her head with frustration. No, she couldn't remember. Though—

There were her shells from Shingle Street. Had they been disturbed? Normally they were grouped together on the window-sill, now they were in a straight line. Had she done that, and if so, when? She shivered. Was she imagining all this? Becoming paranoid? She felt a wet nose against her hand: Ethel had come to investigate.

'What do you reckon, old girl?' said Alex as she fondled the dog's ears.

129

Ethel let out a sigh and a fart and turned back into the living room. A malodorous smell filled the air. Alex laughed and felt the tension leach out of her. If there had been a different smell to her study, disturbed air or whatever, Ethel's wind had certainly put paid to that fanciful notion. Mentally she shook herself. There was nothing to worry about.

Going back into the kitchen, Alex opened the bag of dog food and put some in the new dog bowl. She had no idea how much was enough for a dog of Ethel's size, so she made an educated guess. If it was too much then either the dog wouldn't eat it or she would put some meat on that thin old frame. Alex filled another old bowl with water and put them both down.

She called Ethel, who came towards her slowly, her tail wagging low between her legs, her ears back.

'Here you are, gorgeous,' said Alex. 'Some food for you. I know you're missing Martin, but he'll be back soon and you'll be together again.'

He would be back soon, wouldn't he? Had he been taken by the man in the red jacket and his friend, as it seemed Rick had been? Or was it the lure of a job that had tempted him, and if so, what sort of job was it?

Her phone buzzed.

'How did you get on today? Any progress?'

Cora. Straight to the point.

'I've got a picture of one of the two men seen talking to Rick, and quite possibly to the others.'

Cora gave a sharp intake of breath. 'How?'

'I managed to get a look at the CCTV from the solicitors. It seems as though Rick was taken away in a white van by two men—'

'The two who have been talking to the people on the streets?'

'Quite possibly. Kate Able, from the solicitors, she printed out a copy and—'

130

'I have to see it.' Cora's excitement was palpable. 'Can you email it over?'

'I'll scan it and email it in a minute. I've also got a memory stick with the CCTV sequence on it, I'll try and upload that file to you as well. And I've talked to a woman – Karolina – at the hostel in Magdalene Street, who said she'd had a conversation with them. They're going back there in a couple of days. She said she would tell me what they say to her. Tiger's also got a printout of the photo and he's going to pass it around. Cora, if we can find out who the men are, then I reckon we can find out where Rick has gone.'

'Do you think so?'

'I do. I really do.'

'Alex, when you hear from Karolina you will tell me?'

'Of course. Cora—' Alex hesitated.

'What is it?'

Alex was about to ask Cora whether she knew the Riders better than she was letting on, but if she did that, she would be letting David Gordon get to her. He was probably talking out of his backside anyway. For now, she trusted Cora, and besides, asking her about her past would be better done face-to-face. After all, they hardly knew each other, not really. 'It's nothing, don't worry. Anyway, I've got to go. I'm going out tonight.'

'Ooo, hot date?'

Alex laughed. 'Hardly. A bit of an obligation. Look, I'll talk to you when I've heard from Karolina.'

'Then we can go and talk to her together?'

'Of course.'

Alex put the phone down with a niggle of disquiet. She really needed to get to know Cora better, find out about her relationship with the Riders, how she really knew Boney was Nigel Bennet.

Nigel Bennet. Another look at the clock and she knew she ought to type up her notes and get ready for the evening, but instead she sat down at her computer and typed Boney's real name into Google Images once more. At least she had a proper screen to look at the pictures, rather than her phone.

The page loaded and Alex's heart sank. There were dozens and dozens of Nigel Bennets. There would be, wouldn't there? She began scrolling down. Guitarist. No. Bankers – several of those. A fashion designer. Entries for ten Nigel Bennets in Wikipedia. No one remotely like Boney, if, indeed she would be able to recognize him without his piercings and sharp teeth.

She was just about to give up when a word jumped out at her. Suffolk. She stopped scrolling. It was a photograph of all the rugby teams from a Suffolk school, The Alderton School, and Nigel Bennet was on the front row, fourth from the right. Under 13s. Could that be him? Alex couldn't be sure, she thought she could see a likeness; but what was really interesting was the name of the boy second from left at the back. The under 17s rugby team. Lewis Rider. Well, well, well. She sat back in her chair. Did it mean anything?

Ethel snored and snorted in her sleep. Alex looked up The Alderton School. Co-educational. Independent. Pictures of clean-cut boys and girls in clean and tidy uniform. All smiling. Fees and charges. Eye-watering. She went back to the Google Images tab. There were more photographs. Nigel Bennet in the debating team. Nigel Bennet in the swimming team. Nigel Bennet in *Bugsy Malone*. With Lewis Rider. Simon Rider. Jamie Rider. And then: the school cross-country team, with Lewis Rider and scholarship student Rick Winterton.

Rick Winterton.

She didn't believe in coincidences.

CHAPTER TWENTY

DAY THREE: LATE MORNING

Rick had slept part of the day away, but his sleep had been punctuated with alternate bouts of wakefulness and vivid dreams.

Now he was awake and walking, he was hurting and shivering from the cold and damp. Why hadn't he taken more than one jumper from the farmhouse? Because he wasn't thinking straight, that's why. He could hardly think at all, never mind in a coherent way. His head ached, and he thought if he wasn't careful he would overdose on paracetamol. A couple more wouldn't do any harm. He eased the blister pack out of his pocket, taking care with his hands that were, like the rest of his body, still sore. Fuck. None left. He shoved the empty pack back in his pocket. No point in leaving any clues as to where he'd been. A shiver ran up and down the length of his spine. And the way he was shivering he would probably die of pneumonia before a brain haemorrhage. There. He was making jokes. Perhaps he was getting better.

No. He wasn't. His battered and bruised body also ached and stung with equal intensity. The throbbing in his arm almost overrode the pain in his head. Please God it wasn't getting infected. He would look at it later.

He sat down, his back against a tree, and reached inside the canvas bag for the pot of honey and half-eaten loaf of bread. Dipping the last crust of bread into the dregs of the honey, he hoped it would give him energy for the day ahead. He was trying to conserve supplies, but knew he would have to find more soon. And he was running low on water.

Goddamnit his arm hurt.

He pulled up the sleeve of his jumper. The duct tape was loose. He tore it off quickly, gasping as he pulled the skin.

Fuck.

His arm was swollen and the wound was still open. He could see pus deep down. Worse, the skin around the cut was red, an infection was setting in. He needed antibiotics. He laughed harshly. Yeah, right. And where was he going to get those? Even if he could break into a pharmacy, there probably wasn't one within fifty miles or something.

Leeches. That might help. Were there any rivers near and did they have leeches?

Leeches. His mind must be more muddled than he realized.

He opened the last bottle of water and began to pour it over the wound. Shame he hadn't looked for a bottle of vodka in that house. Alcohol would have cleaned it better. And helped his head. No, wouldn't have helped his head, but give him some warmth. Vodka. He should have taken some. There again, he'd taken so much. He leaned his head back and wondered if they'd discovered they were missing supplies, food, medicines, clothes. He wondered if they knew someone had been in the house, taken a shower, used a towel. He wondered what the woman was saying to her husband. He wondered whether the children walked the dogs. Nice dogs. I heart Labradors.

Shut up. Shut up.

His mind was wandering.

The water was all gone. He hadn't noticed. He'd carried on pouring it over his arm. He hadn't noticed it all going. Fuck fuck fuck.

No good worrying. It was done now.

He dabbed his skin dry with the bottom of his tee-shirt. Very hygienic. But at least the cut was cleaner. Too big to leave open. The infection would get worse. He bit off a strip of duct tape. Wrapped it around his arm making sure he pulled the edges of the skin together. Bite duct tape. Repeat. Bite duct tape. Repeat.

Then a memory hit him, *wham*. He'd been sitting, bound to a chair in an empty room, brought there by the guys who'd bundled him into that white van. But – he shook his head – he'd *wanted* to be there. Had engineered it. Really? Why? And where? He tried to concentrate, willing the memories to come back. Something to do with his family? His sister? And if he'd wanted to be there, why had he tried to escape? Because they'd been coming for him, that's why. They had known who he was all along; they had seen him collecting evidence – evidence he'd had to leave behind.

He sat quietly, trying to ignore the pain in his body, trying to breathe deeply and let thoughts pass by. Trying to remember. There was nothing more.

He had to get some food. More clothes.

He ate the last of his bread and honey.

He walked on.

He looked around.

Fuck.

He had been this way earlier.

He was walking round in circles.

CHAPTER TWENTY-ONE

DAY THREE: EVENING

'So, Ms Devlin, you're a journalist I believe?' Marianne Rider took a delicate bite of her confit duck leg, quite a feat in itself.

Alex smiled to herself. So much for Jamie's assertion that his mother would like a signed copy of her book about couponing – she had obviously never heard of it. Just another chat-up line from the man. She had to admire his front.

'Yes, I am. I freelance for *The Post*, which is based in London.'

'And what do you do for the – ah – *Post*?' The diamonds in her ears glinted in the candlelight.

'I write articles about people, people who have something to say. I also write investigative pieces—'

'Such as?' Marianne watched her closely.

'Ma, don't interrogate her. She has only known us five minutes.' This came from the eldest brother, Lewis, who was helping himself to more of the creamy potato dauphinoise.

Alex flashed him a smile. 'We have met before,' she felt bold enough to say to him.

Lewis turned his gaze on her. His face was so wrinkle-free that Alex thought he must have had work done, and a good deal of it.

'Oh?'

Of course he wouldn't remember. He was in a hurry. He was a busy person. She was not worth noticing. And it had been a fleeting encounter.

'Outside the offices for Fight for the Homeless. In Norwich,' she added, in case for some reason he had forgotten. 'Yesterday.'

'I don't think so.' He flashed her a too-bright smile. 'I would remember you I'm sure.'

'Yes. I was going in and you were coming out. You pushed the door very hard. Almost knocked me over.' She chuckled to show she had found it amusing.

He stared at her. Something dark flashed behind his eyes. 'Ah, right. Of course.'

Alex had the sense the admission had cost him. Why was he being so cagey?

'What were you doing there, Lewis?' Marianne asked. Her tone was mild but her body language was stiff and unforgiving.

'Sorting out some funding, Ma, that's all.'

'I thought—' She shook her head. 'It doesn't matter.'

But the tension still shimmered in the room.

'I understand you live in Woodbridge?' This came from Lewis's wife, Louisa, who Alex knew from her research had been married to Lewis for twenty years. They had three sulky teenagers.

Alex smiled and they chatted for a few minutes about the town and its lovely shops and how super it must be living right by the water.

'You haven't told us about your investigative pieces,' said Marianne before taking a sip of her wine.

Alex noticed bright red lipstick marks on the wine glass. She was not going to be intimidated by Marianne Rider.

'To answer your question, Marianne, one very successful feature I wrote was on the dangers of suicide forums on the Internet. It came about when I was reporting on the death of two people on the Broads. You may have seen the press about it?'

137

'Really? How depressing.' She sipped her wine, dabbing her mouth with a napkin.

'I've also written a book about extreme couponing – Jamie mentioned you would like a signed copy?' Alex smiled innocently.

There was a gratifying break out of coughing from Jamie on her right as something obviously went down the wrong way.

Marianne arched a well-plucked eyebrow. 'Extreme couponing. Hmm. I haven't heard of your book, but I will certainly have a look. Thank you.' Marianne put her knife and fork together neatly. Her fingernails were painted a deep red to match her lipstick.

Somehow the dismissal stung.

'Well I think the book sounds jolly interesting. I might get it.' Claudia, the third wife of the youngest son, Simon, looked as though she was about to burst into tears. Though it seemed to be her default expression – she had looked like that all evening.

'Sweetie, you don't need to cut out coupons from the rags,' drawled her husband, whose expression gave the impression he was chewing on something Ethel might leave in the middle of the carpet.

'I don't care. I think it sounds like a really interesting idea.' Claudia rubbed two fingers up and down the stem of her wine-glass.

'Did you find your scarf?' Marianne gazed at Alex.

'Scarf?'

'Jamie said he asked you to supper when he found you stuck in the mud after looking for your scarf.'

Damn. She had forgotten about that excuse. 'Yes. That's right. No. I didn't find it.'

'Really? No. I don't suppose you did.' Marianne carried on chewing.

Alex tried not to squirm under her gaze.

This 'quiet family supper' promised by Jamie was not turning out at all how she expected.

She had turned away the car that arrived outside the apartment – she wanted to drive so she could decide for herself when it was time to leave. She had learned that lesson. When she arrived at Riders' Farm she was greeted by a silent and unsmiling maid who took her coat and showed her into the enormous and warm kitchen. It was the sort of kitchen Alex would have expected a family like the Riders to have: a cream Aga at one end. Doors out onto a patio and the garden beyond. Gleaming work surfaces with minimal clutter. Plenty of storage space. Pots bubbling on another range cooker. Flowers in jugs. White tiles, wood, stainless steel, granite. All shouting money, and not in the least cosy.

Though she'd had to admit the smell coming from whatever was cooking was delicious.

'Alex.'

Jamie had smiled with pleasure, uncurled himself from an armchair by the Aga and padded across the warm tiled floor to greet her with a kiss on the cheek. 'Thank you for coming. I had hoped I would be able to chase everyone away for tonight, but the brothers and their wives have come along. They'll be here shortly. Drink?'

Her heart had sunk. It was not going to be quite the evening she had hoped for. She said yes to the drink.

'You don't mind do you? About the family, I mean.' He'd opened the American-style fridge and taken out a bottle of wine, pushing the door shut with his foot. 'Only we had a family meeting and so they were all here and before I knew it ...' He shrugged, charmingly. 'Which is a bit of a bore from my point of view when I wanted to see you on your own. But there we have it.'

'I didn't think you were much involved in the family business?'

'No. But I like to dispense advice. Have you been stalking me on Google, then?'

Alex had tried not to blush. 'A little. That's what we journalists like to do. It saves going through dusty files or back copies of newspapers.' Though, curiously, information on the Rider family had been thin on the ground with only the bare bones in Wikipedia and various articles about the success of their expansion and diversification. There was little personal stuff, apart from the basics – who they were married to, who they'd divorced, how many children they had. The family had managed to keep their personal lives pretty much under wraps. Which meant someone like Alex could draw the conclusion there must be parts of their lives they wanted to keep covered. And she wanted to uncover it. Natural curiosity, of course.

'And meeting the family, are you sure you're okay with that?'

'Of course.' She'd hoped she succeeded in sounding upbeat. Besides, it could provide some interesting material.

Now she was trapped at this scrubbed pine table with the silver cutlery and cut-glass wine goblets and linen napkins and all the Rider family giving her the once-over as if Jamie was presenting her as some sort of girlfriend exhibit. It made her feel uncomfortable.

No. Marianne Rider made her feel uncomfortable. She wondered if she did it to all her guests, or maybe only to journalists? Or, and Alex enjoyed this thought more, she was worried about someone unsuitable getting their claws into her beloved son.

'And what are you working on at the moment?' asked Lewis.

His smile, decided Alex, was distinctly Blairite. Friendly and insincere. There was something about him she didn't quite trust. And she trusted her instincts.

What to say? 'I'm looking into homelessness in East Anglia. I want to write some of the stories of the people on the streets. The rough sleepers.'

'Really? How interesting,' said Marianne, not sounding interested at all.

'Yes. You'd be surprised how some people got there – a missed mortgage payment, death of a spouse, a business collapse—'

'Drugs, alcohol—' piped up Claudia, who immediately shrank into herself when given a glare by her husband.

Alex nodded. 'That too. And sometimes people turn to drugs and alcohol to help them cope, to get them through the day.'

'Really?' Marianne arched a perfectly plucked eyebrow.

'Yes really. But more worryingly, some of them are disappearing.'

'Disappearing?' This from Lewis, who had arched both his also perfectly plucked eyebrows.

Idly, Alex wondered if they went to the same beauty salon.

She opened her mouth to tell them about Rick and Lindy and how Martin had left Ethel behind, then realized that these particular people with their yurts and lodges and island probably wouldn't want to hear about it. Or maybe she was imposing a stereotype. However, this was supposed to be a family supper and she must not spoil it. It wouldn't be fair on Jamie. And she wanted to keep him onside. So she shrugged. 'I don't expect it's anything. Probably moved on.' She smiled.

'Ah, pudding,' exclaimed Joe, the Rider patriarch, sniffing deeply and puncturing the tension in the air.

The same unsmiling woman who had shown Alex to the kitchen put down a large bowl of what looked and smelled like sticky toffee pudding.

Joe rubbed his hands with glee. 'My favourite. I love the sauce that comes with the sticky date sponge, don't you my dear?' He beamed at Alex.

Alex couldn't help but smile back. He was an old buffer, but quite endearing. He hadn't lost that Suffolk accent either. 'Indeed I do, Joe.'

'Especially with a splash of thick double cream?'

'Especially with that.'

'Thank you for putting up with my rather awkward family,' said Jamie as he threw another log into the wood burner, making the fire crackle and spit. The flames danced, casting shadows that weaved around the room. Alex nursed a brandy and Jamie a whisky as they sat by candlelight in one of the 'backwoodsmen' lodges. It was where he stayed when he came up to Suffolk, Jamie told her. Especially in the winter when they had few guests. Not many people wanted to play at being 'backwoodsmen' in the cold and the wet and the mud.

Alex had to admit, the lodge was comfortable. Set in the middle of the wood, it had large windows, and thankfully there were also thick curtains. She imagined that during the day the view would be of the trees and the wildlife. There were sumptuous rugs over polished floorboards, fat settees to sink into, the wood burner of course, and a huge television on the wall. There was also, Jamie said, excellent Wi-Fi. Even backwoodsmen liked connection to the outside world these days.

Alex thought that was rather missing the point.

'Your family,' she said, rubbing a finger around the rim of her glass. 'I'm not sure they liked me.'

Jamie laughed. 'They're a strange bunch, I'll give you that. Lewis is mainly in charge of the family business, something little Simon feels resentful about. He thinks he should have a bigger share of the fat pie.' He refilled her glass. She didn't stop him. 'Mum is the brains behind it all. She saw we had to diversify or die and as the farm has been in the family for aeons, we diversified.'

She noticed he didn't reassure her that yes, her family really had liked her.

'You have these lodges?'

He nodded. 'About half a dozen.'

'And the yurts.'

Jamie smiled. 'That was Louisa's idea. She's very much into all that flat-sandalled stuff.'

She nudged him with her foot. 'All that flat-sandalled stuff? That's a bit patronizing.'

He grimaced. 'I don't go in for Indian head massages and holistic therapies and all that.'

'Chakras.' She grinned.

'Indeed. Mind you, they balance all the mumbo jumbo with hunting, shooting and fishing. You see, the farm caters for all. I'm sure we could find something you would like to do.' He looked meaningfully at her over the rim of his glass.

'And the island,' she said, ignoring the heat of his gaze. 'Your family owns that island off the coast.'

Jamie nodded. 'Gisford Ness.'

'And what goes on there? I've heard all sorts.'

'Such as?'

'Well.' She settled herself even more comfortably on the cushions, tucking her feet underneath her. 'That aliens have landed there and the government and you are keeping it under wraps.'

His mouth twitched. 'Aliens? Really?'

'Aliens. Or it's some sort of prison for those who've been put away for life – no tariff – and again, the government is in cahoots with your family. Or it's haunted. Ghosts abound. Or medical experiments go on there. You should see the stuff on Google. Apparently you can hear crying and screaming sometimes over the water if the wind is in the right direction.' She looked at him. He was laughing. 'So which is it? I'll bet it's aliens.'

'I wish.' He refilled their glasses again. Alex hadn't realized she'd drunk all hers. 'Not aliens. Far more prosaic.' He tilted his head on one side. 'No, not prosaic. But not aliens.'

'Go on then.'

'Many, many years ago my grandfather apparently allowed the government—'

Alex raised her glass. 'Told you. The government.' Did her words sound slurred there? Careful, Alex.

'Allowed the government to dump stuff on the island.'

'Stuff?'

143

'Stuff. That turned out to be dangerous chemicals. Anthrax was mentioned.'

She sat up at that one. 'Anthrax? Bloody hell.'

'Exactly. The story goes that scientists exploded a series of bombs during the Second World War. They were tested on sheep – about fifty of them – and they all died within a few days. It was kept very hush-hush. Anyway, the land was officially declared decontaminated twenty or so years ago, but as a family we don't want people going there just in case. Now we are trying to return it to nature.'

'You've been over there?'

Jamie shook his head. 'No, but Lewis and Simon have. And Dad. Not my area of expertise.'

'Interesting.'

'I don't think there's much to write about there,' he laughed.

'I don't know, anthrax and dead sheep and government shenanigans, always good copy.'

'I'm not sure my family would thank you.'

'Maybe not.' She smiled at him.

They sat in a comfortable silence.

'Why aren't you in the family business, Jamie?' she asked eventually.

He sighed. 'It wasn't and isn't for me. Farming I mean. Even the diversification wasn't my bag. I have nothing to do with it, have no say in it and that's fine by me. I prefer playing with money.'

'So your area of expertise is money. You're a banker.'

He grinned. 'To rhyme with wanker, I know. Heard all that before.'

Alex laughed. 'Sorry. It's not very original, is it? What is it you do exactly? In banking. It's not an area I know much about.'

'Are you sure you really want to know?' He gave her a gentle smile.

'Yes, of course. I wouldn't have asked otherwise. Besides, you could be a good subject for me.' She did hope he wouldn't be

144

too dry with his explanation because the way she was feeling she might just fall asleep.

'I'm a trader – part of a team really – and I invest capital the bank has to hold for a rainy day to make as much money as possible within our pretty high-risk limits. Basically we invest in government bonds and punt around in other related markets. Quite often I get to meet foreign governments who try and get us to buy their debt. I focus on USD – dollars – short-end rates – I'm sorry, am I boring you?'

Alex was trying, and not managing, to stifle a yawn. Most of what he said had gone straight over her head. 'Not at all.'

Jamie laughed. 'I can see it's not going to make an article in *The Post* any time soon.'

'It could be if I made it relatable. It would improve my credibility too. A business feature. Heath would never believe it.'

'Heath?'

'My news editor,' she explained.

'I see. Good name.' His face was unsmiling.

Alex looked at him, amused. Was he jealous? Surely not. She swallowed a laugh. 'Yes. Named after Heathcliff, but he dropped the "Cliff" bit.'

'And does he look like Heathcliff?'

'Depends what you think Heathcliff looks like, I suppose.' What an absurd conversation.

'Dark and brooding.'

Alex shook her head. 'No, I wouldn't say he was dark and brooding.'

All at once she had a pang of longing. To be sitting with Heath now, eating good food and drinking good wine, chatting and laughing as they used to do. Well, had done once or twice.

'You mentioned about doing a feature on homeless people? And that some were, what, disappearing?' He refilled her glass.

She looked at Jamie. Was he really interested? His gaze was open and friendly.

145

'Yes. It seems that some of the rough sleepers have been disappearing; and I know you'll say that's not unusual, but I think it might be.' She put her glass down and rifled in her bag, bringing out the picture of the man in the red jacket. 'I'm particularly looking for Rick Winterton.'

'Rick.' His voice was flat. 'Cora Winterton's brother.'

Here we go.

'That's right. I understand you know them?' She aimed for friendly interest.

'A bit.'

Not very forthcoming.

'Rick's been homeless for a while. Here's a CCTV picture of a man I think might have forced Rick to go with him.' She held it out to Jamie.

'Forced?' He frowned, taking the printout from her.

'Maybe. I'm not sure. I know it's a long shot, but do you know this man?'

He laughed. 'Now I feel like I'm on *Crimewatch*.' He looked at the picture before handing it back to her. 'No, sorry. No idea.'

'Oh well.' She put it back in her bag.

'Are you showing that around a lot?'

'A fair bit, yes. Why?'

'Nothing. Just wondered that's all.'

She took a deep breath. 'You were at school with him, weren't you? Rick Winterton, I mean.'

The fire crackled.

'I was. He was a scholarship boy. A couple of years below me. He wasn't a friend.'

'No. What about Nigel Bennet?'

Jamie sipped his drink. 'Nigel Bennet?' He frowned. 'Nope. Don't recall him.' He sipped some more. 'Why all the questions?'

'Trying to build a picture, that's all.'

'Who is Nigel Bennet, then?'

146

'He's called Boney now. Bit of a criminal in the area. Involved with homeless people.'

Jamie arched an eyebrow. 'The headmaster wouldn't like that. A criminal from The Alderton School. You have been doing your research.' He raised his whisky as if in salute.

Alex smiled and put her glass on the table. 'I'd better go.'

Jamie stayed her arm. 'Must you?'

A shiver of – what? anticipation? ran through her. His hand felt heavy and hot on her arm. Her body and mind were relaxed from dinner and the brandy. It was cold outside. She didn't want to go home …

Ethel. She sat up quickly. Which was a mistake as her head swam. 'I've got to go. Ethel.'

'Whose that? Your granny?'

'No, my dog.'

'Dog?'

'She's not exactly mine. I'm looking after her for a friend. You see—' Something stopped her. She didn't want to tell him about Martin, not yet. 'He had to go away, my friend, that is, and it's the first evening she's been on her own, so—'

'You can't leave her.' He stood.

'No, she'll probably be crossing her legs as it is.' She wondered how house-trained Ethel was – if at all. She stood. And swayed.

'You can't drive home.'

'I know that.' Stupid, stupid. Once again. She sighed.

'And I can't drive you.'

'I know that too. And I can't stay.' She frowned. 'You'd better order me a taxi.'

'Because of Ethel.'

'Because of Ethel.' She spoke firmly, wondering for a fleeting moment what it would be like if she did stay. Dangerous.

Jamie sighed. 'I'll get Paul to take you.' He punched some numbers into his phone and spoke briefly. 'He'll be over at the house.'

147

They pulled on the wellies they had taken from the boot room at the farmhouse and went outside into the cold air. A wet fog settled around them, and Alex couldn't see any distance. Even Jamie's torch didn't penetrate the fog, the light bouncing back at them. Alex shivered, and Jamie put his arm around her. She stiffened.

'It's all right,' he said, grinning. 'It's too cold to be doing any ravishing. Besides, I wouldn't be able to see you properly.'

'Just you try, mate,' she retorted, keeping her voice light to take the sting out of her words. She may have had far too much wine and brandy, but she knew danger when she saw it.

Making their way carefully through the wood they heard the hooting of an owl, and rustling somewhere to the left of them. The fog deadened the sound and made her feel disorientated.

'Don't worry, it'll be deer,' said Jamie, pulling Alex closer.

She fit snugly under his arm.

He was warm, comforting.

'I'm not worried,' said Alex. 'Thank you for a lovely evening. And if I don't see her, please thank your mother for the wonderful food tonight.'

Jamie laughed. 'You don't think she cooked it, do you? She has people to do that.'

No, that didn't surprise her. 'Even so, it was delicious.'

'You're very kind.' He kissed the top of her head.

And that, thought Alex, was as far as it was going to go. She knew nothing about the Riders, and as a family they seemed dysfunctional. Perhaps Jamie was the exception. But what did she know about him? Then, how much did you know about anybody the second time you met them? She'd made plenty of mistakes in the past, and it was about time she learned from them.

Gently, she disentangled herself from him. They walked side-by-side, the forest giving way to fields, and the footpath round the edge. On her way to the lodge she had been full of food and wine and very relaxed. Now she knew she had drunk too much and she wanted to get home. To her, the silence was not companionable any more.

'You're divorced, I gather,' she said, regretting the words as soon as they had left her mouth. What on earth was she thinking? His mouth tightened imperceptibly.

'Yes. She left me before you ask. It was painful. Luckily no children.'

'Right,' she mumbled.

'You're a single parent. You've got a son,' he said, as they picked their way through muddy puddles that were just about picked out in the torchlight. 'And a sister who has mental health problems.'

'Had,' she corrected automatically. 'You're very well informed. How did you know?'

She saw his mouth twist into the semblance of a smile.

'You're not the only one who can do research you know.'

How had it come to this? A few minutes before she had felt relaxed in his company, now due to a stupid question on her part the atmosphere had soured. His marriage and divorce was obviously something he didn't like talking about, and she shouldn't have blundered straight in. On the other hand, she didn't particularly want to talk about Sasha. Or Gus, for that matter. Not at the moment. She needed to get the evening back on track.

'I'm sorry if I've put my foot in it,' she said, in a small voice. 'I don't know what I was thinking.'

They walked on for a few minutes. He took her hand, squeezed it, and let it go. She was forgiven.

She tripped over a root; Jamie steadied her.

'Who did cook dinner?' she asked as she clambered over a stile hoping he wouldn't notice her bottom that looked enormous in the coat.

'One of our girls. They're from Eastern Europe. When we were

149

small we had au pairs occasionally, and Mum likes to keep up the tradition, though instead of looking after us, they help in the house. And we get wonderful meals. Makes a change from London takeouts, I can tell you.'

The lights of the farmhouse glowed through the fog at last.

Alex jumped as an ear-splitting shriek suddenly tore through the air, magnified by the stillness of the fog. 'What the hell was that?'

There was another, that was suddenly cut off. The silence was eerie.

'Were they coming from the island?' she asked, thinking back to their earlier conversation. 'They sounded from about the right direction. Across the water.'

'Worried about ghosts?' Jamie grinned.

'No, they sounded all too human to me.'

Jamie shook his head. 'Probably an animal. Or even an owl – their calls can be quite off-putting, you know. They don't all do twit-twoos.'

'I know that.'

'Or maybe a fox with some prey.'

'No,' said Alex. 'It sounded human to me.' She was unnerved.

Jamie shook his head. 'Too much talk of anthrax and dead sheep. There's nothing on the island. Come on, Paul will be waiting in the drive.'

They drew nearer to the house, and Alex made out the shape of a car, its headlights shining in the gloom. She decided to say nothing more about the screams. Perhaps it really had been an owl or a fox. Perhaps.

'Wait, my shoes. I can't go home in these wellies.'

'I'll fetch them for you,' said Jamie.

Then there was a shout.

'Mr Rider, sir?' A man came hurrying up to him. 'Sorry to disturb you. I know it's late and everything, but I need a word.'

'Now?' he said, irritably.

'Sorry, sir, but yes. I can't find your brothers anywhere and your parents are in bed. It's a bit urgent.' The man hopped from foot to foot.

He turned to her. 'Alex—'

'Don't worry,' she said. 'I can fetch my shoes myself.'

She hurried around the back of the house, the outside lamps with their soft coronas lighting her way. Thankfully the boot room was open.

Where had she left them? She peered around. There. In the corner.

She eased off the wellies and slipped them on.

Back outside, Jamie was talking to two men in hi-vis jackets. The second man had his back to her, but was gesticulating. Jamie looked angry, the first man, uncomfortable. As she got closer, Jamie saw her and gave a wave of dismissal to the two men, who hurried off.

'Sorry about that,' he said, as he opened the door of the waiting car. 'Business.'

'Money talk at this time of night?'

'Not my business, farm business. No one else around. Security issues.' He bent forward and kissed her cheek. 'I did enjoy this evening. Despite the family. Maybe we can do it again?'

She smiled. 'Maybe.'

As she watched Jamie and the house recede into the fog, she wondered if her eyes had deceived her. As the second man had hurried away from Jamie, she could have sworn that she had caught a glimpse of a red jacket underneath the hi-vis jacket he wore.

CHAPTER TWENTY-TWO

DAY FOUR: MORNING

'Have you forgiven me for leaving you for so long?' Alex finished the last of her toast, saving a crust for Ethel, who took it, very delicately and deliberately, into her mouth. The dog's large brown eyes still looked reproachful, though.

'Sorry. You can come with me sometimes, but not always. At least you were a good girl.' Ethel wagged her tail. Alex fondled her ears while Ethel sat, her tongue lolling, eyes closed, a gentle *puff* escaping from her backside.

Alex had expected to come home last night to a steaming great pile on the floor or chewed skirting boards but there was nothing. Bonus. Perhaps keeping a dog was not going to be too hard. Though she did have to deal with Ethel's reproachful look when she came through the door.

Her phone rang out David Bowie's 'Heroes'. Jamie.

'Hi,' she said, surprise in her voice. She moved away from the vicinity of Ethel's bottom.

'Alex.' His voice was warm. Chocolatey, even. 'I wanted to talk to you.'

'What about?'

He laughed. 'Nothing in particular, I wanted to hear your

voice. And to thank you for a lovely evening. I did enjoy it. I also want to apologize for stepping over the line, bringing up your boy and your sister like I did.'

He did, indeed, sound contrite.

'I shouldn't have mentioned your divorce, either. It was insensitive of me.'

'Now we've both beaten our breasts, so to speak, can we start again?'

Alex bit her lip. 'Look. My sister's holding an art exhibition at the gallery in Gisford and the preview's tomorrow evening.' She hesitated a moment. Was she doing the right thing? 'Perhaps you'd like to come with me?'

'That's a swish place. Your sister must be good. Tomorrow? Let me see ...'

'No worries if you can't. I mean, I know it's short notice and you have to make your money—'

'I'd love to.'

Alex smiled into her phone. 'That's settled then.'

'Great. Now, Paul is driving your car back this morning. There's a parking space outside your apartment I suppose?'

'Yes, there is. Thank you. Paul will bring someone with him, I hope. You won't make him walk home?'

Jamie laughed. 'He'll bring someone.' He cleared his throat. 'I'm looking forward to seeing you tomorrow night. I'm in London most of the day, but I will be back. For you.' That chocolate voice again. Warm. Odd how important the timbre of a voice was.

Be on your guard, Alex, a voice in her head told her.

'Thank you. I'll see you then.'

She ended the call. Her sister's art exhibition was going to be even more interesting.

Ethel looked at her and whined, her tail thumping on the floor.

'You want to go out, old girl? So you shall.' She shrugged on her coat and pulled on her bobble hat before picking up Ethel's lead.

Calling out a 'hello' to John Watson who was checking his post, she stepped outside. At least the weather had cheered up – only for the day, if the weather forecasters were to be believed. The sky was blue and the air was crisp. It did feel as though the gloom of January was lifting.

She walked past the houseboats moored in the harbour, avoiding tripping over the rusting mooring rings and narrowly missing kicking over the two pints of milk left by the gangplank leading to *The Rose of Tralee*.

Sitting down on a bench at the side of the sandy footpath that ran alongside the yacht club, Ethel down by her side, she closed her eyes, letting the weak, wintry sun warm her face, and tried to clear her mind.

But too many thoughts were clamouring for attention. Jamie Rider was a liar, she knew that. However attractive he might be, he was a liar. Yes, he did admit to knowing Rick, but come on, they were at the same school playing the same sport, there was no way he wouldn't have known him pretty well. And as for denying any knowledge of Nigel Bennet – and that denial had convinced her Bennet definitely was Boney – that was plain ridiculous. They must have known each other.

So why was he lying?

Was the family somehow mixed up with Boney and his criminal activities? Did they have something to do with Rick disappearing? The other homeless people disappearing? She sighed. Surely not. Why would they be?

Why not? A little voice nagged her.

And had she really seen a red jacket underneath the hi-vis jacket worn by the security guard – or whatever he was – on the farm last night? Or was it a figment of her overactive imagination? Perhaps, the drink hadn't helped. She shifted on the bench. And the island the Rider family owned, she would like to find out more about that. There was also Sam Slater. A straight-up sort of guy. But something had occurred to her while she'd been talking to him when they had been out on the road looking for the Land Rover. He had said to her that maybe she was imagining it all because she'd had too much to drink *at the party*. How had he known she had been at the Riders charity do?

And, think about the story. Had she got one here or not?

Certainly she had one about homeless people, there were so many stories to tell. She could take pictures as illustration, too. Not just of the people, but of the surroundings. If she could get to the roundabout on the outskirts of Norwich and speak to the people in tents, well, that would make a fabulous article. She could even trace their lives back to where they came from. It would have to be run by Heath, but she knew he went with anything she suggested. On the whole.

But it had all begun with one event: the disappearance of Rick Winterton, or, strictly speaking, the two disappearances of Rick Winterton.

Before she could puzzle over it some more, Ethel's tail began to thump and a shadow fell across her.

'Cora,' Alex said, looking up, surprised. 'How did you find me?'

'I went to your flat but I couldn't get in. A nice man in a wheelchair told me you'd gone out with a dog and he thought you were going down the footpath. I took a chance.' She bent down and stroked Ethel. 'You've picked up Martin's dog.'

'I couldn't let her sit in a dog pound, I wanted her to be here for when Martin came back.'

'If he comes back.' Cora buried her face in Ethel's coat.

'I wouldn't do too much of that. I've only just given her the flea and tick tablet.'

Cora looked up, a crooked smile on her face. 'I don't mind. She's a lovely dog, aren't you, Ethel? It's going to be a different kind of life for her with you, isn't it? You'd better make sure she will want to go back to Martin.'

Was Cora giving her some sort of warning here? 'I will, don't worry. A few days' pampering won't do her any harm. Anyway, have you come all the way from Norwich to see me?'

Cora looked tired, her skin was grey and her coat crumpled. Her curls were scraped back in a ponytail. The bruise on her cheekbone was turning purple. Alex could see the blue of her uniform at her neck. Alex knew she should be asking her questions.

Cora shook her head. 'No. I've been working overnight at Ipswich.' She brushed away some stray hairs from her forehead and sat down next to Alex. 'I had a call this morning. I thought you'd like to know.' She swallowed and licked at the side of her thumb. 'Tiger's been found dead.'

Alex sat up straighter. 'Tiger? But I only saw him yesterday. When I gave him that photograph.'

Cora nodded. 'He'd been showing it around a great deal apparently.'

'So—?'

'Overdose. He was found late yesterday afternoon.'

Alex slumped back on the bench. 'Oh.'

'No, Alex, not "oh".'

'What do you mean?'

'Tiger didn't do drugs.' Cora's voice was tight.

'What?'

'Booze, yes. Fags when he could cadge them, but never drugs. He always said he had stooped low enough. He wasn't one of those who took drugs to get through the day. You've met Tiger. You know what he's – was – like.'

'What are you saying?'

She shook her head. 'It couldn't have been an accident; he wouldn't have suddenly decided to shoot up some heroin. I'm saying I think he was murdered.'

'Murdered?'

Cora nodded. 'What other explanation is there? He was found

156

slumped in that bloody underpass with a needle sticking out of his arm.'

'Someone must have seen something?'

Cora shook her head. 'Either nobody did see anything or they have been frightened into keeping quiet.'

'I see.' Oh, Tiger.

'I got your email with the CCTV picture, but I didn't recognize either of the men. I was hoping—'

'That you would and it would lead us to Rick?'

'Guess so.'

'Cora,' she hesitated. 'Did it look to you as though Rick got into the van willingly?'

'No. I don't know. Possibly.'

Her answer came too quickly.

'One other thing, Alex—'

Alex looked at her. Was she changing the subject?

'I went to that hostel on Magdalene Street yesterday evening before work to talk to Karolina.'

Alex took a breath in. 'I thought we were going to talk to her together?' For a split second she felt a flicker of resentment. This was her story. Then sense prevailed. It was Cora's brother they were looking for, it was her story too.

'I couldn't wait. Anyway, it was pointless.' She shrugged. 'She's gone.'

'Gone?'

'Yes. Apparently one of those men came back and she went with him.'

'I wonder why?'

'One of the other residents there said he'd probably offered her a job.'

'She did say,' began Alex, slowly, 'that when they first spoke to her they offered her a job cleaning.'

'She must have decided to take it.'

'Except she promised she wouldn't do anything without talking to me. And she has got my number.'

'Obviously you're not as important as you think you are.'

Alex felt as though she'd been slapped. 'What?'

Cora shook her head. 'Sorry, sorry. I'm tired. I don't know what I'm saying. Ignore me.'

Alex nodded. She knew Cora was tired and under enormous strain. 'Though the fact remains that Tiger is dead and now Karolina has disappeared, or, at any rate, gone off without making contact. Of course, you may well be right and she didn't think about ringing me.'

'And you haven't found out anything else that might lead us to Rick?'

Alex could hardly bear the hopeful look on Cora's face. 'No. Except—'

Cora gave Ethel a final pat and stood. 'Except what?'

'Look, I found some glass.'

'Glass? What do you mean?' Her body language was impatient – she was looking around, bouncing up and down on the balls of her feet, touching her hair, her mouth. She looked as though she was about to take off.

'I went back to where the Land Rover crashed. There was nothing there—'

'Of course there wasn't, they would have cleared it all up.'

'Who would have, Cora?'

She waved her hand. 'Never mind, go on.'

Alex decided she would come back to that point. 'I found glass that I think came from either one of the lights or indicators—'

'How do you know it's not an old bottle or something?'

'I don't.' Alex was trying to be patient. 'That's why I'm going to take it to the cops and they're going to examine it forensically.'

Cora looked at her, eyes wide. 'You've told your policeman friend about it, haven't you?'

'Yes, why?'

158

Her face drained of colour. 'So they know we're still looking for Rick?'

'Of course, what's the problem?'

'I thought we were doing it together? Just us two? You're a journalist, Alex, aren't you supposed to chase a story to the very end on your own?'

'I have to ask the right people questions. Sam is going to hurry the glass through forensics. There's a friend of his who—'

'Sam? DI Sam Slater? That's your policeman friend?'

Alex nodded.

'Okay.' She stared into the distance.

'Cora, what's the problem? Tell me about the Riders. Tell me about why it was a bad idea to go to the police with those pieces of glass. Have the Riders got something to do with Rick having disappeared?'

Cora shook her head, then: 'The Riders are poison.'

'Cora, I know that—'

'You can't trust them. Not even Jamie. He might seem harmless, but he's not. They're all the same, the whole lot of them.' Cora was pale and she nibbled some more at the skin on the side of her fingers. Alex noticed that her nails were bitten down to the quick. Cora saw her looking and pulled her jacket sleeves down over her hands.

'Jamie has nothing to do with the family business.'

'Is that what he told you?' She laughed harshly. 'And you believed him?'

'Cora. I know Rick went to the same school as the Riders. Did you know that Boney – Nigel Bennet – went there too? What is it you're not telling me?'

She heard David's voice in her head warning her that there was more to Cora than met the eye.

Cora jumped up. 'I've got to go. I'm going to crash at a friend's for a few hours before my next shift.' She glared at Alex. 'Please. You've got to find Rick. He's all I have. But look—' She shivered and looked all around before her gaze alighted on Alex once more. 'Don't trust any of the Riders as far as you could spit at them.' She leaned down until her face was level with Alex's. Alex could smell the sourness of her breath. 'Listen to me, Alex, that family is toxic.'

She grabbed Cora's wrist. 'Tell me why!'

Cora shook off Alex's hand. 'Ask your precious Jamie. Don't forget, the worst predators hide behind the shiniest smile.' And suddenly she was gone, running down the path.

'Cora, wait,' Alex shouted. 'What do you mean? Tell me, please.' She tried to follow, but Ethel was having none of it. No, siree, she moved in her own good time.

Cora turned the corner and was out of Alex's sight.

Damn. Why wouldn't Cora talk to her?

She walked back slowly to the apartment, the beautiful day now turning grey and misty once more. Rain was in the air. Her good mood had well and truly buggered off, but she was pleased to see her car was in its parking spot, so she was mobile again. Thank you, Paul.

She pushed open the bottom door, Ethel padding in behind her. John Watson came out of his flat. 'I saw you coming, my dear.'

'Are you all right, John?'

'Oh yes, thank you. Having a little trouble with eBay.'

'EBay?'

'Yes. I'm trying to buy this beautiful dish with cascading black glass grapes but it's not going through. And I'm getting threatening emails from eBay saying they will hang, draw and quarter me if I don't pay up.'

He looked so mournful that Alex wanted to laugh. 'I'll come over later and see if I can help.'

'It's this new iPad you see, that my brother bought me. I'm having a bit of trouble.' He shook his head. 'Old dog, new tricks.'

'I'm sure you're better than you think. Take it slowly, that's all I can say. I'll pop over in a little while.'

'Thank you, my dear, but I wouldn't want to spoil your day with your brother.'

Alex, who had started up the stairs stopped. 'My brother?' Her heart started hammering. She didn't have a brother.

'Yes.' John beamed. 'I hope it was all right, to let him in, I mean. He said he had a key to your flat. That you'd given it to him yesterday when he came visiting. He said you were going to do some shopping with him, buy him some new clothes. And, if you don't mind me saying, I think that's a very good idea. He's very alternative, isn't he? I do hope—' He faltered when he saw her face. 'I haven't done anything wrong, have I?'

Alex shook her head and forced herself to smile. She didn't trust herself to speak.

'Are you sure you're all right, dear? Only you look a little pale.'

She nodded and forced her lips into a smile. 'I'm fine, John. Thank you.'

She waited until he had shut his apartment door behind him before she carried on climbing the stairs, Ethel snuffling behind her. Her palms were sweating and her mouth was dry. She was aware of holding her breath. She had been right when she had thought someone had been in her apartment looking round, disturbing the air, touching things. Was she doing the right thing, going up to her flat on her own? Shouldn't she call the police and say there was an intruder in her apartment? Probably. But she wanted to know who it was.

She did have an inkling.

The door to her apartment was slightly ajar. She pushed it open and walked in, hoping the thudding of her heart couldn't be heard.

The door slammed shut behind her.

She whirled round, Ethel's lead still in her hand.

Boney.

Alex almost laughed, thinking of John greeting Boney. 'A bit alternative'. A bit of an understatement. And her instinct had

161

been right. Not that it was any comfort now. 'What are you doing here?' She tried to keep her voice steady. 'Get out of my apartment now, please.'

'Or what?' He grinned. 'You'll set Martin's mutt on me? Come on, let's be friends now. I'm only paying you a social.' He leaned back against the door.

'A social?' She stood her ground.

He rolled his eyes. 'A social call. A bit of a gentle—' He pulled on his long, fleshy earlobe. 'Let's call it a bit of a warning.' Boney gave her a wide smile, his sharp incisors menacing, his piercings wobbling gently. His head had been freshly shaved. All in all, Boney was someone she wouldn't want to meet on a dark night. In fact, she didn't want to meet him anywhere at any time.

'You broke in the other day, didn't you?'

He nodded. 'To get the lie of the land, so to speak. Easy enough, if you know how. If I were you, I'd beef up your security. You wouldn't want just anyone breaking their way in. Now, why don't we sit down and have a cup of coffee? Give the mutt a Bonio. She always liked those.' He held out his hand to Ethel, who thumped her tail and gave his fingers a lick.

Traitor, thought Alex, standing her ground.

Boney sighed. 'So are you going to be hospitable and offer me a coffee?'

'No. I want you to go, *Nigel*.' She would not be intimidated.

Another smile. 'Clever. How did you find that out?'

'It wasn't hard. And you were at school with the Riders and Rick.'

'What a clever little journalist you are.'

'So get out before I call the police.'

'I don't think you'll do that.'

'Try me.' She folded her arms.

'I don't think you'll do that because you don't want anything to happen to that son of yours, do you? Gus, isn't that his name Where is he now? York University, isn't it?'

162

She tried not to gasp. 'How do you know that?'

'Let's say a little bird told me, love. And there's your sister. Wouldn't want anything to go wrong, what with a big exhibition happening and all that.' He clicked his fingers. 'Not to mention Cora. Fucking busybody she is.'

'How do you know all this?' she whispered, her bravado gone.

'Because I'm Boney. King of the homeless.' He puffed his chest out. Alex wanted to punch him. 'I left Nigel behind a long time ago.'

All at once he moved away from the door and seized her wrist so hard she cried out in pain. His skin was soft and clammy. His eyes burned out of the multiple sharply angled black tattoos on his face. He took Ethel's lead out of her hand and dropped it on the floor. Ethel slunk away to her bed, emitting a sharp fart as she went. 'That bloody dog doesn't improve, does she?' he said, fanning his hand in front of his face.

The effeminate gesture made Alex want to laugh. She stopped herself. She didn't want to appear hysterical.

'Now, Alex, let's go and sit down.' He dragged her into the kitchen and pushed her onto a chair.

She rubbed her wrist, but didn't say anything. She wasn't going to give him the satisfaction, wanting to wait and see where this visit was going. Outside the sunshine had well and truly gone and the dark clouds threatened rain. The cry of a solitary gull sounded mournfully outside the window.

Boney put the kettle on and took two mugs and the jar of coffee out of the cupboards. 'See,' he smiled, 'I know where everything is. That's the good thing about scoping a place out first.'

'I could scream, you know.'

Boney sighed. 'You could. And who would help you? The one-legged guy downstairs? It would be a shame if he lost the use of his other leg. Anyone else about? I think they're at work, aren't they? You see, that's the disadvantage of working from home – everybody else works in an office.'

'Except you.' Surreptitiously, she wiped her palms on her jeans. Keep calm, that's what she had to do.

'I have my office. It's not conventional, that's all.' He smiled. 'I like being among the dead. They are most interesting to talk to.'

The kettle boiled and Boney made the coffee, opening the fridge for the milk. 'You know, I'm a bit disappointed in you, Alex. I thought you'd have a fancy coffeemaker, or at the very least one of those pod things. Instead I have to slum it with instant.' He reached up into a cupboard and brought out the sugar, giving himself three heaped teaspoons.

'I know what you're thinking,' he said, seeing Alex watching him. 'I'm sweet enough already.'

He pushed a mug across to Alex, some of the liquid slopping over the sides. 'And don't even think about throwing it at me. I'll have people looking for – and finding – your Gus before you're out of the door.' He smiled.

That smile was getting on her nerves. 'You still haven't told me what you're doing here.'

'Giving you a friendly warning, like I said.'

'A warning?'

He crouched down in front of her. 'Stop looking.' His breath, at once rancid and fetid, assaulted her senses and it took everything she had not to recoil from him. She would not show any fear. She'd been in worse situations than this.

'What do you mean?' Her voice did not wobble one bit. This man thought he had power over her, he thought he was something special. He wasn't. He was a sad specimen of a man. She looked him in the eye. 'You're a nasty piece of work, do you know that? Peddling your drugs around the city, getting people hooked. Giving them even more problems than they already have.'

He gazed at her for a long minute, then stood and took a noisy sip of his coffee. 'Stop meddling. Don't look for Rick Winterton any more, it's not worth it. We will find him eventually.'

He drained the mug and put it on the table. 'And, as for Cora—' he left her name dangling.

'What about Cora?' Her jaw ached from gritting her teeth, thanking the moon and the stars that she had met Cora on the walk and not here, at the apartment.

'Persuade Cora to give up on the search.'

'How do you expect me to do that?'

He shook his head. 'I don't fucking care, just do it. Tell her he's no good. Best left, dead or alive. Tell her he got in touch with the hostel to say he didn't want looking for.' He stroked her cheek with two soft fingers. She tried not to flinch. 'Or tell her she'll get hurt again if she doesn't. Like you will. Goodbye Alex. Don't make me come here any more. It's a long fucking way from Norwich.' He went to the door.

'Who sent you, Boney? Somebody did. You haven't got the brains for this.'

He turned, eyes flashing. 'I have, Alex, believe you me.'

'But you're still someone's jumped-up messenger boy, Nigel.' Why was she doing this? Putting herself in jeopardy when he was almost gone? Because she was furious her space had been invaded. Had it not been for his threats against Gus she would have thrown him out, not caring if she hurt him. And she could hurt him. She hadn't taken self-defence lessons for nothing.

He shook his head. 'Oh, Alex, you don't know the half of it. I almost feel sorry for you.' He grinned. 'But not quite.'

He shut the door quietly behind him.

Alex sank to the floor and put her head on her knees, the adrenaline making her feel sick. She would not cry. She breathed deeply and evenly.

A wet tongue licked the side of her face. She tangled her hand in Ethel's fur, waiting to hear the slam of the downstairs door. She got to her feet. Trying not to shake, and not entirely succeeding, she found her phone and tapped out a message to Gus on WhatsApp. It took several times to get the letters right.

Hi darling. Give me a ring when you get this message xx

She went to Sasha's chat stream.

Hi Sash. Looking forward to the exhibition tomorrow. What time does it start?

Her phone rang almost immediately. 'Hi Mum, you okay?'

She gripped the phone hard. It was so good to hear her son's voice. 'I'm fine, Gus. I only wanted to …' What to say? She hadn't thought this through. 'Check everything was going well.'

'All good here, Mum. I might be able to get back in the next couple of weeks.'

Next couple of weeks? Whereas a couple of days ago she would have welcomed Gus saying that, now she would rather he was safely far away in York than near danger here.

'There's no rush, love.' There. She hadn't thought she'd be saying that in a month of Sundays. 'Whenever you can make it. And Martha. I might even come to you.' Yes, that was it. 'That would be nice, wouldn't it?'

'Yeah, that's cool. We could go out for meals and stuff. I could show you around. Me and Martha could show you around,' he corrected himself.

'I'll let you know. And, take care, won't you, Gus. Don't speak to any strangers.'

He chuckled. 'What do you think I am? Six? I'll be very careful who I talk to, don't you worry. See you, Ma.'

'See you darling.'

Maybe not six, but he would always be her baby.

Putting the phone down onto the table, she saw her hands still shaking.

166

Stop it. Take control.

She had rattled someone's cage.

And now she had to know more about Cora and Rick and the Riders. Sitting at her computer, she brought up the search engine and typed in 'Cora Winterton'. Nothing. Rick's name brought up a couple of stories about his time in Afghanistan and a little bit about the injuries he suffered while he was on duty. Before he went into the army, before he was married, he had lived with his parents and Cora in Bury St Edmunds. But they had lived near the Riders when they were children. Rick had been at school with them. She drummed her fingers on her desk, thinking. He had been part of the school cross-country team. So had Lewis Rider. Different age groups but same team. She would start there. Lewis Rider's name gave her little more than she already knew – successful businessman, farmer, diversification. She carried on looking. There had to be something. More articles about Lewis Rider the successful businessman, the philanthropist – he really did have an excellent PR department.

Bingo.

An image buried deep in the search engine, probably deliberately pushed down – a clever lawyer could ensure good news stories rose to the top and bad ones were buried. It was a blurred reproduction of a press photo. 1994. Twenty-four years ago. Captioned: *Lewis Rider leaving court today*. And, if she wasn't much mistaken, standing behind him, a young Rick Winterton with a murderous look on his face.

167

CHAPTER TWENTY-THREE

DAY FOUR: LATE MORNING

The sand was soft beneath his feet and the sun high and hot on his head. Too hot. It hurt so much. The wind was swirling around him. He had to screw up his eyes to see anything.

He rounded a corner and there was a small village. Is this where the girl with the gentle brown eyes lived? Surely it had to be a mirage.

He blinked. Once. Twice. Three times. His eyes were gritty and the taste in his mouth sour. The sand turned to loose stones mixed with sand. tufts of grass tripped him up. The sun was not high and hot. There was no sun. The sky was grey, with a black promise in the distance. The wind was cold, icy, briny.

His arm was throbbing. As were his head and legs. He was weak with hunger. He had been walking for God knew how long. He'd had to stop so often. Had he slept? He wasn't sure. How many days had it been? One? Two? Three? More? He wanted to see his children, oh, how he wanted to see them. If he got through this, he would be a better Dad to them, that he swore. A much better Dad.

Now here was a village. Not so much a village but a ribbon of houses huddling together for warmth beside a windswept beach. He had found the coast. Did he want to be here?

The wind was pushing and pulling at him, slicing through his wet clothes. There were other people around. Walkers. Birdwatchers, maybe. There were kites in the sky. Or maybe they were kitesurfers.

Rick heard his teeth chattering. He stumbled along a track. Past the line of cottages – one that looked like an old coastguard look-out. There was a Martello tower in the distance. Defensive forts built to protect the British Empire.

Soon he found himself on a shingle beach dotted with vegetation. Sea kale. Yellow stonecrop. These names came to him, he knew them. He'd been here before, a long time ago. When the sun was warm and the wind not so fierce. He had swum in the lagoon-like waters. The waters were not lagoon-like today. The wind was whipping up the waves that crashed down onto shore, sucking back the shingle as it moved angrily out again. White horses raced across the water out to sea. Large ships lay sluggishly on the horizon. A few brave souls were standing by the shoreline, jumping the waves. A couple of walkers. And yes, in the distance, a group of kitesurfers, their red kites flying and swooping. And if he looked over there, barely visible through the sea spray and mist, an island.

The blood roared in his head. It roared around his body.

There was something …

'Are you all right, mate?' A man in a thick eiderdown coat, backpack slung over one shoulder, a camera over the other and a bobble hat jammed on his head, looked at him, a frown on his face. 'Only you don't look too good.'

'I-I, I lost my stuff.'

'Lost?'

Rick nodded. 'Lost. Taken.' He shrugged. 'I don't know. I can't remember.' He was so cold and tired and hungry he had stopped shivering. Not a good sign, he knew.

'What's your name, mate?'

Name? He knew his name, but something made him bite it back. 'Dan. It's Dan.'

The man gripped his bad arm. It took every ounce of strength he had not to cry out in pain.

'Come with me, Dan. I'll get you a cuppa.'

'A cuppa?'

'Yeah. There's a little café at one of the cottages. C'mon. I'll buy. I might even throw in a cake. At least you can get warm there.'

As if in answer, his stomach rumbled. He nodded, and followed the Good Samaritan.

The café was in the front room of one of the cottages. Four scrubbed wooden tables with a vase of early daffodils made for a cheerful atmosphere. A ruddy-cheeked older couple were sitting at one table with a pot of tea and a plate of sandwiches in front of them. A couple with a baby in a high chair at another. The third table was taken up by four young men in running gear. A fire cheerfully crackled and burned in the grate.

The man guided him to the last table. Rick lowered himself down gingerly onto one of the hard chairs.

The man put his camera on the table, his rucksack on the floor. Rick stared at the camera. Photographs. That's what he'd been doing. Taking photographs over on the island.

'Mate?'

The man was talking to him. 'Sorry. Yes?'

'What can I get you?'

Rick worked hard at not wincing at the pain from his cuts and bruises and infected arm. The man had a kind face. A worried face. He must look like shit. 'Any chance of a full English?'

The man winked. 'I'll see what I can do.'

'So,' said the man, sitting down, having reappeared after presumably ordering something from someone somewhere, 'I'm Mike.'

'Hi, Mike.' Rick smiled weakly.

'What's your story?' He looked expectant.

'I have no story. Just someone down on his luck who can't remember what happened.'

'If you don't mind me saying, Dan—' Mike leaned forward, 'you look as though you need a friend.'

'Maybe.' He tried to smile, bit his lips were cracked and sore. 'I wonder if you've ever thought about bringing the Lord into your life?'

He looked puppy-eager.

Rick felt world-weary.

A thin woman with a large smile and a frilly apron rescued him. She bustled forward with a tray loaded with plates and teapots and cups and milk and toast. 'Here you are, my lovely. A full English with extra toast for you and muesli with almond milk for you, sir.'

Rick ate in silence, trying not to shovel the food down. It was good, very good. Every mouthful made him feel better. He had to figure out what to do next.

'The Lord can help you, Dan. I know he can. If you would let Him into your life.'

Rick ignored him. Carried on chewing. He could feel his clothes drying on him. He thought he probably smelled.

'So how about it?'

Mike was persistent, Rick had to give him that. He meant to keep his head down, avoid getting drawn in, when a sudden cold breeze made him look up.

Two men had walked into the little café. Rick's stomach lurched. The two men who were hunting him. Rick buttered his toast, not looking at the two, wondering what they would do. And what he should do. There were too many witnesses for them to take him by force.

At that moment, the elderly couple vacated their seats and gestured to the two men with a smile.

They sat down.

Now they were only metres from him. They fixed him with a stare.

Rick felt the violence and dislike radiating off them. They wanted to take him back to the island. That was it. That was where he'd escaped from. He was starting to remember now. Memories like shadows, but they were becoming more solid minute by minute.

The thin woman with the large smile and frilly apron bustled up to the two. 'What can I get you, lads?'

'Tea,' said the one in the too-red jacket.

'Please,' said the man in the smart coat.

This was said without taking their eyes off Rick.

Rick knew he had to do something. If he didn't he thought the men might cause trouble, hurt some of these people.

Red-Jacket stood up, far too close to him. Invading his personal space was what he was doing, thought Rick. 'You need to come with us.'

'Why?' asked Mike.

'Not you, him,' Red-Jacket said, pointing at Rick.

'I know that's who you meant. And I'm still asking you why?'

'He needs to come with us.'

Mike turned to Rick. 'Do you need to go with them?'

Rick put his knife and fork together and wiped his mouth with one of the paper serviettes. 'No.'

'Come on.'

'You heard the man,' said Mike. 'He doesn't want to go with you.'

Rick had to admire the strength in Mike's voice.

Red-Jacket bent down and gripped Rick by the arm. The second time he'd been held by his bad arm. Again, he could feel himself sweating with the effort of not crying out.

There was a scraping of chairs against the floor and the four runners appeared at the table. The room was beginning to feel very claustrophobic.

CHAPTER TWENTY-FOUR

DAY FOUR: LATE MORNING

Alex had wanted to clean the flat from top to bottom after Boney left, so contaminated did it feel, but she needed to get that glass to Sam Slater. He'd said he would be at Bethel Street station today and she didn't want to wait any longer. If he wasn't there, she would bloody well find forensics herself. And she would not have her family threatened. By anybody. She bundled Ethel into the car and set off for Norwich.

Wait a minute. What had Boney said? *We will find him eventually.*

Bloody hell. She banged the steering wheel. It was obvious now. Whoever Boney was being messenger boy for was also looking for Rick. He must have got away from those men who'd picked him up at the accident. He was probably trying to get away from them in the first place. Rick Winterton must know something that someone, somewhere wanted to keep quiet. But what? All she had to do now was to find out who and why. She felt excitement fizz through her veins.

Finding Rick was even more important now. They had to get to him before those men.

Where to go to from here?

After she had parked the car she tried to ring Cora. No answer. Damn. She left a message on her answerphone. Then she walked as quickly as she could to the police station, telling the dog to wait while she went inside. Ethel dropped to the ground immediately, her head on her paws, her look one of abandonment. Alex tied her to a post. Ethel would be used to lying and waiting, she thought.

It was the same police officer on the front desk. Still the same smell of sweat, vomit and fried food. Alex gave the officer a wide smile.

'Hello officer, I'm here to see DI Slater.'

'Is he expecting you?'

'Yes.'

The officer raised a disbelieving eyebrow, but picked up the phone.

'I put in a missing person report the other day for Rick Winterton. Do you know if anything has happened on that one?' said Alex.

'Nope.'

'Nope?'

'Nothing has happened yet. Not a priority.'

'Says who?'

He stared at her. 'Says Norfolk Constabulary.'

'Alex.'

Alex turned at the sound of Sam's voice.

'Come on,' he said, buttoning up his coat. 'Let's brave the wind and the rain and go and get a coffee.'

'What have you got, then?' Sam asked as they sat down in a booth away from other customers with their coffee – cappuccino for him, mocha for her. Alex had also picked up a very squidgy-looking brownie.

At least the café was warm and snug, with the smell of fresh baking in the air. The decor was plain and simple – scrubbed tables, leather benches in the booths. A vase with a single artificial flower. Alex liked it. It was in the Royal Arcade so it meant Ethel was out of the dreary, drizzly weather.

She brought out the hanky-wrapped glass from her pocket and pushed it over the table to him. He unwrapped the cloth and carefully put the pieces of glass in an evidence bag.

'I'll do my best. But as I said to you, our budgets are shot to hell so it won't be easy to get it looked at, especially as there is no ongoing investigation—'

'There should be.' Alex took a bite of her brownie. It was every bit as chocolatey as she had hoped. 'Anyway, I'm pretty certain it came from the Land Rover, I feel it in my gut.'

He smiled. 'You're tenacious, I'll give you that. Again, as I said, I'll do my best, but it'll be days before they come back with anything.'

She swallowed her cake. 'Come on, Sam. I'm sure you have strings to pull.'

'You flatter me.'

'What about the Land Rover? Was it stolen?'

Sam nodded. 'It was found burnt out in Ipswich. Joyriders, they reckon.'

'Joyriders?'

'There is no evidence to suggest otherwise.'

'Hmm.' She thought she would leave that one for now and try a different tack. 'What do you know about Boney?' She thought she would see what his reaction would be.

'Boney?' He looked amused. 'You mean the man with the shaved head, the piercings and the Dracula teeth?'

'So you know him?'

He drank some of his coffee, as if considering what to say. 'Let's say he is known to the police. I trust you haven't had any dealings with him?'

'Cora Winterton—'

'The sister?'

'Yes.'

'You should be careful around her.'

'Why, Sam? What do you know?' Why was everyone telling her to be careful around Cora?

He shook his head. 'It doesn't matter. Tell me about Boney. Has he threatened you?'

'And why do you say that?'

'Because that's what he does best. Threatens people. And my best advice to you is to stay away. He's a drug dealer. Oh, some people say he's got a heart of gold because he helps people find a place to stay, food to eat, but he also gets them drugs and anything else they want.' He laughed harshly. 'Boney is a piece of work.'

She played with the spoon on her saucer. 'Cora and I went to see him, to ask about Rick—'

He closed his eyes. Shook his head. 'Goddam it, Alex, why don't you leave it to the professionals?'

'Because the professionals are doing damn all about it,' she retorted. 'And if you know he's a drug dealer and all the rest, why haven't you arrested him before now?'

'Because—' He lowered his voice an octave. 'Boney is small fry. He likes to think he's Mr Big, but he's someone's bitch, that's all. We want to catch the top man. Or woman. Whoever he reports to, works for. That's why we haven't brought him in yet.'

'I see. You know his real name is Nigel Bennet? And he went to school with the Riders?'

'Yes, Alex. Dammit. Stop meddling.'

'Meddling?' She leaned forward. 'He broke into my flat. Told me to stop looking for Rick.'

'He broke into your flat?'

'Yes.'

'Broke in? Did you call the police?'

'No.'

'No.'

'Sam, you've told me how stretched the force is.'

176

'That's one thing, Alex, but when someone like Boney forces his way into your flat, that's quite another.'

'He didn't force his way in. Well, I suppose he did the first time—'

'The first time?' Sam's face was a picture. Apoplectic, she'd have called it. 'Alex. You could have been hurt. Boney is a nobody in the scheme of things but he does hurt people. I don't want him to hurt you. He didn't hurt you, did he?'

She shook her head. 'No, not physically.' She had to stop herself from shuddering as she remembered his menacing tones, his threats to her family.

'Look,' he said. 'I will get him picked up, bring him in for questioning, put the frighteners on him and—'

She shook her head. 'No, I see why you need him out on the streets. And I'm a big girl, I can cope. And he didn't hurt me. Anyway, that's not why I told you. Don't you see, he must be involved in Rick's disappearance somehow, otherwise why would he threaten me? And also—'

Her phone buzzed in her pocket. She took it out. It was David Gordon's work number.

She frowned. What did he want? 'Do you mind if I get this?'

He shook his head. 'More coffee?' he mouthed.

She gave him the thumbs up.

'Alex? Alex Devlin,' whispered a woman's voice. Not David. Someone else calling on his line.

'Yes. Who is this? Can you speak up?'

'No. I can't. I need to talk to you. About the jobs homeless people are being offered. I know something about them.' There was trembling in the voice.

'Who is this?'

'Sadie, from Fight for the Homeless. You gave me your card. I didn't know whether to phone—' The young girl from behind the reception desk at David's office, she remembered. 'And I haven't got much time.'

'Okay. Shall I ring you back?'

'No. I have to go now. Can you meet me? Today. After work?'

'Yes, of course. Where?'

'In the wine bar on Inkerman Street. Do you know it? About six?'

'I'll be there. Can I have your mobile number, just in case?' But she was talking to dead air.

Sam sat down with some more coffee. 'Trouble?'

She shook her head, looking at her phone. 'The receptionist from David's work wants to see me.'

'David Gordon?' He sipped his coffee, leaving a frothy moustache on his top lip.

'Yes. David Gordon. Fight for the Homeless. I went to the charity event at Riders' Farm with him. How did you know I meant him?'

She couldn't help it, she pointed to his top lip, and he laughed and wiped the froth away.

'Our Assistant Chief Constable said she'd seen you both at the event. I deduced that you probably only knew one David with a receptionist. Of course, I could have been wrong, but I am a pretty good detective.'

She thought back and remembered David pointing out the top copper. 'Small world.'

He grinned. 'You can't do a lot in this area without someone noticing. Carry on.'

'That's right. Anyway, I went to see him – David – in case he could help.'

'About Rick Winterton?'

She nodded. 'An obvious choice, really. He is involved with people on the streets at all levels. If anyone knew anything about people disappearing, I thought he would.'

'And did he?'

She shook her head. 'Nope. He said not. But listen, when Boney was in my flat he said something like "we'll find him eventually".'

'"We'll find him eventually"?'

'Yes,' she said eagerly.

'So?'

'Don't you see what this means? Somehow Rick got away from the two men who were supposed to be taking him to hospital, but I suspect they were never going to do that anyway, and now these people – I don't know who – are looking for him, and Boney was sent as a messenger boy to frighten me and Cora into not looking for him. There's something going here, Sam, don't you think?' The words had all come out in a rush and she hoped she had made some sort of sense.

Sam shifted around on his chair. He drummed his fingers on the table. 'Don't you think you're getting a bit obsessed about this?'

'Obsessed?' Her heart sank as she saw the sceptical look on Sam's face; that was okay, he was a police officer, he needed hard evidence. Alex crossed her arms. 'Sam, I was threatened by Boney earlier, now this girl – Sadie – is whispering she wants to meet me in the wine bar on Inkerman Street. Come on, surely you must think there's something in it?'

'Hmm.' He sat back and they both drank their coffee. 'And this receptionist – what did you say her name was?'

'Sadie.'

'And she's meeting you after work?'

'Yes. She sounded—'

'What?'

Alex hesitated. 'As if she needed to talk.'

Sam smiled. 'She will have a good listener in you.' He looked at his watch and stood up. 'I've got to go.' He took out his wallet.

Alex shook her head, taking out her purse. 'This is on me. But Sam, I really believe there's something in this. If you could get that glass looked at quickly and think about what I've said, please? There must be a reason for Rick to have gone missing. I really think he escaped from those men and is on the run. Please, think about it.'

179

He nodded. 'I will. But think, Alex, why hasn't Rick gone to the police if there was something dodgy going on?'

'Because he's homeless and he thinks you won't listen?'

He rubbed his forehead. 'We would listen. *I* would listen. He's not stupid. He would know that.'

She bit her lip. Could Sam be right? Maybe she was obsessing. After a moment she nodded.

'See you around,' he said.

'See you around.'

'Come on, Ethel,' Alex said to the dog, as she untied her from outside the café. 'I guess we've got a fair bit of time to kill before we meet Sadie. I'll take you for a walk somewhere. Whitlingham, maybe. Or around the university lake.'

As they came out from under the cover of the Royal Arcade, it had come on to rain heavily.

'Is this ever going to stop?' she muttered.

Ethel whimpered in reply.

'I know, old girl, but we're not far from the car.' She pulled the collar of her coat up around her ears and stepped out onto the sodden pavement. Everybody was hurrying, umbrellas poking their way through the crowds.

A girl dressed in a thin mac, her hair plastered to the sides of her face, hollow cheeks and feverish eyes, stood in front of her. 'Alex, isn't it?'

'Yes?' Alex smiled.

'I'm Emmy.'

'Okay.'

Emmy looked as though she was about to burst into tears.

'And you've got Ethel. Martin's dog.'

'Yes.'

The girl sniffed, and wiped her nose with her sleeve. Her hair was dripping water.

'Emmy, do you want to go somewhere and have something to eat?'

180

The girl shook her head and didn't look as though she was going to say anything else. Was she worried about the dog, perhaps? 'I'm only keeping Ethel until Martin comes back.'

Emmy's shoulders drooped. 'I don't know if he'll ever come back.'

'He will.' Alex sounded surer than she felt.

'Why did he leave Ethel? He would never leave Ethel.'

Alex couldn't answer that.

'And now Tiger's gone.'

Alex put her hand on Emmy's shoulder. 'I was so sorry to hear that.'

'And did you also hear it was an overdose? How did someone who hated drugs overdose? First Lindy, now Tiger. I hope it's not Martin next.'

'Hang on, did you say Lindy?'

'Haven't you heard? She was found strewn across the railway line somewhere between Stowmarket and Ipswich. She was identified by her tattoos. Suicide, I heard. Her mum came across from Wales. Such a long way. At least her mum might have enough money for a funeral. Or maybe someone'll set up a JustGiving page. Or there won't be enough money and she'll have a pauper's funeral. They still have those, you know.'

Alex did know, and she couldn't say anything. Her mouth was dry. Two dead. Lindy and Tiger. Within days of each other. Both suicides. Supposedly. And where had Lindy been before she died?

'I don't expect you know where Lindy had been? You know, all those days she was missing?'

Emmy was crouching down patting Ethel. 'No.' She looked up at Alex. 'I think she had a new job, though. She was right excited and said it was a new chance for her. That was about two weeks before she left her pitch. She didn't tell me what it was. I didn't ask, you see. I was a bit jealous.' Tears flowed down Emmy's face, mingling with the rain. 'She was happy, you know. Really happy. And I was jealous of her and her happiness. But if she

181

was happy, why did she kill herself?' She straightened up and wiped the wet off her face. Rain or tears, Alex wasn't sure. 'Gotta go now. Nice seeing Ethel.'

'Emmy, if you hear anything about Martin, or anything that seems strange to you about Tiger's and Lindy's deaths – anything else strange I mean – you will let me know?'

'How?'

'Do you have a phone?'

'Stolen.'

'I'll call by at the underpass every so often, see if you're there. Or you could go to the police and—'

'The cops? Don't make me laugh.' She fluttered her fingers. 'I'll see you.'

Alex watched her go. Emmy was right. Why did Tiger overdose on drugs when he wasn't any sort of user? Why did Lindy go to the railway line to end her life when, if Emmy was right, she was happy for once? Why?

182

CHAPTER TWENTY-FIVE

DAY FOUR: EVENING

Alex relaxed in a leather chair in the wine bar waiting for Sadie. She had bought herself a glass of Sauvignon, which was going down very nicely. There was also a jug of water and another glass on the table – she wasn't going to be able to drink wine all evening. She stretched her legs out in front of her and admired the black and white photographs of the iconic sights of Paris hanging on the whitewashed walls. Cheesy, but effective. The place was full, mainly with people who had come in for a glass or two after work. Classical music played gently in the background.

It was no good. She couldn't sit here doing nothing. The island. She wanted to know more about the Riders' mysterious island. And there was the screech she had heard. Dismissed by Jamie, but for her it was both human and not human. And why would Jamie never have been over there as he'd claimed? Surely even idle curiosity would make him want to see what was on an island owned by his family?

She took her laptop out of her bag and began searching for anything to do with Gisford Ness.

There was the inevitable Wiki entry that didn't tell her any more than she already knew. *A spit of land ... hostile and potentially dangerous site ... privately owned ... closed to the public.* Then there were the Google entries she had seen before about aliens on the island, about government experiments, experiments on monkeys. Screeches heard in the middle of the night – well, she could certainly vouch for that.

Then she found an old *East Anglian Daily Times* article reproduced on a blog called *Alien Suffolk* that talked about the anthrax testing on Gisford Ness during the Second World War. *Island leased from the Rider family ... more than fifty sheep killed ... locals told to keep away* ... okay, she knew all that. The blogger asked if there was a government conspiracy going on and thought the island was like Area 51 in Nevada in the USA – where UFOs that had landed on earth were taken for examination. Alex rolled her eyes at this.

She looked at her watch. Then at the door of the pub. More people were spilling in. She'd been waiting half an hour. Perhaps Sadie had changed her mind. Maybe she had decided it was too much trouble. Alex tried ringing the Fight for the Homeless number. Then David's direct line. No answer from either, and of course she didn't have Sadie's mobile number. The receptionist must surely have left the office by now, and it would take, what? ten minutes to walk to the wine bar?

Anything could have happened. Sadie might have had to take a detour. See someone else first. Perhaps she was ill. She would wait a little longer.

Back at her laptop, Alex found another article from the *East Anglian* reproduced on a different blog, this time about the Suffolk coast. The article dated from the 1980s and quoted Joe Rider as saying they wanted to return the island to its original state, and the family planned to 'nurture the wildlife and the shingle vegetation for the public to eventually enjoy'.

They were taking a bloody long time about it then. And she wondered how much 'nurturing' had gone on and how much more was needed. No member of the public was allowed near the island, that was very clear from her conversations with Jamie.

She googled some more, but didn't find anything else interesting. She needed to dig deeper, but hadn't the resources. It was time to ask for some help.

Her wine was finished. Another look at her watch told her it was seven o'clock and there was still no sign of Sadie.

All at once she was beginning to have a bad feeling about Sadie.

CHAPTER TWENTY-SIX

DAY FOUR: EVENING

Red barriers and a police accident sign cordoned off the road between the pasta place and the Thai restaurant. A white forensic tent had been placed over the victim. An ambulance stood nearby, a man and a woman wrapped in foil blankets sitting on the open edge of the vehicle, paramedics chatting to them. A police car with its flashing blue lights was stationed either side of the tape and officers were directing the traffic away from the area. Queues were building up on the roads around the scene. Onlookers held up their phones as if at a concert, which made Sam Slater want to go and tear them off each and every one of them.

'Ghouls,' he muttered, as he flashed his warrant card at one of the officers standing guard. 'DI Sam Slater. I was in the area and—'

'Of course, sir.'

He thought the officer looked pissed off, standing there in the pouring rain and the cold when he'd probably been thinking of his supper and a pint. Didn't blame him.

The officer let him through.

'Who's in charge?' he asked a man with 'Police Collision Investigation' emblazoned on the back of his neon yellow jacket.

'DI Paterson. He's in the tent.'

Slater nodded and donned a paper suit he'd taken out of the boot of the car parked behind the cordon.

The tent was cramped and smelled of blood and fear and death. The pathologist, police photographer and two police officers were huddled under its roof.

'What are you doing here, Slater? Thought it was your day off,' said Paterson.

He nodded. 'It is, but I was in the area and heard the commotion. I thought I'd come and see what was going on.'

'Hit-and-run. Young girl. Aged about twenty. Dragged under the wheels of a van. Witnesses said the van seemed to go over her twice. Made a good job of it.'

Slater glanced at the girl's body. Her head was crushed, one eye hanging obscenely from its socket. Her jaw had been pushed to an unnatural angle. Her limbs were twisted to impossible positions. Blood all over her. He was thankful he had a strong stomach. 'Accident or deliberate do you think?'

'From the sound of it, deliberate.'

'Though drivers do odd things when they think they've hit something. Go backwards, forwards, trying to get away from the body. Especially if they've got previous motoring convictions or are under the influence,' said Slater.

Paterson pursed his lips. 'All true.' He was thoughtful. 'But, I don't know. Something seems "off" about the whole thing.'

Slater nodded. Paterson was good. 'Anything I can do?'

'No, all under control. Thanks for stopping by.'

Slater exited the tent and pulled off his suit when he got near to the barrier, shrugging his raincoat back on.

'Nasty business, sir,' said the police constable, rain dripping off his nose.

'Yes, Constable. Nasty business.'

He pulled his collar up and walked off into the night. He would be seeing that young girl's face in his dreams.

CHAPTER TWENTY-SEVEN

DAY FIVE: MORNING

The beeping was soothing, gentle. What was it? An alarm? Should he be getting up to go to work? What was his work?

Rick opened his eyes slowly. White all around him. He blinked and turned his head slowly. Machines to one side, monitoring his vital signs. That was the beeping noise. Not work. He hadn't been to work for a long time. He hadn't had a proper life for a long time. But he had a purpose. He remembered that now. More importantly, he remembered what that purpose was.

A table with a plastic jug and a plastic cup. A straw. Bare magnolia walls. He turned his head the other way. A window streaked with rain. Granite sky. Nothing else. A door in the corner. To a bathroom, perhaps? Three more beds in the room. No one in them. Another door to the side. Open. He could hear chatter and laughter. The smell of antiseptic. The rattle of trolleys. Blue uniforms – dark and light – hurried past his open doorway.

Hospital.

What time was it? How long had he been here?

He licked his lips. His mouth and throat were dry. He turned to reach for the jug. His body protested. That was the trouble with lying on a soft bed in clean, cool sheets, you grew weak, couldn't cope with pain. His arm was heavily bandaged. There was a tube snaking into his other arm. The tube led to a drip. Antibiotics, he guessed. He managed to pour water into the cup without spilling too much, and then was able to drink some through the straw.

A nurse bustled into the room. Probably in her late thirties, early forties. Lines were beginning to appear. Dark curly hair pulled back into a pony tail. She reminded him of—

Cora. It was the curls because Cora didn't have dark hair, she had glorious flame-red hair. He remembered at last. His sister. That's who he was doing all this for.

'Nice to see you awake, Dan.' The nurse put a blood pressure cuff around his good arm. 'A cuppa will be along soon.'

Dan?

Yes, Dan, the name he'd given to the man at the café.

'How long have I been here, nurse—' He peered at the name badge pinned on her boobs. 'Thelma Johnson'

'The ambulance brought you in yesterday. Your friend is waiting for you outside.'

Yesterday? He'd been out that long? And friend?

'Which friend is that?' He tried not to wince as the cuff tightened. He was still so sore all over.

'I'm not sure. I can find out for you, though. He followed the ambulance.'

'Thanks, Thelma.'

'Nurse Johnson to you. He's been here all night waiting for you to wake up.'

'All night. Right.' That didn't sound good. He didn't have those sort of friends.

'The man who came with you in the ambulance had to go home. He said he would try and visit in a day or two. Mike, his name was.'

Mike? God squad, that was it. Wanted to save his soul and

189

ended up saving his life, not that he probably knew that. He leaned back against his pillows. 'Where am I?'

'Ipswich Hospital. You were in a bit of a state. You've obviously been in the wars. Dehydrated, hypothermia, lots of cuts and bruises. That arm was badly infected and you had nasty burns on your hands.' She stood, looking at him.

'I can't remember what happened to me.'

'Hmm. Well, we will want more than just the name "Dan".'

'Like?'

'A surname. An address. How you came by your injuries. Medical history. It looks as though you might have some.' She nodded towards his hand.

He waggled his fingers – what was left of them. 'You mean these?'

'And the shrapnel scars on your body.'

'Army.'

'I thought as much. And you haven't been looking after yourself well. You're quite malnourished. Have you been living on the streets?'

'Yes.'

Nurse Johnson began writing on his chart at the end of the bed.

Rick remembered being in the café. The man in the red jacket with the bull neck – Gary. That was his name. And there was a man in a good coat. Pete. Yes! He felt like punching the air, his memory was coming back in small pieces. The runners in their Lycra facing up to the two goons. The world starting to spin. Mike telling him he looked pale, like death. His arm throbbing. Wanting to throw up. Hearing Mike's voice telling him to hold on, that he was going to call an ambulance. The blackness swirling up.

'Shall I get your friend in now?'

'Not at the moment, Nurse Johnson.' He gave what he hoped was a weak and feeble smile. 'I don't feel up to it.' If the friend wasn't Mike, then that left Gary or Pete, and that wasn't good news, not good news at all. 'Actually,' he said, 'I don't want to see him at all. Can you send him away?'

Nurse Johnson raised her eyebrows. 'Really?'

He tried to look pathetic. 'Please. He's not really a friend.'

She nodded. 'I'll tell him you don't want to see him, but I can't force him to go. Anyway, we don't expect you'll have to stay here long. Don't want you blocking the bed for someone more deserving, do we?'

'No, Nurse Johnson.' He tried to smile at her.

She smiled slowly. 'Enough of the charm, Dan. Now rest. Lunch will be along soon, and although it's not exactly gourmet it is nourishing. So eat up. The doctor will be doing his rounds later and I expect he will want to sign you out.' She frowned. 'We'll try and get you a bath before you go.'

She bustled out of his room, leaving the door open.

They were busy on the ward. He could hear people calling out for attention, the ping of a lift somewhere, people walking past his door purposefully. He lay quietly for a minute. Nurse Thelma Johnson would call social services soon enough. Ex-army and homeless, she would reckon he needed help. There were more deserving than him, far more. And he couldn't afford to get caught up in red tape and do-gooders. Not in any way.

He swung his legs over the side of the bed, gasping at the pain shooting through his back, his hip, his arm. He winced as he yanked the catheter out. He steadied himself, wishing away the nausea that was rising in his throat.

Where would his clothes be?

In the bin.

All he was wearing was a hospital gown. He felt around the back. Thank God it wasn't one that left his arse exposed. Now all he had to do was to walk out of his room and find a cupboard with some spare scrubs in it – just like they did in the movies. It was going to be that easy.

Sure it was. But he had to try.

But first—

He pulled open the drawer on the bedside cabinet and found his watch and gold chain in a bag. He managed to put his watch on, but the chain was more difficult. His thumbs felt like great fat sausages as he tried to fasten it around his neck. He nearly gave up, but then thought of Cora. She had given him the chain, years ago, and he had never taken it off. He wasn't going to start now.

Two agonizing minutes later, he had managed it.

He sat, breathing heavily. Christ, if it took him that sort of effort to put on a fucking necklace, he stood no chance out there.

He wanted to sleep.

No. He could do better than this. Besides, he couldn't stay here, he would die. Whoever it was posing as his friend – Gary or Pete – wasn't going to give up.

He stood and took a few tentative steps. Okay, not too wobbly. Bit shuffly. Stand up straight. Breathe through the pain. Ignore the throbbing in his arm. At least he'd had a fair dose of antibiotics.

He reached the doorway. No one was taking any notice of him. He walked out with as much confidence as he could muster, sure that someone was going to ask him what he was doing. Shoulders back. Stand up straight.

He was on a long corridor with rooms either side and a nurses' station at the top. He walked in the other direction, peering into rooms as he went. At the fourth room he got lucky. A man was lying asleep, his mouth open, snoring. On the chair by the bed was a coat.

Rick hobbled in, swiped the coat and put it on over his gown. There was a pair of slippers under the bed. He put them on as well. A little small but they would do. The man in the bed kept on snoring. Rick hoped he would forgive him when he woke up.

He tried to walk normally back down the corridor; no limping, no striding, no breaking into a run. The idea was for him to blend in with the crowd. As he rounded the nurses' station he saw a couple of chairs against the wall. Gary in his red jacket was sitting in one of them, flicking through a magazine.

There was nothing else for it, Rick had to walk past.

At that moment a gaggle of medical students came along, laughing and joking. Rick stuck himself to the far side of the group and walked on, leaving the waiting Gary behind. He didn't dare risk a look to see if the goon had seen him, but there were no running footsteps, no shouts, no knife pricking the skin at his side.

He kept on walking. Found the lift. Made it to the ground floor.

Out in the hospital forecourt he stopped for a minute and patted the coat pockets. A wallet, surely? He took it out and found five tenners and a fiver and a credit card in the name of Clive Nixon. 'Sorry, Clive. But I think I need the notes more than you do at the moment,' he muttered.

The painkillers he'd been given were beginning to wear off and his whole body throbbed. He thought he could feel a wetness on his torn arm. It was drizzling. A teenager hooked up to a drip was under a shelter smoking furiously. 'You okay, mate?' he asked.

Rick nodded. 'Bad morning.' He sat down on a nearby bench, the cold and wet seeping through the coat.

'Tell me about it.' The teenager inhaled on his fag some more before crushing it underfoot. He began to walk back to the hospital, then stopped. 'Hey, mate, there's someone waving at you. That window there. Where the stairs are.' He pointed.

Rick looked. It was Gary, gesticulating and shouting, obscenities probably.

'He looks as though he really wants to talk to you,' said the youth.

Rick watched as Gary began bounding down the two flights of stairs.

He thought quickly. 'Do me a favour, mate. That bloke is after

193

me. I slept with his wife, you know how it is.' He smiled ruefully and held out the £5 note, his heart hammering.

The boy tapped ash onto the floor and took the money, pocketing it quickly. 'I know what you mean. These things happen. I'll trip him up or something.'

'Cheers.'

Rick began to limp away as fast as his injuries and ill-fitting slippers would allow him.

CHAPTER TWENTY-EIGHT

DAY FIVE: MORNING

It was all very well crashing at a mate's place between shifts, thought Cora, but it wasn't anything like having your own bed. She groaned as she leaned over the side of the sofa and stabbed at her phone to turn off the alarm. She didn't want to wake Bunny and Bev, not at five o'clock in the morning when it was still as black as bloody pitch outside. The winter seemed interminable. She thought of Rick and wondered where he was spending his night.

Yawning, she tiptoed to the bathroom for a quick wash and brushing of teeth before slipping into the clothes she'd left out the night before. Then she let herself out of the house and began to walk to the hospital on the outskirts of Ipswich.

It was cold and drizzling and Cora wondered where Rick was, wondered how badly hurt he might be after the crash. He could have internal injuries, anything. Alex said he should have gone to hospital. Oh God. Perhaps he was hiding out somewhere? He was nothing if not resourceful. And, despite his weeks on the streets, he was pretty fit. She sent a silent prayer to God – any bloody god – that he was at least safe. Not for the first time she regretted the path she had let Rick go down.

When he had first gone missing, she had panicked and had been only too glad of Alex's help, whether she was a journalist or not. But now … now Alex was too involved, too tangled up with the whole thing and Cora was scared about what might happen. If Alex knew the truth, knew how much danger she could be in, what would she do? She might put Rick in even more danger. Alex had already twigged that it wasn't only them looking for Rick. Still when all this was over, she would have her story. It just might not be the one she thought it was.

The good thing was that Alex liked working on her own, she hadn't bleated on about bringing in the police, though there was the problem of her having been to see Sam Slater about some bits of glass. Not that it would get anywhere, she was pretty certain of that, but they would have to be careful – she, Cora, would have to be careful.

Alex was not stupid and would not be fobbed off much longer regarding the Riders. She would have to tell her the whole story soon to keep her onside. She needed her help. She couldn't do this on her own.

The Riders.

They had been there all through her childhood. She and Rick played with them during the school holidays when the Rider boys were bored shitless because their fancy friends weren't around. They were allowed to swim in their pool, use their swings and slides. Even play tennis on one of their courts. But the brothers would always make it clear that she and Rick needed to know their place. Their father was the farm foreman. Their mother was the cleaner and the odd-job woman. Their house was a tied cottage. It didn't matter that Rick had more brains than the lot of them put together, that he went to the same school, that he had worked hard for his place. Their lives belonged to the Riders.

Of course, Rick wouldn't play by the rules and committed the cardinal sin of stealing Lewis Rider's girlfriend from right under his nose. That did not end well. Even now Cora grimaced as she remembered the stand-off at the beach, the girlfriend telling Lewis that Rick had made her go with him. The hurt on Rick's face. The sneer in Lewis's voice when he told them they were dirty pikeys, that Rick was only a scholarship boy with a hand-me-down uniform. Was that where it all started? Or had the seeds been sown when they were young children and were only allowed to play with the Riders when the Riders wanted them to? Everything was on the Riders' terms.

There had been a time when she thought that Lewis Rider could have been a friend, a real friend. They had shared secrets over cigarettes. But maybe he had regretted that, which had made him act even more nastily towards her and Rick.

Nastily. That was one word for it.

She wanted to shake away the memories.

The lights of the hospital burned brightly through the dark and the rain, and she put away all thoughts of the Riders and tried to think of the day ahead.

Even at this early hour, the hospital was busy. Cora got to work checking the folders and drugs charts for the latest patients. A child with a bad wheeze who needed a nebuliser and a teenager waiting to have her inflamed appendix taken out. She was not allowed anything to eat. Her mother hovered nearby, anxious, and Cora did her best to reassure her.

The morning whizzed by in a flurry of ward rounds, recording observations and talking to the doctors about the plans in place for the patients until finally Cora was able to take a lunch break down in the canteen. Then she thought she would nip outside and have a fag.

It was still drizzling as Cora went through the hospital doors, so she pulled her cardigan tightly around herself and walked along a path and down the side of a building to an area where she couldn't be seen by any nosey parkers. She wasn't really supposed to smoke on hospital premises, but she and her smoking colleagues had found this sweet spot where no one would see them.

She leaned against the wall to keep out of the drizzle as much as she could and closed her eyes. Some days she thought she could fall asleep this way. Today all she wanted to do was not to think about anything, if only for a few minutes.

Ten minutes later she ground the cigarette under her foot, picked up the stub and then made her way back towards the hospital entrance. As always, the area in front of the hospital was busy with people milling around and ambulances pulling up next to the nearby A&E department.

A group of people came out of the doors and among them she saw a man, half running, half limping. He was vaguely familiar. The group surged towards her, and she lost sight of the man for a moment, then spied him sitting on a bench. He was clean-shaven and his hair was short, but ... She stared. Her heart jumped into her mouth. It was Rick. She had found him.

Cora opened her mouth to shout just as two ambulances set off from A&E, their sirens blaring. She began to run, but became tangled up in the group on the path.

'Excuse me, please,' she said, trying to shoulder her way through, then she tripped, banged her knee, hit her head on a sapling. She looked up, dazed, to see a man in a red jacket race out of the hospital doors, pushing people out of the way, looking left. Right. Looking for Rick.

Where was he?

She clocked him at the same time as the man, who had his hand in his pocket. Not a gun, surely? Not in a crowded place with all these witnesses around?

Oh God, it was like watching a silent film. Or having a dream where you know it's going to end badly.

The man ran towards Rick – he would catch him, Cora was sure. Then the youth with the fag tripped him up. The man got up slowly, the youth with the fag looking as though he was apologizing, preventing him from moving away. Meanwhile she could see Rick disappearing from her sight down the road.

'I'm sorry, miss, are you all right?' A woman helped her up. A sea of faces looked at her, concerned. 'Your knee. It's bleeding.'

Strands of hair had come out of its ponytail. She swept them back off her face. She had to go after Rick. Stop the man in the red jacket. 'I'm fine,' she said. 'I'm fine.'

Her legs began to work again, and she ignored the pain in her knee as she ran to the front of the hospital, looking around her everywhere. But there was no sign of Rick, and no sign of the man in the red jacket.

She put her hands on her knees and hung her head down, breathing heavily. She had missed him. Her chance to find him, talk to him, see what was happening. She'd bloody well blown it.

Oh, Rick.

'Are you all right miss?'

It was the smoking youth.

Cora nodded, catching her breath. 'Did you see which way the man went? The one who was talking to you earlier?'

The youth grinned. 'You mean the guy who was being chased?'

Cora nodded. 'Rick. He's my brother. Did you see where he went?'

He shook his head and Cora's spirits plummeted. 'I think he might have got on a bus. The other geezer was right mad. Tore his trousers. He ran after him. But he's gone, too. Your knee's bleeding by the way. All down your leg.'

Cora was very glad the man in the red jacket wasn't anywhere near. She didn't know how much he would know about her, but she didn't want to chance it. She smiled weakly at the youth, who was now grinding his fag butt under his shoe. 'I know, I'll get it seen to. And thanks for the information.'

'No probs. I hope you find your brother soon,' he called as she walked back towards the hospital.

She waved her hand in acknowledgement.

She hoped so too.

She had to find him, and quickly.

CHAPTER TWENTY-NINE

DAY FIVE: MORNING

After a broken night tossing and turning, Alex was back at David's offices again. A different girl was on reception.

'Hi,' said Alex. 'I'm looking for Sadie.'

'She hasn't come in today.' The girl smiled pleasantly.

Alex felt a hollow in the pit of her stomach. 'Is she ill?'

'I don't know. I was called in from the agency to cover. Temporary, like.'

'Alex, what are you doing here? Again.'

'David.'

He took her by the elbow and led her away from the reception desk. 'Considering you and I have nothing to say to one another you seem to be around here an awful lot.'

'Actually, I was looking for Sadie.'

'Sadie?' He frowned. 'Receptionist Sadie?'

'Yes.'

'Why?' He was suspicious.

'She wanted to talk to me, I don't know what about,' Alex said brightly. 'She phoned me yesterday and set up a meeting. But she didn't turn up.'

'She didn't come in this morning. She let us down quite badly as a matter of fact. I've got a big meeting later and I needed her to take the minutes.'

'She hasn't called in sick?'

'No. Not a word. Always was a bit flaky.' He sighed. 'I really don't know what I'm going to do—'

'About your meeting, I know. Would you like me to come and take the minutes?'

David's eyes were so wide with disbelief Alex wanted to laugh. 'Don't be so silly. I'm not having a journalist at a top-level meeting.'

Oh, the pomposity.

'I'm going to do a series of articles on homeless for *The Post*, and I hope I'll be able to include you and the organization?'

'You've already done a feature on me.'

'I know. I'm thinking a more general piece about Fight for the Homeless and the people you help.'

'Maybe.' His face was closed.

'But first I want to find Rick Winterton. And talk to Sadie. And find Karolina.'

'Karolina? Why do you want to find Karolina?'

Was it her imagination or was he sweating? 'I met her at your hostel on Magdalene Street, and she was going to let me know me when the two men who are offering jobs to your clients turned up again. But apparently she hasn't been seen around for the last couple of days.'

'She could be anywhere. Like Rick, she will have moved on.' He enunciated the words carefully.

Alex cocked her head to one side. 'How did you know who I was talking about?'

'What do you mean?'

He was dissembling, Alex could see it in his face. And he was very definitely sweating. 'When I said Karolina, you knew who I was talking about. You didn't ask me anything about her.'

'I know many of our clients,' he blustered.

She wasn't going to let him get away with that. 'Really? It's possible, I suppose. Anyway, Karolina was willing to talk to me and to Cora Winterton. And now she's gone. Sadie wanted to tell me something. She was frightened, whispering on the phone. And now she seems to have disappeared. That's a lot of people who've disappeared in a short time. What did Sadie want to tell me, David?'

'How the hell should I know?' His face was red and there were beads of sweat on his forehead. He was clenching and unclenching his fists. Alex thought he was a good candidate for a stroke.

'It seems to me, David,' said Alex, evenly, 'you're frightened of something.'

'Don't be so stupid. Look, running a charity in this day and age is no picnic. The rules and regulations, the safeguarding issues, the sheer amount of paperwork—'

'David. I'm on your side. If you'll let me be.'

'Alex, I—'

For a second Alex thought he was going to tell her something meaningful. But he blew out his breath and seemed to deflate. 'There's nothing, Alex. Absolutely nothing.'

She looked at him, unflinching.

'Look, Karolina has got a new job.'

'As?'

'A cleaner. At the Riders' farm. Marianne Rider likes to give homeless people an opportunity. She's a great supporter of the charity.' He looked everywhere but at Alex.

'So you said before.'

Alex thought back to the charity event and remembered some of the silent but attractive waitresses. Probably cleaners when they weren't needed as waitresses. It made sense now.

'Do they have two heavies who go around trying to recruit people?'

'Heavies?'

'The Riders. Do they have two men who do their recruiting. One who wears a red jacket and has a bull neck, the other wears a smart coat?'

'No.' His answer came too quickly and Alex didn't believe him.

'David—'

A cold blast of air announced the entrance of two police officers into the reception area. Both had solemn expressions. Alex's heart sank. She'd seen that sort of look on police officer faces before and it didn't tend to signal good news. Could it be something to do with Sadie, or was she jumping to conclusions?

'Mr David Gordon?' asked one of them, a thin blonde woman who looked as though she could do with more sleep. The other officer looked as though he hadn't started shaving yet.

'Yes.' David's eyes darted from one officer to the other.

'I'm Detective Sergeant Ash and this is Detective Constable Jackson. Could we go somewhere more private please, sir? Not you, madam,' she said, as Alex made to follow.

'Is it something to do with Sadie? The receptionist? Is that why you're here?' Alex didn't have a good feeling about this.

'And you are?'

'Alex Devlin. Sadie was supposed to meet me last night, but she never turned up.'

DS Ash pursed her lips, then nodded. 'Very well.'

Alex could hardly contain herself as they made their way through to David's office. 'Has something happened to Sadie?'

'How well did you know her?' DS Ash asked, sitting on one of the more uncomfortable chairs in David's office. David himself was sitting behind his grand desk, as if he needed protection.

Alex shook her head, noticing the past tense. 'Not well at all,' she said. 'I spoke to her here, but only briefly, when I came to see David, then yesterday I got a call from her. As I said, she didn't turn up for our meeting. When I spoke to her on the phone she did seem frightened, though.'

DC Jackson was making notes.

'I see. Do you know what or who she was frightened of?'

'No idea. Look, what has happened to her?'

'Why did she want to talk to you in particular?'

'Probably because I'm doing an article on homeless people and I'm also looking into some disappearances. What's happened to Sadie?' She wished the officer would spit it out.

'I'm afraid Ms Hartley was found dead last evening. Hit-and-run in Tombland, near the cathedral. She was crossing the road and it's thought the driver didn't see her.'

'Did the driver stop?' asked Alex.

The officer shook her head.

Alex glanced across at David. He had turned green.

'What time was this?'

'I'll ask the questions if you don't mind,' DS Ash said. DC Jackson carried on scribbling, occasionally pausing to look around the office. Alex wondered what she was looking for. 'So you had no idea what she wanted to talk to you about?'

'She said she wanted to talk to me about homeless people being offered jobs. She sounded frightened. I arranged to meet her last night in the wine bar on Inkerman Street but she didn't turn up. I tried ringing reception here and David's office – I didn't have her mobile number – but there was no reply.'

'Who else knew she was meeting you?'

'No one. I was talking to Detective Inspector Slater when she phoned, I might have mentioned it to him.'

'DI Slater? What were you talking to him about?'

'He is helping me with a story,' said Alex, smoothly.

'Hmm. And she would have to go through Tombland to get to the wine bar?'

'Yes.'

DS Ash turned to David, who was looking greener by the minute. 'Mr Gordon, have you any idea what was troubling Sadie?'

David spread his hands as if in supplication. 'There was nothing troubling Sadie, as far as I know. She worked on reception. She was good at her job, but I didn't really know her. I mean, it's not as if she was privy to anything important.' He stood up. 'I need a drink.' His filing cabinet held whisky and glasses. 'Officers?'

'We're on duty, sir. And maybe a cup of sweet tea would be better?'

David took no notice. He waved the bottle at Alex.

'Want one?'

'No, thanks.' She felt numb. What had Sadie wanted to tell her? And was it only a coincidence that she was knocked down? It must have been, surely? 'Have you any leads on the car that killed her?'

DS Ash sighed. 'According to witnesses it was a white van. Sped away. We will find it, though. It will have been damaged and if the driver takes it anywhere for repair then we will know about it.'

'No licence plate?'

'The plates were muddy according to witnesses and the CCTV in the area wasn't working, though we may pick the van up elsewhere in the city.'

Alex saw David's hands shaking as he drank his whisky.

A white van. Muddy number plate. Exactly like the van that may or may not have taken Rick Winterton away.

'Look,' said Alex. 'I'm trying to find a homeless man, Rick Winterton – his sister and I have reported him missing – and—'

'Ms Devlin, what has this got to do with the hit-and-run?' DS Ash's face was pinched with impatience.

'I have CCTV of a white van that may have taken him away. Its number plate, too, was impossible to read because of the mud. Surely no coincidence?'

'Surely,' DS Ash said, obviously unconvinced.

'If you talk to DI Slater, he knows all about it.'

'Does he indeed.' DS Ash still didn't look impressed. 'Very

well. If you let me know where I can get hold of that CCTV we will have a look at it.' The subtext written on her face was 'but I think you're leading us up the garden path'. Alex gave her the name of the solicitors in Unthank Road, not ready to give up her memory stick with the CCTV on it.

'Mr Gordon. Tell me more about Sadie. Did she have a boyfriend? Girlfriend?'

'Sadie?' said David, looking surprised. 'I don't know. I didn't see anyone and she didn't talk about anyone. But—' He shrugged.

'And she had worked here for how long?'

'A couple of months. She kept herself to herself, you know how it is.'

'Indeed.' She stood up. 'That'll be it for now. I am very sorry for your loss. I will need both of you to come to the station to give a statement. In your own time. As soon as possible.'

David sat at his desk with his head in his hands as soon as the detectives had left. 'Sadie. Hitandrun. What a tragic accident.'

'If it was an accident,' said Alex, almost giving in to the lure of the whisky bottle.

David looked up at Alex. 'What do you mean?'

'It seems a bit of a coincidence, don't you think, that Sadie had something to tell me, something she obviously thought was important, but she never made our meeting. Was it a coincidence?'

'Has to be,' said David, sitting up, his voice firm, as if he'd suddenly acquired backbone.

'As I told the coppers, she said it was about the jobs homeless people were being offered. Do you know what she meant by that?'

'Nope.' He poured himself another whisky, this time with a steady hand.

'I didn't know Sadie, I only met her here. She knew I was a journalist and she wanted to talk to me. She was desperate to talk to me.'

'What are you implying?'

'That you do know what it was about. And it has something to do with Fight for the Homeless.'

David looked at her steadily. 'If it did, I have no idea what. Now, I'm sorry, Alex, but you will have to go. I have a meeting to cancel.' He poured more drink.

'What was Lewis Rider doing here the other day, when I saw you?'

'Funding meeting. Not that it's any business of yours.' The answer came quickly, as if he had been expecting her question.

He stood and opened the door of his office.

'Goodbye, Alex.'

CHAPTER THIRTY

DAY FIVE: AFTERNOON

Alex didn't know what to do with herself. She probably ought to go home, take Ethel out for a walk, maybe do some work. Or perhaps she could go and see Sam Slater, see if he knew any more about poor Sadie. Perhaps he might have some answers from forensics about the glass. No, he said it would be days at best.

She sat in a coffee shop with a mocha and a slice of passion-fruit cake and rang Heath.

'How's it going?' he asked. 'Have you started on those features for me yet?'

'Not yet. Still gathering material. Look, Heath, could you look someone up for me? I've found out a certain amount, but if you could get any more it would be helpful.'

'Me? I'm the bloody news editor, not your lackey.' He sounded amused.

'It wasn't that long ago that you were my lackey.'

'I think you will find, if you search your memory properly, that it was the other way round.'

She laughed. 'Maybe. Whatever. I know you're a very busy man, so perhaps you could put someone else on it, but I don't have the resources here to do it. And you have. Please.'

'Will you buy me dinner?'

'Yes, yes, of course.'

Heath gave a sigh which seemed to smack of satisfaction. What had she agreed to? Only dinner. Nothing more.

'What's the name?'

'Boney.'

'Boney. What sort of name is that?'

'You should see him, too. A sight for sore eyes. Maori, or something similar, tattoos all over his face. Incisors sharpened to a point.'

'Easy to spot then?'

'And known to the police. Low-level fixer and drug dealer. His real name is Nigel Bennet and he went to school with the Riders. I want to know if there's any more of a connection. I need to know his story. Who his acquaintances might be, that sort of stuff. It's a long shot and probably won't have any bearing on anything, but, you never know.'

'I'll get on it.'

'You or a minion?'

'For you, my dear Alex, it will be me.'

'Sure. One more thing—'

'Alex, please.'

'Sorry, making you work, I know. Gisford Ness.'

'What's that?'

'An island off the coast here. I'm sure there's more to it than I've managed to glean.'

He groaned. 'Alex. I have meetings to go to. Decisions to make. Palms to grease.'

'Come on, Heath, think what you owe me. And don't tell me you don't miss the cut and thrust of actually writing stories.'

She was laughing as she pressed 'end' on the call.

Her phone rang immediately. Not even Heath was that fast. She looked at the display. It was Cora. Damn. She ought to have told her about Sadie.

'Alex, where are you?' She sounded breathless, hardly able to get her words out.

'I'm in Norwich—'

'Great. Can you call by? Now?'

'Cora, what is—'

But she had gone.

'I saw him.' Cora's eyes were bright, almost feverish as she handed a cup of coffee to Alex.

'Who?'

'Rick.'

'What?' Alex began coughing – the hot drink had gone down the wrong way. 'You've seen him? Where? How?' she said eventually, though her eyes were watering and her throat was on fire.

Cora sat, her hands curled around her cup. 'I was at work in Ipswich and was coming back from a break outside when Rick barged out of the main doors, then I lost him and I saw him being chased by a man in a red jacket, but by the time I got to the hospital forecourt, they'd both gone.' She stopped, her eyes wide. 'It was the man from the CCTV, I'm sure of it.'

'And you've no idea where they went?'

Cora shook her head, deflated. 'Rick could have got on a bus, in a taxi, anything. The man in the red jacket might have caught up with him. Anything could have happened to him, Alex. Anything.'

Alex frowned. 'Rick must be heading somewhere, but where? Have you any idea?'

Cora shook her head.

Alex was convinced Cora knew more than she was saying.

'He's alive, though, Cora, that's great news. And somehow he managed to get away from those men.'

She was shaking her head. 'He's on the run. Maybe they've caught up with him again. Oh, God.' She buried her face in her hands.

210

'Are you sure you don't know where he might go?'

Cora shook her head again.

'Cora, if there's something you're not telling me—'

'There's nothing,' she said stubbornly. 'Honestly. I only want Rick back. That's all.'

'Cora—'

'If you're not going to help me, then I'll do it myself. Find him, I mean.'

Alex looked at Cora, at her thin, bird-like figure, her hollow eyes and her tired skin. 'Of course I'll help you. But you're not telling me everything.'

Cora bit her nails. 'There's nothing else to know. I only need to find Rick.'

'What about the Riders?'

Cora flinched. 'What about them?'

'You told me when we first met that they liked to control women. That they were, "smug bastards". What have they done to you, Cora? I know there's something there.'

She wouldn't look at Alex as she took a squashed packet of cigarettes out of her pocket and lit one.

Alex sighed. What a bloody contrary woman she was. Was now the time to bring up the photo of Lewis Rider and her brother she had found? 'Look, if you're expecting me to go out of my way to help you, then you have to give me something in return.'

'Have to? I don't think so, Alex. Besides, you'll be getting your story, won't you?'

'Will I?'

'A front seat.'

'I'm seeing Jamie Rider tonight.'

'Tonight?' she said sharply. 'Why?'

'He's coming to my sister's preview for her art exhibition.'

She blew five perfect smoke rings. 'Where's that then?'

'In Gisford.'

211

'Did you ask him to go with you?'

'Yes.'

She stood up. 'Then you'd best go and get yourself ready, hadn't you?' The spikes were out again and had been sharpened even more.

Alex sighed. 'Cora, I wish you'd tell me about the Riders. I might be able to help.'

More smoke rings. 'I doubt it.'

'Do you think they've got something to do with Rick's disappearance?'

'Think?' She laughed harshly. 'I fucking well know.'

'So tell me,' pleaded Alex. 'Look, I know I messed up by not taking him to hospital. That's why I'm here.'

Cora looked at her steadily and for a moment Alex thought she was going to spill all.

'I found a picture,' she said quickly. 'Of Lewis Rider leaving court, twenty-four years ago. Your brother was in it too.'

Cora winced, opened her mouth. Then closed it again.

'Was that to do with you, Cora?'

Cora gave nothing away. Frustrating, to say the least.

'Why was your brother in the picture?'

'You ask too many questions, Alex.'

Alex could hardly speak. 'But you wanted me to get involved.'

Cora looked straight at her. 'Did I? Did I actually ever ask, or did you hang on to my coattails wanting to "do good"?'

'That's not fair, Cora.' Alex tried to quell her rising anger. Cora was worried and tired. She didn't know what she was saying. She mustn't let it get to her.

All the air seemed to leave Cora. 'It's not your fight, Alex. Really.'

'What do you mean? Rick brought me into this by giving me your number. You made me interested in the plight of people who are homeless. I'm interested in Fight for the Homeless too because I'm not entirely sure it's the charity it says it is.'

'What do you mean?'

Alex shook her head. 'I don't know yet. But David was acting cagily when I went to see him after Rick disappeared. And then there's Sadie.'

'Sadie?'

'The receptionist from David's office. She's dead. Killed by a hit-and-run driver.'

'What?' Any remaining colour drained from Cora's face.

'She phoned me up wanting to talk. She was frightened. I should have gone to her straightaway, but she said she would meet me after work and then never turned up. The next thing I heard was that she had been killed. Cora, the hit-and-run vehicle was a white van. And nobody could read the number plate—'

'Because it was smeared with dirt?'

Alex nodded. 'And the van went backwards and forwards over Sadie's body. Making sure she was dead.'

'And you think it's somehow connected with Rick? Because of the van?'

'It has to be, don't you see? Look, I know there are hundreds, thousands of white vans in the country, but in my book it's too much of a coincidence. We saw a white van going round to where Rick was sleeping, then Rick vanishes. Rough sleepers are disappearing. Sadie, who works for a charity for the homeless, is killed, conveniently, by a white van just before she is coming to talk to me. Come on, Cora, it's all linked. And I have a feeling the Riders are in the mix there somewhere.' She looked at Cora despairingly. She had to get through to her somehow. 'You've got to talk to me.'

Cora was silent for long minutes. She played with the cigarette packet, turning it over and over in her hands. 'I don't know how much I can trust you, Alex. You're a journalist. I know you want a story out of this. But whose story?'

'Yours, Cora. Yours and Rick's and Tiger's and Martin's. Nobby too.' She clenched her fists and took a deep breath. How could she make Cora understand that she was speaking the truth?

Cora blew out a breath. 'Let's just say Lewis Rider tried to ruin my life. I tried to ruin his. Tit for tat. Being the sort of man he is, he won't ever let that go. Even though he won.'

'And what sort of man is he?'

Cora remained mute.

'What game are you and Rick playing, Cora?'

Cora stood. 'You go and meet your precious Jamie Rider, Alex, and I hope you have a good evening. Perhaps you could ask him about that summer, twenty-four years ago and what happened after.' She laughed, but it was a false laugh. 'But I don't expect he will tell you the truth. He's his brother after all. I want you to go now.'

Alex nodded.

'And, by the way—'

Alex, at the door, turned.

Cora stood, eyes blazing. 'It's not a game. It never was.'

CHAPTER THIRTY-ONE

DAY FIVE: AFTERNOON

Rick stood at the edge of the lay-by just before the roundabout that fed onto the A12, holding out his thumb, ignoring the anthracite skies and the fine drizzle. Did lorries stop for hitch-hikers these days? Did people even hitchhike? He was still in pain, so if he could get a lift even a little of the way he had to go, it would help. He had to be careful, though, who he accepted a lift from. At least he'd been able to swap his slippers and hospital gown for a pair of trainers and jeans and a shirt from the Relate charity shop he had passed.

The woman behind the counter had thrown in a thick jumper as well. He hoped she wouldn't remember him, though why anyone would think of asking about him in a small charity shop in the centre of Ipswich he couldn't imagine.

The only trouble was, he only had a few pounds left.

It didn't matter. He knew who he was now. He was more than his name, more than Rick Winterton. He was Cora's brother. He had been in the army. He had been married. He had children. He had a life. Yes, he remembered he had fallen on hard times, that his time in the army had affected him, had sent him almost mad for a number of years. How long had he been on the streets?

How long had it been since Helen – yes, Helen, the woman with the golden hair and the sweet smile – how long had it been since she'd been part of his life?

That part was still hazy.

He knew he had escaped from the island. That he had watched people die there and he had vowed to get away and tell the world. Slavery. Exploitation. That's what it all amounted to. He looked at the pink skin of his healing burns. He remembered how he had got those, too. How he had been chained up, put to work like an animal. And he knew he had to get back to the island to pick up the evidence he had collected. No one would believe him without those pictures. If he went to the police, the family would only clear up the evidence before the coppers got there.

He shivered as he remembered how one of the men he was imprisoned with had heard the guards talking about him. Somehow his cover had been blown and Lewis Rider had discovered who he was. That he needed to be got rid of. That's when he knew he would have to escape somehow and get his evidence to the cops. The trouble had started when he realized he would have to swim to the mainland so would have to leave his camera behind. He laughed. How fucking naive he'd been. Thought he could get onto the island with his spy camera bought off the Internet and get off again without any problem. He had underestimated them all. But he managed to bury it and escape. He was going to contact Cora. She would help him.

But then he'd crashed that sodding Land Rover and lost his sodding memory and now he had to go back and retrieve the camera.

Cora. She had changed so much. She had been a lively teenager, keen for new experiences, to seize the world and see what it could give her. But then Lewis Rider happened and Cora lost her spark, and he swore that one day he would get their revenge. But that day had never come. Until now. And now it was much more than revenge.

A large lorry carrying hundreds of squawking chickens wheezed to a stop in the lay-by.

'Where are you off to, mate?'

'I need to get up the A12 a bit – somewhere near Gisford?'

'No problem. I'm going to Wickham Market. Hop in. Shouldn't take long. Could've walked it, mate.'

The lorry driver, big and burly with tattooed knuckles, nodded to a bag on the floor. 'Some sarnies and a couple of packets of crisps in there if you're hungry. You look as though you could do with a bit of a feed. There's water, too.' He patted his obvious belly. 'You get hungry doing this job.'

Rick smiled. His stomach rumbled. 'Thanks.' Bending down, he took out a cheese sandwich and some cheese and onion crisps. Food had never tasted so good. It seemed to have been days since he had finished the last of the muesli bars. And he hadn't stayed long enough in hospital to sample any of its meals. He washed it down with a bottle of water, thinking an explanation was in order. 'Yeah, I know I could have walked. Truth is, there are some people who I don't want to see. Looking for me. Want to be out of sight as much as possible. Women. You know?'

The lorry driver chuckled. 'Tell me about it. No, don't. Too depressing. So, what's at Gisford, then?'

'People I need to see. Something I need to sort out.'

'Another woman?'

'Got it in one.'

'You've been in the wars though. I can see those burns on your hands from here. Must've hurt.'

Rick curled his hands into fists. 'Yeah. A bit.'

'How did you get them?'

'Bonfire. Petrol. Being stupid, really.' Too many questions. Far too many questions.

'Right.'

Rick closed his eyes, hoping the driver would take the hint, even if it was only for a few minutes.

217

All too soon he heard the clicking of the indicator and they were turning off the A12.

'This is where you're going to have to hop out, mate.'

The lorry pulled up by the side of the road. 'Take a bottle of water with you,' said the driver.

'Thanks,' said Rick, as he slammed the door.

The lorry trundled away.

He took a deep breath and began walking. Again.

Would Gary and his sidekick still be looking for him? He guessed so, but would they realize he was on his way back to the island? Surely they would expect him to try to get as far away as possible.

Filled with fresh determination and fuelled by the sandwiches and crisps, Rick put his aches and pains to the back of his mind. He thought it would take him three to four hours to get to Gisford, and it would be well and truly dark by then. He just had to be careful, keep a look out. The road was busy – traffic, cyclists, pedestrians. For the moment he felt safe.

But he soon realized that trying not to think about how much his body hurt wasn't going to work. Realistically, he had been beaten, starved, filled with fuck knew what sort of crap to keep him sweet and it had taken a great deal of will and effort to lift him from that lethargy. Not to mention a vicious car crash. And his body and mind had paid a price. A few hours' sleep in a hospital bed was not going to cut it.

His arm had begun to throb, but the stitches the nurse had put in were holding. He probably hadn't had enough antibiotics to stave off infection, so he would have to be careful. At least he was warm now and hypothermia was not a danger. How he had survived the last few days, he had no idea. Inner strength and determination. Grit. All three.

Across a roundabout and the road was a little quieter. There was no pavement, and he was walking on the muddy verge. Past a pub that was doing good business, despite the fading light. Smoke was curling out of its chimney, and welcoming lights shone out of the windows. Soon, he promised himself, soon he could go back to a normal life.

Whatever that was.

The road narrowed. He sat down, tempted to take off the ill-fitting trainers, but he knew if he did that he would never get them back on again.

Neat houses with neat hedges and gardens began to appear either side of the road, then he was out in the countryside again, with ploughed fields either side.

He sensed a change in the air. Colder, sharper, a tang of brine, perhaps? He knew that smell, it brought back his childhood. The land was flatter, the sky wider, space opening out, the vegetation scrubbier. The drizzle had stopped. For now.

The light was fading. He had to keep walking, but he had to be more careful – he was getting near, and there was only one road in and one road out.

Houses. One painted Suffolk Pink. A couple white. Beams. All thatched. Why was he noticing those details? To keep his mind occupied, to stop him thinking about the constant ache in his legs, his arm, and the pounding in his head that had returned.

Gorse bushes, trees. Hedges. Was that where he had hidden that first night? How could he remember that, he'd been barely conscious then.

The wind was getting up.

The cheese sandwich and crisps seemed like a very long time ago.

He imagined himself eating crumpets dripping with butter. Unsalted butter. Perhaps some jam. Or maybe a bacon sandwich with ketchup between two slices of soft, white bread. A mug of tea. He could taste that tea. Eating in front of a fine fire, piled high with logs, enveloping him with heat.

Keep walking. Keep walking.

More cottages huddled together. Cars parked outside. A blue car to match a blue garage door. A petrol station. Ferry Road.

He had arrived.

CHAPTER THIRTY-TWO

DAY FIVE: EVENING

There was a quiet buzz of conversation in the art gallery as Alex and Jamie walked in, his hand warm on the small of her back. As if she was a possession. It irritated her. But she had to keep calm, smile, relax and remember the evening was an ideal opportunity to do a bit of digging, find out more about the family business. And more about Cora. Especially about Cora. It had to come out naturally, though, not like an interrogation.

'Alex, Alex, it's so good to see you.'

Sasha came over, waving a glass of wine and looking stunning in a shimmery green dress that clung to her curves and showed off her blonde hair and pale skin. It had the long sleeves her sister always favoured. Alex knew they were to hide the silvery threads of scar tissue where she used to cut herself when she was at her most unhappy. She needed to remember that, first and foremost, tonight was about her sister.

Sasha pulled Alex towards her in a hug. 'Thank you so much for coming.'

Alex pulled away and held Sasha at arm's length, examining her. 'Look at you. All happy and glowing.' And she was, she really was. Alex couldn't remember when she had last seen her sister this relaxed and with such a big grin on her face.

'You look lovely too, Alex.' Her sister briefly put her hand on Alex's cheek. 'Now, enough of this love-in, introduce me to this man.' Sasha was staring at Jamie with a frankly admiring look on her face.

Alex laughed. 'Jamie, this is my sister, Sasha. Sasha, this is my friend, Jamie.'

'Friend?' said Sasha laughing. 'Okay, I'll run with that. Nice to meet you, friend Jamie. What do you think of this place, sis?'

The gallery was a large white space, with padded benches strategically positioned here and there. Sasha's paintings hung from a picture rail that ran all the way round the white walls, which were perfectly lit with spotlights. Several paintings had red dots on them, meaning someone had bought them. There were also plinths with sculptures on the top.

'Fabulous,' said Alex. 'Fit for a soon-to-be famous artiste.'

Sasha nudged her. 'I wish.'

'My parents have arrived,' said Jamie. 'I'll just go and say hello.'

Alex looked up, and sure enough, Marianne and Joe Rider were taking off their coats at the door. Marianne looking as graceful as ever in bright red palazzo pants and white blouse, and Joe looking, well, like Joe Rider in trousers and a rather loud yellow shirt. They were accompanied by Lewis and Simon – no wives in evidence – and they were all being fawned over by a small dapper man in a bow tie, who Alex presumed was Pierre, the gallery owner.

'What are they doing here?' She nodded towards the Riders.

Sasha looked. 'The famous Rider family, I do believe. You're not the only one to meet Suffolk's answer to the royals. Pierre said he was going to invite them. And some more local notables, I think. He said it was good to have influential people at these things. There'll be a couple of restaurant owners, the presenter of the local TV news, the owner of a bookshop and some sort of comedian who I hope won't tell any jokes because they're bound to be unfunny. Oh, and a couple of authors.'

It was, thought Alex, the Riders' charity event all over again, without the boring people. Or mostly.

'Jamie is a Rider,' she said.

Sasha gave her a wicked look.

Alex nudged her and smiled. 'You know what I mean. He's one of the Rider family.'

'That's good. Mind you, there doesn't seem to be a lot of love lost between them.' Lewis, Jamie and Simon were in a huddle, Lewis was angry about something, judging by the expression on his face, and the other two were having to listen. Jamie looked bored.

'Three brothers, yes.' Bloody hell. That family seemed to stick together like barnacles on a slimy rock.

'I look forward to meeting the rest of the family then.' She looked around. 'I don't think the actual critics have arrived yet, though.' She pulled at her sleeves. Alex could see she was nervous. 'Come on,' she said, taking Alex's arm. 'Let's have a proper look at my daubings.'

They began to walk round the room slowly, not taking anything in. Alex sensed Sasha had something on her mind, so she waited until her sister was ready to speak.

Sasha stopped. 'All this,' she said in a low voice, sweeping one arm around, 'does not mean I have forgotten my babies. Harry and Millie.'

'I know.' Alex caught hold of her hand and squeezed.

'I think about them all the time. What they would have become. What sort of people they would be.' Her lip trembled. 'It's a long time since they died, I know that, but they're always with me. And I'll always have to live with what I did. Some days I can hardly bear to live with it. But that's my punishment. I've done this for them.'

Each painting was a swirl of colour – blues and greens and

222

yellows. Reds, purples, cream, brown, even black. But each one made Alex feel something. Joy. Sadness. Waves being whipped up by the sea. There were portraits too: an elderly couple sharing a sandwich behind a windbreak, their love for each other caught by the artist; a fisherman mending his nets, the lines on his face showing the ravages of weather; the twins – Sasha's dead twins, laughing, eating ice creams. Alex brushed a tear away.

'Do you like them?' Sasha's voice was quiet, as she stood shoulder to shoulder with Alex.

Alex nodded. 'Wonderful, Sasha. They are all wonderful. I—' She could hardly speak.

'You didn't know I had it in me, did you?' she grinned.

Alex shook her head. 'Honestly, I had no idea. When you said you'd taken up art, I didn't realize this would be the result.'

'I took classes while I was at Leacher's House.'

Leacher's House: the mental health unit Sasha was sent to after finally admitting to having killed her twins during what had become clear was a bout of postpartum psychosis.

'Your sister is very talented,' said Jamie, returning to Alex's side, bringing her a glass of champagne.

The sombre atmosphere was broken.

Sasha laughed and nudged Alex. 'He's probably a keeper if he carries on being charitable about my art.'

'I mean it,' he said. 'And I apologize for not bringing you a glass, Sasha.'

'No worries, I am drunk on excitement and adrenaline. Oh look, Pierre is waving at me, I'd better go.'

'Pierre?' asked Jamie over the rim of his glass.

'I think he's plain old Peter at home, but he likes to bring a bit of the exotic to Gisford.' Alex grabbed a couple of canapés from a waiter who was gliding around the room. 'Here,' she said.

Jamie took the mini hot dog and popped it in his mouth. 'Perhaps we could have supper somewhere. Afterwards, I mean.'

'That would be lovely, thank you.' Had she accepted too

quickly? Sounded too keen? 'I know Sasha is going to dinner with Pierre and a couple of "patrons"', Alex pronounced the word in a mock-French accent, 'of the gallery, so she won't miss me.'

A waiter glided by and refilled her glass. The string quartet in the corner was playing soothing classical music. There was the tinkle of laughter, the chinking of glasses.

Alex took a sip of her wine. 'Jamie, do you know a woman called Karolina?' Go straight in there, why don't you? She could have bitten the words back.

'Karolina. I don't believe so. Should I? I rather like that painting over there.' He pointed to a landscape of sea and sky.

'She's a cleaner. For your family business.'

He laughed. 'A cleaner? And why would I know one of the cleaners?'

His tone set her teeth on edge. 'Karolina is a homeless person who I met at one of David's hostels.' What was she doing? This was absolutely not the right time for this.

Jamie sipped his drink. 'Well, Ma does tend to try and find jobs for what she calls "the deserving".' He appeared to be thinking. 'But, as I said, I usually stay in one of the cabins when I'm home, and I have been in London a lot lately. Working. So I haven't come across anybody new at the farm.'

'Of course.'

'When did she start, do you know?' Jamie appeared mildly interested.

'Karolina? Probably in the last couple of days.'

'There you are then. I've been moving money around lately.' He grinned. 'Rather successfully, as it happens. Look, if my mother has employed her, then she will be treated properly. Is that what you're worried about? She'll have somewhere to live on the farm—'

'Where?'

If he was surprised at the sharpness in her voice he didn't

show it. 'We have caravans, in one of the fields, for temporary workers.'

'In the winter?'

'Oh, don't worry. They are state-of-the-art caravans. Heating and lighting and everything.' He smiled gently. 'Why are you asking about this Karolina woman?'

'Doesn't matter.' She tucked her arm into his. 'Let's enjoy the evening.'

'Come on, you have to tell me now.'

She looked at him. She really didn't want to go into it.

'I'm curious,' he said. 'I'm going to stand here until you tell me. And people will think I'm very odd if I stand on the same spot all evening. Not moving.' He struck a pose and stood stock still, staring into the distance.

Alex laughed. 'Very well. You asked for it. I met Karolina originally in a Fight for the Homeless hostel and I was supposed to talk to her about the homeless people who have gone missing—'

'You're not still following that old path, are you?' He grabbed a mini fish and chips in a cone off the tray of a passing waiter and popped it into his mouth.

She nodded. 'I told you, I have to.'

'Why?'

'I feel guilty about Rick Winterton. I didn't tell you before, but I first found him, injured, by a crashed car. Two men took him away – one of them was in that picture I showed you – and he hasn't been seen since.'

'This was before he was whisked away by men in a white van?'

'That's right.'

'Okay.' He nodded, licking his fingers.

'And David Gordon told me Karolina had a job with your family.'

Jamie was looking at her, puzzled. 'I don't know what you're trying to say here. Are you suggesting that Karolina disappeared after she got the job with my family?'

225

Alex looked at him. 'I'm saying that Karolina was recruited by the men who picked up Rick Winterton at the accident.'

'And you think these two men are what, working for my family?' he said. 'Seriously? You think my family is involved in making homeless people disappear off the streets? And what would they be doing with them? Experimenting on them? Selling their organs? Sending them to alien ships?' He shook his head, then leaned forward and kissed her lightly on the lips. 'If I didn't like you so much, I might be offended. But I do, so I'm not. However, if it would set your mind at rest, we can always go and ask them.' He looked across the gallery to where his parents were talking to two couples. Lewis and Simon Rider seemed to be stalking around in front of the paintings.

'No,' she said hurriedly, 'that won't be necessary.' She was making a right mess of this, sounding stupid.

'Alex, I think you're conflating too many things. Homeless people disappearing, which isn't unusual because they move around all the time—'

'I know, but this feels different.'

'Instinct, huh? Gut feeling? The journalist in you?'

Did she imagine it, or was there a sneer in his voice? She imagined it, she decided.

'Something like that, yes. But I did see your brother coming out of David Gordon's office.'

'The Rider family donates to various charitable causes. Fight for the Homeless is one of them. You know that.' There was a touch of impatience in his voice.

Alex sighed. 'David did tell me.'

'There you are, then.'

'One more thing—'

'Go on.'

She hesitated, but she couldn't help herself. 'You know I went to change out of my wellies the other night in your boot room, where I had left my shoes?'

226

'Er, yes?' It was clear he didn't really remember.

Alex ploughed on. 'When I came out, you were talking to two men. Arguing even.'

He wrinkled his forehead. 'Yes, I remember, there was a security issue.'

'One of the men – I didn't see his face – he was wearing a red Puffa jacket underneath his hivis.'

'A red Puffa jacket? So what?'

'The other man who I believe picked Rick Winterton up from the streets – before the accident – was wearing a red Puffa jacket.'

'And, what? You think there is only one such jacket in Suffolk?' He laughed at her.

'Well, no.' She was beginning to wish she hadn't started the conversation. 'It seemed a massive coincidence, that's all.'

'My dear girl,' Alex tried not to feel patronized, 'it was a red jacket. Probably completely different to the one belonging to whoever took Rick Winterton away. Even if it was like that one, it doesn't mean it's the same one.' He pushed a hand through his hair. 'Look, this is ridiculous. It is only a jacket. That's all.'

Alex looked at him. 'Maybe. I'm most likely putting two and two together and making five.'

'Seven, I would say. Jackets, cleaners, homeless people disappearing, honestly, Alex.' He shook his head in mock despair.

She smiled. 'Seven, then.' Perhaps she was seeing ghosts and monsters where there were none. Or perhaps she wasn't. 'You might be right. It's not as if those sorts of jackets are a rarity, are they?'

'Precisely. Now let's have another drink and marvel at your sister's show.'

He was right. Those sorts of jackets were common enough. Yet there had been something about Jamie's quick dismissal of the whole thing that sat uneasily with her.

They wandered around the gallery, Alex enjoying overhearing

people saying how much they loved Sasha's paintings, and what a find, what a talent. She was filled with happiness for her sister, but also filled with doubt about Jamie Rider. She couldn't shake off a feeling that she was missing something that was right in front of her eyes.

White van. He had mentioned a white van. How did he know that?

'Alex, darling.' Her mother arrived at her side and kissed her cheek.

'Mum.' Alex was delighted, and pushed thoughts about Jamie Rider and white vans out of her head. 'I didn't realize you were coming.'

'I wouldn't miss it for the world. It's a shame your father couldn't be here to see it.'

Alex felt a familiar pang of loneliness. She was close to her father, but felt she had lost him. His mind was moving further and further from life every day. When she went to visit him at the home, the times when he recognized her were becoming few and far between. It broke her heart. And her mother found it hard, for all the brave face she put on things. 'He's all right, isn't he? I haven't been to see him this week.'

'He's fine. Same as usual really. Not getting any better.' She smiled sadly, then seemed to shake herself. 'And this is?'

Her mother, she thought, looked far too interested, in a mother sort of way.

Alex laughed. 'Sorry. Jamie, this is my mother.'

'Lovely to meet you, Mrs Devlin.' They shook hands.

Her mother gave Alex a less than discreet smile and then turned to Jamie. 'I'll leave you to it; I ought to get home now anyway. Nice to have met you, Jamie.'

'Your father's ill? Is it serious?' asked Jamie, once Alex's mother was out of hearing.

Alex nodded. 'He's in a home. Dementia.' She didn't want to give any other explanation, didn't want to go into the ins and

228

outs of his condition, didn't want to share what she had left of her father.

'I'm sorry.'

'Thank you. It's been hard, but we're getting there. He's much happier in the home. He knows where everything is. Nothing much changes. And Mum goes to see him every day.'

Jamie nodded and was quiet for a moment.

'Right.' He pointed at the gallery wall. 'I want to buy one of these paintings. Which do you think, Alex?'

'Whichever one you like.' She smiled at him.

'Come on, let's check them out.'

It took Jamie only a few minutes to settle on one of Sasha's oils of the sea at Southwold. 'There,' he said, as the red sticker went on. 'I reckon I've got a bargain from an up-and-coming painter. Will be worth a few quid in a year or two.'

Alex laughed. 'I love your confidence, thank you.'

'No worries.'

There was a sudden commotion at the door.

'Jamie Rider. She said you'd be here.' Cora pointed at Alex while weaving towards them, eyes blazing, clearly drunk.

'Cora, what on earth are you doing?' Alex tried to steer her away from Jamie. 'Everyone is looking at you.'

'I don't fucking care.' Cora shook off Alex's hand.

'Well I do.' Alex felt the anger rise up in her. How dare this woman spoil her sister's evening? 'This is my sister's show.'

'I told you, I don't fucking care. I wanted to see him, look him in the eye.' She pointed to Jamie and walked up to him and stood right in front of him. 'You thought you'd seen the last of me all those years ago, you and those brothers of yours. Always treating us like dirt. And as for that slimeball Lewis—'

'What about me, Cora?' Lewis stood in front of her, a twisted smile on his face.

His eyes, Alex noted, were cold. Chips of ice.

Cora seemed to shrink in front of him. Then she stood tall.

'You are the worst of them. Well, almost.' She flicked her eyes across to where Marianne and Joe Rider were standing. Joe was talking to a woman in a jumpsuit who had a bandana tied around her hair. He glanced over at Cora for only a second before resuming his conversation. Marianne stared at Cora before she, too, turned away.

'That's enough.' Jamie's voice was low, controlled. 'You're making a show of yourself and you're not welcome here, Cora.'

'Where's Rick? He hasn't contacted me. Something must have happened to him.' She stood as close as she could to Jamie, trying to intimidate him with her small frame.

'I don't know, Cora. Really.'

She stared at him, then collapsed in on herself. He took her very firmly by the arm and led her out of the gallery.

Alex watched them go as the buzz of conversation started up again. She was glad to see that Sasha had shrugged it off.

'Friend of yours?' she'd mouthed at Alex. 'Rival in love?'

Alex shrugged and looked as apologetic as she could. 'Sorry.'

Sasha laughed and resumed her conversation. She was so happy it appeared nothing, not even a drunk, angry woman could spoil the evening for her.

But it had spoiled it for her.

She was burning to know what Cora was talking about and why, and the way the Riders had reacted to Cora, their sheer *disdain*, made her blood boil. Careful, Alex, she told herself. Relax. Don't frighten him off. The time to ask will come. She made a deliberate effort to bring her shoulders down from round her ears.

Jamie reappeared and smoothly took her arm, guiding her around the rest of the exhibition.

The evening carried on, and more of Sasha's paintings were graced by a red dot. Alex did a lot of nodding and smiling. The critics – two of them – turned up from London, and the invited guests soon ate and drank all the supplies.

230

'Supper?' Jamie eventually asked.

Alex nodded. 'Could we have a walk first? The evening is still young and I would like to have a bit of fresh air, if it's not raining too much.' And she was burning to find out why Cora was so angry with the Riders. But she had to tread carefully.

The rain had relented for once and the air was cold, the sky above clear and studded with stars. Alex and Jamie began to walk slowly towards Gisford Quay. Jamie had his arm around her waist, and Alex leaned in, wanting him to relax with her.

'So what is the history between your family and Cora? And presumably her brother Rick?' Alex asked, watching her breath float on the night air.

Jamie sighed. 'You're tenacious, I'll give you that. Her father was the farm foreman, in the days when the farm was just that, a farm. None of this diversification that we all have to do to survive these days. Their house was a tied cottage and they didn't have a lot of cash. Their parents worked hard, but Cora and her brother were jealous of us. Resentful. They would bad-mouth us in the village, and Rick even stole Lewis's girlfriend – look, you don't want to hear this, let's not spoil a lovely evening.'

'I know, but she was so angry with you all. I mean, what have you done to make her like that?' She tried to sound light and curious, not that she was desperate to know.

'Bloody Cora.'

'She said to ask you what happened twenty-four years ago.' She tucked herself further into the warmth of his body, determined not to give up.

'Twenty-four years ago? What are you talking about? Look, can we stop for some food? Please?'

She got the impression he was playing for time. 'Yes, after you've told me what happened then.'

He stepped away from her. Something – fear? Irritation? flitted across his face. 'You're not going to stop, are you?'

231

She shook her head. 'Tenacious, remember?' She smiled, hoping she sounded non-threatening.

He looked up to the sky and then back at her. He shrugged, letting go of her. 'Twenty-four years ago Cora accused my brother Lewis of rape.'

'Right.' A big deal then. And it explained the photo she had found and why Rick had that look on his face. 'And?'

'Well, of course it wasn't rape.' He was dismissive. Or defensive? 'They'd been friends for years, but she'd always been jealous of us because of where we lived, how we lived. All that. Things went a bit far one evening after the pub and ...'

'And what?'

'Do you really want me to go on?'

'Please.'

'And they had sex.' He shook his head angrily. 'All right? But she regretted it. Cried rape.'

'Why would she do that? We've all done things we regret but we don't necessarily accuse someone of a criminal offence. Especially not rape.'

'Don't ask me, ask her. She put our whole family through it.' He sounded bitter.

'Through what?'

'A trial. Okay? A bloody rape trial, complete with headlines in the newspapers and on local telly. And although we won, it did us so much damage. Lewis still carries the taint around. No smoke without fire and all that shit. Do you know enough now?' He had raised his voice and was almost shouting.

'She went to court. That's no easy decision.' She tried to keep her voice mild, not wanting to antagonize him further.

'So what are you saying? He was in the dock so he must be guilty?'

'It takes a lot of guts to take someone to court for rape. Especially then.'

'It was revenge, pure and simple. Honestly, you have no idea

232

about that woman. She and her family hated the Riders. If you ask me it was that damn brother of hers that put her up to it. Look, I've told you now. That's what happened twenty-four years ago. If you don't believe me, then—' He shrugged. 'Then perhaps we had better leave things here.'

Alex's head was full of Cora's anger, Jamie's anger, thoughts of Cora battling life and its rubbish on her own, her brother off the radar. Poor Cora. What she must have been going through. Though Jamie seemed to be sure of his brother's innocence. Perhaps Jamie didn't know the full details. Maybe the Rider brothers were bastards. It all kept coming back to how well did she know any of them? Not well at all. And she needed to stick with both Cora and Jamie.

She reached for his hand. 'I'm sorry,' she said softly. 'Of course I believe you.' She surprised herself how sincere she sounded.

'Good.' Petulant voice, but hopefully he was mollified. Alex was glad it was dark so he couldn't see her roll her eyes. She tucked herself back under his arm.

'Tell me, why are we walking in the cold when we could be having comfort food in the local pub?' he said.

'I want to have a look at the island.' Time to calm the waters, so to speak.

'The island?'

Was it her imagination or did his arm tighten around her imperceptibly?

'Yes. Your island. The one over the water.'

He stopped walking. 'Why on earth do you want to do that? It's dark, there's nothing to see.'

'I know.' She shrugged. 'I suppose I want to get a feel for it. After all those stories you told me, you know.'

'Why now?'

'Why not?' She knew it sounded lame. 'Maybe we'll see some ghosts. It'll be very atmospheric. Come on, let's get closer.' She grabbed his hand and started walking again.

When they arrived at the quay, Alex smelled a familiar mix of salt and vegetation and fish and diesel. They picked their way around fishing boats that had been pulled up on the shingle. There were a couple of lamps lighting up the car park to the left with a sickly yellow glow and the sea was gently slapping against concrete.

She walked to the edge of the water. 'Gisford Ness. A prosaic name in a way for an island surrounded by secrets and myths.'

'We always just called it The Island. It's a shingle spit. Separated from the mainland by the river that goes into the sea. Longshore drift and all that.'

'Oh,' said Alex. 'I was never any good at geography, I didn't listen in class. Did you say you've never been across? I find that hard to believe.'

'I might have been when I was younger, but as I said to you, there's nothing to see over there. Now, can we go? I'm getting chilly.' He stamped his feet and rubbed his hands together.

Alex nodded, then climbed up the three steps onto the car park and stood for a minute, looking out over the water, gazing at the outline of the island.

A flicker of light. Had she imagined it? She stood still, watching.

Another flicker. As if someone was walking around with a flashlight.

'Jamie? Did you see that?'

He came to stand beside her. 'What?'

'A light, flickering. There.' She pointed to the light, which had moved along the shoreline.

'It's probably one of our men checking the fences.'

'I thought there wasn't anybody there?'

'There isn't as a rule, but the island is protected by fences all around. We don't want people going on there and disturbing the wildlife or stealing the plants. Or hurting themselves – there are some pretty unstable buildings over there. Then we'd be sued.' He shrugged. 'Occasionally one of the staff goes over to check all the fences and gates, make sure they're secure.'

'At night?'

'Not always, but obviously it was the only time free they had. Now can we go and get something to eat? Please. I'm starving.'

Alex turned away and walked across the car park, passing a white van. She stopped. But there were hundreds of white vans on the road.

Still.

Getting down on one knee, she looked at the number plate.

'What are you doing?'

'Here. This number plate is completely covered in dirt.' She took a tissue out of her pocket and wiped the dirt away, then got up and walked around to the front of the van. 'And this one.' She wiped that plate too, and took a quick picture with her phone. 'This isn't one of your vans, is it? From the farm?' She peered through the dirty windows, but there was nothing out of the ordinary on the front seats, only a couple of empty crisp packets, a discarded takeaway coffee cup and a plastic bottle full of what she hoped was water.

'How the hell would I know that?' She heard the impatience in his voice from round the other side of the van. 'I'm bloody freezing now.'

She bent down again. There was a dent in the bumper, and the paintwork was streaked with dark marks. Alex shivered.

She straightened up. 'Sorry. But Jamie?'

'What?' His voice was shot through with irritation.

'Nothing.' She shook her head. 'It doesn't matter.'

Jamie favoured the pub around the corner, which was packed and noisy with the sound of chatter and clinking glasses and music, but they managed to find a table a couple had that minute left free.

'What would you like?' asked Alex. 'My treat. No arguing. I kept you hanging around in the cold for long enough.'

'Absolutely not—' His body was still stiff and angular.

She touched his shoulder lightly, wanting his anger to drain away. 'I insist.'

He sighed and seemed to visibly relax, his shoulders dropping and the tension leaving his face. 'I'm sorry. About earlier.'

'I shouldn't have brought it up.'

'It's fine. The thing is, I hate it when it's dragged up again and people doubt my brother. We went through enough then, yet it has followed us down the years, however hard we try to shut it all down.'

What about Cora? She wanted to ask, but didn't.

'How did you know it was a white van?'

'I'm sorry?'

'Earlier, at the exhibition, you said Rick had been taken away in a white van.'

'So?'

'How did you know?' She smiled at him in what she hoped was a non-threatening way.

'You told me.'

'Right.' Alex smiled and handed him the menu.

'I think the fish and chips sounds good,' she said.

As she elbowed her way to the bar she was aware of an unsettled feeling in her stomach. Jamie's insistence that the Rider family were in the right when it came to Cora. The whole bloody family. Jamie knowing about the white van. The dent on the bumper of the van in the car park at the quay. And the mark on the paintwork. Could it be the van that had hit Sadie? Or was it merely a coincidence?

She didn't really believe in coincidences.

She found herself at the bar and tried unsuccessfully to catch the barman's eye.

'You with that Rider lad?' The voice came from the old boy sitting next to her who was nursing a pint, gnarled but thick and strong-looking fingers curled around the glass. He was wearing a thick jumper, despite the heat that was coming from the roaring log fire to the side of the bar.

She glanced back at Jamie, who was frowning at the screen on his phone. 'I am. Do you know him?'

''Course I know him. Know all the family. Used to work for them.'

'On the farm?'

He nodded.

In for a penny, in for a pound. 'Did you ever go over to the island?'

The old boy snorted. 'Wouldn't go there now if you paid me. They reckon it's haunted.'

'Haunted?'

'Screams in the dark of the night. Lights. There's not supposed to be anything over there. But if there's nothin' over there, then why are there ruddy great fences and gates? Pardon my French.'

'Jamie says it's to protect the wildlife.'

The old boy snorted. 'Ain't no wildlife over there. Nothing out of the ordinary anyway.'

'How do you know?'

'I do, that's all.' He looked at her sideways. 'All right. When I was a bit younger I used to go over there. Sneak about a bit. Try to find the ghosts. Only do it in the daytime, mind. Never found any. I wouldn't go now. They have men patrolling the fence. Electrified for all I know.'

The barman finally noticed her. She gave her order for the fish and chips and asked for a bottle of wine and two glasses. And a pint for the old boy.

'How did you get across?' Perhaps she could learn more about the island. Perhaps tease a story from him.

The old boy chuckled. 'I used to go, that's all. Snuck round by the lighthouse. There weren't no fences there then. Had me own boat. No one to bother me.' The old boy took a deep draught of his beer, then wiped the back of his hand across his lips. 'That had to go, though. Everything had to go when old Joe Rider sacked me. He found out I'd been across there, you see.'

237

'But there wasn't anything worth seeing when you went over there?'

'Not really. Like I said, no ghosts. They were doing some building work, making some of the buildings so they could use them. Storage someone told me.' He sucked on his teeth. 'Though I do think summat peculiar's going on over there. Why else have all that barbed wire and stuff? Some even say there are landmines. Mind you, believe that, and you'll believe anything.' He looked at her slyly. 'Seems to me you're right interested in the island. Did you want to go over? Because if you did, Reg over there in the corner might take you for the price of a pie and a pint. He's still got 'is boat. I'm Seth, by the way.' He held out a gnarled hand.

Alex shook it. 'Alex Devlin. I'm a journalist.' She looked over at Reg. White beard, woollen jumper, beanie hat, supping a pint.

Seth nodded. 'That's why you're interested in the island.' He took a deep draught of his pint. 'Reg,' he called. 'Over here.'

Reg looked up, frowning, then picked his glass up and walked with bandy legs over to Seth and Alex.

'You'd take this girl to Gisford Ness, wouldn't you, Reg.' Seth nodded towards Alex.

'Depends.' He drained his pint and looked meaningfully at her.

Alex nodded. 'Pint of Adnams?'

'Aye. I'm usually in my hut by the quay in the afternoons. Best time to come is when the light fades.' The barman put a pint down in front of him. 'Cost you more than this, though.'

Alex thought for a moment. It was tempting, but dangerous, too. Who knew what was over there, even if Reg could take her in his boat? Goosebumps ran up and down her back; someone walking over her grave. No, to confront possible danger with no safety net would be foolhardy – a bit like those young girls in horror films who venture down into the dark, dank cellar and you're screaming at them not to because everyone knows you

238

don't go down into a dark cellar in the middle of a horror film. Her inner voice was screaming at her not to be tempted even if there was a great story to be had, even if it might solve the mystery of what was happening on the island. There had to be another way.

She shook her head. 'No, Reg. I don't think it's a good idea, to be honest.'

Really? Was she absolutely sure?

Yes. She had put herself in danger in the past, time she learned to look after herself. She would find another way into the story.

Reg shrugged and picked up his beer. 'No skin off my nose.' He went back to his seat.

'Are you sure?' said Seth.

'I am, but thank you.'

'If you change your mind, you know where Reg is. And miss?'

Alex was out of her seat, ready to go back to Jamie. 'Yes?'

'Don't trust them Riders whatever you do.' His voice was gruff. 'Wouldn't like to see a pretty little thing like you hurt.'

Alex held back a smile as she weaved her way through the drinkers back to Jamie. It had been a long time since she had been called 'a pretty little thing', if ever.

'You've been a while,' said Jamie looking up from his phone and stretching out his legs as she sat back down. He frowned. 'And I saw you with Seth Goodwin.' He unscrewed the wine and poured it into the glasses. He took a sip.

'The old boy? Yes, he was lovely.'

Jamie's eyes were dark. 'Dad dismissed him for stealing.' He drank some more of his wine.

Alex watched him over the rim of her glass. 'Really?'

'Yes, really. And he's a bit gaga. Losing his marbles.' Jamie leaned back in his chair. 'He likes to talk all that rubbish about screams and lights in the night over on the island. I'd take anything he said with a pinch of salt if I were you.'

'Right, I will. But—'

'What?'

'There are lights at night. You told me yourself. Security.'

'Yes, but he – oh never mind. Steer clear, that's what I'm telling you.' He refilled their glasses.

Was she being overly sensitive, or had Jamie sounded vaguely threatening?

The fish and chips arrived.

As she dug into the plateful – mushy peas on the side – Alex knew she wasn't going to be intimidated by anything Jamie said.

CHAPTER THIRTY-THREE

DAY SIX: LATE MORNING

Alex put her phone down and gazed out of the window. Another dreary day and a dreary walk with Ethel returning home wet and muddy. Never have a long-haired dog again, particularly a long-haired dog in a flat, she thought, as she rummaged in a cupboard to find a towel for the dog and began to rub her under her tummy and down her legs. She would mop the floor later.

The call from Sam Slater hadn't been what she'd wanted either. He had told her the glass she'd found on the roadside was not from a Land Rover, but from a Mini, and yes, they were certain about that. He'd been very sympathetic, but it appeared to be a dead end. Damn. She could scarcely believe it. After all that. She rubbed at the back of Ethel's legs even harder, grimly satisfied as the towel became dark with dirt. She had also told Sam about the van in the Gisford car park with the dent in its bumper and the dark marks on the paintwork that she had convinced herself were blood. She sent him the photo of the number plate. He'd sighed and told her – very gently, as was his way – that he had already used up a pretty big favour persuading someone to analyse the glass she had found, he really couldn't waste resources racing to Gisford to look at a van that very likely wasn't even there anymore. He said he would run the number plate number through the system but didn't expect it to yield anything. Bugger and more bugger, she thought, trying to wipe the mud from under Ethel's chin. Reluctantly, she had agreed with him.

And what about the investigation into Sadie's death?

No progress, he told her. But it was early days.

She was on her own, then.

Tossing a couple of dog biscuits on the floor for Ethel, Alex sat at her desk and turned on her computer, looking out over the estuary as it clicked and whirred. Seagulls wheeled and screeched in the misty air. She saw Patricia pick up the milk from the end of her gangplank. A couple sauntered alongside the harbour, arm in arm. A woman swaddled in coat, hat and scarf and holding on to a buggy, fed the ducks bobbing up and down and in the water.

The water. She thought again about her conversation with Seth and Reg in the pub. Had it been the drink talking? The idea of taking a boat around the spit of land that was Gisford Ness had been interesting, but her instinct then was that it was a step too far, and she remained of that mindset. Definitely. Absolutely. She had already seen the so-called 'mysterious' lights, and Jamie had explained them away as being a couple of men making sure everything was secure on the island. But why did it have to be secure? Protecting wildlife and flowers and vegetation didn't necessitate the building of fences and the employment of guards, did it? Look at Shingle Street, that was an SSSI – a Site of Special Scientific Interest – with rare plants growing among the shingle on the beach, but that didn't have fences and guards. No, there was definitely something slightly off about Gisford Ness; however Jamie had tried to dismiss it.

And wouldn't it be something to land on the island and have a sniff around? Yes, but stupid too.

And Jamie Rider. How did she feel about him?

He was attractive and entertaining. Certainly different to the sort of men she'd had relationships with before, mostly disastrous it had to be said. But she didn't trust him. Not at all.

Her emails finished loading, and she found the one she had been hoping for from *The Post*. She was impressed, she didn't think she would get the information that quickly.

From: Lauren Clark
Re: Gisford Ness
To: Alex Devlin
　Hi Alex! Hope all good with you. Attached are a few bits about that island place you asked for. Hope it's okay. Anything else you need, give us a shout!
　Lauren x

Alex smiled. She might have known Heath would get a junior to do the research. She opened up the document. National Archives files. Good. The official documents, many from government departments, were often opened as public records after thirty years had passed. These files related to Gisford Ness. Thankfully Lauren had cut through the crap and given her a precis of its history. Apparently the anthrax story was one peddled by the government of the day to keep people away from the island. She whistled when she read that one. The Riders must know the story was a pile of crap, yet they were still repeating it. How very convenient. According to the archives, during the Second World War the island was leased by the Ministry of Defence and used for testing bombs and ammunition, and for developing chemical weapons.

During the Cold War, the island had been home to the Atomic Weapons Research Establishment to help develop the atomic bomb and carry out tests on it in half-buried concrete buildings. The Americans also used the island for 'research' during the sixties and seventies. No details about that – presumably still very much under wraps. It was also thought there were areas with buried landmines, though many of the areas had been cleared of the mines. The Rider family, Lauren wrote, was given the island back in the late eighties.

Her mind was buzzing. All at once she wanted to get into a boat with Reg and go across to the island. She would find answers there, she was sure of it.

Lauren had also attached an old map of the island. Alex opened it up. Like a child's drawing, it showed the lighthouse and an assortment of old buildings. Three were called 'pagodas', whatever that meant, and there were several labelled as 'bunkers'. A control room. A bomb ballistics building – that sounded alarming. Where they tested the bombs? Airfield site. A Bailey bridge. Marshes. A network of paths criss-crossed the island. There were even three 'Danger – Landmines' signs.

Bunkers. A perfect place to hide things. Or people.

God, how she wanted to get across there.

Her phone vibrated on the table beside her.

'Have you got Lauren's email?' Heath said.

'I have. I'm reading it at this very moment.'

'Good. Good. Interesting, don't you think? All that guff about anthrax. Pack of bloody government lies. Though why should we be surprised?'

Alex could hear phones ringing in the background and Heath typing at his computer.

'Lauren's done a great job. And fast, too,' she said. 'She's saved me from wading through dry and dusty documents by managing to weed out what is and what isn't important. Say thanks to her for me.'

'I will. She's a good kid. Will go far. She reminds me of you before you got soft.'

'Before I got soft? What are you talking about?'

'Making money from populist books.'

Alex didn't know whether she should be angry with him,

whether he was being serious. It was difficult to ascertain over the phone. 'Enough, Heath.'

'Now, about Boney, aka Nigel Bennet.'

'Yes?'

She heard him sigh at the other end of the phone. She imagined him leaning back in his chair, crossing his ankles and tapping a pen on the desk. 'Obviously there was nothing on Google about him.'

'Obviously.'

'But the Dark Web threw up a couple of shadowy references. Drugs. Supplying women. Trafficking. He's heavily into Internet porn, too.'

'Watching it or providing it?'

'Both, I expect. No pictures of course. Shame. I was looking forward to seeing his tats. No known associates. And anyway, as you know, the Dark Web usually means the end of any investigation. Impossible to crack.'

Alex wondered if Boney did, indeed, have a wireless router in that shed of his. 'Any idea who his customers are?'

'No. But he's dangerous, Alex, that's for sure. Leave him to the police.' Heath had his serious voice on.

Alex fervently hoped she need never see Boney again.

'So, what else besides missing people, UFOs and secret government experimentation is going on in deepest, rural Suffolk?'

Ethel started making whinnying noises and her legs paddled madly. Dreaming of chasing rabbits. 'I'm not one hundred per cent sure, yet. Look, I've got to—'

'Alex, you're not going to do anything stupid, are you?'

'Like what?'

'Go over to that bloody island. I don't want you being washed up on a beach somewhere and languishing in a mortuary because you can't be identified.'

She sighed impatiently. 'Don't be so macabre.'

'I mean it.'

'I won't.'

'Good. Because it would be stupid. And you'd have to fill out a health and safety form.'

She smiled. 'And I've got a ton of them hanging around.'

She looked out of her window. Raining again. When would it ever stop? There were flood warnings for some of the water courses in the county. Rivers threatening to break their banks. High tides washing away sand from the beaches, undermining houses perched on the edge of dunes. The roads swilling with water. Every time she looked at a weather map there were black clouds with great fat drops of rain dripping from them. She didn't envy anyone who was sleeping rough through it all. She thought of Emmy, who had looked as though she really needed a few square meals, dry clothes and someone to hug her. Alex really didn't want her to end up in a pauper's grave.

Emmy homeless.

Lindy. Tiger. Dead.

Where was Martin? Nobby? Karolina? Rick?

Lindy on a railway line. Tiger with a needle in his arm. What had Heath said? Don't get washed up on a beach. And didn't she read a story on the local pages of BBC News Online the other morning about a body on a beach?

She opened up her computer again. There it was.

Mystery surrounds the identity of a man whose body was found washed up on a beach in Suffolk.

The man, described as white and middle-aged, was found near Southwold Harbour.

Suffolk Police say the death is not believed to be suspicious.

She leaned back in her chair and gazed out of the window for inspiration. She started to look for news stories about bodies found on East Anglian beaches.

These are the eleven unidentified bodies washed up on Suffolk beaches in the past fifty years.

It was an article about the unidentified remains found: 'A bone, believed to have been in the water for less than six months,' she read, 'a body thought to have been in the water between two weeks and two months. White European male, aged over forty, 185 cm (6 ft) tall—'

She scanned the rest of the article: a one-eyed man, a woman with arthritis, a man with one leg. All sorts.

So, eleven in fifty years, not that startling. The article had been written in 2011.

She clicked around some more.

Rise in number of bodies on beaches

In the last year, wrote the author, *more than six unidentified bodies have been found washed up on the beaches of Suffolk and Norfolk.*

Alex sat back in her chair. So, eleven in fifty years, now six in the last year.

Detective Inspector Sam Slater, in charge of a task force looking into the rise in the unidentified bodies said he and his team were still investigating. 'It is a worrying trend, and we are looking into one or two possibilities,' he said.

Well, well, well. Sam Slater. She would have to ask him about that. Another coincidence to add to a string of coincidences.

She typed 'railway line suicides' into the search bar.

She discovered there had been a rise in the number of people jumping in front of trains over the last two or three years. Some of the journos speculated it was because of the economic slump, hard times, families not coping. Alex suspected that was true for some, but did it explain them all?

Then she found a couple of articles about bodies found on railway lines that had not been struck by trains. Frustratingly, there were no follow-up stories, so no way of knowing what they had died from. Presumably not deemed murder, otherwise there would have been more written about them.

She poked around. No mention of any increase in washed-up bodies in Cornwall or Dorset or Yorkshire. Two or three more in Lincolnshire and Essex. Nor an abnormal number of deaths on the East Coast London to Edinburgh line.

She sat back in frustration. She was looking for negatives. Non-stories. Still. A lot of bodies washed up on beaches. Bodies on railway lines. All in the area. Almost as if it was deliberate. As if someone was making these deaths look like suicide or even an accident in order to hide something more sinister.

Like murder.

But why?

Her intercom buzzed, interrupting her thoughts. Ethel scrambled up, startled awake by the noise.

'Hello?' she said into the speaker.

'It's me, Cora.'

Alex hesitated, then pressed the button to open the downstairs door and waited for her to reach the top of the stairs.

'I need to talk to you,' said Cora.

Alex held the door open wide, shocked at Cora's bedraggled and haggard appearance. She looked as though she had been sleeping under a hedge, the purple bruising under her eyes even more noticeable than before and her skin waxy. Her beautiful red curls were hanging limp and dirty and her boots were caked with mud. She was wrapped in a thin coat and misery.

'Sorry, I don't look great, do I?' she said, obviously noting Alex's shock as she followed her into the flat. 'I've been walking all over the place, trying to find Rick, but with no luck.'

'Sit down. What do you mean, walking everywhere? Since when?'

Cora sat at the table. 'Since the early hours.' She hung her head. 'I'm so sorry about barging in like that. To your sister's exhibition, I mean. I was brooding from the moment you said you were going with Jamie Rider. It built up from there. Then I went to the pub and downed drink after drink until the landlady refused to serve me any more. But the booze had given me Dutch courage. I had to come and say something.' She smiled ruefully. 'I'm suffering today, though. This', she pointed to herself, 'is not only the early morning and worry.'

Alex smiled, realizing Cora hardly dared look at her. 'Don't worry about it. Nothing you could have said or done would have marred Sasha's evening. She was having a wonderful time.'

'I'm also sorry if I spoiled your evening,' she said, awkwardly.

'You didn't, I promise. I've got a lot to tell you, but first let me make you some food while you fill me in on where you've been.'

Alex took bacon and eggs out of the fridge and put a frying pan on the cooker. Soon the little kitchen area was filled with the noise and sound of sizzling bacon. She deftly cracked two eggs into the pan, then turned on the kettle to make a coffee.

'I've been looking for Rick,' Cora said eventually, tracing patterns with her finger on the table top. She sighed. 'I seem to have spent a long time lately looking for him. I went to Norwich. I even went to poke around Riders' Farm. Cost me a fortune in taxi fares.' There was the glimmer of a smile on her face.

'To the farm?'

Cora nodded.

'And did you find any sign of him?' Alex poured milk into two coffees.

'No. Nothing. I tried everywhere. I tramped around the city again – God knows I know that place like the back of my hand – then at the farm I looked in barns, sheds, peered through the windows of a couple of those stupid lodges. I even tried to get into one of those ridiculous yurts. Nothing. I did have to dodge out of sight more than once as there were a couple of thugs who looked as though they were patrolling the area. Trying to keep people like me away, I suppose.'

'Did you find any caravans?'

'Caravans?' echoed Cora.

'Yes.' Alex slid the bacon and eggs on a plate and put it in front of Cora before sitting at the other end of the table. Ethel slunk in and sat by Cora's side, her chin resting on Cora's thigh. 'When I was talking to Jamie about Karolina, he said she was employed at the farm as a cleaner and that their staff – or some of them at least – live in "state-of-the-art" caravans as he called them, in a field. Did you see any?'

'No, nothing like that.' Cora was shovelling the food into her mouth as if she hadn't eaten for days. 'I could have missed a field of caravans, I suppose, but it seems unlikely. I went all over that farm.' She pointed to Ethel. 'Does she always drool this much? My thigh is soaking.'

'Always,' Alex confirmed.

'Do you think Martin will come back?' Cora pulled gently at the dog's ears. Ethel shifted her body, whimpered, and settled her chin complete with drool back on Cora's damp thigh.

Alex put the pan in the sink, letting it sizzle. 'I hope so,' she said quietly. 'Because if he doesn't it means something's happened to him.'

Cora nodded.

She finished her bacon and eggs. 'Thank you for that.' Her fingers drummed the table. Alex knew she was itching for a smoke.

'Have a cigarette if you like.'

'Trying to give up. Haven't got any with me.' Her fingers drummed some more. 'But I could kill for one now. Look, I owe you an explanation.'

250

Alex took a deep breath. 'Cora, I know a little about what happened twenty-four years ago. Jamie told me.'

Her face was stony. 'I bet he loved that.'

Alex shook her head. 'Not really.'

Her fingers stopped their drumming. 'What did he say?'

Alex's heart was thudding. She had started on this path, and now she had to carry on down it. 'That you took Lewis to court because you believed he'd raped you.'

'Believed. Such careful language, Alex.' Her lips settled into a thin line. 'Is that the journalist in you? That I *believe* he raped me, but it might not be so?'

'I'm not the enemy here. Honestly.'

Cora ran her hands through her hair, her fingers becoming tangled in the rats' tails. 'Lewis Rider raped me. Sex without consent. Rick persuaded me to go to the police and they wanted to prosecute. But of course, he had the big fancy pants lawyer. I didn't. He won.' She closed her eyes and shuddered. 'I was like a fish on a slab. Flapping this way and that without the means of breathing. I wasn't so much stitched up like a kipper as boned and filleted – just to keep the fish metaphors coming.' Her smile was sad. 'It was awful. Beyond awful. I'll never forget the smirk on Lewis Rider's face as I crossed to the witness box. I had to concentrate to even put one foot in front of the other. I thought I wanted to see his face when I testified. I wished to God I hadn't.' Her face was ghostly pale. 'It haunts my dreams most nights, even now.'

Alex found her emergency stash of cigarettes and handed one to Cora. 'You don't have to go on, you know, if you don't want to.'

Cora's hand shook as she lit the cigarette. 'I do. Now I've started. I've never told anyone the whole story before. The thing was, it – the rape – happened after a late-night shift in the pub. A rowdy night. Hot. Sweaty. So, of course, in court I was asked the usual sort of questions. *How much had you had to drink, Ms*

Winterton? You regretted the sex act, didn't you, Ms Winterton? Why didn't you call the police straightaway, Ms Winterton? Ms Winterton, Ms Winterton, Ms Winterton, even my own name sounded false when he'd finished with me.' She dashed away some tears with the heel of her hand.

Alex put an ashtray in front of her.

'And can you imagine what it's like to have details of your sex life laid out in front of your parents? Mum sat through the whole thing, tears pouring down her face. Dad's face – oh God, Dad's face—' She closed her eyes, trying to compose herself. 'His face was a mixture of horror and revulsion and it took every ounce of strength I had to keep my knees from buckling; I could only imagine what it must have been like for him to have heard about his daughter's sex life, to have his daughter accused of being *provocative*, of *bringing it upon herself*, to have *consented to sex and then regretted it*. What must it have been like for a father to hear that?' The tail of ash on the end of her cigarette dropped into the ashtray.

Alex sat completely still, absorbing Cora's words.

'Actually, I can tell you what it was like.' She pulled on the cigarette as if her life depended on it. 'Devastating. But do you know what was worse? He blamed me for the rape. He became more and more morose and drank, oh God how he drank.' She rubbed her eyes with her free hand until they were red and sore-looking. He used to ask me questions like "why did you have to encourage that Rider boy?", as if it was all my fault.'

Alex got up and poured them both another cup of coffee. She felt weighed down with sadness.

'It killed him, literally killed him. Because of me he lost his job with the Riders, so we lost the house. And he never worked again. That's when we moved to Bury St Edmunds. My mum's sister rented us a place, so at least we had a roof over our heads. Rick took all sorts of jobs to help my mum out and to help me get my nursing degree. Dad sort of faded away to nothing.'

'Lewis Rider has a lot to answer for.'

'Not only Lewis, but the whole family. Look, I know you like Jamie and maybe he's not as bad as the others—'

Alex shook her head. 'I'm not so sure.'

Cora gave her a sharp look, then carried on. 'Marianne and Joe sat in that courtroom every single day. Staring at me.' She shuddered. 'I was a wreck by the end of it.'

Alex gave Cora a hug. 'Your poor, poor thing. What a terrible ordeal.' She leaned her chin on top of Cora's head. She could not imagine how much it had cost Cora to talk about the rape and its aftermath.

'Do you believe me?' she asked in a small voice.

Alex rubbed Cora's back as though she was comforting a child, thinking how close she had come to questioning Cora's story. 'Yes. Absolutely. I never doubted you, Cora.' She sat back down. 'I'm guessing all this is connected to whatever it is Rick's doing now?'

Cora nodded.

'And you've no idea where he might be?'

Cora rummaged in her pocket and took out a gold chain. 'Eventually I went to the quay at Gisford and found this on the ground. It's Rick's.'

'How can you be sure?'

'Look here,' she pointed at the chain. 'See that catch and the extra piece that acts as a safety chain?' Alex looked, and sure enough, there was a safety chain and the gold links didn't match the rest of it. 'I bought him this some years ago and he never took it off. He lost it one day, that's when we had the safety catch put on, but the jeweller made it very chunky and it doesn't match the – oh, for fuck's sake, it's his, okay?'

She nodded slowly. 'I believe you. He was wearing the chain when I found him by the Land Rover.'

'So that means he's gone back over to the island, doesn't it? And I think that's where the other missing homeless people might be, too. I mean. Martin. Lindy. Nobby. It makes sense, doesn't it? A deserted island with stories about ghosts and UFOs—'

'And anthrax.'

'Anthrax?'

'I'll tell you later, but go on.'

'That's where they ship these people after giving them offers of work. But why?'

'If that's so, why was Lindy's body found on the railway track?'

'Perhaps they—'

'Whoever "they" are,' interjected Alex.

'All right. Perhaps "they" had no further use for Lindy for some reason. Oh, I don't know, Alex.' She viciously stubbed her cigarette in the ashtray. 'We need to find out.'

The increase in bodies washed up on the coast. The number of bodies on the railway line. She shook her head. Surely not?

'I need to go over there.'

Alex looked at Cora. 'Go over there?'

'To the island. Somehow. There has to be a way.' She gazed at Alex earnestly. 'And you know something. I can see it in your face.'

Alex shook her head. No, there was no way—

'He's my brother.' Cora's shout made Alex jump. 'He's the only family I have left and I need to find him. If you know a way to get across to the island and land somewhere out of the way that doesn't involve me swimming, then please tell me. Alex, I'm begging you.'

Cora's stare was making her feel uncomfortable. 'There might be a way. But it's too dangerous.'

'You don't need to come.'

Alex sighed. 'There's a man – Reg – who spends his time in one of the fishing huts on Gisford Quay. He might do it. Take you over, I mean.'

A slow smile spread across Cora's face. Her skin had lost its waxy look. 'That's brilliant, Alex. Brilliant. Will you take me to

254

the quay? I haven't any transport and – look.' She reached inside her pocket and took out a piece of paper that she spread out on the table. This was a completely different Cora to the one a few minutes before, as if a switch had been flicked. From depressed to manic in one jump.

'A map,' said Cora, 'of the island.'

Alex nodded. 'I've got one of those. Lauren from the paper sent it to me.'

'Ah, but this map is different. Look.' She stabbed at the map with her finger. 'I've marked where there are security cameras, at least the ones I've seen. And these buildings here, and here,' more finger stabbing, 'are where I have seen lights, very occasionally. And these buildings?' Another stab. 'They're underground and I reckon something goes on in there. I've spoken to people who say sometimes they've seen a mysterious and ghostly mist hanging over the middle of the island. I don't think it's mysterious and ghostly. There's something substantial to it, I'm sure of that.' She stared at Alex, her face flushed, her eyes bright.

'How do you know all this? And why haven't you said anything before?'

Cora had the grace to lose the smile. 'I had to get you onside, didn't I? I had to be sure you were genuine. For all I knew, you could have been in the Riders' pockets. After all, you went to their charity thing and you've been on a couple of dates with Jamie Rider. How did I know you weren't working for them?'

'What makes you so sure now that I'm not?'

'Instinct, mainly. And your passion. I really believe you mean to write about people on the streets.'

'Thanks,' Alex replied, drily.

Her sarcastic tone was lost on Cora. 'The thing is, I've taken a boat over there before. I haven't landed it, obviously, but I was able to take pictures.'

'Didn't they see you?' Alex couldn't believe what she was hearing.

She grinned. 'Once. I waved as if I was a day tripper and didn't realize I shouldn't be there. The guard waved back, can you believe it? The Riders should pay more and then perhaps they would employ people who had a bit of brains. It's that thing, isn't it, about being confident and looking as though you belong in a place. A bit like holding a clipboard when you want people to think you're important. I also sat on Gisford Quay for hours on end, watching. And strong binoculars help.' She looked pleased with herself.

'When did you do all this?'

'A while back now,' Cora admitted. 'I know the Riders are not all they seem—'

'And you wanted to get something on them.'

'Precisely. I knew they were up to something, but I couldn't find out what.'

'And Rick helped you?'

Cora's shoulders slumped. 'He wasn't meant to, not this way.' She looked at Alex, eyes shining with unshed tears. 'And now I'm so worried about him.'

'I think it's time you told me what Rick has been doing.'

Cora took another cigarette out of the packet Alex had left on the table and lit up. She nodded. 'Rick came to Norwich to live, as I told you. He said it was his favourite city and he needed to get his head together. But, like I said, it all went wrong and he ended up on the streets. That's when he saw Lewis Rider again for the first time since, well, since, you know.'

Alex nodded. Since Cora was raped.

'He was with a couple of his bodyguard types. Luckily Lewis Rider didn't see him, but later Rick saw the bodyguards – henchmen I suppose – going round the city talking to rough sleepers. That's when they started disappearing.'

'How long ago?'

'About a year. Maybe less.'

'Okay.'

'Rick heard rumours they were being made slaves of some sort. Taken to the Riders' farm, he thought, and made to work in God knows what. Have you heard about that? In this day and age? I mean, slavery? Didn't that go out hundreds of years ago?'

Alex nodded. 'Sadly, it is still around. Modern day slavery. Usually it's people trafficked from abroad for the sex industry. Though there are families who've been imprisoned for holding people against their will in this country – vulnerable people – and making them work for nothing. Building work, mostly. Tarmacking drives. They usually live in foul old caravans, which is why my ears pricked up when Jamie said the workers at the farm lived in them.'

'It's a fucked-up world, isn't it?'

'Not entirely.' Alex smiled. 'Why didn't he go to the police?'

'Police? You are fucking joking, aren't you? For a start he was a homeless guy and who would believe him? Especially when pitted against the most influential family in East Anglia. A family whose social circle includes the Assistant Chief Constable.'

'Are you suggesting she's involved in some way?'

Cora shook her head and blew smoke into the air. 'Not necessarily. Though it makes it difficult to know who to trust. Especially when it comes to the Riders and their friends. I told you how that family crushed me. And my parents. They would pin Rick under their shoe and grind him to dust if he'd gone to the authorities. No, he came up with his own fucking stupid plan.' She dashed away tears on her cheek.

'Go on.' Alex hardly dared think what the plan was.

Cora swallowed hard. 'Rick would accept a job from Lewis's two men and see where he was taken.'

'So he wasn't forced into that white van?'

Cora shook her head. 'He'd bought a buttonhole camera off the Internet—'

'He did what?' Alex wanted to bury her head in her hands.

Instead, she took a deep breath wanting to hear the rest of the sorry tale. 'And what if Lewis saw him?'

'I know. Stupid. He was convinced Lewis wouldn't recognize him with his horrible long hair and beard. Filthy clothes. Smelly. And people don't notice the homeless, the down-and-outs, the beggars, do they? How often do you walk past someone sitting on the streets? Especially if they're rattling a jar or a tin. Sometimes all they want is a look, a smile, maybe a few coppers, but people look the other way. They don't want to be involved.'

Alex was uncomfortable. It was true: how much notice did she used to take of rough sleepers? None, in all honesty. And she often justified to herself that she shouldn't give money because it would be spent on drink or drugs. That gave her the excuse to walk on by. But she should make more effort, like she had with Tiger. Oh, God, poor Tiger.

'Anyway,' Cora continued, 'he was going to take photographs with his camera—'

'Bought online.' Alex shook her head in despair. 'How did he know it would even work properly?'

'He tried it out first. He's not that stupid.'

'Really?'

'But I knew it wouldn't work. How could someone who was suffering from PTSD and who'd been living rough for weeks expect to take on hardened criminals? For all he told me he kept himself fit, he wouldn't have been any match. I told him he should give up on it. We had a row. But he wouldn't stop. He wanted to see it through. For me. He was doing it for me, and now it's all gone wrong. I don't even know if he's alive or not. Whether he managed to find and photograph any evidence. Whether the whole thing has just been one mega fuck-up.'

Alex made up her mind. 'We'd better go and see then, hadn't we?'

'What?'

Alex looked at Cora. This was ridiculous. Irresponsible. Stupid.

What if something happened to Cora? What if they never found out what happened to Rick, could she live with herself? It was a chance she was willing to take. And besides, she was itching to know what was going on over at Gisford Ness. 'Let's go and find Reg, see if he'll take us over to the island.'

The adrenaline surged through her, but a little voice was asking her if she had made the most reckless decision of her life.

CHAPTER THIRTY-FOUR

DAY SIX: AFTERNOON

A mist was rising off the water and swirling around the land as Alex pulled up in the harbour car park at Gisford.

'Are you okay?' She reached across and took Cora's hand in hers. Perhaps this trip over to the island would answer some questions. Perhaps it would put them in too much danger. Was this the most stupid thing she had thought of doing? Alex almost turned the car around. Back to safety. To home. She would collect Ethel from John and then – and then she remembered Lindy and Martin and Nobby and Rick. And Tiger.

'Cora, do you think Tiger was murdered?'

Cora put her head back against the headrest and closed her eyes. 'I'm certain of it. Showing that picture around? Bad move. Got him noticed. Got him killed.' She held her hand up. 'Before you say it, I did report my suspicions to your friendly police officer and he said he'd look into it, but that it seemed like an open-and-shut case of accidental overdose.' She shrugged. 'I don't suppose they spent more than five minutes on it.'

Alex's stomach dropped. She had shown Jamie that picture. No use dwelling on that now. Perhaps the island would give them the answers they were looking for.

She unbuckled her seat belt. 'Come on. Let's do this.'

They made their way down to the shoreline and to the fishermen's huts. There was a light in one, so Alex peered through the door. Reg in his beanie hat was mending one of his nets by the light of a paraffin lamp.

'Reg?'

He concentrated on mending his net. 'Who wants to know?'

'It's me, Alex Devlin. I met you in the pub yesterday. With Seth. You said you might be able to take me to Gisford Ness.'

'I did.' His gnarled but nimble fingers continued with the net. 'But then I got to wondering, why would you want to do that? It's haunted, you know.'

'I think there's more to it than that.'

He stopped working on the net and looked at Alex for the first time. 'You may be right at that. Lights. Odd noises, especially out of the fog or the rain. I've been round the other side of the island a few times, though everyone says we're not to. Even been shot at.'

'Shot at?' This from Cora.

Reg narrowed his eyes. 'And who may you be?'

'I'm Cora. And I think my brother is being kept prisoner on that island.'

'Do you now. Prisoner, eh? Like in one of them thrillers?'

'A bit,' said Alex. 'More serious, though. Real life.'

'Real life, eh? Well, well, well. Yes, I've bin shot at. They don't want anyone anywhere near their precious island, those Riders. They say they're protecting the wildlife. Though why they need great big fences with barbed wire on the top and men with guns I don't know.' He shook his head as if to emphasize how stupid people were. 'I know a nice little landing place. Round the other side. But I reckon it's a mite dangerous for you ladies. We have to navigate out of the channel, see.'

Alex had to curb her impatience – men like Reg didn't like to be rushed, she knew that, but, oh Lord, she wished he'd just say yes. 'For a few minutes perhaps?'

'You want me to hang around waiting while you go and get yourself caught and thrown off the island, is that what you want? Didn't you hear me? It's dangerous. And cold. We'd have to take the fishing boat or they might smell a rat. They need to smell the fish, you see.' He chuckled.

'Please, Reg,' said Cora. She put her hand on Reg's arm. 'It's my brother. I need to find him.'

Reg sniffed. 'I think you're being fanciful. Prisoner? Though I do hear some strange noises at night when I'm here late, or doing some night fishing.'

'A few minutes. To spy out the lie of the land. Please.'

Alex held out three £20 notes.

Reg eyed them and sighed. 'The sea's calm tonight and the forecast says it will be for a while yet. The fog could be a problem, or a blessing. It could get us there without being seen. Though there are the currents we have to be careful of. I don't want your money. You can buy me a pie and a pint in the pub.'

'Agreed,' said Alex.

'We'll wait till it's darker, a lot darker. Can't do no night fishing in the afternoon.'

Two hours and copious cups of tea made with water heated on a primus stove later, they set off in Reg's small fishing boat, Reg at the helm. Thankfully the water was calm. At first, Alex was tense and nervous. She hadn't been on a boat since she had almost died on one on the Broads some months before. She made herself relax. This was nothing like that experience. It wasn't going to happen again. She was here with Reg and Cora. No one was going to hurt her. Not on board the boat at any rate.

Not having the stomach to call him, she fired off a quick text to Heath telling him what she and Cora were doing, before she lost the signal. He would be furious, but at least someone knew where she was going.

A spotlight at the front guided them along the river towards the sea. The earlier mist had become thick fog and a blanket

262

of eerie silence wrapped itself around them, with only the thrum of the engine to keep them company. The fog was good, it meant they were less likely to be seen, though it made it harder for Reg to find his landing place. Maybe he wouldn't go through with it. Maybe he wouldn't be able to. The guards on the island were used to seeing his boat around at night, Reg said. They didn't like it but they would probably ignore him. Alex wasn't sure she liked the 'probably'. She shivered, pulling her coat around her. The wind and the rain had stopped, at least for now, but the damp and cold of the fog were seeping right into her bones. Reg had oilskins on over his jumper; Cora wore her thin coat still. Neither seemed affected by the cold. None of them spoke.

The lights of Gisford gradually faded behind them, and, as they rounded the corner of the spit that was Gisford Ness, disappeared altogether. Now they were out in the open sea and rolling more, although Reg was hugging the land as much as he could. Alex fancied she could feel the currents tugging at the little boat. She put her hand on the inside of the cabin to steady herself. The stench of fish was beginning to make her feel nauseous. Cora was standing on the deck of the boat, looking at the island. She appeared deep in thought.

A sea breeze suddenly rushed around them. Alex could taste the salt. The sea was not the pond it had been earlier: waves were forming, with tips of white horses. The fog was clearing, to reveal a dark grey sky that was quickly changing into black. She peered through the boat's window, now splattered with sea spray and saw the outline of the island, together with the abandoned light-house. There were no lights at all, as far as she could see.

'How close can you get to shore?' she asked Reg, pushing her wet hair out of the way and wishing she had a more waterproof coat, wishing she had come better prepared.

'Pretty close. I'll have to row you the rest of the way.' The small rowing boat was tied up to the back of the boat and being pulled along. The stern, she should probably think of it as, but she had never been good at boat jargon.

'Aren't you worried they'll see your light?'

He shook his head, while expertly tugging the wheel this way and that. 'If they do, they'll only think I'm fishing. We have to be quiet in the rowing boat, though. Then if I take you to the right spot, I'll show you how to get through the fence.' He grinned and tapped his nose. 'I've been around far too long not to know how to get into places.'

Alex returned his smile.

Five minutes later Reg threw the anchor overboard. They were as close as the fishing boat could get to the island.

Reg hauled the rowing boat alongside. 'Hop in.'

She and Cora managed to jump in making the little boat wobble alarmingly. Reg followed suit, taking up the oars.

None of them spoke as they neared the shingle beach of Gisford Ness.

Reg hauled himself out of the boat and pulled it onto the stones before helping her and Cora.

He put his finger to his lips. Alex could just about make him out by the light of the shadowy moon.

Reg led them up the beach, their feet crunching on the shingle. They clambered up the high dunes. Surely someone, if there was anyone around, would hear them coming? Maybe no one was checking the fences tonight. It could just be, as Jamie had told her, that all they wanted was to keep the place safe from people who might damage the delicate ecosystem. This clandestine trip could all be for nothing.

A tall fence, topped with barbed wire, loomed out of the dark. They crept along its perimeter, until they were in the shadow of the decommissioned lighthouse.

To one side of the lighthouse and outside the fence were three tumbledown sheds. Reg led them into one. It smelled musty and of decay. The concrete floor was pitted in places, and loose bricks and what looked like old sacks were lying around and about. Alex heard a scurrying noise and tried not to think about how many rats there might be hiding in the dark corners.

'See, at the back,' he whispered, 'where the bricks are loose, or have fallen away completely, there's a hole in the fence. You can get through there. Easy. There are no floodlights at this end.'

'You'll wait for us?' Alex whispered back, as Cora moved towards the back of the shed.

'Aye. I'll wait here. Don't be long mind.'

Alex felt in her pocket for her phone and was glad to feel its reassuring presence. She hoped she wouldn't have to use the light, there was no way she wanted to attract attention to them both.

Cora beckoned to her. 'We can go through here, look. It's been cut with wire cutters.' She grinned at Alex. 'Reminds me of turning up at Boney's place.' She pushed with her shoulder and shimmied through sideways.

Alex looked back at Reg. There was an odd, thoughtful look on his face. 'You will wait for us, won't you, Reg?'

He nodded. 'You take care.'

'Where now?' whispered Cora, once they were standing inside the fence.

Alex stood and listened. Had all this been too easy? She could hear nothing but the sound of the sea pulling on the shingle behind her and the wind now whipping through the air. In front of her and about fifty metres away was the shape of a building that looked solid enough. They should make their way there and think about their next move. With a sinking heart Alex realized she hadn't actually thought this through; she had done her usual thing of stampeding forward without a plan. Why hadn't she taken more time to consider what they were doing? She shouldn't have dragged Cora along. Too late now.

'We'll head for that building and take stock. Come on. Quickly and quietly.' She almost laughed at her own words. So difficult to be quiet on these stones.

They crept towards the building, sticking to a well-trodden path.

As they reached it, Cora grabbed her arm. 'Did you hear that?'

Alex shook her head. She had been concentrating so hard on getting to safety, she hadn't been aware of anything else but the building that was to be their sanctuary. She wanted to look at the map of Gisford Ness she had brought with her, make her way to the concrete bunkers. She had a feeling about those.

'I thought I heard a noise, like a cough or something.'

They stood for a couple of minutes, listening hard. Nothing.

They reached the building. It certainly was solid. Dark.

The door was unlocked.

She pushed it open.

The lights came on.

CHAPTER THIRTY-FIVE

DAY SIX: LATE

It was as if he had never left.

Except this time, he would never leave.

He was back on his cold, hard bed in the underground building, his wrists and ankles chained to convenient posts that had been hammered into the ground. His whole body ached, only marginally relieved by the drugs that had been shot into his system by a grinning goon.

How could he have been so stupid?

It had all started to go wrong when he was standing on the quay, looking across the river to Gisford Ness …

'I thought if I waited here long enough you would turn up. Like a bad, bad penny.' The whisper was behind him, in his ear. There was a sharp prick through his clothes below his armpit. A knife, he guessed.

Rick froze. He'd been careless, so focused on getting to Gisford that he had forgotten to keep in the shadows.

'So, keep very still and walk when I tell you to walk, and jump when I tell you to jump. What we're going to do is walk towards that boat over there, get in nicely and I'll take you back to the island and we can put you to work. Again. If that's what they want.'

Gary. Fucking Gary.

'And if I don't?' he asked through clenched teeth.

'If you don't,' Gary pushed the knife in a little more and Rick felt it pierce his skin and a drop of blood run down his side, 'I will push the blade just below your armpit here.' The point of the knife was sharp. Rick tried not to flinch. 'And if I twist it I will sever your arterial system. Might even put a neat hole in your heart. Instant and efficient death with minimum blood loss. You would be on the floor and I would be away on the boat before anyone realized you were dead. Understand?' His voice was low and menacing, but with an undercurrent of pleasure.

Rick nodded.

He had been inching his right hand up towards his neck while Gary was talking. He took hold of his gold chain with two fingers and pulled it, as surreptitiously and as hard as he could.

It snapped.

'Good. You're not the only one to have been in the army. And after you, I would go after that sister of yours. Cora, isn't it? Although her death wouldn't be quite so quick. Now, let's move.'

Nausea rose in Rick's throat. He was dizzy and hot. His arm throbbed. He was getting an infection, he thought. At this rate he wouldn't last over there, on the island. Even if they did decide to put him to work, and then they would work him until he dropped dead. He had seen that happen, he remembered now. He remembered everything now, when it was too late.

He had failed.

He'd wanted to do right by Cora, to expose what was going on over there, on the island, the nastiness, the disregard for human life and dignity, where money meant more than anything. Where human trafficking and drug manufacture took precedence over everything. It had all been for Cora. She needed – what was that Americanism? – closure, and he wanted to give it to her. But now he was here, on the quay, about to get into a boat to an uncertain future. No, it wasn't uncertain, he knew exactly what would happen to him.

He would never return home.

He pretended to stumble. Gary caught hold of him and hauled him upright, but not before Rick had managed to drop his chain onto the concrete, praying Gary wouldn't see. It was a long shot, maybe no shot at all, but he had to try something. He could only hope his sister might find it and realize where he'd gone.

A chance in a million.

The small motorboat was tied up alongside a wooden jetty and rocked from side to side as the two men clambered on board. Rick had half-thought he might be able to rush Gary when they were on the boat, because he would have to steer it as well as make sure he didn't jump overboard or attack him. What he hadn't bargained for was for the second man – what was his name? Pete, that was it – for Pete to be on board. Grinning. Waiting for him.

'You're so predictable,' Pete said as he started the motor and cast off. 'We knew you'd be back here. Couldn't keep away, could you? What were you hoping to do? Storm the island single-handedly or something?'

He shook his head. He didn't know himself what his plan was. He just knew he had to somehow get his camera out of its hiding place and make sure the evidence on it reached the police. And not the bent ones. Because he'd promised Cora he would get evidence against the Riders. Somehow.

The weak sun was low in the sky, but Rick felt the rush of fresh air on his face and across his scalp as they crossed the river. The last fresh air he would feel for a while, he thought.

His whole body ached.

Perhaps he would die of blood poisoning before they could do anything with him …

He shivered as he looked around the miserably cold bunker. None of the other beds were occupied – they must all still be at work. It was still night-time.

269

He had to think of Cora. He knew he had to try for her sake. But he had escaped the island once, escaped the thugs twice, did he have it in him to do it all over again?

That wasn't the point. The point was he *had* to do it all over again otherwise everything he'd done over these last months, all he'd done to try and make some meaning of his life, would be for nothing.

It had all seemed possible when Cora found him and he told her how he had seen Lewis Rider and a couple of his henchmen around Dragon's Hall one day. That he'd kept out of sight, but had then seen Lewis's men talking to some friends of his who had pitched their tent on wasteland near Dragon's Hall. Behind a crumbling old wall so the tent couldn't be seen by a casual observer. It wouldn't take the plods long to find them, but until then, they were safe. Thing was, a couple of days later, the tent and his mates had gone. Never seen again. It happened a few more times, and that's when he started to hear the rumours. That the people who were disappearing were not being moved on or leaving by choice. They were being taken and forced to work for a family. Rick immediately thought of having seen Lewis. Then more rumours: people were being offered 'jobs' and were taken to a mysterious island from which they never came back. Yet despite the rumours, people on the streets were accepting these 'jobs', hoping for a better life. Who wanted to sleep on cardboard, wrapped in newspaper and magazines, being spat on, pissed on, beaten up if a warm dry room and a job was on offer? Some, sure. But many wanted out if they could see a way out.

That was when he'd come up with his plan.

Why had he told Cora about seeing Lewis Rider? Why had he told her what he was going to do?

Because she was still hurting: twenty-four years later still nursing such a grievance in her heart that it consumed her. All Rick wanted for his sister was for her to meet someone and be happy. Have a family. Move away. Forget the Riders. Forget their parents – or, at least, forget the way in which their lives ended. But she couldn't. Wasn't able to move on. And he understood that – after all, the woman he saw in his dreams wasn't his wife, but the young girl from the checkpoint in Afghanistan. He thought he would never be able to forget her and the exact moment of her death, so it stood to reason Cora couldn't forget the day Lewis Rider shoved himself inside her body. And he thought it would help if he told her his plan.

He, too, hated the man.

He ran his tongue around his dry lips. God, he was thirsty.

CHAPTER THIRTY-SIX

DAY SIX: LATE

Alex blinked, the sudden bright light searing itself onto her retinas, blinding her momentarily.

What was happening? Did opening the door trigger the lights? She hoped no one was watching from on the island, otherwise they would know someone had entered the building. She groped behind her for some sort of switch to turn the brightness off.

'Welcome to Gisford Ness, Alex.'

She froze.

Lewis Rider with that phoney smile, his face and forehead plastic smooth.

On either side of him stood two men. She recognized one of them as the man from the solicitor's CCTV. The other was wearing a red Puffa jacket and was holding a gun, pointed unwaveringly at her.

Where was Cora? She couldn't see her, couldn't sense her in the room. She had been behind Alex when she pushed open the door. Could she hope she had seen something, heard something and hadn't followed her in? Alex prayed that it was so.

Okay. Let's see what she could do.

'Lewis,' she said brightly. 'How lovely to see you.' She made herself appear shamefaced. 'I'm sorry, I know I shouldn't be here, but I was so interested in the island and its history that I had to come and see it for myself.'

'In the dead of night?'

'Well … it was the screams and the lights and the possibility of aliens that I wanted to explore. Only get them at night. And I wanted to take a few photographs.'

'No camera?'

'Phone. I always use my phone. Top of the range. Perfect photographs. Don't need to carry excess equipment. Makes it easier.'

'Really?'

Fuck it, she was gabbling.

'Yes. I didn't expect anyone to be here. I knew there was a fence around the island, but I found a hole and thought I would slip through. I'm sorry. I haven't harmed anything. I was only interested, I thought it would make a good piece—'

'For your paper?'

'Yes. For *The Post*.'

'Hmm.'

'Do we really need the gun?' She pointed at the man in the red jacket.

'For the moment.'

She shrugged, as if it didn't matter one way or the other. 'Is it only you here?'

'Oh yes.' He chuckled. She didn't like the sound of that chuckle. 'Only Gary and Pete and me. Here at any rate. There are some others who want to meet you, however. Who did you expect?'

Who did she think would be here? Immediately the cold and haughty face of Marianne Rider came into her head. Ice-cool. Merciless. Keeping her family afloat any way she could. 'Your mother?' she ventured.

Lewis Rider laughed. 'No, my mother leaves the island to me. The lodges and yurts are more her field. That and attracting funding for our various charities. But you know all about those, don't you, Alex Devlin? Our charities. You do understand we have to be seen to be above board. Eager to help. Socially responsible. That's what makes it so perfect.'

'What is so perfect?' she asked, warily.

He gave her a quick smile. 'Unfortunately I will probably show you.' He shook his head and tutted. 'It's such a shame you didn't take notice of the warnings I sent you.'

'Warnings?'

'Boney. Terrible name. Mind you, he's not so nice. And those teeth. Jesus.'

'You sent Boney round to my flat?'

'I did. He was supposed to frighten you.'

'It didn't work.'

He looked at her consideringly. 'Evidently not. Even the threats to your sister and your son didn't work. You are obviously a hard person to scare. But don't you care about them?'

'Of course I care,' she said, gritting her teeth so hard her jaw began to ache. What had she done? She had always known that Lewis Rider was not to be trusted, had his finger in some rather nasty pies. Surely he wouldn't really hurt her family or her, would he?

'And that poor girl from Fight for the Homeless, what was her name?'

'Sadie,' said Gary, leering.

Lewis clicked his fingers. 'Correct. Sadie. That was a shame. But she was going to blab to you, wasn't she? I thought if I stopped her then maybe you would go away, because, you see, you have become quite a problem to us.'

Alex wanted to throw up. The white van. It really did have a dent and blood on it, she had been right. Why couldn't she have persuaded Sam Slater to look into it? Why hadn't she told him where she was going?

She was beginning to realize she had made a big mistake.

274

She tried to look around surreptitiously. The room was bare. Concrete walls, concrete floor. Two windows either side. A set of open stairs in the corner. It didn't smell of anything but damp and the sea.

'Anyway,' said Lewis Rider. 'I've had enough of this.' He nodded at Gary and Pete. They came forward and seized Alex by her arms.

'I think you'll get your wish,' said Lewis Rider. 'You were so desperate to see what goes on here that I will show you some of the island.'

Alex tilted her chin. 'Why show me?'

He smiled. 'I'm proud with what we have achieved. And I can't tell many people that. But since you won't be leaving ...'

She had to swallow hard to stop the bile rising in her throat. 'I don't know what you're planning,' in truth, she didn't want to know what he was planning, it was bound not to be anything good, 'but there is someone who knows I am here. Someone who brought me over.' She tried to loosen the men's grip, but to no avail. She had known it wouldn't work, but she'd had to try.

'You mean Reg?' Lewis Rider didn't only laugh, he guffawed. 'Old Reg. Been working for me for years. Like Seth.'

'Seth?' Now she was confused. 'He said your father had dismissed him. Jamie said he had been sacked for stealing.'

'Yes. They did both say those things, didn't they? No, Alex. Reg has gone straight back home. Back to his smelly little hut but five hundred pounds richer. He turned tail as soon as he'd shown you the handy hole in the fence. Funny you didn't smell a rat. A convenient old man in the pub who conveniently told you about another old man. The second old man happy to take you across to an island in his fishing boat that most people wouldn't visit if they were paid. Then hey presto, a cut in the wire and you're in. No guards, no lights. No dogs. We do have dogs here, you know. I may introduce you to them at some point. They get very hungry this time of year. Mind you, the plan very

275

nearly hit the rocks when you didn't immediately take him up on his offer of a lift. What made you change your mind?'

Alex stared at him, refusing to say anything, although her heart had plummeted into her boots and she felt sick. Seth and Reg. Stooges. Why hadn't she stopped and thought about it properly? Because she was so desperate to get her story, get an exclusive. She was so focused on getting across to the island that she didn't stop to think that Seth and Reg were a little too convenient.

And what about Jamie? He must be involved too, otherwise how would Lewis have known to plant Seth at the pub? She shook her head. How stupid she had been. How bloody, fucking stupid. She had been so right not to trust him, but she had been too slow.

Lewis Rider sighed. 'I've had enough of talking. Let's go. Gary, Pete, bring her. Any sign of trouble, you know what to do.'

There was no relying on Reg. He wouldn't be phoning the coppers when she and Cora didn't turn up. The only other person she had told she was coming here was Heath, but he was back in London and no bloody use at all. And he certainly wouldn't be worrying about her in the middle of the night.

The only hope she had was Cora. Lewis Rider didn't seem to know she had come over with her and Reg.

She prayed Cora was lying low.

Gary and Pete pulled her along so fast, her feet hardly touched the ground. They were out of the building and making their way along a defined path, the moon giving just enough light to see by. It seemed nobody wanted to put their torch on. The gun wasn't pointing at her, it was pointing at the ground. Alex desperately wondered what she could do. Kick out at the gun? Twist and turn to get out of their grips? Lean down and bite Gary or Pete's arm? Scream. That was it. She should scream.

She took as deep a breath as she could manage, then opened her mouth. But before the scream could emerge, Gary and Pete had dropped her, and Gary had put his hand over her mouth.

Their grip was looser.

She bit hard down on Gary's fleshy hand.

'Fucking hell,' he shouted. Letting her go.

She took the opportunity to twist away from both of them and run. She could hardly see where she was going.

'Don't stray off the path.' Lewis Rider's voice followed her, sounding bored. 'There are a fair few hidden mines. You must have read about those, during your research? Or perhaps not. Not everybody knows about them. So, go on, run. But be careful where you put your feet. We've had people try to escape before. It didn't end well.' His laughter carried over the air.

The mines. Did she really believe there were any on the island? Why not? After all, plenty were laid on Suffolk beaches during the Second World War when the coast was fortified for an expected German invasion.

She stopped dead.

'Stay still, your feet are off the path.'

She looked down, and sure enough, she could just about make out that the path was to one side of her, and her feet were on the sandy scree.

Lewis Rider sauntered up to her, holding the gun. 'We don't want an explosion that could cause people across the water to ask questions, do we now? Not yet, anyway. Come on, there's a good girl. And there are some friends of yours here.'

Gary and Pete took hold of her once more and guided her along the path until they reached a one-storey building. There was no light coming from it at all.

Inside, it was lit up like, as her father would have said, a gin palace. There must either be good blackout blinds at the windows or no windows at all. She was led along a long corridor, through a door and down a flight of steps. They were going right underground. The tunnel, which was well-lit, was damp and lined with brick, and the walls were glistening with condensation. She began to shiver.

'These tunnels criss-cross under the island,' said Lewis Rider from behind her. 'They come up into several of the buildings that you can see from Gisford. Some open out into the underground structures. It was helpful for all the secret work that went on here between the two world wars.'

Alex could hear the echo of her footsteps.

They turned a corner, and Gary or Pete – she couldn't see who it was – pushed her up a set of stairs. They emerged into a long room, a bit like a warehouse. Moonlight was shining through glass in the roof. Partitions lined one side. It smelled of rust and damp and something else. Loneliness. It smelled of hollowed-out loneliness.

'Here,' ordered Lewis Rider.

Gary and Pete pushed Alex forward.

The side of the warehouse had been carved up into several three-sided rooms. In each room was a large double bed, a chest of drawers with tissues and baby oil, and a computer perched on a table with a camera on the top. The rooms were decorated too, some with wallpaper, others with paint. The bedding ranged from deep purple to clean white. There were women in all of them, writhing on the beds and two men were hovering, presumably to set up the cameras and check on the Internet connection. Alex knew immediately what she was seeing. Women selling sex on the Internet. Except she would bet the women here were not willing participants and would see very little of the money made out of their bodies.

Lewis Rider smiled. 'I believe you were asking Jamie about Karolina?'

Alex could almost hear her heart thudding. Please God, no. Please don't let Karolina be in one of these makeshift rooms.

'I'm sure she would have made a very good cleaner, I have to admit, and my mother was not pleased when we insisted on having her for this little enterprise. Thing is, she is so beautiful. Perfect, in fact.'

278

He pointed at a figure lying on a bed in stockings and suspenders. Push-up bra. Nothing else. Alex ran up to her. One of the men quickly turned the camera off.

'Karolina.'

Karolina looked at her with dead eyes.

'What have you done to her?' shouted Alex at Lewis Rider, then, quietly: 'What have the bastards done to you?'

'I am fine,' said Karolina. 'Now leave. I cannot make any money if you stand here. I need to make money so I can go home. See my family. They said I could go if I made enough money.' Her voice was as dead as her eyes. She had been given something to make her compliant.

'Oh, Karolina.' Alex was despairing. She caught her hand in hers and turned Karolina's arm over. Sure enough, telltale needle tracks.

'I am fine,' she said again, pushing Alex away. 'I need to make money so I can go home to my family. Now leave. Go.'

Alex felt herself being pulled away by Gary or Pete.

'This is how you make your money,' she said, bitterly, looking at Lewis Rider. 'Not the yurts or the lodges or even the farm. But this. Forcing women into the sex trade. And you find these people through your charities. Is David involved?' She thought about how he had lost weight recently, how he had seemed almost afraid of the Riders – he was certainly under their spell. She guessed he and his hostels were ripe for the picking.

'That's unfair. I don't force them. I simply tell them I have a good little job for them and they come willingly.' Lewis smiled, almost proudly. 'I mean, look at them. They're perfectly happy, aren't they? No one is jumping up and running away.'

'That's because they're pumped full of drugs.'

Lewis Rider shrugged. 'They want it. Eventually. Look.' There was a hint of impatience in his voice. 'I give them a chance to make good money—'

'That you mostly take off them.'

'They have to pay for their bed and board, don't they? Nothing's free in this world. As I say, they jump at the offer of a job.'

Alex hated the self-satisfied look on his face.

'They wouldn't if they knew what it entailed. And how many do you take off the streets?'

'Well, now. That's the brilliant thing. No one misses them, do they? – as you have found.'

'And the men you "recruit". What do they do for you?'

Lewis Rider smiled as he licked his lips. 'You must have watched *Breaking Bad*?'

Alex nodded.

'A very good series I've found. A great story. Good characters. And the idea of a chemistry teacher making crystal meth to provide for his family. And you know when Walter starts work at that new, purpose-built and illegal meth lab?'

Alex nodded.

'We have one of those.' His smile was one of pride. In fact, Alex could have sworn he puffed out his chest. 'It's the perfect place. Underground. Nothing suspicious to see, you know. Looks just like a winery in fact. All stainless steel vats and pipes and a control panel of red and green buttons. Simon is the brains behind that. A PhD in Chemistry. Did you know that?'

Alex closed her eyes briefly. Simon. She heard David's voice in her head telling her about Simon's chemistry degree. But she hadn't listened. And she had been so fixated on finding out more about Lewis and Jamie, she hadn't looked at Simon.

'It's perfect you see,' he continued. 'Any unusual smells go out to sea; there are plenty of places to dump the toxic waste – so many underground chambers to use. And we have successfully put anyone off coming here.'

'The high fences, the anthrax story, the ghost stories.'

'Yes,' he beamed. 'Sometimes we have the dogs.'

'But what happens when you've no need of the women or they outlive their usefulness?' The horrible truth dawned on her. 'You get rid of them, don't you?'

He nodded. 'Indeed we do. Don't look so horrified. We don't always kill them. Much easier to send those commodities we don't need abroad. Men or women.'

'Abroad?'

Again that sinister, stiff smile. 'You must realize the whole of the coast is filled with nooks and crannies where we can land a boat with impunity. We can bring stuff in, we can ship people out. And no one knows anything about it. And the money. Oh, the money. Keeping people away from the island over the years has proved invaluable.'

'You haven't answered my question about David.'

'Ah. Well of course he's involved. If it wasn't for his hostels we wouldn't have half the right people for our little jobs. He wasn't keen at first, but a few promises of the good life, plenty of cash in an offshore account and he'd do anything. Though I have to admit he's getting a bit troublesome of late. And now can I ask you a question?'

Alex glared at him, wondering what was coming.

'Cora. Where is she?' His tone had hardened.

So, they didn't know she had come with them.

Alex shrugged. 'How should I know? I haven't seen her for a day or two.'

Lewis Rider narrowed his eyes. He was suspicious, she thought. 'I thought you two were as thick as thieves.'

'I was trying to help her find Rick, that's all. My guess is he escaped but you've found him again.'

Lewis Rider nodded as if in approval. 'Good guess.'

'And Cora, well, she was high-maintenance.'

'I suppose she sold you a sob story about being raped?'

'She told me about the court case, yes.'

'I was friends with her once. Then she set out to ruin me. She

281

should have known that my father would employ the best to annihilate her.'

'He did that all right.'

'She shouldn't have told lies.' He sounded like a petulant child. Twenty-four years had passed and he still believed his own story.

'That's not what she says.' Alex was not going to let him get away with it. 'She says you raped her, Lewis. You got off. It destroyed her and it destroyed her family.'

Alex felt a sharp blow and heard a crack before pain exploded in her head. She staggered backwards, white spears of lightning streaking across her vision, bile rising again in her throat. She couldn't even shout with the pain, only moan. Lewis had hit her, hard, in the face with his elbow. He stood, watching her, breathing heavily. Her whole face hurt like hell and it felt as though a few teeth had been loosened. There was a trickle of wet at the corner of her mouth. She wondered if he had fractured her cheekbone.

Fuck this. She may never get off this bloody island, but she wasn't going to go quietly.

She licked her mouth and tasted the sweet metal of blood. Before she let herself think, let herself give into the pain that was threatening to overwhelm her, she bent her hand back at her wrist and drove the heel of her palm under his chin as hard and fast as she could.

He gave a cry like a wounded animal as his lower teeth were slammed into his top teeth. He swayed on his feet, stunned.

She had a moment to think that the self-defence lessons she'd taken had come in useful after all before Gary and Pete caught her and slammed her down on the floor.

She howled in pain as her damaged cheek hit the concrete.

She was grateful for the blackness that descended.

CHAPTER THIRTY-SEVEN

DAY SIX: LATE

Cora could only guess at what was going on as she heard both a man and a woman scream out, swearing, a scuffle, then moments later, a noise that sounded as though something or someone was being broken, followed by a body thudding onto the floor.

Alex?

Had to be.

'Take her away.'

That was Lewis, though his voice sounded strange – slurred and weak and full of pain. But there was no mistaking the menace in those three words. Had Alex done him some damage? She did hope so. But then Alex had obviously paid for it.

She held her breath as she heard something being dragged across the floor and wondered what she was doing here, hidden behind an old rusting filing cabinet, sure that they would soon hear her heart thudding. Why hadn't she run when she'd had the chance? Because she knew Rick was here somewhere, and Alex would lead her to him.

She'd been right behind Alex when the lights had gone on in the building, almost blinding her, but she hadn't followed her.

As soon as the lights went on and she heard Lewis Rider's voice – there was no mistaking it – she shrank back, listening at the open door.

His voice took her back to the last time they had spoken. When he had been psyched up by drink and fuck knew what else and he had taken his anger about Rick stealing his girlfriend out on her. Lewis had confronted her while she was having a sneaky fag after her shift, and he'd become more and more obnoxious, before pushing her up against the brick wall and telling her that she, together with the rest of her family, belonged to him, to the Riders.

She had pushed him back, telling him to sober up, and thought for a moment she had penetrated the fog and rage in his head. But he had slammed her against the bricks and tore at her clothes, before pushing himself into her. Afterwards, while he was zipping himself up, all he had said to her was 'droit de seigneur, baby' in a flat voice. When he'd gone, she'd retched until she could bring nothing else up.

Hearing his voice again, with that same threatening tone, Cora felt she would be sick all over again.

No. She'd had too many years of Lewis Rider dominating her life. Now was the time to stand up to him and that bloody family and make sure they got what they so richly deserved.

She had managed to use the shadows to follow Alex, Lewis and the two henchmen to this warehouse, though it hadn't been easy when they made their way through the tunnels – there had been nowhere to hide and although she kept herself flat to the wall, one of them only had to turn round to see her.

Her luck held.

Why were there not more guards? People with guns around?

Not needed, she supposed, a feeling reinforced when she crept into the warehouse behind the old filing cabinet to see the women on the beds. Compliant. Uncomplaining.

When she heard Lewis talking in that glib way about the

women who were selling their bodies and their souls for nothing in this miserable place, for absolutely nothing, she wanted to run out and do some serious damage to him. But she knew that would be foolish.

A door slammed shut. There was nothing more from Lewis or the henchmen. Or Alex, for that matter.

Had she been badly hurt?

Cora's legs were beginning to cramp up from the crouching, she needed to move. She considered her options. There was no hope of getting off the island at the moment, thanks to Reg's betrayal. She might have known it had all been too easy. The Riders don't run this sort of operation for some old man with a boat to scupper it. Alex had been well and truly taken in, too busy thinking about the story she could break.

For a moment, she felt a surge of rage against Alex. Why the fuck hadn't she done more homework?

She tried to roll her shoulders. She was being unfair. She hadn't looked beyond finding Rick and had been ready to grab the chance – any chance – to get over to the island.

And now she should be looking for him, not crouching behind this cabinet getting cramp thinking about things she couldn't change.

Did she feel bad about leaving Alex?

She wrestled with her conscience for all of ten seconds. Well, sort of. But if she could find Rick then they could go back and rescue Alex and somehow escape the island. With evidence. How, though? And how many of the Riders were here on Gisford Ness tonight? What was the betting old man Joe would call a family conference – he was fond of doing that when his boys were young. When they had been friends, in their early teenage years, Lewis had confided in Cora that his dad used to make them all sit around a table and discuss things like division of chores, bullying, rudeness. Lewis always said he found the conferences excruciating.

She had liked Lewis then.

Enough of that.

She needed action. She needed evidence to bury the Riders forever.

Ignoring the protest in her calves and knees, Cora crawled back out of the warehouse. She was lucky the Riders thought their island was impregnable, it meant there were few guards around and it would make her task easier.

She had to find Rick.

CHAPTER THIRTY-EIGHT

DAY SEVEN: EARLY MORNING

He had found Seth Goodwin in his little sitting room in Gisford in the early hours, slumped in front of the electric fire. The TV was still on. An empty mug was on its side by the chair, the threadbare carpet wet with the contents. Tea? Coffee? He sniffed. Something stronger. Whisky, perhaps. Gently, he pushed up the old man's sleeve to see if he could find the telltale pinprick in the crook of his arm. Sure enough, it was there. He cast his practised eye around the room. They must have got the old man drunk as there was no sign of a struggle, no telltale signs at all.

The death of an old man from a heart attack, that's what it would be. Who would bother to look for the mark of a needle in his arm?

DI Sam Slater had always known it was going to end badly, but he hadn't thought it would come to this. Not so soon. He thought about the first voicemail he had received late last night, and put it away in a compartment in his head to take out later. There was nothing he could do about that. Not now. Not ever.

Sam pulled off his nitrile gloves and went out the same way he had come in, stealthily and quietly, leaving no trace.

He looked again at the text he had received a mere hour and

a half earlier, the text that had made him first of all drive round to Seth's house and now to the quay and to Reg's fisherman's hut.

The door was hanging off its hinges.

Sam stepped in.

There was blood spatter everywhere – the walls, the floor, all over the few, miserable sticks of furniture Reg had in his hut.

And there he was. The old man. Lying on the mattress in the corner, hacked – and there was no other word for it – hacked to death by someone who had obviously enjoyed his work. He shuddered, trying not to breathe in the smell of blood and shit and death. Reg's face was turned towards him, and there was fear and desperation in his dead eyes. How frightened he must have been when his killer came in with his knife and there was nowhere for him to go. Had he been woken up by the killer's presence? Or did the first blow from the knife wake him?

It didn't bear thinking about.

Why was Seth's death relatively peaceful, yet Reg had to go with fear and horror? Perhaps he would never know; there might be no answer. Or maybe there had only been one syringe of drugs to use, so they tried to make Reg's death look like, what? Robbery gone wrong? More like the work of a psychopath.

And they had killed the two old men in case they talked. Told anyone about the two women Reg had ferried over to the island.

That was it. Enough was enough. He couldn't and wouldn't put up with all this senseless killing any longer.

He left the hut.

This time, he didn't bother to cover his tracks.

Time to call it in.

CHAPTER THIRTY-NINE

DAY SEVEN: EARLY MORNING

Alex didn't know how long she had been kept handcuffed to the hard chair in that airless room. She had drifted in and out of consciousness, then had tried to sleep in between the waves of pain in her face. Her whole head was on fire, her arms, pulled tight around the back of the chair, numb. A small window, high up on the wall was letting in watery grey light. Must be morning then.

Her mouth was dry and she was desperate for a pee.

Hungry too.

Head aching. Feeling dirty.

What was happening?

Why were they keeping her here?

Where was Cora?

Cora. Perhaps they hadn't caught her yet. There was a small leap of hope in her heart. She would go back to the mainland and – wait. Reg had left. Reg was one of them. She remembered that. So, she couldn't have gone back with Reg. Where might she have gone?

The door opened, and in walked Jamie Rider. He saw her and went white. He was holding a cup of coffee and a paper bag. He put them both down on the table in front of her.

Alex wanted to cry. She had held out a small hope that Jamie Rider was going to be one of the good guys. That he really didn't have much to do with the family business. Evidently she was wrong.

She stared at him.

Still he didn't say anything, still he couldn't look at her. Instead he took a key from his pocket and undid the handcuffs.

She tried to shake her arms, and bit her lip to stop herself from crying out as the blood began to flow. The pins and needles began, too. She wanted to cradle her cheek, but suspected if she touched it she might cry out.

'Coffee and a couple of doughnuts for you,' said Jamie, sitting down on a chair opposite. 'I'm sorry it's come to this. And I'm sorry that Lewis did this to you.' He made as if to touch her, but she flinched and jerked away from him, pleased to see the hurt in his eyes.

At the mention of Lewis's name, her cheek throbbed even harder. 'Are you?'

'Yes. But. Too much meddling. You didn't know when to stop. You shouldn't have listened to Cora Winterton. Then he wouldn't have … you wouldn't have …'

She had a sudden urge to spit at him. 'What are you trying to say, Jamie? That your psycho brother wouldn't have slammed his elbow into my face and almost broken my cheekbone?' It hurt to talk. It hurt to do anything.

Had they captured Cora? Was she, at this very moment, sitting in a room similar to this wondering what was going to happen to her?

He must have seen something in her face because he smiled. Was it a sad smile or was she imagining it? 'Cora must be somewhere on the island. We now know she came over with you. Of course, you know that we know and all that. Unless she swam back.' He laughed, but nervously, she thought. 'I don't think she'd do that, not without her precious Rick. You know, I really liked you when I first met you, though when I realized you were a journalist I knew I had to be careful. Then there was the problem of you being there when Rick crashed that bloody car. That really complicated matters, but it also played into our hands.'

'I bet it did.' She heard the bitter tone in her voice. 'You knew I'd been there all along, before I told you?'

'Not straightaway, obviously. But then you showed me that picture from the CCTV.' He nodded towards the doughnuts. 'Eat.' There was a slick of grease on the paper bag that made Alex nauseous and her jaw ache.

She shook her head. 'I can't.'

He frowned. Then shrugged. 'Up to you.'

Her head hurt from talking. Still, she had to carry on, find out more, a bit like catching a tongue ulcer on your tooth. The hurt felt delicious in some way.

'What's your role, then?' she asked.

'What do you mean?'

'You told me the family business wasn't anything to do with you, yet it obviously is. I was wondering what? I mean, you are a wanker banker, aren't you?'

He laughed. 'Yep. And a real wanker banker. I launder the money that the family makes from the girls and the meth. Make sure there's a long tangle that no one – if they did decide to investigate – could untangle.'

'Do you enjoy it?'

He stared at her, puzzled. 'What, laundering the money?'

'Yes. Handling dirty money made out of the misery of others? Knowing you are ruining the lives of so many?'

'Don't be so moralistic, Alex, you're no better.'

If she could have, she would have gasped. 'What do you mean?'

'You can't tell me the reason you hitched up with Cora Winterton was out of some pure desire to do good? You wanted the story behind Rick's disappearance. You wanted to splash all about the homeless on the pages of a newspaper. Opportunist, I would call you.'

'Don't be such a dickhead. At least I can do some good with the story, draw people's attention to what's happening on the streets, get them some help. And maybe I'll look into the court case.' She moved her head from side to side in an effort to ease the pain.

'Court case?' Jamie's voice was sharp.

'Lewis and Cora.'

'Why would you want to drag that up again?'

She shrugged as best she could. 'Because I can? Because your family shafted her.'

'Lewis did that.'

'Don't be crude, Jamie, it doesn't suit you.' Or maybe it did suit this new Jamie she was beginning to know. 'I think we might be able to re-open the case. Look for witnesses.'

'From twenty-four years ago?'

'I can try,' she shouted. Though she knew she would probably never get the chance.

Jamie thrust his face near hers. 'That's what I liked about you, Alex, your passion.'

'I need a pee.'

'Come on then.' He jerked his head towards the door.

She stood up and the room swam around her, she was as weak as a kitten. Any thoughts of trying to escape Jamie flew away. He took hold of her arm and led her out of the room.

The toilet was dark, dank and smelly. No window. No lock on the door. Alex didn't hang around and was soon sitting back in her chair looking at the bag of doughnuts that made her stomach turn.

She closed her eyes, wondering what, or who, they were waiting for. Marianne Rider, she supposed. Who she was convinced was the brains behind it all.

How long was she going to be in here for? What was going to happen to her?

She heard the door open.

'Alex Devlin.'

She opened her eyes. Joe Rider stepped into her line of vision. He didn't look in the slightest bit avuncular or like Marianne Rider's poor, henpecked husband. He stood tall and straight and his smile didn't reach his eyes.

Joe Rider? Where had the jolly man who enjoyed his sticky toffee pudding gone?

'Joe,' she said, flatly. 'I didn't expect to see you here.'

'No.' He sat down on the only other chair in the room before looking around, wrinkling his nose in distaste. 'I'm sorry you're here. I rather liked you, you know.'

'Really? That's exactly what your son said.' She tried to look bored, though inside her heart was beating fast and her palms were slick with sweat.

'The question now, is what do we do with you?'

Alex didn't want to think about that. 'The farm has been in your family for years, you've diversified, you've got a good business. Why did you need to turn to sex and drugs?'

He looked surprised. 'The two most lucrative businesses in the world, of course. And with farming being what it is these days and even with the diversification, well,' he shrugged, 'you know how it is. We're doing these people a favour, giving them employment, getting them off the streets.' He laughed heartily at that. 'It's what's wanted, according to the cops. Look at it this way, it's business, that's all. It's not personal. And I'm afraid you've got in the way, so we have to deal with you as well as the two Wintertons.' Joe Rider shook his head. 'It's a shame, Alex. But what can I do?' He spread out his hands as if in apology. 'Put the handcuffs back on.' His voice had gone from genial to uncompromising. 'We'll deal with her later. When we've found the Winterton girl.'

'What do you think you can do with me? You can't kill me and put me on a railway line or throw me in the sea, no one would believe I would kill myself.'

'Really? Are you sure about that? After all, you've had a lot on your plate lately, what with your father's Alzheimer's, your sister battling mental illness, your son leaving home, your career not exactly on a great trajectory—'

'None of that, none of them, have anything to do with you.' Alex tried to jerk her wrists away from Jamie, but he deftly caught them and snapped the handcuffs on the sides of the chair.

Joe Rider sighed. 'No. But we can make out a good case for it. Jamie will help, won't you, Jamie?'

Jamie nodded. 'You were in a very low mood after the exhibition. Conflicting emotions. Not sure your sister could bear the public scrutiny, plus, deep down, you were jealous of her success.'

'And that's just for starters,' said Joe. 'You'd be surprised at how convincing Jamie can be. Oh, and there's David.'

'David? I can't see him killing me.' The situation she was in, here, in this airless little room with her aching face and the Rider father and son talking about killing her and Cora and Rick made her want to giggle. Laugh out loud. Was she becoming delirious, perhaps?

'May I have some water, please?'

Joe Rider gestured to his son, who went out of the room, coming back with a bottle of water a minute later. He unscrewed the cap and held it to her lips. She drank quickly, greedily, wanting to get some sort of strength back, just in case. In case of what? She thought of her mum looking after her dad who one day wouldn't recognize the woman he had been married to for so many years. Then Sasha, getting on her feet at last, her delight at the success of her art work. And Gus. Her wonderful Gus, setting out in life, the arrow that she shot flying to goodness knows where, but she hoped she had done enough to make sure it landed in the right place.

How could she bear not to see any of them again?

It was not an option.

'No, you're right about David. Can't see it either. But he will help to spread the story of your anxiety. And your obsession with trying to find Rick Winterton. An obsession that led you here.'

She was confused. Perhaps she didn't hear Joe Rider properly. 'What do you mean? Then the police'll come here and you'll be found out.'

Joe Rider smiled. 'It's time to quit while we're ahead. We're going to close this particular operation down and move everything abroad. We have begun packing up and transferring the girls and much of the equipment to boats to get out of here. This coast is marvellous, isn't it?' Alex thought he was going to rub his hands with glee. 'Then, boom! We'll cover our tracks.'

'How?' Though, with a creeping dread, she thought she knew.

'It is well known there are mines all over the island. A few Second World War bombs as well, I shouldn't wonder. Ordnance they call it.'

'But they'll come over, the police, I mean. They'll find evidence of the lab, the Internet sex.'

'Will they? Are they going to look that hard? Perhaps Slater can come in useful one last time. And if not, it doesn't matter. We'll be a long way away by then.'

Through the fuzziness in her head Alex almost missed the name. 'Who did you say?'

A smile curled on Joe Rider's lips. 'Detective Inspector Sam Slater. Good-looking police officer – I expect you noticed that? He's one of us. Misdirects, seeds doubt in inquiries, keeps us one step ahead. He's good at that.' He looked at his watch. 'Should be here soon. To help.'

Jamie had stayed silent through all of this. Alex looked at him, at once pleading and horrified. 'Jamie? Surely you can't let him get away with this?'

Jamie stood up. 'I'm so sorry, Alex.'

Was it her imagination, or were his eyes wet?

'Jamie,' she said, desperate now, 'you're not that kind of person.'

'I am,' he said, almost sorrowfully. 'Money corrupts, you know that.'

'Absolutely.' Joe Rider grinned.

Jamie put the bottle of water down on the table.

The Riders left the room.

CHAPTER FORTY

DAY SEVEN: EARLY MORNING

Cora was shivering, not only from the cold and early morning mist that was settling on the island, but from sheer exhaustion. Finding Rick had been a much more difficult task than she'd imagined. For a start, there was much more activity than she had thought there would be, more people around even though they were concentrating on carrying equipment or pushing people down the paths towards the beach behind the lighthouse. It meant she'd had to duck and dive more times than she'd wanted, trying to hide behind buildings, lying flat on paths, making herself small and insignificant against large lumps of concrete that were dotted around, all the time remembering that there could be old mines anywhere off the beaten track.

She had searched for Rick in deserted and tumbledown sheds. She had crept into a long, low prefab, somehow avoiding the odd armed guard but did not find him. Another long, low building was too heavily guarded for her to even attempt to break in – and she had scratched her hands and knees trying to look through boarded-up windows. She had to hope he wasn't in there. A Second World War pillbox yielded nothing but old sacks and a bird's nest.

Now she was crouching outside an underground building – there were four squares of concrete covered with wire that seemed to be shafts down into the structure. She crept towards one of the openings and peered down.

It was a dormitory with cots arranged in several rows. Most of them were empty, bar one. Was that Rick down there? Yes, yes, she was sure of it. She wanted to call out to him, give him a sign that she was here. Wait. There were men, scurrying around, doing – what were they doing? She couldn't make it out, but whatever it was, they were in a bloody hurry.

Her stomach turned over.

It wasn't going to be anything good.

She crept round the edges of the concrete shafts, hoping to find some clue as to how she could get in. There. One of the shafts had a ladder against the brick that seemed to lead down into the chamber. She tried to prise away the wire cover. It was loose at one side, having rusted away from the edge. She pulled at it, breaking her nails in the process. She tugged again. The skin on her fingers was scraped off. They were bleeding and stinging and she could see flakes of rust embedded in the wounds. This is for Rick, she told herself grimly, trying not to make any noise for fear of alerting someone, though she didn't know what she was going to do once she had gained access to the shaft.

She looked again. Rick was still there. The other men had scarpered. Good. There was no one to see or hear her now. She hoped.

She put all her effort in to one last pull of the wire cover.

At last.

One more look to make sure the coast was clear before she swung herself round and began to climb down the ladder.

After what seemed an age she reached the bottom. Still no sign of anyone. She ran over to the cot where Rick was lying. He was still and his eyes were closed. She shook him, hard.

Slowly, so slowly, he opened his eyes. They were unfocused.

He opened his mouth, but nothing came out. She shook him again. 'Rick, come on, now, please, we've got to get you out of here.' She looked around, frantic. Someone was sure to come along at any minute. 'Rick.' She shouted as quietly as she could in his ear.

He opened his eyes again and smiled. 'Cora. What are you doing here?'

'I've come for you. We've got to leave. Something bad is going to happen. I can feel it.' She gritted her teeth, put her arms underneath his shoulders and tried to heave him up off the cot.

It worked. Sort of.

He rolled off the cot, landing on the floor with a loud bump. He cried out in pain, then closed his eyes again.

Cora looked around, hoping no one had heard his shout. Then she kicked him in the ribs. 'Up you fucking well get, now. I haven't come all this way so we can get murdered on this godforsaken bit of bloody land. Up. Now.'

Rick sat up, rolled onto all fours. He stayed like that for a second or two, and then, with what looked like a monumental effort, he hauled himself up onto his feet and stood there, swaying.

'They gave me something, Cora. So thirsty. So thirsty.'

She ignored him. 'We have to get out of here. There's a ladder. You can do it.' She draped one of his arms across her shoulders and somehow, with a combination of shuffling and pulling, they reached the ladder. How she was going to get him up there, she didn't know.

CHAPTER FORTY-ONE

DAY SEVEN: EARLY MORNING

Alex was pulling at the handcuffs and trying to move the chair towards the door when it opened.

'Sam.' A core of volcanic rage rose in her chest that almost overwhelmed her. 'Come to finish me off, have you?' she shouted, making her cheek throb even more. She rocked the chair back and forth. 'You needn't bother. I'm going to go up with whoever else is left. I can't get out of this, but that's what you wanted. They're going to blow half the island up and I'll go with it. Unless Cora finds me.' But she didn't think Cora would find her. She had either been killed or had somehow hightailed it back to Gisford. Or she could still be looking for Rick, which would mean she, too, would be caught in the inferno.

Sam ran over to her chair and looked down at her wrists.

'Handcuffs, Sam,' she spat. 'I expect you provided these, didn't you?' Then, annoyingly, she felt the tears start. 'Why? I thought you were one of the good guys.'

'I was. I am.' His eyes were darting about the room.

'Then why throw your lot in with the Riders?'

His eyes settled on her. 'Rosie.'

'Rosie?'

'My wife. Look, there's no time. Here. The key.' Sam picked it up from by the water bottle on the table. Jamie must have left it deliberately, moving the bottle so his father didn't see it. Alex knew she should feel grateful, but she had neither the time nor the inclination.

Sam went behind her and unlocked the cuffs. 'Come on,' he said. 'We've got to go. The meth lab is about to blow and one or two of the other buildings.'

He pulled her out through the door along a corridor and into the cold, damp open air. 'Follow me,' he said. 'I've got a boat hidden near the lighthouse. There's a quick way, but we've got to get past the meth lab before it goes up.'

'You never did analyse the glass, or get Sadie's death investigated, did you?' she said bitterly.

'No. Now will you come on.'

They began to run, Alex following behind, not deviating from his path.

Suddenly there was a loud explosion from behind them. They both fell to the ground. Alex covered her head as stones and mud and shingle and sand rained down on her. It lasted forever. There was ringing in her ears. Then it was eerily quiet. She looked up. Sam was already standing, blood from cuts on his face running down his cheeks, his body covered with grime and grit. She guessed she looked similar.

'We're not there yet,' he said, his voice coming from far away. 'And there'll be more explosions to come.'

She got to her feet. They were both coughing, but there was no time to think about it. They had to get to Sam's boat.

But where was Cora? Was she still here? And Rick? After all this, she couldn't leave Rick.

'Sam,' she shouted. 'I need to find Rick. And I can't go without knowing Cora is safe. I can't.'

Sam looked at her, undecided. 'You go. Find somewhere to hide. I'll go and look for them.'

'But Sam—'

'Do as you're told,' he roared.

Alex nodded.

Sam turned away.

Joe Rider stepped out from behind one of the nearby buildings.

CHAPTER FORTY-TWO

DAY SEVEN: EARLY MORNING

Rick picked himself up off the ground after the so-called living quarters were blown sky-high. A part of him was pleased that hell-hole no longer existed. He knew the meth lab was next – he had heard the men talk about it as they rigged the room in which he was lying. The Riders wanted to cause chaos and confusion on the island so that the emergency services – police, fire and ambulance – would be so tied up they wouldn't see the family ride off into the sunset in their fuck-off speed boat. The women and the men – the slaves – were already on their way abroad, and the goons would melt away into the countryside. He had to get to Gisford.

He looked around for Cora. She was sitting up, cradling her head, blood trickling down her cheek. Then he noticed her leg was at an odd angle, and the white of bone was sticking through her trousers. He felt sick. How was he going to get her off the island? Perhaps they should wait it out until the coppers arrived.

But he had to stop the Riders if he could.

'Cora?'

'I can't move, Rick. I can't move. You'll have to get help.' She was white with dust and pain.

'Help will come now after that lot went off. But I have to stop that fucking family from winning.'

'Rick—' A spasm of agony crossed her face. She waved at him. 'Go on, then. I'll be okay. That's what all this has been about anyway. Get that camera.'

Rick glanced at her one more time, then loped off towards the lighthouse. That's where he'd buried the camera, to the left of the door.

'Keep to the paths,' Cora shouted after him. 'Mines.'

He waved his hand in acknowledgement.

He could see three figures in the distance, and as he got closer he realized one was Joe Rider, the other was the woman with the soft voice who had tried to rescue him when he crashed the car. The man was that detective bloke, what was his name? Sam Slater, that's it. He was the crooked copper he'd heard talk about and who had come to the island to watch them work in that death-trap of a meth lab more than once. But he seemed to be arguing with Joe Rider. Joe Rider was gesturing with a gun in his hand. Rick knew Rider wouldn't think twice about firing it. He kept on running, adrenaline giving him strength and speed for the first time in a long time.

He ran as fast as he could, ignoring the pain in his shoulder, the weakness in his legs. All he could think about was the woman with the soft voice. He had to save her.

It wasn't until he was close to the three that they noticed him.

Joe Rider levelled his gun at him. At any moment he expected to suffer the slam of the bullet, feel it tear through muscle and sinew, blood vessels, vital organs.

Don't think. Don't think. Run.

He saw Slater jump towards Rider, knocking him down before he had any time to react. They grappled on the shingle, rolling over and over until they were well off the path.

Run.

Joe Rider was a fit man for his age and knew how to fight

dirty. He could see the woman was about to join in, to try and help Slater. He knew she shouldn't.

'Don't,' he yelled at her. 'Stay where you are. It's too dangerous. Mines.'

She looked up, startled, but stopped moving towards Rider and Slater.

Now the fighting pair were several feet off the path and for Rick, time slowed. He saw what was happening as if in a dream.

He saw himself reach the woman, knock into her, fly through the air, fall away and tumble into a heap. Safe.

A bang. A white light. Rick felt the heat. Rider and Slater were tossed twenty feet up into the air before landing, like ragdolls, down onto the earth. There were pieces of bone, flesh, clothing scattered around. Something – a shoe? – was hanging grotesquely from a thorny bush. Neither of them moved. He wanted to cover his ears. This is not Afghanistan, he told himself. This is not Afghanistan.

He was aware of the woman lying beside him. Shrapnel wounds in her arm, her side, her shirt soaked in blood. Her leg was bleeding pretty badly. He made himself get up, tore off his shirt and made a tourniquet to stem the bleeding. He felt for a pulse.

Nothing.

'Come on, come on, stay with me,' he muttered.

There. A flutter, maybe?

He heard the whir of a helicopter crossing the water.

CHAPTER FORTY-THREE

THREE WEEKS LATER

She took the stairs very slowly and very carefully followed by Ethel and Ethel's unique stink. Alex still wasn't used to the crutches, though Gus was watching her every clunky move.

Gus. He'd come very quickly after the hospital had called him and was now her guardian and her minder. She was loving every minute of his attention. Almost every minute. There was a tiny part of her that would be glad when she was on her own again and could draw breath and relax.

'Take it easy, now, Alex.'

Heath was guarding and minding her too. He had come charging to her bedside when he'd heard what had happened.

'Worried about your story, Heath?' she'd managed to ask.

'Don't be an arse, Devlin,' he'd replied. 'And your text didn't come through until it was too late.'

She could have been mistaken, but she thought she saw tears in his eyes as he held her hand.

Now both Gus and Heath were trying to outdo each other in their solicitousness.

They reached the bottom of the stairs and freedom was through the door.

John Watson came out of his flat, walking on his one leg and his prosthetic. She almost laughed. What a pair they must look.

'A couple of disableds, now, Alex, eh?' he said, trying and failing to get low enough to fondle Ethel's ears.

'Don't make me laugh, John. It still hurts.'

'How are you doing?'

'Getting there, John, getting there.'

And she was, she thought, as she emerged from the door of her apartment block and into the weak February sun. Better than that bloody rain, anyway. She knew she was lucky; she had nearly died on Gisford Ness, her life saved by Rick to whom she would be forever thankful. Her injuries would have been so much worse had he not hurled himself on top of her and rolled her out of the way. As it was, she'd had to have several pieces of metal removed from her body, though doctors had warned her they couldn't get it all. Some would work their way out over the years, some would get inflamed and she would need further treatment. But she was alive, and the bandages and crutches would be gone soon. Rick, too, had many wounds and was recovering at home with Cora. She'd also heard from Cora that Rick's wife and his two daughters were staying with her. Alex hoped he and Helen could build some bridges.

She didn't know what to feel about Cora. She knew from Rick that Cora had been ready to abandon her to her fate. And although she could understand her reasoning – Rick was her brother after all – she wasn't sure she was ready to meet with her yet. But Rick had saved her life, had pushed her the right way. And she would make sure Rick was cared for properly. If she could get near him. She rather thought Cora might be too protective. At least the brother and sister had achieved what they had set out to do – the ruin of the Rider family. Though that damn camera had never been found.

Of course, Joe Rider and Sam Slater hadn't been so lucky, both blown apart. There was no chance of DI Slater being awarded any sort of medal for bravery; he had confessed to his crimes as he called the emergency services to Reg's hut. And that had meant they were nearer than they might have been when the explosions tore through the island.

Sam's wife had died two days after Sam. And for that, Alex was glad. Heath had told her what he'd heard: that the home where his wife was living with Huntington's was expensive, and the Riders had come up with the money in return for spreading a little bit of misinformation, making sure his colleagues looked in the wrong places when bodies turned up. 'There may have been more,' said Heath. 'But that's why he did it.'

'For his wife.' Alex had nodded, had grieved a little for him.

She hobbled around the harbour and towards her favourite bench.

Sitting down, thankful for the rest, she took out her phone and scrolled through BBC News.

There it was. The story about the arrest of Lewis, Jamie, Simon and Marianne Rider for slavery offences. Marianne was pleading ignorance. Somehow Alex thought that wouldn't wash. Two boats of men and women had been intercepted in the North Sea, their captors arrested. Then a story detailing the charges: forced labour, money laundering and conspiracy to traffic with a view to exploitation. A family slavery gang.

'I'm glad Karolina's back with her family,' said Heath, stretching out his legs and turning his face to the weak sun.

'And that Nobby turned up on one of the boats.'

'And has been given a decent screw for his story,' said Heath, wryly.

'Come on, it was worth it.' She gave Ethel a biscuit, then wiped the drool on her jeans.

'Do you think Boney will ever turn up?' asked Gus, scratching Ethel under her chin. 'Because if he ever does—'

'You won't do anything,' said Alex, sharply.

'He'll turn up' said Heath. 'His sort always do. Maybe then he'll be arrested and join the rest of them in prison.'

'And talking of prison, I wonder what'll happen to David Gordon's charities when he goes down.' Alex put her phone back in her pocket.

Heath mumbled something.

She turned to him. 'What did you say?'

'The hostels have been taken over by another charity.'

Alex was surprised. 'So soon?'

Heath blushed. 'Pulled a few strings,' he mumbled.

Alex leaned across and planted a soft kiss at the corner of his mouth. He blushed some more.

'I thought I was the one that blushed,' she said, laughing.

'Mum! Purleese!' Gus gave a mock shudder.

Heath laughed too, then was sober. 'But I'm afraid there's no news about Martin.'

'I'm writing their stories,' said Alex. 'The people on the streets. Their families, too. I owe it to them. The ones who died and the ones who survived.'

'They'll be published, Alex. We owe them that.'

A couple walked by with a little dog on the end of a lead, somewhere between a Jack Russell and a chihuahua. Ethel perked up, wagged her tail. A lot.

She was ignored, so she went back to lying at Alex's feet, her chin on her paws.

'Sasha's doing well,' said Heath, after a silence.

Alex nodded. 'Got an exhibition in London now, later in the year.' She paused. 'Come with me if you like.'

'Okay,' he said.

'Good.'

Suddenly, Alex had the unsettling feeling that someone was watching her. She turned her head. Sure enough, a man was standing on the path, looking her way. He was slim, clean-shaven and dressed in jeans and a waterproof coat.

He raised his hand and waved enthusiastically.

Alex smiled. Who was it?

The man walked towards them.

All at once Ethel leapt to her feet and started to wag her tail so much it almost felt as though she might take off.

The man reached them and dropped to his knees, burying his face in her fur. 'Ethel. Ethel. I've missed you so fuckin' much.'

Alex frowned. Was it – 'Martin?'

The man looked up. 'Yeah. That's me. They told me you had 'er.'

'Where have you been?' she said.

'At me sister's. She didn't want Ethel, and Tiger was supposed to take care of her, but he forgot, din't he? And then he was got by them murdering bastards. I didn't know till I came back to fetch 'er. Me sister's changed her mind, you see. Saw how unhappy I was without her. I told her she wasn't no trouble. Apart from her farts. But I didn't tell her about those.' He took her lead. 'Thanks ever so for looking after her. She looks great.' He beamed, then frowned as he caught sight of her crutches. 'I heard what happened and that. Glad you're all right.'

'Thanks, Martin.'

'S'okay. See ya.'

'Right.'

Alex watched sadly as Ethel trotted away by Martin's side without a backwards glance. Gus took her hand and gave it a gentle squeeze.

ACKNOWLEDGEMENTS

Heartfelt thanks to my agent, Teresa Chris, who is always on my side and is a fierce champion of my writing. Thanks also to my editor, Sarah Hodgson – your insight and support is invaluable. And to all the team at Killer Reads/Harper Collins – what an incredible job you do! There has to be a special mention for Claire Fenby for helping to launch the book, and Janette Currie for preventing several gaffes going out into the world.

Love and thanks to Jenny Knight, with her coffee/pastries/flowers/Prosecco and all round fabulousness, for reading an early draft, for digging me out of a plotting hole and for keeping my spirits up. You are rightly having your turn in the sun now. And to Jamie Knight for letting me borrow his name for a rather nasty character – you are, of course, nothing like my Jamie…

Thanks to Beth for keeping me entertained with baby pictures and James for advice on money markets and banking and to Georg Childs for her brilliant Booksmart site on Instagram.

Thanks to Kate Rhodes, Valentina Giambanco, Chris Curran and Jackie Baldwin who are always a support.

Thank you to the book bloggers who do a fantastic job reading books and writing reviews for the love of it, to Emma Welton of damppebbles.com for organising the blog tour, and to you, the readers, without whom there would be no book.

To Melanie McCarthy – always love and thanks.

Thanks to my children, Edward, Peter and Esme, and their partners Emily, Jenni and Nick, who unfailingly love my books and shout about them at all times.

And to my husband Kim. I couldn't have done any of this without you.

KILLER
READS

DISCOVER THE BEST
IN CRIME AND THRILLER

Follow us on social media to get to know the team behind the books, enter exclusive giveaways, learn about the latest competitions, hear from our authors, and lots more:

/KillerReads  /KillerReads